OVERWHELMING PRAISE FOR
THE SOUL OF VIKTOR TRONKO

"A SEDUCTIVE NOVEL . . . consummately developed characters."

—*Booklist*

"SUPERIOR TO MUCH OF DEIGHTON AND LE CARRÉ
—more authentic and less mannered."

—David Rains Wallace, author
of *The Dark Range* and *The Wilder Shore*

"WITH THIS COMPLICATED, MASTERFULLY WRITTEN TALE OF INTRIGUE, QUAMMEN LEAPS TO THE FRONT RANK OF ESPIONAGE WRITERS."

—Gregory McNamee, *The Bloomsbury Review*

"A FETCHING PREMISE FOR A THRILLER . . . staying with *The Soul of Viktor Tronko* does pay off. Quammen, whose natural history essays for *Audubon* and *Outside* have brought him deserved kudos, writes posh prose."

—*The Washington Post Book World*

"SHARP, GRITTY GLIMPSES OF LIFE IN THE WORLD OF INTELLIGENCE."

—*Publishers Weekly*

"SINUOUSLY INTRICATE AND COMPELLINGLY REALISTIC."

—*Library Journal*

Also by David Quammen

THE ZOLTA CONFIGURATION
TO WALK THE LINE
NATURAL ACTS
THE FLIGHT OF THE IGUANA

The Soul of
VIKTOR
TRONKO

David Quammen

A DELL BOOK

Published by
Dell Publishing
a division of
The Bantam Doubleday Dell
Publishing Group, Inc.
666 Fifth Avenue
New York, New York 10103

The trademark Dell ® is registered in the U.S. Patent and
Trademark Office.

ISBN: 0-440-20177-2

Reprinted by arrangement with Doubleday

Printed in the United States of America

Published simultaneously in Canada

December 1988

10 9   8   7   6   5   4   3   2   1

KRI

to R.P.W.

AUTHOR'S NOTE

This is a work of fiction. The characters are invented creatures. But a certain amount of factual detail informs my story (I hope) as texture and background. For that sense of texture and background, I am indebted to more sources than can be mentioned here; but I want especially to acknowledge the helpfulness of published works by Alexander Dolgun, Petro Grigorenko, Michael Voslensky, Mark Azbel, Aleksei Myagkov, Oleg Penkovskiy, Peter Deriabin, Vladimir Sakharov, Ladislav Bittman, Alexander Solzhenitsyn, Arkady Shevchenko, Eugène Marais, Robert Ardrey, Norman Malcolm, John Barron, Henry Hurt, Robert Conquest, Thomas Powers, William Hood, David C. Martin, Edward Jay Epstein, Anthony Summers, Tom Miller, Patricia Johnson McMillan, and Anthony Cave Brown.

The quotations concerning the life of Eugène Marais, on pp. 182 and 183, come from a brief preface written by his English translator, Winifred de Kok, in 1936.

The Soul of
VIKTOR
TRONKO

I

This much was oddly appropriate: it began with an exchange of symmetrical lies. The Russian claimed he was a lost man if he did not come across now, right now, today or tomorrow, before his own people could get him on board a plane. And the other side, who were Americans, claimed to believe him.

By "lost" he was understood, correctly, to mean dead.

But still they put him off for another two days. Go back to the hotel. Rejoin your delegation. Behave normally. This was all for their own convenience—certainly not for the Russian's. A bit of time was required for communications, consultations with home, deliberation on that end. Assumption of the weight of responsibility. You'll see us again on Wednesday, they instructed him; same time, same procedure, a different address. The Russian had no choice but to comply. Meanwhile in Langley, within a glass-walled cubicle that was itself within a secure communications room on the seventh floor, three men were faced with deciding precisely how clever they thought they were.

The cubicle was hardly bigger than an elevator, and there was only one chair. That was occupied by the junior officer of the three, a pug-faced man named Melvin Pokorny, forty years old and bald and drastically ugly in an affable, unthreatening way. As deputy to the chief of Counterintelligence, Melvin Pokorny did not ordinarily serve as a code clerk; but circumstances this evening were not ordinary. Pokorny sat at a teletype keyboard. The encryption machine before him dominated the space of the cubicle, hulking up tall and smoke-gray like an old Univac crossed with a jukebox. It was identical to a dozen other machines in the larger room, except that its printer made no carbons. Tending the cubicle's glass door, from the outside, was a discreetly alert security officer in a business suit. The two older men stood behind Pokorny, hovering.

The station chief from Bonn had flown over to Vienna upon first word that the Russian—after one and a half years of utter silence—was reestablishing contact. The Bonn man spoke Russian, it was he who hosted the first of these latest meetings, and it was he therefore who passed along to Langley the first quantum of startling news: that the Russian was now in a froth to defect. Startling in its own brief moment, but nothing at all compared to the second quantum. That was reserved for Jed McAttee, who had gone roaring over at once from Langley.

McAttee was a former chief of the Bonn station himself, now very much senior to the new man, and coyly but unmistakably vain of his own fluency in the Russian language; more important, he himself had handled the original contact that year and a half earlier. McAttee knew this Russian. Or rather, they had met. McAttee would try to persuade the Russian to remain in place. After all, the Russian himself had been adamant against defection just eighteen months ago, hadn't he? Wife and child in Moscow? Brilliantly promising trajectory to his KGB career? All right then. Let him stay put and tell us some stories. At least for a while yet. Let him *earn* his defection. Little junket out to Vienna was no reason for getting giddy and reckless all of a sudden. Just let him remain in place. But talk to us. Stories.

Thus it was figured in Langley. McAttee would know how to hit the right note. McAttee would be good. So Jed McAttee flew into Vienna and hosted the second meeting, in a furnished flat just off the Concordiaplatz; and to him was entrusted the second quantum. McAttee rushed immediately back to the embassy, where he locked himself up to cable Langley, and coming off the machine in the glass-walled cubicle it read like this:

SUBJECT CLAIMS INFO RE OSWALD

The two older men watched over Pokorny's shoulder as these words were pecked down. For a moment no one said anything. The air of the cubicle already tasted galvanic and sour, from three men and an electronic machine all confined at hard labor —the new difference in that atmosphere might have passed notice by even a good hound. For another moment no one said anything. Then a repeat of the transmission was requested. *Please clarify,* Pokorny typed on his keyboard. *What did you say?* he typed. The encrypted tape was fed back to the machine, which sucked it away like a noodle, and the message went off in a burst. McAttee's next cable read:

SAYS HE WILL TELL US ABOUT OSWALD

Of the older men, one was a gnomish creature, barely taller as he stood than Pokorny in the chair. This man had the lean features and flushed fair skin of a child who has spent too long in the hospital, but the strong underbite of his jaw suggested quiet ferocity of the adult sort. He held himself in the desperately straight posture of very short folk who happen also to be very proud. His hands were buried beyond sight in deep pockets of a camel-hair overcoat. The coat was finely tailored and came almost to the floor; it had a collar of soft fur; by any sane standard, it was more than a little too warm for the glass-walled cubicle of the room on the seventh floor. The gnomish man only wore it because he was on the verge of leaving the building, and because he insisted stubbornly on letting the other man be reminded of that fact. He had been on the verge of leaving the building now for five hours. Since just after 9 P.M. It was entirely unnecessary, in this second month of 1964, for Pokorny to type *Oswald Who?*

To McAttee's message, the gnomish man offered his own comment in the form of a snort.

"Yes," said the other, a man of far more abundant silhouette. This one sighed. He was tall enough, broadly enough framed, to carry almost as much weight as he was presently carrying; not badly kept, that is, for someone of his age and station. He played golf without a cart—a point of pride. Beside the gnomish man, though, anyone would have looked like a comic baritone out of Gilbert and Sullivan. "What's your impression?"

"Bogus," said the gnomish man. "Sent."

"Yes, well. Maybe. Jed seems to agree."

Earlier messages from McAttee had already warned Langley of reasons for doubting the Russian's whole line. For instance the telegram of recall, purportedly summoning him back to Moscow on the last Aeroflot flight of the week, and thereby setting such a conveniently intractable deadline for his coming across to the West. McAttee found no evidence that such a telegram really existed. There were other questions too, minor ones but nagging. Wife and child at home, career trajectory, and the earlier strong opposition to the notion of defecting. What had changed so drastically in eighteen months? One an-

swer to that question was now—after McAttee's last two cables
—obvious. But hardly reassuring. The Russian was being
sniffed at skeptically.

"Even so. Even with Jed's concurrence." This was a small
barb of sarcasm fired into McAttee's back, latest in a long series, after which the gnomish man's mouth bent primly up at
one corner.

"We can't very well turn it down."

The gnomish man said nothing, implying his firm but defer-
ential disagreement. Silence was as far as he generally went by
way of expressions of deference. The gnomish man was laconic
by nature and often too by calculation; since he was also calcu-
lating by nature, it was really all one. The mere act of remaining
silent, like most else in his life, was seldom done for only a
single reason.

"We can't. Sorry. That's definite," the big man repeated. "We
just cannot. Picture me facing Earl Warren and his group a
month from now. Telling them we had a source on Oswald, a
potential source at least, possibly veracious and very possibly
not—from *inside the KGB*. And we turned it down. Lord. Because the man didn't smell right. 'Well, you see, Mr. Chief Justice, we passed on that one. Turned him down. Fellow didn't
smell right. Fishy. We were dubious. Thought he was probably
making things up. So we just spun him around and sent him on
back home. Sir.' Christ alive. Picture that for me, would you,
Claude?"

Maybe the gnomish man pictured it, maybe not. He remained
silent.

"What would *you* do?"

"Nothing," said the gnomish man. "Leave him be. Watch.
Wait."

"That I know. What's your second choice?"

"I have none."

The big man made a flatulent noise through his lips: acute
frustration muted by four decades of bureaucratic composure.
That the conversation continued was testimony that this gnome
in a camel-hair coat, however abrasive, however unhelpful,
could not simply be ignored. Melvin Pokorny sat quite still,
willing himself invisible.

"Jed says bring him across," said the big man. "Discount
everything. Hear the stories and disbelieve them and see where

they might lead. Where they might be *meant* to lead. Extrapolate backward. Then crack him. Crack him right open. What about that?"

"I wouldn't," said the gnomish man. "It's just what we're being asked to do. Therefore I wouldn't."

"No it's *not*." A large fist was slapped into a fleshy palm, like a softball landing in mud. "What we're being asked is to accept him at face value. Open arms. Friendly debriefing, then a house in Bethesda and a consultancy. Paagh. I'm not proposing any such thing, and you know it."

"Asked by him, yes," said the gnomish man. "I mean what we're being asked by *them*."

"*Them*. Of course. But in the present instance, Claude, we simply don't know that *they* are asking *anything*."

"So we must infer," said the gnomish man, at which familiar incantation the other rolled his eyes. In Vienna, Jed McAttee was waiting for an answer, and Pokorny was waiting to send it.

"Infer the look on Earl Warren's face. Infer that one for me."

Both of the standing men already knew precisely what decision would go out. They had known from the start. But it was psychologically necessary to their mutual sense of professionalism that, first, the thing be properly anguished over from all conceivable angles.

"You are very goddamned hard to please."

Silence from the gnomish man this time indicated his total and mildly flattered assent. The skirmish was lost but he had affirmed, for later, his hold on certain high ground. Which was as much as he had hoped for. He began buttoning the camel-hair overcoat; now finally it was possible to leave the building.

"Then again," said the gnomish man, "I'm not the Director." A small careful brush stroke of conciliation.

"That's correct," said the Director.

Still the gnomish man lingered. It would be rude, exceeding even his standard degree of rudeness, to stalk off before the offending message was sent. Beyond that he was expected for reasons of protocol to remain, to be present during the actual transmission, so that later he could not be tempted to claim suggestively that he hadn't been. For the record: he had been overruled, but not circumvented.

"All right, Mel," said the Director. "Let's tell Jed to bring the little stinker across. A great big American welcome for comrade Viktor Semyonovich Tronko."

So the third meeting was, for the Vienna phase, the last. That one too was hosted by Jed McAttee. The Russian was tucked and zippered into the uniform of an American Army major, best available fit, and assisted in ducking quickly from the door of the safe house into the rear seat of a Buick with diplomatic plates. He stayed squashed on the floor of the car until they were an hour outside the city, speeding westward along the winter-gray Danube Valley. McAttee was right there beside him, for the entire ride over to Frankfurt and then again for the flight back to Washington. McAttee kept himself practically handcuffed to the Russian until they had passed through the gates of a certain Agency compound some fifty miles southeast of Washington along the Chesapeake Bay.

As the gnomish man had intuited, there was much to be known and much to be doubted about this particular Russian, beyond merely his two startling quanta of news. But the full truth certainly wasn't offered to Jed McAttee, not in Vienna and not during that sleepless journey west, and not in the months following. Nor was it offered to anyone else, on what might be called (though imprecisely) the American side of the matter, for a very long time thereafter. The journalist Michael Kessler did not come into it, in fact, until seventeen years later.

2

Michael Kessler stands frozen in his own doorway. He does not own a gun.

He is still holding out against that and a word processor, though he recognizes as an ineluctable truth that in both cases the barbarians are at the gates. In his old age—actually it was just after his thirty-sixth birthday—he has relented only so far as to buy a TV. Death of principle, the greased track downward into darkness and entropy, but there you are. Yes I've bought a TV. The crucial thing about owning a television, Kessler rationalizes, is to refrain from pretending you got it for the news. That way lies gibbering self-delusion. Besides, it's not his idea of news, some jasper posing by moonlight on the White House lawn in a Burberry and a razor cut, reciting the day's official boilerplate in oracular tones. No, Kessler bought his set for the bright colors, which play soothingly across his frontal lobe after a bad day. He has heard by grapevine that a certain precocious vice-president at NBC does all his own watching with the volume turned off. No sound at all. Colors and shapes. Obviously the man has thought a few things through. But right now Kessler is wondering, suddenly, whether he shouldn't perhaps have gotten the gun instead.

His keys dangle from the lock. The door is open. Surprising a burglar at work can be more costly than letting him surprise you, Kessler thinks. Possibly it isn't too late, though, to reverse course and gallop discreetly away down the wooden stairs. One aspect of a television is that, however pernicious, it can't be used to blast a hole in your face when you stumble home with drastically bad timing. Kessler has been startled on his own threshold by the sight of a burning light, in the kitchen, which was not lit when he left.

Or was it? No, definitely not. And muted noises now audible

from the living room. Kessler advances warily. On the kitchen counter, bare this morning or Kessler is losing his mind, is an empty beer bottle and the sheet of butcher paper that was wrapped around the piece of Stilton cheese that he put away carefully last night. Either an arrogant burglar, then, or a starving one. Some desperate junkie from the alleys of New Haven who has jimmied his way into Kessler's place for a fast rip-off, a snack, and maybe a few restful minutes of browsing the bookshelves—the sort of calm felon who would pass up five cans of Budweiser in favor of a Beck's from the door shelf, though the Beck's would have required a bottle opener, a rifling through drawers. Obviously it's a case of white-collar crime. Of course there is another possible explanation and by now, breathing easier, Kessler is gropingly inclined toward that one. Somebody has come to visit.

Somebody for whom a door, when locked, is not quite really persuasively locked. Even this doesn't tell him. The woman named Nora has no key, doesn't drink beer, and would be highly unlikely to pay Kessler a surprise evening visit, alas. Far out of character that she might let herself into his empty apartment and settle cozily down awaiting him—though the image is enough to make Kessler's blood hum in his ears. She could be barefoot, shoes cast aside, legs tucked up under her on the sofa. She could be sleeping. He remembers quite vividly what she looks like when she is sleeping. Yes, if only. But he knows that this visitor isn't Nora. Crazed with her own (incomprehensible, to Kessler) brand of remorse, crazed with caution, she hasn't let him get within arm's reach since that first and rather puzzlingly chaste night. Which by now is, what, almost six months back and a hemisphere away? He literally has not touched her since Ecuador. Maybe it was the Coriolis effect that played some sort of magic role, sweeping Kessler and Nora up in its centripetal suck, spinning them so closely together for that short bit of time: don't vortices all flow in the opposite direction, down on the far side of the equator? Maybe what he should do is kidnap her, drag her back down to Guayaquil, and make his best bid again there. Spanish guitars, fragrance of mangrove, the tropical evening heat raising a light sweat on the nape of her neck, and a candlelight dinner of roast guinea pig with popcorn. Would the Hotel Alfaro even let them back in? Anyway, no—no, the unexpected is always possible and Kessler could win a sweepstakes and die of the shock and be born again as a Hindu cow but this brazen guest, tonight, definitely cannot be Nora.

Who, then? Who else would come to call?

No one, not in New Haven at least, a town where Kessler is still the lonely stranger. Not a student, certainly. Not Fullerton, the dean who lured him here, just an acquaintance socially. Kessler's mind is empty: he has been too long away from the world of Washington and its spookier players and the sort of journalism he used to do down there. Too long since he promised anonymity to a terrified source or lied over the telephone about who he was. His metabolism is different now. His body has made adjustments, no longer producing such quantities of the hormone for suspicion and paranoia. That or his memory is simply failing with age, like his principles. It could only be one person, after all.

And lo. Seated comfortably in the good chair is Mel Pokorny, wearing an orange mohair wig and a pair of Groucho glasses.

The glasses are of high quality as those things go, presumably from some strange little shop that only Pokorny would know—real hinges to the frames, real synthetic hair for the mustache and brows. They don't make them like that anymore, Kessler thinks passingly. On the floor nearby is an attaché case, lid up, in which Kessler can see a *Wall Street Journal* and a simple professional lock tool.

Pokorny has taken the liberty, among others, of removing his shoes and socks. A grotesque travesty of the image just savored —Nora, drowsy and soft—and it makes Kessler cringe. Pokorny's wide naked feet rest on the coffee table, from the far end of which Kessler's new television is showing highlights of the day's celebrations in Washington. Fireboats on the Potomac pissing out great rainbow arcs of water, large buses pulling into the White House drive, a festive and emotional crowd on the South Lawn. Fifty-three folding chairs, one for each returned hostage. Ronald Reagan is making a speech of welcome. Pokorny's suit has endured a long day's rumpling, probably much of that on the train, but to the conservative gray lapel is affixed a crisp yellow ribbon. He is holding a second Beck's steadied on his stomach. Now he raises it in salute, whether to Kessler or to the TV isn't quite clear.

"It's a stirring day to be American, Michael."

"Wait. Don't start. Let me get one myself."

"Two," Pokorny calls after him. "Thank you."

"Six years, Mel," and Kessler raises his own beer. "I can honestly say it's good to see you. What are you doing now?"

"Plotting," says Mel Pokorny.

"Besides that, I mean."

"I'm a *consultant.*" The word is pronounced in italics of self-mockery. "Risk analysis. That's what they call it in the trade: 'risk analysis.' I hire out through a group with a bland name, a name you've never heard, to advise multinational corporations. About their assets in the fringe countries."

"What's the bland name?"

Pokorny shakes his head gently, suppressing a smirk. "One you've never heard."

"Same old Mel."

"I tell them when to start getting concerned. How to shift their weight prudently. When to go further in, when to hunker, when to pull out. Not just plant and employee security, thank God. It's more a political forecasting role. Tolerably interesting. Only tolerably. Shamefully lucrative."

"I'm glad the private sector found a place for you."

"Yeah," says Pokorny. "Believe me, so was I. Forty-nine years old and a résumé with a big empty space where it doesn't even say CLASSIFIED. Not a situation I recommend."

"But the Agency always has friends."

Pokorny's eyes widen earnestly. "Judas, yes. The Agency's friends. That was part of the problem. I could hardly expect any favors from those boys. I was persona non grata. I had gone out on my ass."

"I heard you walked."

"On my ass. I went out on my ass. What all else did you hear, exactly?"

"Bits and scraps," says Kessler. "Just the *Post* version, plus a few annotations by word of mouth." Kessler himself had already been easing away from the whole subject by that time, no longer so avid as once, sated with intrigue, put off at last by the numberless layers of coy machination, the lies and denials and tactical no-comments and more lies, the leaks and exegeses that only turned out to be further lies, all of which had begun to remind him of the glutinous multiple laminations of a hunk of baklava. Still, he recalls being mildly shocked when he heard about Sparrow's downfall. "Claude Sparrow dismissed summarily," says Kessler. "Called onto the Director's own carpet and fired cold, suddenly, one Monday morning, for abuses of his position as Counterintelligence chief. The very same abuses, not coincidentally, that had just been announced to the American public by way of Joe Delbanco's column. Namely, unauthorized wiretaps against certain U. S. Government officials, in clear violation of the Agency charter. That was the big lead, the sacking of Sparrow. In the gossip a person heard also about Mel Pokorny and a couple other close aides following their boss through the door. As a matter of principle. I've seen you once since then, remember?"

"I like that 'matter of principle.' It's gratifying to hear that. So often the press wants to take only the most cynical view of these things."

"We bumped at the Capitol in '75," Kessler says. "During the Church Committee uproar. You were haunting the corridor outside the hearing room. Wearing a tweed cap and a toupee, as I recall."

"Certainly not testifying. Right. And I gave you a story."

"You *told* me a story," Kessler corrects him. "A story about a story. About the great purge two years earlier. About the moves behind the moves. You wanted me to know that McAttee, the new DCI, was not such a constipated Boy Scout as he was contriving to seem. That the ghastly breach of security by a relentless adversarial press, which had been so well advertised, was charade. The damage control, the security tightening, the bastardly new rules regarding even innocuous, insignificant leakage to journalists—all charade. So you said. That it was McAttee himself—not the syndicated righteousness of Joe Delbanco, nor even the best muckraking work of Delbanco's young staff—who had given this story to the world. No breach: on the contrary, an intentional leak. A deliberate and well-calculated leak, from the Director himself. Do I have all this straight?"

"You sure do."

"And that tapping a few phones at the sub-Cabinet level had not been the most outrageous of Sparrow's sins. He had also been listening to some of his own CIA colleagues. Some of the big boys. People in corner offices. For which impudence, Jed

McAttee had simply fed your boss Sparrow to the hogs, by way of Delbanco's column. Revenge. Fratricide. According to Mel Pokorny, at least. That's what I remember."

"Your memory is pretty good."

"A case of the CIA biting its own tail, like a demented snake. It sounded intriguing at the time, but I didn't do anything with it."

"You should have."

"It was unverifiable. Also self-serving."

"So what? Self-serving doesn't make it false." Dropping his feet off the table, Pokorny sits forward. "And there's more."

"I'm sure there's more. There is always more."

"Aren't you even interested, Michael?"

"Not really. I'm a different sort of writer these days."

"I know." He composes his face to a pitying glower, slightly theatrical like most of Pokorny's expressions. "I've seen some of the stuff you turn out lately."

"What was it, Mel? I gather you loved it."

"I forget. Something about a tiger. A guy who got eaten."

"That was three years ago," says Kessler. "And for your information it won a goddamn award."

"I skimmed it. Very pretty and all, toodle toodle, but I mean who really gives a shit?"

"Who gives a shit about what happened to Claude Sparrow?"

"I think you do," Pokorny says coldly.

They drink at their beers while seconds pass and then Kessler, impulsively and for the sheer pleasure of goading, says: "Now I'm writing a book about termites." But he wishes immediately that he had kept quiet. It's going slowly enough, badly enough, and Kessler is superstitious.

"Termites."

"Sure," Kessler says. "Toodle toodle."

Fortunately Pokorny doesn't believe him.

"All right," says Kessler. "Assume that I am interested. For the sake of discussion. Assume that as a member of the press I prefer to take only the most cynical view of these things. What are you going to tell me? That the Joe Delbanco revelations were only a pretext?"

Pokorny says nothing. He sits there as though deaf.

"That Sparrow was thrown out for some entirely different

reason? Possibly—just as a wild hypothetical—because he had brought the whole Agency to a standstill? Because the Counter-intelligence staff, under him, was running amok? Because he and his people—*you* guys—had put everyone else into a state of paranoid catalepsy? Because McAttee felt that Sparrow had finally, literally, wobbled over the brink of sanity?"

"Not hardly. Where do you get such ideas?"

"Cocktail chatter. These were the annotations," says Kessler. "What, then? That Jedediah McAttee himself is, in reality, a Soviet operation? And only Claude Sparrow was keen enough to smell it?"

"No," says Pokorny. Then he is quiet again. He scowls with one eye down into his bottle, as if watching the past through a telescope, and slouches sulkily. Evidently the bottle is empty. "Never mind."

"Sorry, Mel. I'm a crank on conspiracy theories, is all. You know that. They're the muscatel of the mind, and they make me impatient. Always did. Even when I was fascinated by people like Claude Sparrow."

"There are no people *like* Claude Sparrow."

"You know what I mean."

"Sure I do. You're a hard-ass. That's exactly why I came up here." The tone now is aggrieved. "Washington has journalists like cockroaches, but do I take this to one of them? No. No, I spend a long wasted day on the train." Peeling away the comic glasses, Pokorny drops them dispiritedly into the attaché case. His real nose is much smaller but hardly less comic. He gropes halfheartedly for his shoes.

Kessler decides to wait out this shameless gambit. In the meantime he strolls to the kitchen and returns. Keeping a Budweiser, he sets the last Beck's at Pokorny's elbow.

"Bless you, Michael Mikhailovich." An old nonsense nickname invented by Pokorny, who had one for everybody, and invoked now no doubt to play upon nostalgia. After a few meditative swallows of beer, he says: "Where were we?"

"The purge."

Pokorny nods, gathering back his focus.

It is almost the way they used to transact their business, information passing in layers and scraps, each scrap coyly withheld and challenged and bartered over as to value, other scraps moving back and forth too at the same time. Kessler recalls having relished the process, even on those occasions when it led him nowhere. Dealing with Mel Pokorny—as he believed he knew, in those days after the splash made by his second CIA story—dealing with Mel entailed roughly the same mixture of satisfactions and perils as dickering with a cheery fellow in a plaid jacket over a '55 Mercury coupe with wonderful paint.

But that was the view of a foolish young man. Later Kessler came to suspect that the perils had been very much greater.

"All right. The purge. We'll start at the end," says Pokorny, and proceeds directly to the beginning. "How much do you know about Viktor Tronko?"

Not much, Kessler admits. A Russian defector. Came across sometime in the sixties. There was a ripple of controversy within the Agency—by Kessler's dim recollection of what were even then dim signals—as to whether or not he was real.

"A ripple, the man says. God's bones. The ripple you heard about, Michael Mikhailovich, was Niagara Falls. That's a ripple. This Tronko thing, on the other hand, was a certified shit-storm."

Viktor Tronko, Pokorny explains with uncharacteristic vehemence, was one or the other of two things. *Could only have been* one or the other. "Either he was the biggest beluga we ever landed," says Pokorny—the most significantly placed KGB agent who ever came West, shedding new light on a range of old questions, including two especially perplexing ones of paramount delicacy, a priceless resource, in other words, this Tronko, as Jed McAttee would claim—"or else, option two, he was the greatest fraud since Piltdown." And therefore the worst catastrophe—the very worst of any sort, Pokorny stresses fiercely, even including Watergate and Senator Frank Church—that has ever befallen the CIA. Total disaster. And worse than total. Worse than if Congress had voted the Agency out of existence. Worse than if they had disbanded the whole staff, burned all the files, pulled the plug on every agent and every spy satellite, sent the Corps of Engineers out to rip down the building and salt the earth. Worse. Tiny sparkles of spit fly in diving parabolas from Pokorny's mouth. His high fat little cheeks have gone red.

"As Claude Sparrow would claim," says Kessler. "And Mel Pokorny."

"Either this or that. Choose one. No middle possibilities. Yes

I would. You bet I would. Michael, the place isn't just wrecked. It's inside out."

"Where's Viktor Tronko now?"

"Inside," says Pokorny. "Contract employee. A high-level analyst for the Soviet Bloc Division. McAttee's old bailiwick, of course. Trusted, relied upon, confided in. Cleared for a staggering breadth of access."

"And you ask me to believe that Tronko, all along, is simply a Soviet hoax."

" 'Simply' is not the word I would use. Anyway, no. I don't ask you to *believe* a goddamn thing. What I ask you to do is *wonder.* I ask you to *doubt.*" Without warning Pokorny pitches his empty bottle to the far end of the room, where it shatters smartly against an old whiskey barrel that is part of Kessler's bachelor decor. For a moment Pokorny's eyes bug slightly, as though he has shocked himself. "I ask you to listen."

Deft aim and no real damage. That was rather good, Kessler thinks.

"From here on we're into cans."

"It's okay," says Pokorny. "Don't get up." And he goes to the kitchen for a round.

By its bare outline the Tronko case does not seem to offer prospect of infinite befuddlement. "In that sense you're right," Kessler is told. "In that sense I suppose you could call it simple." The overt facts are stark. The moves are brusque. The potential permutations of uncertainty would not appear to be so very numerous. Either it's this or it's that. Either the man was what he claimed he was, or he was something other. "That much is obvious. Correct?" says Pokorny.

"Maybe," says Kessler.

"Hah. Don't be sucked in."

The first contact had been made in Rome, during the summer of 1962. Viktor Tronko was there on assignment—a plum assignment for any KGB officer—as chief of security for a trade delegation touring industrial sites in the Tiber Valley. In other words, he was watchdog for a busload of Soviet junketeers. Technically, it was a counterintelligence post, with responsibility for protecting the delegation members from being spied upon or blackmailed; realistically, his chores amounted to keeping those other comrades in line or reporting on them when they stepped out, and by a nice irony the primary chore was to watch for defections. Entirely unsolicited, Tronko passed a letter to an American diplomat—actually, and presumably not by coincidence, it was a CIA man under embassy cover—volunteering himself as an agent in place.

"What we call a walk-in," says Pokorny. "Maybe ten percent of our useful agents come from the walk-in trade. Maybe less. We don't altogether spurn it but we begin those cases with the presumption that, well, you know, more likely than not here's a guy who is out to diddle us. Most of the diddlers are free lance. Just trying to peddle phony intelligence for a quick dollar. Some are bait, in nasty little traps set by the opposition. They're hoping we'll give something or somebody away." Kessler wonders if there is significance to the fact that, immediately upon beginning this talk about tradecraft, Pokorny has lapsed into the present tense. "For instance, they might kidnap the case officer. Or a safe house gets blown, and then we're stuck holding the lease. So walk-ins are special. We tread carefully." For that first contact, Tronko was handled by what amounted to remote control. No very precious U.S. intelligence assets, either human or in terms of real estate, were compromised.

Then the Italian junket ended and the Soviet delegation went home, Comrade Tronko along with the others. Arrangements had been made for him to continue the contact in Moscow; he had a signal code that would alert an American case officer to a rendezvous. But the signal was never used. "So we assumed it had just been a KGB trawl," says Pokorny. "Halfhearted and inept."

Eighteen months later Tronko turned up in Vienna, again as security chief for a trade delegation, and this time he used a telegraph message, also in prearranged code, to ask Langley for another contact. Promptly and discreetly granted. At which meeting Tronko abruptly declared his eagerness to defect. No word for a year and a half, and now he wanted to jump on the first plane for America. Just couldn't wait to go. Langley was uncomfortable with this Tatar impulsiveness. "We were still calling it impulsiveness then," says Pokorny, implying murky reversals to come. Impulsive or not, Tronko was unmistakably an adroit professional, and he danced Langley into a corner. He effectively made it impossible for them to turn him down. So

Jed McAttee brought him back to Washington and then the Soviet Bloc Division had—

"Wait," says Kessler. "How did he make it impossible?"

Mel Pokorny for a moment gives at least the impression of weighing his answer. "He dropped names."

"What names?"

"Lee Harvey Oswald, for one."

"He knew something about Oswald?"

"Yes. No, not exactly. I'm getting to that."

"Who else?"

"Who else what? Who else knew about Oswald?"

"Don't pull that on me. You said *names*. Plural."

Pokorny's eyes shine as he hides his mouth behind a beer can. "Did I?"

Back to Washington with McAttee, and then the Soviet Bloc Division had its shot at debriefing him. Last week of February until the middle of June 1964. Meanwhile the Warren Commission was also in session, Warren himself and the other members getting summaries of summaries of evidence while the staff scrambled to put some sort of findings together by LBJ's deadline, which was September. Let's get it settled, the President was saying. Get something out fast; reassure the citizenry. Also of course September was before the election. So there was heavy pressure to make sense, quickly, of the new Oswald lead. After three days of routine processing at an Agency compound near Washington, Tronko was booked into a safe house out in Annapolis, with a couple of nannies from the Office of Security; and the first phase of debriefing began. It was conducted by a clever fellow from the Soviet Bloc Division named Sol Lentzer, Russian by extraction and by manner, though he had been born in Paris. Lentzer was chosen because he was the best that Jed McAttee had. Throughout this phase McAttee himself remained in Langley, reading the daily reports and conferring with Lentzer personally, sometimes listening to the raw tapes, but having no further direct contact with the subject. For now. Tronko was treated as a man with information to offer and a certain claim to pampering.

"Which is not to say," Pokorny interrupts himself, "that we expected the information would be true. Not at all. We still assumed he was some kind of devious fake. Sent across by the KGB. On a mission of disinformation, as yet unspecifiable.

Even goddamn *McAttee* still assumed that. But we didn't want
Tronko to suspect our suspicions. Get him to dump his load
first. As he had been programmed to do, back in Moscow. After
which we would break him, see, was the idea. And figure out
what to make of it all." Pokorny drinks. A long languid tilt that
must very nearly have drained the present can.

Then he says: "But the man drank. That was the first problem. At least it seemed to be. You know how drunks are."
Pokorny offers a broad smile. "Mendacious and crafty."

Denied other options, Tronko took his pampering in the form
of alcohol, which Langley then believed, foolishly, would be
harmless and not involve troublesome complications. So after
each hard day of answering questions, Tronko dragged the nannies out on a pub crawl. He boozed his way through every bar
in Annapolis, every country roadhouse in that corner of coastal
Maryland. Between February and June, Tronko was drunk or
hung over most of his waking hours. And the debriefing, according to Pokorny, was a total mess.

"Why?"

"His story was full of holes. Contradictions, factual mistakes,
minor implausibilities. Exaggerations of his own importance.
And some other things, crucial things, that just defied belief. It
was obvious that he was lying through his teeth."

"What sort of crucial things?"

"Partly about Oswald, during his time in the Soviet Union.
Oswald at this point was still the main focus. We were in a
sweat to know anything at all about Oswald. How much KGB
interest had the guy attracted while he was living in Russia? It
was inevitable that there had been some. Oswald, you know, he
was once a radar operator at a U-2 base in Japan. Just before he
left the Marines. Only natural to assume that the Soviets—well,
here's a creep from the U.S., calling himself a defector, he
wants Russian citizenship, and it turns out the kid spent a year
tracking U-2s. Definitely the Soviets would pick his brain.
Right? Wouldn't they? Sure. There would be contact. But *how
much* contact? Under what circumstances? To what end?
Tronko claimed no. Unequivocal *nyet.* Claimed the KGB never
so much as interviewed Lee Harvey Oswald. And Tronko at
that time had been in precisely the position to know. Rather,
again, he claimed he had."

In June, cold sober and with a margin of four days for drying out, Tronko was given a polygraph test. Which he failed.

Then began what Pokorny refers to as "the first hostile interrogation." Quickly Pokorny adds: "Compared to the second one, though, this one was still almost cozy."

The pretense of benign credulousness was abruptly dropped. Tronko was allowed to know that the Agency disbelieved his story; had always disbelieved it, in fact. And "allowed to know" is an understatement, Pokorny explains, since the sessions now included a good deal of shouting, badgering, other varieties of verbal and psychological abuse. Sol Lentzer was still in charge but the sort of role he played was much different. No longer an amiable and patient debriefing officer; now he was an inquisitor. More demanding, more unpredictable. Much more strident. They might have replaced Lentzer altogether and started fresh, sent in a cold new face at this point, if it hadn't been for one consideration: they wanted Tronko left without hope. Wanted him devoid of any suspicion that he might still have a partisan, a single believer, somewhere out there within the Agency. So Lentzer stayed on, merely changing his own face. His personality. His whole approach. Of which, being the division's own Dostoyevskian Russian, he was quite capable. All this was plotted out premeditatively at Langley, Pokorny says.

Tronko now heard himself called a liar, repeatedly and at high volume. He got no more pampering, no more booze. He was not even free to go out on the street. Handcuffed and blindfolded, he was moved to a different location, a place of decidedly more spartan atmosphere than the safe house in Annapolis, but still within an hour's drive of Langley. There he was slapped into a single bare room with a window boarded over and a naked bulb dangling from above, of which he did not control the switch. The only furniture was a cot with a rough wool blanket. His Annapolis clothes were taken away and he was issued military fatigues—first a set that were too small for him, then when those grew fetid a set that were too big; after the next washing the small set again. Once a day he was allowed use of a chamber pot, brought in by armed guard at an arbitrarily varied time, waited for, taken away again. Once a week he was permitted to shower and shave. No toothbrush. No washbasin in the room. Nothing to read. No heat—which was not a bitter hardship when he arrived there in June but became one before he left. No cooling and no ventilation through the summer. He was observed constantly through a door peephole by his guards, who were laconic and under instructions to scowl. They took turns watching television in the far front room of the house, wearing earphones, while Tronko was left rotting in silence. Awakened at 6 A.M. with boot-camp stridency, he was forbidden to sit or lie on the cot again until ten at night. Mainly he leaned. Sometimes he paced. In every way possible the point was made to Tronko that he was no longer—never had been—a valued defector. He was a prisoner. He was a captured enemy in the spy wars.

Every few days he was visited by Lentzer, put through a long and exhausting session, sometimes three or four days in a row, then maybe no session at all for a week. Less often, Lentzer was joined by another, these two working on him like lumberjacks with a crosscut saw. On those days the language jumped wildly back and forth from abusive to conciliatory, and from English to Russian. The second man was Jed McAttee.

Together Lentzer and McAttee attacked Tronko's story in its—

"Was this legal?" says Kessler.

"No," says Pokorny.

"He was on U.S. soil. Subject to and protected by U.S. laws. But incarcerated against his will."

"You bet he was."

"Charged with no crime."

"Not in a courtroom, no. Not officially."

"What was the legal justification? You guys keep a lawyer or two on the payroll, don't you?"

"No justification. We couldn't think of one," says Pokorny. "We just did it."

" 'We had to,' " Kessler quotes from imagination in a voice not his own.

"We did have to," Pokorny says blandly. He shrugs. "Sue us."

Together Lentzer and McAttee, day after day stretching finally into months, attacked Tronko's story in its every vagueness and flaw. Hammering at—

"Oswald in Russia," Kessler interrupts again. "No KGB interest. What else? What are these famous flaws?"

"I'm getting to that."

"No you're not. You're filling my head with crap. Details of the cell. Psychological warfare stuff. Your own methodology. CIA methodology doesn't interest me that much, Mel. Not even when it's mildly illegal. I want to know the payoff. Skip ahead. We can always go back."

"This is a godawful convoluted story, Michael. I'm trying to give you an overview."

"Fog. Fog." Tracing a diaphanous shape in the air with his beer hand, Kessler notices that the can is empty. "Becloud the man's mind, spin him around twice, then lead him where you want." Through fog Kessler gropes his way to the refrigerator and back again safely. "What exactly did you learn from this Russian? And why has it taken seventeen years before you were ready to breathe it out?"

"Eleanor Roosevelt was a Soviet agent," says Pokorny. "A man."

"Tronko came over. All right. He told a phony story. All right. He was locked up and spat upon and interrogated and broken. All right. Or he wasn't broken. That's all right too. Just give me the punch line and then I desperately need to go take a leak."

"It isn't nearly that simple."

—hammering at what were then still considered the weakest points, and therefore the most critical points, of Tronko's story. Had he or had he not held the KGB rank of colonel? Had there or had there not been a recall telegram forcing his hand in Vienna? Did or did not the KGB interview Lee Harvey Oswald during the two and a half years Oswald spent as a lonely expatriate in Minsk? If not, why not? Before Tronko began getting these cushy trade-delegation assignments, had he in truth been a desk man within the Seventh Department of the Second Chief Directorate—also known as the Tourist Department—which was, by great coincidence, that very office of the KGB that would have handled the Oswald file, if one existed? Had he? Or had he not? If so, why was he unable to describe the physical layout of that wing of KGB headquarters? Why had he given the wrong patronymic for the man who had supposedly been his boss's boss? Who did he think he was trying to fool?

And in addition to all these minor evidential matters, says Mel Pokorny, there was always a single dizzying question that had to be settled in connection with the Tronko testimony.

Even during McAttee's try, even with LBJ and Earl Warren
breathing heavily in the background, despite all the headlines
and false leads and preoccupations, this question laid its weight
upon every move in the case, every hour of interrogation, every
new theory or suspicion applied to Viktor Semyonovich Tronko
and all his confusing signals. "It was the real question behind
every other question we asked him," says Pokorny.

"Of course it was. 'Did the KGB program Oswald to pull the
trigger on Kennedy?' " Kessler postulates.

"Don't be pedestrian," says Pokorny. "No. Not that at all.
Considerably more dizzying."

The September deadline came and passed but Tronko, in
spite of the harsh treatment, the snags in his story, the demon-
strable falsehoods that were thrown back at him, refused to be
broken. He just wouldn't collapse. Wouldn't confess. He was
the one person involved who was quite indifferent to LBJ's time
line. So the Warren Report was duly issued, containing no mention whatsoever of the name Viktor Tronko or of the perspective he claimed to offer on Lee Harvey Oswald. Better to ignore
Tronko entirely, the Commission decided, than to link their
conclusion to his credibility. By November, Tronko still wasn't
broken. "But McAttee was," says Pokorny. "He had become a
believer."

"In what?"

"The reality of Viktor Tronko."

"How could he?" says Kessler. "With all these inconsistencies and manifest lies you talk about."

"White ones, according to Jed. Yes, okay, the man lied about
his rank. Lied about his work history. About KGB interest in
Oswald, the former U-2 flunky. About certain other personal
and professional matters. These were just the predictable falsifi-
cations of a desperate defector and an alcoholic, according to
Jed. Nothing more. Nothing so very ominous. Tronko is a bit of
a liar, yes, all right—McAttee conceded that much. But he's his
own liar, says Jed. Not Moscow's. He was not sent. He walked
across to us under his own power. We can believe part of what
he tells us, says Jed. We can believe that part which seems
otherwise plausible. Nice? That was the Archangel Jedediah's
carefully measured and supposedly well-informed assessment.
Which of course was just fatally dumb. Wrongheaded. Naive. It
was the first dingdong of doom. Because part of what Tronko

was telling us—and it seemed *plausible* enough, sure, it just happened to be false—was his answer to that single preeminent question. The dizzying one," says Pokorny.

"The one which you, coy bastard, are going to keep from me as long as possible," says Kessler. "Maybe right up to the moment my hands close around your throat."

"I thought you'd never ask. It had to do with a penetration, Michael. Of the Agency. Tronko came over to us with a very curious assertion about the possibility of a high-level penetration. That was the big issue—not Oswald. That was why we were all ripping out handfuls of hair to decide one way or the other about this guy."

"Tronko claimed there was a KGB mole way up inside the CIA?"

"No," says Pokorny. "He claimed there wasn't."

3

Pokorny has disappeared toward the kitchen but a few seconds later he is back in the corridor, bracing himself against one wall. He hovers there momentarily, adding what seems to be an afterthought:

"We had reason to believe otherwise."

The television all this while has been flashing and chattering. Kessler notices now that either the late news has begun, the midevening special report hasn't yet finished, or tonight there is no distinction. Ronald Reagan stands at a dais above the South Lawn saying: ". . . entered the ranks of those who throughout history have undergone the ordeal of imprisonment—the crew of the *Pueblo*, the prisoners in two World Wars, and in Korea and Vietnam. And like those others, you are special to us." When Kessler glances up, Pokorny is gone. Not altogether beyond possibility that, for reasons obscure and perverse, he might slink away at just such a juncture, as quietly as he arrived, and one of the nerves in Kessler's right calf twitches in response to that thought. But Kessler remains seated. Hears the refrigerator door smooch open reassuringly. Pokorny returns to his spot in the corridor, which is narrow enough for the walls to keep a man upright.

"Fortunately Jed's view wasn't the only one. Not the prevailing one, even. Not yet. Herbert Eames was unconvinced."

"Eames was still Director then," Kessler says with the crisp pointless certitude of someone pretending to be sober. Pokorny pays no attention.

"So Eames turned him over to Counterintelligence for a try. This was November of '64. Tronko was moved again. To a place that had been built special." He allows himself a sneer of sadistic nostalgia. "We called it the Vault."

"The Vault," says Kessler. "That sounds just real friendly."

"Exactly. Because here we begin the second hostile interrogation. Much different from the first. This one lasted three years. Every bit of three goddamn long years. During all that time Tronko did not get his nose outside this Vault thing. Literally didn't. Three years of solitary confinement. Surrounded only by concrete and questions. There was nothing else to his life. Concrete and questions. He saw no other human being, practically, except his latest new inquisitor. Almost no one else. Three years, Michael Mikhailovich. Imagine the kind of psychological dependence that could foster." Pokorny squints pityingly at the recollection. "And the new man, he was a genuine asshole. Not smooth and deft like Lentzer, with an ingratiating Mother Russia manner that he could turn on when he wanted. Forget it. None of that filigree. Not as smart as Lentzer either. But tenacious as all hell, this one. Murderously cunning, maybe, in his own way. Tough. Relentlessly unsympathetic. Just a weatherproof, cast-iron asshole. About the last person Tronko would have chosen."

"Who was it?"

"Me," says Pokorny. "Now I have a piece of truly appalling news for you."

"We're out of beer."

"I'll go," says Pokorny. "Just tell me where."

Kessler gives him directions to a neighborhood grocery on the corner of Chapel and Howe, a place that has earned Kessler's affectionate loyalty because it combines the best aspects of a convenience mart and a fine Italian deli. The old man who runs it is a widower and evidently sees no reason to rush home at seven. From greed or loneliness, more likely the latter, he stays open till all hours reading Jacob Burckhardt and listening to good music on FM. Get some nosh while you're at it, Kessler tells Pokorny. Cheese or the artichoke salad or whatever looks good. And there's one other thing.

"What?"

"You should probably take off that wig."

Kessler loses himself in a trance of confusion and boozy exhaustion with his eyes on the TV, part of the time even focused there. His brain roams and stumbles. The thing to do now, he senses distantly, is assemble a mental list of the more pertinent questions, then contemplate each in turn, making decisions

about which should be asked and which are better just guessed
at. *Why has Mel come to me with this stuff?* He wants an article
written, obviously. He wants to use me. Wants the Tronko thing
to break into print, finally, as a public stroke in some dark little
private battle he happens currently to be fighting. Fine. That's
nothing new. Every disgruntled bureaucrat in Washington has a
grudge article of some sort he would like to see written. Mel's is
undoubtedly more juicy than most. *What dark little private battle?* That's an easy one too. By his own account, Mel is out on
his ass. Risk analysis for the multinationals is deadly boring.
His man Sparrow is still in disgrace also. But they haven't given
up. They want back in. Maybe it's even as Mel has claimed: he
might really believe that the Agency has suffered a catastrophic
inversion, with Tronko and other nefarious influences now on
the inside, and Mel with a brave dream of setting things right.
Then why wait eight years? That one is more difficult. The purge
of Claude Sparrow and his minions is by now very old news.
Why should Mel's self-interested calculations dictate that this,
at last, is the very moment to go public? Why not last month?
Why not last year or five years ago? Why, why not, why. And
at the tail of the list there is another question, long pending,
more important to Kessler personally than any of those others,
and which still has the power to make him uncomfortable. *Just
what IS the mix of perils and satisfactions entailed in dealing
with Mel Pokorny?*

Kessler's own first big CIA story, an exposé of illegal mail
interception conducted against certain U.S. citizens, had been
virtually a gift from Pokorny. Moderately damning in its por-
trayal of the Agency—or at least of one part of the Agency—it
ran as a cover story in *Harper's* and gave Kessler the start of a
national reputation. The piece was unexceptional in all but its
factual content, no masterwork of elegant prose or sage analysis, yet it greatly increased his professional options. Opened
other doors. Kessler was twenty-four years old at the time. He
asked himself even then why Mel had done it. Of course he
asked. But he didn't worry much about that until somewhat
later.

The TV has finally moved on to other subjects, and Kessler
begins to feel more hungry than drunk. When the ring of the
telephone jangles him from his stupor, he thinks at once of the

woman named Nora, so ferociously serious and remote, in her little house across town.

Kessler has only on one occasion gotten past her front door. Made it as far as the living room but wasn't offered a chair. That was in daylight, and still she seemed flustered by his (admittedly uninvited) presence, pacing away her embarrassment or ambivalence or whatever it was in a circuit between the piano and the stairs, while he leaned in a doorway, watching; she wasn't rude to him, she wasn't quite cold, but clearly she didn't want him to linger. Conflicting emotions seemed to be moving through her like thunderclouds and patches of blue on a gusty afternoon. My daughter, she said nervously, as though it explained something. What *about* your daughter? he thought. Nora's daughter is nine years old and rather owlish, he gathers, and evidently must be protected from the trauma of seeing her mother in company with questionable gentlemen, of which Kessler has repeatedly been made to feel one. Nora's divorce was still recent at that point. The marriage had been stone dead for a couple of years, by Kessler's understanding of those few facts she had vouch-safed him, but the divorce was recent and Nora believes ardently in formalities, vows, due process. Down in Ecuador, the week they met, she had still carried the pale mark of a wedding ring, lately removed from her finger. That was erased quickly by sun and sea water. The internal marks, as Kessler began learning during their night at the Hotel Alfaro, would be much slower to fade. It seemed that she had only begun, that night, to learn the same thing herself. Then in September, when he appeared on her New Haven doorstep, she seemed thrilled to see him and allowed him the living room, then within ten minutes asked him to leave. A confused and confusing woman. My daughter, she said. Please don't show up here like this, she said. Reach me by telephone if you like, she said (forgetting all his long-distance tries), but don't just show up. Or I'll call you, she said unconvincingly. We'll talk, yes. Just give me a bit of time and space. I need some time and space. She was gnawing her lip. The door of the little house closed quietly as he went down the walk. That was September and they have spoken only a half dozen times since, once indeed on her initiative. Now, as the phone rings persistently, he imagines a single light burning in, say, the left downstairs window of her place.

What time has it gotten to be? Too late for Nora to call, even if planets have shifted and her emotional astrology now again favors Kessler—or maybe just the right time of night, because by now the child is asleep. He wonders how Nora would look in a flannel robe. Serenely maternal, no doubt—a nice complement to the oversize T-shirt that kept her modest in Guayaquil. Snatching up the receiver, Kessler warns himself that more likely this is Pokorny, somehow diverted or lost, wandering half sodden in a far neighborhood.

Neither. It is Fullerton, the dean, calling to remind Kessler of the master's wife's tea scheduled for the following afternoon, at which Kessler has agreed to make himself present and answer earnest student questions about the romantic life of globe-trotting journalism, or whatever it is they perceive him as doing. A promise he would have been grateful for the chance to forget. The master's wife, Kessler asks—does she serve anything stronger than tea? Fullerton laughs politely as though someone has made a joke. The whole conversation lasts three minutes. As he leans to set the phone back, Kessler sees the face of the clock. He hasn't had lunch or dinner. He can feel his body sinking into a torpor, an edgeless sour limbo, neither drunk nor alert. For God's sake, Mel, where are you?

He is aware suddenly that Pokorny has been gone much too long. It does *not* take forty-five minutes between here and Biaggio's. Not even for a slaloming drunk.

By the time Kessler reaches Chapel and Howe it is midnight. A van and two evidence technicians from the New Haven PD are already at the scene, as well as three squad cars (one of those parked up across the sidewalk), a pair of detectives, and a small crowd of gawkers. Aqueous light strobing through red plastic, and the silent keening of a flash camera. Angry and rude, Kessler elbows his way through the crowd. After a brusque exchange with one patrolman he is welcomed inside the little market, among the detectives and Mr. Biaggio, because he can identify the victim. This deceased person in question was carrying a pocketful of rumpled twenties, a set of house keys, a small Dictaphone, but no wallet.

Mel's body lies in a dark marbleized slick of blood and wine near the reach-in cooler, looking as though it arrived there by catapult.

Legs and arms twisted with the ungainly abandon of the

dead. Though his black wing tips are neatly tied, he hadn't bothered, Kessler notices now, to put on his socks.

God knows how many times he has been shot but the first official count, otherwise, will be made by the medical examiner. Whoever did it seems to have emptied at least a magazine into Mel in particular and that end of the room generally. Shattered glass from the cooler doors, broken wine bottles, crockery shards from the cheap Liebfraumilch; dry-roasted nuts, of which Mel apparently took down a rackload when he fell. The cash register has of course been looted, a detail that Kessler hears with numb and faraway skepticism. He feels as though he is watching the whole scene from a crane bucket overhead. Beyond supplying a name, he has nothing much to say.

The dead man was a friend of his, yes. That's close enough for forensic purposes. Visiting him tonight, yes. A social visit? Kessler hesitates. Then says yes. Pokorny may have had other business in town, or maybe at some corporate headquarters down in Stamford, but the stop to see Kessler was purely social, yes. He had come up that day from Washington. Where he works as a consultant to large corporations. Worked. Well, sort of an insurance and security adviser, Kessler explains. No, he cannot tell them the company's name. It was a new job since he last saw the man. Yes, he will gladly check his apartment for a wallet or a business card; or they can search it themselves. At this point Kessler recalls—but does not mention—the attaché case. There is no immediate family, no. He tells them the name of Pokorny's ex-wife, who to the best of his knowledge still lives in the Washington area. One of the two detectives takes notes on a clipboard. Both of them are polite and seem very young. He gives his own name and address, doubting that he will hear from them unless the body goes unclaimed. It's such an obvious sort of crime, crude and brutal and heartbreakingly banal, and he is not even so much as an eyewitness.

All of which is saddening but acceptable to Kessler. He cannot honestly mourn in a personal way. Pokorny had long since become a stranger. And if any recourse exists, in the name of justice or national security (as the phrase goes) or maybe just truth, certainly the New Haven police do not offer it. Who does offer it? Kessler exerts a conscious effort to avoid thinking in such terms. Blah. Beware of words like "recourse" and "truth."

At the same time he is altogether fascinated. No use denying that: he is even more fascinated than before. Pokorny has had the bad grace to leave his story tantalizingly incomplete. They moved Tronko to the Vault, okay. Began the second hostile interrogation, okay. Damn it all, what then?

Kessler attempts to stretch his lungs free from the grip of this ambivalence with several deep breaths, which the old man mistakes for bereavement. A hand is laid gently on Kessler's sleeve. "He shouldn't have panicked," says Mr. Biaggio, intending it somehow as solace.

Mr. Biaggio himself is covered with blood, a splotch in his hair that has sent runnels down over the ear and along the jaw line, and across the front of his blue shirt a heavy maroon stain, still sticky as fresh paint. But he seems to feel just fine, thank you. Glad to be alive. The blood is evidently from Mel.

"It was a white man this time," Mr. Biaggio confides.

A man of medium height and slender build, according to Mr. Biaggio, dressed in faded jeans and a nylon jacket and wearing the obligatory ski mask, navy wool with the eyes and mouth outlined in cheery yellow. Caucasian hands. There was no one else in the store just then, only the two of them, Mr. Biaggio in his chair by the register and the bald fellow, what was his name, down a far aisle by the smoked meats. This white man in the ski mask appeared. Ordered them both over to stand in front of the cooler. Held the gun on them for a minute or two before any move was made toward the cash. Said a few pointless things, like "That's good" and "Everybody stay easy" and "How much in the till, old man?"—as though the robber just wanted to hear his own voice. All right. Let him hear it. Mr. Biaggio had no inclination to rush him.

"Your friend," says Mr. Biaggio. "He shouldn't have panicked. I know. I know about these things." Mr. Biaggio is by now a postgraduate fellow in the study of urban mayhem: seven shots from a .45 automatic, blood and glass sailing everywhere, and he sneaks through unscathed. "These jittery dope eaters and screwballs. I know. I come up here, it's six years ago now, from Bridgeport. Whatever you do, you don't panic. You got to relax. Panic is suicide. Because it's contagious, see?"

Kessler walks home with that wisdom in his ears. Does it apply to journalists as well as grocers? He wonders what he can do to be granted, in this whole affair, the same magic immunity as Mr. Biaggio.

4

By noon the next day the body has already been claimed and is on its way down to Washington in a private hearse. Kessler learns that much from a phone call to the medical examiner. Yes, the hearse was hired locally. Left here about an hour ago. Wasn't there an autopsy? asks Kessler. Of course there was. Nine o'clock this morning. The medical examiner has that report on his desk. No need to hold the corpse. Massive trauma and bleeding, the result of five shots from a .45-caliber pistol, three of those five each delivering a wound that, alone, was potentially fatal. The report is public record; Kessler can come in and get a copy made for twenty cents. There is no great mystery involved, so far as the medical examiner is concerned, in this death.

"Thanks anyway," says Kessler. "Who was it that claimed the body?"

Two men from Washington, he is told.

"Who were they? Relatives?" Kessler is a friend of the deceased and he wonders—so he says—about funeral arrangements. These men were government officials, he is told. What sort of government officials? Is this an FBI case for some reason? The medical examiner doesn't answer that one; still bland and condescending and impatient with questions, like every coroner Kessler has ever talked to, he has come to the limit of required cooperativeness. He refers Kessler to the New Haven police.

Instead Kessler spends a few hours at his desk, leafing his way through a thick pile of typescript, penciling in a few inconsequential revisions and drinking too many cups of coffee. He feels as though he is breaking rock with a sledge hammer. His concentration is bad. He gets nothing much written. He makes a pretense of some meager accomplishment, finally, by retyping

several pages grown sloppy with arrows and insertions. This is
the work he spoke of to Mel, misleadingly but not too inaccu-
rately, as his termite book. When the doorbell interrupts, Kessler is almost relieved.

The scowling fat man on his threshold waves a leather ID
folder in Kessler's face, snaps it closed before Kessler can read
the card, and walks in without saying a word.

A total stranger. This character swaggers toward the living
room. His brown checkerboard suit is too long in the legs and
looks as though it has been serving him as pajamas. His hair is
curly and wild as a pile of meringue, but clipped down short
over the ears and gone totally bare on the crown of the pie. He
wears oxblood wing tips with tap heels, which clack gratingly
against Kessler's bare hardwood floor. His swagger is really
more of a noisy waddle, and he seems to walk bowlegged as a
matter of principle, arms held away from his sides as though
that way the hands are ready for something, a fast-draw encounter maybe, or perhaps a banana proffered through bars.
Halfway down the corridor he turns to tell Kessler:

"Close the door."

He is not the pear-shaped variety of fat man, however, the
lifelong hopeless endomorph, but the sort who gives evidence of
having once been an athletic specimen. The belly hangs low yet
the chest is still held high, the shoulders arched back militarily.
He couldn't button the brown jacket if he tried. Under one
armpit Kessler can see a dark holster and a pistol. The gun's
handle, unless Kessler's glimpse has deluded him, is some shiny
light material the color of ivory. The man has seated himself in
the good chair by the time Kessler catches up.

"Everything you can tell me will be useful," the man says.

"You're going to have to start over," Kessler says.

The man only blinks, and scowls harder.

"I'm glad to cooperate. Within reason," says Kessler. "But
you're making a bad impression. Could I see that identification
again?"

The man's eyes are small and close-set as two finger-pokes in
a snowman. He flicks his gaze from Kessler to the room's far
corner, then out the window, back to Kessler. His mouth hangs
slightly open for deep breathing after the stair climb, a narrow
mouth over a thick lower lip, like a vending slot for quarters.
He reaches again for his proof of identity, somewhere back un-

der the jacket, not the holster side but the other. Throws his folder onto the coffee table in roughly Kessler's direction.

It is a standard CIA credential of the type that Kessler has seen before, sandwiched in plastic and attesting that someone named Dexter Lovesong is an employee of the Office of Security, Directorate of Management and Services, Central Intelligence Agency. The official Agency seal is printed across it in pale gray ink, like a watermark. The photograph seems to show a younger and thinner man, but Kessler is willing to believe that any aging thug claiming the name Dexter Lovesong must certainly have come by it honestly.

"Okay. Thank you," says Kessler.

"Don't mention it."

"You want to know about Mel."

An exaggerated slow nod from Dexter Lovesong, who sits sideways in the chair, one arm slung over the back, belly stressing his shirt buttons. His face is still empty. At least he has closed his mouth.

Kessler tells him virtually everything. The surprise visit last night, the long acquaintance between himself and Pokorny, the accidental encounter outside Senator Church's hearing room, then the six-year lapse in contact since Kessler began working a different sort of beat; the talk yesterday about Claude Sparrow, about Viktor Tronko, about the first and second hostile interrogations, about the Vault, about the Agency having been turned inside out—even, for good measure, that sensitive part about the dizzying question which Tronko had been expected to settle. Pokorny believed there was a Soviet penetration, Kessler explains. Mel talked as though Sparrow and others believed it too. Tronko was saying no, no mole, and that's why they distrusted him. Kessler dredges his memory for detail from last night's conversation, for exact phrases that Mel used. As a preemptive tactic, he hopes to bury this Dexter Lovesong with information. He offers nearly all he has—with only two conscious omissions.

For reasons of professional ethic he does not mention the old mail-interception story, or any of the several others for which Mel served as his primary source; even dead, Pokorny has a right to the protection Kessler once promised him. And he says nothing about the locker key from Mel's briefcase.

Dexter Lovesong takes no notes. He doesn't cross-examine. He doesn't interrupt Kessler, or force him to repeat, or badger him for enlargement in crucial areas. For Lovesong it seems there are no crucial areas. He asks only enough questions to keep Kessler talking—under his own momentum and directing the focus as he wishes—for roughly an hour. During that hour Lovesong shifts restlessly in the chair a few times, sprawling each time at a new angle, and glances once at his watch. Kessler wonders: Am I boring this guy, or what? Lovesong shows no particular interest in the notion of a Russian mole on the seventh floor at Langley—no interest in what Mel Pokorny believed on the subject, nor Claude Sparrow, nor Viktor Tronko. That sort of talk seems only to give the man heavy eyelids. When Kessler comes back around to the attaché case, though, Lovesong sets both hooves on the floor.

"Where is it?"

Kessler brings him the case. Lovesong makes a point of snatching it away before Kessler can release the handle, a willfully rude gesture that seems intended to say that Kessler's very grip on the thing is illicit. By this bit of crude force, Kessler is faintly amused. Dexter Lovesong seems to be a different subspecies of CIA officer from the others he has known. Laying the case flat on the coffee table, Lovesong hesitates, his hand on the latch. He appears to be thinking. First evidence of this that Kessler has seen.

"Did you open it?"

"It was open," says Kessler. "Open when I found him here. Open when he left for the grocery."

"Did you go through it?"

"Yes," says Kessler. Unless there is some sort of fancy false bottom, he knows exactly what Lovesong is going to find: a train schedule, a wallet, copies of *The Wall Street Journal* and *Business Week,* several file folders containing computer printouts that describe such banal matters as the flow of agricultural-technology imports into Saudi Arabia, one lock tool, and one orange wig. He will also, with help from a forensic lab, find Kessler's fingerprints, so no sense in being too coy. "I was looking for a phone number. Some way to reach his people. That's still you all, evidently." The pair of Groucho glasses must have gotten misplaced, perhaps hidden themselves under the sofa. The locker key is in Kessler's pocket.

"Don't be so sure," says Lovesong. His little brown eyes flick up. "Didn't take anything out, did you?"

"No. Of course not," Kessler lies.

5

By four o'clock he has an agreement for the story. It took him three phone calls. The *Atlantic* has just run a CIA piece, a long one about paramilitary involvement in Central America, so nothing more for a while, thanks; besides, what's the news value today of a gloss on the Claude Sparrow firing? Kessler didn't argue. At this point, and over the telephone, he was not offering his most dramatic datum—that Sparrow's deputy had been shot dead last night almost on Kessler's doorstep. The new fellow brought in at *Harper's,* the latest Bigbrain there, a man younger than Kessler with whom he has never dealt, turned out to be cordial but also uninterested in what Kessler had come to peddle. This one said:

"I thought you wrote nature stories."

After wincing, Kessler said: "Sometimes. Not always. I broke into this business writing about spooks. For *Harper's.*"

"Tigers and that sort of thing," the man said. "I've seen your work. Liked it. Like to get you in the book. Come back to me with something on the environment. Rainforest destruction or the grizzly bear or something."

"I'm doing this Russian defector thing," said Kessler. "That's my current project."

"Stay in touch," the man said. "Call me again with three or four ideas. For instance, have you done anything on acid rain?"

"Good-bye."

Then he dialed a number at *Rolling Stone,* talked with a managing editor he has known for years by voice but never met in person, and within ten minutes the story was sold. The editor tossed out figures for an expense check, to be in the mail tomorrow, and an article fee payable on delivery—in both cases decent sums but not extravagant. Fine, Kessler said. The money is unimportant. Kessler expects to spend so many days and so many dollars chasing leads around Washington and God knows where else that he will be lucky to break even overall, but that is fine. The demographics of the magazine's audience are also unimportant. Kessler's story can be sandwiched amid all the turntable advertisements and drug-bust gossip aimed at teenagers with blue hair but eventually it will get read by a few serious grown-ups anyway. Or at least by a few grown-ups. What *is* important, in any case, is that Kessler trusts this particular editor to accept collect calls from jail and send someone else out to look for him if Kessler himself should suddenly disappear.

So selling the piece has been relatively easy; the writing shouldn't be difficult; it's just that little part in between. His real struggle begins with the fourth phone call.

He has surrendered himself to the main switchboard at Langley and been transferred between extensions more times than he can recall, so far reaching no one authorized to say yes or forthright enough to say no. He knows it is all merely standard treatment, nothing extraordinary or personal, and the name Viktor Tronko has not even been uttered. Nor have the names Claude Sparrow or Mel Pokorny. The name Jedediah McAttee was quite sufficient to bring him up against resistance.

Kessler has spent twenty minutes on hold, spared of Muzak but paying long-distance rates, before the latest new voice in a long series comes on the line to say: "Mr. Kessler?"

"Still here."

The voice identifies itself in the unctuous tones of someone who has budgeted time for the likes of Kessler, a few minutes anyway, into each efficient workday. At least now we're up on the seventh floor, Kessler thinks. But what he pictures is a far outer antechamber. "I'm sorry," says this voice. "The Director is not presently granting requests for interviews."

"Why not?"

"He simply gets too many. I'm sure you can understand. It isn't a matter of security. Not entirely. People think so, but no. We do them occasionally. It's more a matter of his time."

"I'll settle for a half hour in his limousine on the way to an NSC meeting," says Kessler.

"No. I'm sorry. Here's what you need to do. Put your request in writing. You can submit it to this office. Mark it for my attention. Specify the subject area you want to explore and what publication employs you. Your request will then be routinely considered through channels. When the Director's schedule allows, some requests will be granted. If yours is one, you would then hear from us." A subtle shift, Kessler notices, from the future-indefinite tense to the subjunctive-improbable.

He has heard the same speech, years before, from a different but interchangeable flack. It's what he expected. In fact there may be even now such a letter, from him, written ten years earlier, still making its way through those turbid channels. He says: "Thanks. I'll be sure to do that."

With Claude Sparrow he fares better, to his own considerable surprise. On a scrap of notebook paper from deep in his old files he finds a number with the same area code as Langley and the notation "CS" beside it in Kessler's own hand. He remembers: it was bartered to him once as Claude Sparrow's unlisted residential line, the sort of precious arcana that journalists covering the intelligence world traded among themselves like contraband icons. Kessler can't recall anymore what he might have given away to earn this particular treasure. A stray fact that happened to fit nicely into some colleague's jigsaw puzzle, probably. Or maybe he had offered Mel Pokorny's unlisted number—a voluble deputy being at least equal in trade value to a chief who was legendarily reticent. Kessler is quite sure he never used the Sparrow number himself, never spoke with the man or even tried to; but again, he can't recall why not. It must have come into his hands too late, when Kessler was no longer eager, when he was edging away from that whole racket. Even so, the number has got to be almost ten years old. A cold trail. How often do you sweep your tracks, change your telephone number, and perform all the other such routine measures, if you are an unemployed spook with a lifetime accumulation of fanatically secretive habits? Kessler is not optimistic.

But after four rings there is an answer, a soft male voice which says only: "Hello?"

"Mr. Sparrow?"

Not the correct password. For a few seconds Kessler hears nothing but silence and a decision being considered, on the far end, about whether or not to hang up.

"Mr. Claude Sparrow?" Kessler says again. He gives his own name and adds quickly: "I'm a friend of Mel Pokorny. I'm calling from New Haven." If Sparrow has gotten any news at

all through his own sources in the last twelve hours, that pair of
facts should catch his attention.

"This is Sparrow."

"I'm a journalist," Kessler says, and again he pauses. The
idea is to be reassuringly direct, steady stride and both palms
showing empty. I'm crowding you but you have your lines of
escape; therefore it's not necessary to use those lines of escape,
is it? At least not yet. Kessler waits for a reaction.

No reaction.

"I talked with Pokorny last night," Kessler says. "He came
to see me. Then he left. Do you know about what happened?"

Instead of answering that question, Claude Sparrow asks one
of his own: "What happened?"

"He was killed. Shot. In a robbery. Or what was—"

"Give me your number," Sparrow interrupts.

"Excuse me?"

"Give . . . me . . . your . . . *number.*" Sparrow presses
the words out with exaggerated precision, the third one among
them flattened to a braying *yaaa,* but he doesn't elaborate. By
now Kessler has heard enough to detect a shading of accent,
either genteel Southern drawl or the faintest bit British. He is
momentarily befuddled. Then he recites his phone number. The
connection is immediately broken.

Kessler sits at his desk, not daring to move. He decides
against even a trip to the bathroom. Fifteen minutes later he
takes the phone on its second ring.

"All right," says Claude Sparrow from somewhere. "Now."

I'd like to talk with you, Kessler tells him. Pokorny gave me
some interesting information last night. (Best to be vague for
the present, Kessler figures, about how much Pokorny *didn't*
get time to give him.) I intend to learn more, Kessler says. I'm
referring mainly to the Viktor Tronko case. And the events that
led to your own resignation. I may write an article and I may
not, depending on what I find. (Kessler's standard disclaimer at
this stage in research.) I would like to have your help. If not
that, then I'd like at least to hear your side. I'll be in Washington beginning tomorrow, Kessler says (having only decided that
as it came off his lips). I'll be speaking with a number of other
people. (Who? Got to think of some.) I've covered CIA matters
before, though not recently.

"Mail surveillance," says Claude Sparrow.

"Yes, sir. Your memory is accurate."

"August of 1968. All across the magazine's goddamn cover, as I recall."

"Your memory is quite good."

"Freedom Airways and the Laotian counterinsurgency movement."

"And the Laotian heroin trade. Yes, sir. That was mine also."

"I'm mystified that you think I might lift a finger to help you, Mr. Kessler. I give you credit for gall, but I am mystified. In your time, you have caused me a fair parcel of grief." The word is pronounced *paw-sull*. The accent, like a fragrance of verbena, is seeping in with the emotion—or else being applied for effect. Kessler thinks he can hear west Tennessee, or perhaps Mississippi.

"Those weren't your operations."

"It was my Agency, sir," says Claude Sparrow.

Another moment of empty air. Too bad, Kessler thinks; it's not going to happen. What next? If not this guy, then who? He listens for background noises beyond the silence, wondering idly whether Sparrow has called him from a public phone on a street corner. There is no background noise.

"I will give you three days," Sparrow says abruptly.

Kessler crooks his head back against the ear piece. What? The tone sounds more like challenge than generosity, as Sparrow continues: "In that much time I can show you the bare outlines. If you aren't too dense, in that much time you can grasp them. Anything less would be travesty. Take it all or take nothing."

"I'll take it."

"No tape recorders. No cameras. But especially no tape recorders," says Sparrow. "You may make all the handwritten notes that you wish."

"All agreed."

"After three days, I'll have nothing further to say. No followups. No further contact."

"Agreed. Tell me where and when I can find you."

"You tell me where *you* will be staying, Mr. Kessler."

Kessler mentions a hotel on N Street near 17th and then again, instantly, the line is dead.

* * *

He is late for the master's wife's tea, but not disastrously so, not enough to claim later in good conscience that he forgot the thing altogether. Kessler grabs a tweed jacket and gallops off for the college. They won't hold forty-five minutes against him; academic people *expect* writers to be self-important and rude. Anyway, it seems a good place to begin his search for Fullerton. And sure enough, Fullerton is there, along with the master's wife and her three-gallon silver teapot and a dozen slick-faced undergraduates. The master himself evidently has a better use for his time. Kessler salutes the master's good sense.

He shakes a few hands and answers a few questions about the tiger book, which is what those present have read who have read him at all, and then a couple more general questions about the financial and contractual side of his particular craft, which seems to fascinate them inordinately. These Yale students have already been exposed to an overrich diet of celebrity novelists, shambling world-class poets, and syndicated political oracles; someone like Kessler is a different and more puzzling dish. He is neither wealthy nor famous, not even quietly eminent. He isn't employed by a newspaper or a magazine or, until recently, a university. He teaches only the single seminar, two hours weekly, and that arrangement is known to be temporary. To them, he has no visible means of support. A marginal figure on this hallowed campus. Doesn't seem to own any corduroy. The subtext of their gentle probings is: if you are so goddamned independent that you can write what you want, live where you want, tolerate the fact that we've never heard of you, what the devil are you doing in New Haven, Connecticut?

"I came here chasing a woman," he wants to tell them, but forbears.

After a decent interval he pulls Fullerton aside and explains that he's going AWOL for two or three weeks.

6

"I think he's lying," says Dexter Lovesong.

"You always think they're lying," says the younger man.

"What's wrong with that? You went to college. Didn't you ever hear of a logarithm?"

The younger man smiles greasily.

"I suspect you mean *algorithm,*" he says. "It's not a bad line. I congratulate you. Would have been downright good if you'd had the words straight. Algorithm. I say, 'You always think they're lying.' You say, 'You went to college. Haven't you ever heard of an algorithm?' I like it."

"He is lying. This time, Buddyboy, I'm right."

"That's another thing you always think."

Maybe I'll just choke him to death right here in the restaurant, Lovesong considers. No, I'll drag him outside and whop holy hell out of him in the gutter, then choke him to death, and then throw the body in front of a bus. Witnesses everywhere. They'll put me away, but it will be worth it. Sure. Lovesong shifts his gaze out the window, checking for bus traffic on Chapel Street. He has these thoughts frequently. They help to relax him.

"Let's go back to Washington," says the younger man. "There's nothing here."

"Kessler is here."

"But Michael Kessler is not going to lead us to anything. He doesn't know anything. Pokorny is dead and that's that. Let's go home and wash."

Lovesong swivels his attention back to the younger man, upon whom it rests coldly. Sometimes, for brief periods, Lovesong allows himself to believe that there may still be hope for Buddyboy. Today isn't one of those periods. Today it gives Dexter Lovesong heartburn to contemplate what a glorious future he has ahead of him, this kid, among the cretinous Ivy League whooping cranes up on the seventh floor.

"No," says Lovesong. "That is *not* that."

7

Kessler culls a few items from old files. He packs a bag. Then, before leaving town for Washington, he contemplates making one further call: to the woman named Nora.

He persists in labeling her within his own mind as "the woman named Nora," despite the fact that he might be considered to know her a good deal better than that phrase suggests. They have shared a hotel bed for one night, after all, amid exotic and even romantic surroundings, although they didn't manage on that occasion to become lovers. Not then, not later. "Didn't manage" is another editorial formulation as framed in Kessler's mind; he realizes that Nora would have her own, a different one. Probably hers would involve words like "hasty" and "my moment of bad judgment" and "what might have been a disastrous mistake" and of course the familiar "I need a bit of time and space." He can only guess the exact phraseology. Having committed his own piece of bad judgment down there in Ecuador—when he imagined that this Nora Walsh was a straightforward person, decent at heart but slightly jaded, much like himself, and that he could therefore know her quickly and easily—Kessler, like Nora, has latterly withdrawn to a position of caution. But his is epistemological, not emotional. Designating her mentally as "the woman named Nora" helps him to remember that caution, and dampens his expectations. Ecuador was a false start. Ecuador with its low comedy and its tears and its frustration was just a misunderstanding, a mistake, though not the disastrous one that she claims it might have been. This one was easily rectified. She drew back. Denial set in. Their night at the Hotel Alfaro, like the band of paleness around Nora's fourth finger, has been erased.

Kessler had gone down there for a glossy magazine, on one of those shameless travel-writing assignments that feel like something halfway between play and prostitution. He had accepted only because it was the Galápagos. He was reading Darwin again when the offer came, by coincidence, and he had never himself seen the islands. For Nora the trip was neither work nor really quite play; for her it was more like therapy. A brief sabbatical, an escape from responsibility and decisions. That had been the intent, anyway, until she met Michael Kessler. Never before having traveled anywhere more exotic than France, she had taken a lump of her divorce settlement and bought a ticket to Quito. Such impulsiveness was uncustomary but it felt (as she eventually told Kessler) overdue. The young daughter, named Emily, had been left with family friends in Boston. Nora and Kessler each boarded the ship at Baltra, along with eighty other strangers, for a week of cruising the archipelago. It was well into the third day before Kessler began to notice her. On the fourth night he got himself seated near her at dinner. The fifth and sixth days, tromping across one island to see blue-footed boobies, climbing another to molest iguanas, they spent entirely in each other's company. The seventh night, last of the cruise, Kessler and Nora sat up until very late in the ship's bar, talking. The eighth night they were back on the mainland, at the Hotel Alfaro in Guayaquil. Neither of them, that night, got a great deal of rest. They talked on for hours, to the point of exhaustion, then slept for a while in each other's arms, woke, talked again until around three in the morning, when Nora was briefly, quietly hysterical. At four she got dressed and went back to her own room.

When Kessler came down to the lobby at nine, he found that she had checked out, a day earlier than planned. Yes, the signora had gone up to Quito, he was told. He spent a ludicrous afternoon making long-distance calls to Quito hotels, groping his way through the cultural and technological labyrinth of the Ecuadorean telephone system, asking in his clubfooted Spanish about "a gringa named Nora Walsh." No trace of her in Quito. She had already caught a flight north. Kessler followed. No trace of her at the Miami airport. She had made her connection. Luckily he knew at least her destination; she had told him about returning to graduate school, about the little house in New Haven, about sharing it cozily with the daughter. She was listed in the New Haven directory, last name and initial. When Kessler called her from his own place in Vermont, the first of those numerous times, she sounded pleased and surprised to hear his voice. Momentarily so, anyway. She apologized for what she called her "rudeness." It was a rather formal apology, sounding like boilerplate. Rudeness? he thought. Hello, what are we talking about? "Never mind. *Rudeness?* Listen, I want to see you," Kessler said. No, she said. What? he said. No, no, I think that would probably be a bad idea, she said. The second time Kessler called, half an hour later, she hung up.

And in five months, since he accepted the offer from Fullerton and moved himself down to New Haven, it hasn't gotten much better. She is still opaque and changeable and his very proximity seems to make her nervous. He has gotten past the front door of the little house, once. He has been permitted to meet the daughter, once. He has had Nora out for a pleasant if rather stiff evening of dinner and theater, once, and seen her home very properly, said a stiff good night on the front step, and then for two weeks afterward she dodged his calls. So far as Kessler knows, she is seeing no other men. Maybe she is still bitterly, incurably in love with the ex-husband. Maybe she has somehow been grievously hurt. Well, haven't we all, Kessler thinks. Haven't we all. Obviously she is a lunatic.

His interest in this creature remains extremely high but his patience, and his stamina, are finite. In a sulky mood Kessler leaves town on his journey to Washington, the following morning, without phoning the woman named Nora.

God only knows, maybe she will notice his absence for herself.

8

He has decided to travel by train. For this there is an ulterior reason. Pokorny came up by train. Kessler wants to retrace the route: New Haven Station, Grand Central, Union Station in Washington. He is interested in finding that coin-operated locker to which belongs the key—stolen from Mel's attaché case before Dexter Lovesong could get to it—that now rides in Kessler's pocket.

Of course the locker it opens might be out there on some sterile corridor at LaGuardia, or at any other airport in America, or even amid the Styrofoam flotsam of a bus station. But Kessler is betting otherwise. He is betting his optimism. He wants to believe that the key was fresh in Pokorny's possession. He wants to view the key as a bit of spoor from the very day of the man's death. And if Mel had stowed something in a coin-op locker just that day, during the course of his journey toward Kessler's door, acting either premeditatedly or on a desperate spontaneous impulse, chances are it was something more interesting than an overcoat.

At the New Haven station there are only two dozen lockers and Kessler knows, without needing to peek again, that Pokorny's key bears the number 553. Also the design is wrong —solid aluminum keys at New Haven, versus a yellow plastic grip on the one in his pocket. He boards an express to New York.

For ninety minutes he has nothing to do but read the newspaper and think about Viktor Tronko, the poor schlemiel who spent three years alone in a concrete cell in custody of the CIA. And about Mel Pokorny, crashing down dead in a puddle of wine and glass and cashews. Two days ago at this hour Kessler was thinking about termites, and about Eugène Marais, the troubled naturalist whose ghost he has chased for almost three years. Today, so quickly, a new set of ghosts. A new set of hormones awash in his blood. Kessler feels them already, those mood juices, including the one for knee-wobbling fear. On balance, the feeling is good.

At Grand Central he decides to take a precaution. He climbs to the mezzanine bar near the Vanderbilt Street exit and plants himself there for a cup of coffee, with a commanding view out over the main waiting room.

In its midmorning lull, the great room is still busy enough. Late commuters striding briskly and college girls who sit on their suitcases and individuals of ambiguous profession, like Kessler himself. He watches people. He recognizes no one. He spots no lurking mysterious characters wearing trench coats or cheap shiny suits who inspire in him a vague sense of alarm; the lurking characters all look relatively benign and, for here, very much standard. So he goes down again to browse the lockers.

He feels a silent thrill when he sees that the key design matches: yellow plastic grips. For a rather long while, though, he cannot find 553 or any numbers in that range.

He crosses the main room to check more banks of lockers tucked in among the train gates and the shops on the east side —no, still not the right numbers—and crosses back again to see what he missed on the west side. Here he finds lockers numbered into the eight hundreds, but no 553. This is aggravating. Kessler walks faster, his bag in one hand and now holding the key clutched in his other fist, that fist pushed down out of sight in a pocket of his overcoat. As though the touch of the key itself will help him home in. His nostrils are wide. He knows he must be very close to discovering something, some significant bit of data, Pokorny's secreted item. Physical evidence. Certainly it must be in this train station, somewhere, the yellow plastic is too much for coincidence. He must be very close to the path Mel himself followed two days ago. Under the next archway Kessler is going to find something—or else miss something, passing heartbreakingly near. Three hundreds, two hundreds, eight hundreds; four hundreds on the far side. It's maddening. He goes downstairs to the subway level, where there turn out to be no lockers at all. Back upstairs. The scent of discovery is fading. He shouldn't have gotten so hopeful. Maybe yellow plastic is standard for this brand of locker everywhere in the United States. He has a discouraging vision of a bus terminal somewhere in Illinois, and Mel Pokorny's last gift waiting there forever unclaimed. Hold on a minute, though: three hundreds, four hundreds, eight hundreds. What about that?

Kessler heads back toward the claim-ticket baggage room that he has already passed three times; he'll ask directions, always just a desperate last resort in New York. But as he passes the mouth of a long marble corridor leading downstairs, a rampway toward the lower level, he glances that way. And stops walking. Thirty yards down the ramp, marked by its sign and its red curtains, is the Oyster Bar. And opposite its doors stands another large bank of lockers. They are neither downstairs nor upstairs but in between, which is how he has managed to miss them.

He finds 553 at eye level amid the others.

It occurs to him that the close resemblance between these coin-eating boxes and a wall of mausoleum drawers is in one sense pathetically apt: Mel Pokorny will now speak from his tomb. Kessler experiences a crescendo of curiosity and excitement as he inserts the key; that goes abruptly flat when he opens the door. The locker is empty.

He slams it and opens it again. Still empty. He brushes his hand across the light film of grit on the floor of the box. Very thoroughly empty. And now after his few seconds of feeling thwarted, cheated, robbed, Kessler begins to worry.

Someone else has been tracing Pokorny's path. Yes, well, we knew that from what happened at Mr. Biaggio's, didn't we. But this is different. Kessler himself has just walked into the line of fire, possibly. He had wanted to avoid that. His own fault: all at once it seems drastically indiscreet to have marched blithely up to this locker and produced the key. Smug fool, he thought he was one step ahead. Evidently he is one step behind. Grabbing his bag, Kessler moves for the trains.

He figures to climb aboard his connection for Washington, stay out of sight in the dining car, and then be gone—but after one more trek across the vastness of the waiting room he is met with the disconcerting fact that they haven't yet opened his gate for boarding. Half an hour still to be killed. No, Kessler thinks, that's a bad choice of words.

He swings back, feeling trapped, and the sudden turn brings him around just in time to see a slender young man in a gray suit break stride, diverting himself smoothly into line at a newsstand. Kessler doesn't like that. He saw the same young man five minutes earlier, he thinks, in line at the baggage window. Kessler returns the way he came. He is stepping briskly.

He mounts the stairs toward the mezzanine bar and then, halfway up, reverses course: whoops, forgot something. Comes back down as fast as gravity will pull him, his shoes slapping hard on the marble. Out on the waiting-room floor a shape in gray stops suddenly, turns to the information booth, but Kessler only notes this at the corner of his vision and doesn't twist around to gawk. He doesn't need to. The charade is now on. Two hours into the first morning, Kessler already being stalked like a victim, and this assignment is getting off to a very damn breathless start. Move, feet. Think, brain. Kessler feels like a high diver with failed nerves standing far above a pool full of cold panic. Move, feet.

He wants witnesses.

Lots of people, the safety of companionship—something more than a single Italian grocer.

He yearns to sprint for the street but now, alas, he is pointed the wrong way. Another reversal on these stairs will tell the man in the gray suit, if the man perhaps doesn't know, that Kessler is now aware of his presence and duly terrified. Maybe it's better the man not know that. Kessler keeps moving. He can turn right and streak out toward 42nd, try to lose himself in the sidewalk crowds. Forty-second Street at noon is not the best place to shoot someone dead without arousing notice. But instead Kessler follows his feet, damn them. There is another set of steps, there is an unconsidered impulse, and suddenly he is skittering downstairs to the subway.

Christ, and I don't have a token. I don't even have correct change. Kessler does a slow blink without slackening his pace, astonished by his own stupidity and poor taste. The smooth marble steps and floor have given way to filthy concrete. The air is now steamy and the smell is familiar. The ceiling is low and the posters are vehemently, maniacally defaced. I always knew it, Kessler thinks: I always knew that this place is what death would look like. Truth is, he was always more optimistic than that about death.

But at least there are people. Kessler shoves past a few and an old lady barks at him obscenely. He finds himself running down a septic gullet of white tile, following signs for the shuttle, sweating lavishly into his cumbersome wool coat. It occurs to him he should drop his bag so as to be able to run faster. Ditch it right here, let it be stolen, who cares? Open your hand, moron, drop the bag. But he doesn't have the heart to do that because it would truly announce his panic, his total relinquishment of dignity and the pretense of normality and a clean set of underwear for tomorrow, if there is a tomorrow. Let them all think he is just a rude hurried businessman. No one shoots rude hurried businessmen in the back with a .45 automatic. For better or worse, it isn't done.

Kessler pauses to glance back. Seeing a flash of gray come off the stairs, again he runs.

Down the white gullet, around the curve, dodging and weaving in and out, bashing a few folk blind side with his bag, leaping a little riffle of stairs and then thirty yards later another. This labyrinth goes on forever, Kessler realizes; if only he knew how to use it. Run on. Evade. Improvise something ingenious, you're an imaginative guy. Gack, but what happens when I come to a turnstile? thinks Kessler. Certain death or at least castration and, if not that, then arrest. Instantly Kessler has a brilliant idea, definitely his first today.

He will vault the turnstile, yes, and then surrender himself at once to the transit police. The guys who jump out of nowhere with choke holds and truncheons when some kid in black sneakers tries to cheat the system. Don't they also carry guns, the transit police? He believes they do and it is a wonderful, comforting thought.

Kessler breathes deep. He stretches out his stride, purposeful now, pouring on effort to widen the gap and give himself a couple precious extra seconds. Running literally for his life. Every move will need to be perfect. He leans into the last turn, he kicks for the tape, and he is dropped hard there on the concrete with a roll tackle by Dexter Lovesong, diving out from the doorway of a shop that sells pornographic T-shirts.

Kessler has lost most of the skin from the palm of his right hand, replacing it with gravel pressed into the raw flesh like cloves in a ham. The left hand may be all right. He isn't sure, he can't see that one, because Lovesong has it reefed high up in back between Kessler's shoulder blades. Kessler's nose and cheek are squashed against the concrete. He can't move. This is very unsanitary, he thinks. And all his fear has gone, miraculously transformed to anger.

"Gimme," says Lovesong.

"Give you what?" In immediate response to that question, which is only partially disingenuous, he feels the ball joint of his left humerus rise grindingly toward the lip of the socket as Lovesong levers up on his arm. "Gaaa. Nnnnh. Oh," Kessler says. He drools on the pavement, can't help it.

"Gimme."

"It was empty," Kessler says hoarsely.

The arm is jacked higher and Kessler departs momentarily to the edge of unconsciousness as though Lovesong were squeezing with two fingers the very base of his brain. With the pressure eased slightly, he comes back. Evidently Lovesong has a fine practiced touch for that threshold. Kessler sees feet. He hears voices, one of which says:

"Good lord. What did you do?"

"I stopped him," Lovesong answers.

"Clearly. Let him up. Get off him. Jesus, Dexter." This voice comes from the airspace above a pair of black Italian pumps. The pumps gleam with fresh polish and gray trouser cuffs break gently over them; sharp crease, a good conservative twill, Kessler is in position to notice. The voice belongs to a man who is younger than Lovesong and knows a better tailor. Kessler feels a knee placed in the small of his back as Lovesong turns to address the other man.

"He had you beat, Buddyboy. Ten steps and he was gone. Plus which you spooked him, upstairs, with your clumsiness. Hell, he was gone."

"Does that mean you get to break his arm?"

Kessler waits with interest for the answer to this one.

"No." The leverage releases, blessedly. The weight goes. Kessler's good arm is taken hold of around the biceps and, with a single smooth and powerful motion, he is hoisted all the way to his feet. He is still shaky but Lovesong, surprisingly strong, supports him. Lovesong brushes some dirt from Kessler's right knee, a token gesture since the left knee is torn and bloody and the trousers are definitely ruined.

"You're all right," says Lovesong.

"It was empty," says Kessler.

"He's all right," says Lovesong.

The man in the gray suit stands back about six feet, wearing a solicitous, queasy expression. He seems to be in his middle or late twenties, with ginger hair and a rectilinear jawline and the same sort of quasi-rugged handsomeness much favored for cologne ads in some of the magazines for which Kessler writes. "Mr. Kessler, I can only apologize. This was a mistake." Lovesong emits a contemptuous snort but the younger man ignores him. "We just wanted to talk with you."

"Never run after a guy like that, Buddyboy," says Lovesong. "It only makes you conspicuous."

"So talk with me," says Kessler. "The locker was empty. I have a train to catch. Talk with me." The small covey of onlookers, now that they understand that Kessler is neither a purse snatcher apprehended nor a mugging victim, are moving on. Kessler dabs at his bloody palm with a handkerchief. He looks around for his bag, which Lovesong is holding. "Tackling me doesn't make you conspicuous?"

"I know it was empty. I saw," says the younger man. "Let's go upstairs. We'd like to take you to lunch."

"You're out of your mind," Kessler says.

But he allows them to walk him back up the white gullet. When the younger man presents his own credential, Kessler pulls it from his hand to read the name carefully: Matthew Hay Henderson. Office of Security, Directorate of quack quack quack, just like Lovesong. Kessler intends to remember them both. He is almost more annoyed with this younger man, for the terror induced during that run, than he is with Lovesong for crunching him. Almost. And he is already wondering, practical-minded, whether the chase and the bloody palm can be somehow converted to use. "Does the Director know that you boys are up here in New York? Operating on American soil? Assaulting innocent citizens?"

"Drop dead," says Lovesong. "It won't work."

"Yes he does, as a matter of fact," says the younger man. "On a security investigation, we have standing to function domestically. It's quite legal."

"And besides which you were concealing evidence," says Lovesong.

"What evidence was I concealing?"

"A locker key. That you stole from Pokorny's briefcase. Along with who knows what all else."

"Is that part of your security investigation? That locker key?"

"Possibly."

"Why? What was supposed to be in the locker?"

"Come to lunch. We'll talk," says the younger man.

"If I do, are you going to answer my questions? Or is it supposed to be just me answering yours?"

"We'll talk."

"We're talking now. What was it? What was in that locker?"

"We don't know any more than you do. We didn't empty it."

"I'm sure you do. Take an educated guess."

"Classified material."

"Of what sort?"

The younger man pinches his lips. Kessler watches indecision flicker like heat lightning in his pale blue eyes, but there is no reply. Then Kessler turns to Dexter Lovesong, who puffs up his chest and tries to draw his belly back in under it. Lovesong's lower jaw shifts forward like an automatic pinsetter. From him also, no answer.

"Give me my bag," says Kessler.

9

He checks into the Tabard Inn, a little bohemian wren-house squashed between more serious buildings on a quiet block of N Street, a place where they know him from previous stays, and is greeted immediately with Sparrow's note.

The woman in the cubbyhole office has had it waiting, propped atop her old plug-and-socket switchboard: a sealed envelope marked only with "Mr. Kessler" in a fine script. No, the woman isn't able to say when it was delivered, or by whom. Kessler thanks her. He climbs to his room on the fourth floor and spends a monkish evening there reading a few clips he has brought along, groping through a few books, scanning everything he could find from his old files that might contain a mention of Claude Sparrow or of a Soviet defector named Viktor Tronko. There isn't much. Sparrow in those days was a powerful government baron with an inordinate share of outrageous opinions and bizarre personal habits, true, but he abhorred publicity unambivalently, for plausible professional reasons and no doubt also by disposition, so that even back then, while chasing tales of CIA malfeasance down some very long alleys, Michael Kessler like the rest of America was never much more than vaguely aware of the man's existence. Kessler stares again, and then later again, at the sheet of cream parchment on which are written a few lines of instruction—a suburban park in McLean, a concrete bench, a time of day. He stares, as though with sufficient concentration he might learn something more about Sparrow from this page itself. What most fascinates Kessler is the grace of the hand.

By one o'clock the following afternoon, as instructed, he has found his way to that bench in that park.

Claude Sparrow is a small peach-colored man with the fingers of a concert pianist. He wears a camel-hair overcoat bundled lumpishly around himself and a plaid wool scarf, which give him the look of a doddering alumnus wrapped for an afternoon in the stands of a college stadium at the very worst time of year. He holds one hand clamped tightly on the other wrist, both of those hands turning pink from the cold, which is unusually harsh for Washington even in January. Noticing that pinkness, Kessler wonders how long Sparrow might have been waiting here, and why. The man's feet don't reach the ground except when he points his toes. He makes no move to rise or to offer a handshake. When Kessler announces his own name, Claude Sparrow only says:

"Of course you are."

Sparrow glances off toward the wooded end of the park, through which a paved path winds away toward tennis courts and a community center. The trees are bare with the season, the path and the courts are empty of humanity. Absorbing the view, Sparrow looks as if he might be bored or soul-weary. He turns back to inspect the other direction, a browned lawn stretching forty yards to a footbridge, empty, then a sidewalk, and then the moil of traffic along Old Dominion Drive. Cars full of bureaucrats and other suburbanites rushing back from lunch or handball at the health club or a noontime errand at the computer store, thriving and preoccupied folk with better things to do than gape at an old man in a park. Satisfied, Sparrow stands quickly, producing a compact electronic device—like a portable calculator crossed with a bicycle lock—from one coat pocket.

Though Kessler has experienced these things often, at airport security checkpoints, he doesn't know a name for them and he doesn't like them.

"Raise your arms, please."

And with several quick passes it is done, technological verification that Kessler is carrying keys, a pocketknife, loose change, but no concealed recorder or microphone. Without thanks or apology, Claude Sparrow sits back down. Fine, so we know where we stand on the matter of mutual trust. Kessler decides to be amused. He sits too.

"You're curious about the Tronko case."

" 'Curious' is a good enough word," Kessler says. "Yes. And about the Sparrow case."

Sparrow is silent for a moment, only the first of many. This initial one seems long to Kessler, and discomfiting, though he will be growing accustomed soon to Claude Sparrow's highly individual sense of conversational rhythms.

"The Sparrow case," says Sparrow. "That's very much more complicated, I'm afraid." Another stretched pause. "And I'm sure it's none of your business."

Ignoring the second part, Kessler answers: "You said we have three days."

"Three days is for the simple version." And another pause, as Sparrow adjusts the coat back up snug, settling himself like a hen. The hand is again locked on the other wrist, which is delicate, Kessler can see—a knot of bones standing out through the skin. If Sparrow has gloves he chooses not to wear them. "Are you a student of history, Mr. Kessler?"

"A student of history. Well, I suppose I'd like to think so."

"And what *is* history?"

Now it's Kessler's turn to be silent. The expression Claude Sparrow presents to him is benign and bland, fit for a parish priest catechizing schoolchildren.

"According to whose theory?"

"Choose any you like."

"Bunk. Henry Ford."

"Is that also your own view?"

"No," Kessler says. "If it was, I wouldn't be here. My own view is less cynical. I believe in the enterprise, if not always the recorded product."

"That's a sensible distinction," says Sparrow. "What most people think of as history, it's precisely what you call 'the recorded product.'"

"I agree. Their mistake."

"You agree. Good. Good. Now let me offer you another view. I am quoting. 'History is a fable agreed upon.'"

"Napoleon," says Kessler, and for this bit of tenth-grade erudition he earns a small smile from Sparrow. Kessler adds: "I think he was on St. Helena by then. Being secretly poisoned to death by the British." The smile wanes.

"Anyway he was wrong, it has nothing to do with agreement," says Sparrow severely.

"But you like the fable part, I gather."

"Victors write history. A cliché, but it happens to be true.

Victors write the books. They shape the popular understanding. Even sometimes in cases where the vanquished remain blithely unaware that they *are* vanquished. Are you following me?"

"No."

"I'm talking about appearances. Appearances have enormous importance, Mr. Kessler. The creation and maintenance of appearances. Appearances govern. And I don't mean in merely the civil sense. Now what about this notion: 'History is the control of appearances.' "

"Are you quoting?"

"Yes. Claude Sparrow," says Sparrow. "I've said it often."

"If history is just appearances, then what—"

"No," Sparrow interrupts. "Excuse me. I said 'the control of' appearances."

"All right. The control of. The recorded product. Then what do you call the effort to see through the appearances?" Kessler has especially in mind Mel Pokorny's appearance as a victim of random violence on the floor of Biaggio's grocery. "What's that, then? Philosophy?"

"No. But you're close," Sparrow says. He seems delighted to be asked. "I call it counterintelligence."

Here is a man with his own agenda. There will be no gain, Kessler senses, in trying to rein him around or hurry him on. Kessler has come hoping to hear what Claude Sparrow knows but prepared to settle, at least initially, for hearing what Claude Sparrow wants to say. The rest, at least initially, he will just have to guess at and wonder over—including the question of why Sparrow consented to meet him at all. At least initially, he will need to let Claude Sparrow control the appearances.

"First I am going to tell you about two arrivals. Two comings," says Sparrow in his strongest Confederate drawl. "Without knowledge of these, you can understand none of the rest." He has straightened his spine, his eyes are widened and lit. He is straining so hard with that left hand on that right wrist, a nervous habit, a displacement of fervor, that Kessler imagines how the hand might come popping off. Alarming, but not impossible. Sparrow does seem to have the brittle and angular anatomy of a marionette.

"Two arrivals."

"Bogdan Kirilovich Fedorenko. I'll make an assumption, Mr.

Kessler. I'll assume that you've never heard of Bogdan Fedorenko."

"You're right," Kessler says, and again Sparrow is clearly delighted.

Bogdan Kirilovich Fedorenko was a Ukrainian, a KGB officer assigned to the *rezidentura* in Paris during the early 1960s. He had diplomatic cover at the Soviet Embassy, Sparrow explains, a middling post within the visa section, but his real assignment was to service an agent. The agent was an American. Not an important man, not an influential diplomat or a high-ranking military officer, Sparrow insists; the truth of that, in fact, was ludicrously and maddeningly the opposite. This American, Fedorenko's agent, was a nonentity. An aging Army corporal attached to the U.S. forces on NATO assignment, with a drinking problem, a dysfunctional personality, and a corrosive grudge against the officer corps of that service in which he himself could not even rise to the rank of sergeant. The man's name doesn't matter, says Sparrow. The man himself doesn't matter. He was angry and ignorant enough to want to pass information to the Soviets, out of sheer blind spite, but that wouldn't have mattered much either, in a sensible world, because the nonentity would have had no information to offer. He had been a rifleman in Korea, undistinguished, and had reenlisted for lack of alternative prospects, and turned up next as a clerk-typist at the U.S. command headquarters in West Berlin. In a sensible world he would have stayed there, Sparrow says, typing with two fingers and answering the phone. Or been shipped back to a quartermaster assignment in Arkansas, better still, handing out helmets and canteens to fresh-shaven draftees. Kessler can't help but notice the personal bile in which these facts have been marinated. But of course this is not a sensible world, Sparrow tells him emphatically. And so our corporal, having applied for reassignment, saw his request granted. He came down to Paris as a guard at the Armed Forces Courier Center, the nexus for all sensitive NATO communications between Washington and the other nation members. This courier center was no more than an inconspicuous cement blockhouse within a chain-link fence on a far corner of tarmac at Orly Airport, but through it passed a breathtaking volume of quite secret cable and pouch traffic. Sparrow wrinkles his nose at the thought. He squints as though his eyes are burning from sliced onions. One or two nights a week for almost a year, he says, the corporal pulled graveyard shift guarding the cipher-room safe. It was there that Fedorenko ran the corporal as an agent, collecting his product and doling out meager payments. Not right there at Orly, these contacts, of course—they would meet at various points of safe rendezvous in the city. It was Fedorenko who taught the corporal, despite a certain doltishness toward any mechanical task more delicate than shoving a magazine into a .45, to take impressions of keys. To use a Minox camera. And it was Fedorenko who played nursemaid and counselor whenever the corporal undertook one of his crude joyless booze-and-whores crawls across Paris, the corporal doing his best, against all Fedorenko's efforts, to get himself cashiered. The corporal was a mewling, self-pitying sot with a streak of harsh venality that might have been comic if relieved by the least touch of personal charm, which it was not. Fedorenko despised the man, Sparrow says with a vehement immediacy as though the sentiment were his own.

Kessler says nothing. He is waiting to see where it will go.

But Fedorenko shared one trait with the corporal, says Sparrow. He was disgusted by his own situation. He was angry. This traces back to a whole network of factors in Fedorenko's personal background, his career, his family history, which we needn't go into right now, says Sparrow. His nationality, even. Fedorenko wasn't a Russian, you should understand at least that. Emphatically no. He was a Ukrainian. And the KGB itself had never been his own dream of high bliss. Not like it is for some. He was in fact rather poorly suited to the role because, among other reasons, he was too direct. Too ingenuous. Some would say he was downright mulish. Well, yes, he could be. He hated subterfuge and dissimulation of any stripe, says Sparrow; no talent whatever for sycophancy, or for the sort of ever-calculating awareness of one's own position in the crosscurrents of favoritism and disfavor that a KGB career seems to demand. Blunt-minded Fedorenko always wanted to say just whatever was in his head, spit it right out, Devil take you if you didn't care for it. Of course he had learned early on, from necessity, to stifle this inclination—otherwise he would have long since been counting the trees, as he used to say. That was a Russian expression, one of Fedorenko's favorites, Sparrow explains, meaning: Hello, Siberia. Or he would have joined the truly and permanently lost souls in the cellars of the Lubyanka building. But no, Fedorenko could control himself, at least to that measure required by good sense. He was mulish but not suicidal. For that matter, he was mulish about survival. Kessler has heard the tone of rough fondness creeping in. Now Sparrow stops talking altogether.

Sparrow doesn't seem to be silenced by any gorge-tightening accession of emotion; merely to be thinking. He frowns unself-consciously. It gives Kessler time to listen backward again over the last thing he heard: Fedorenko was mulish about survival.

"One day he came across to us. An impulse that day, but an impulse that had long been contemplated, even long prepared for. His tour of duty in Paris was ending. He would be back in Moscow soon, at a desk—possibly for the rest of his life. A tidy little office on the third floor of the Lubyanka, beneath portraits of Lenin and Dzerzhinsky. No, Fedorenko wasn't going. So he made his leap. Just took a taxi across the city and walked into our embassy. Where he all but handcuffed himself to a table."

"He defected," says Kessler.

"Yes of course. Not a social visit, no." Sparrow doesn't grace his own sarcasm with a smile. "Within eight hours we had got him over to Frankfurt, where there was a reception facility, a place for handling these things. Preliminary debriefing. By that time the Paris *rezidentura* had sensed something amiss and his colleagues were just frantic. Charging around the city, jostling people in bars, desperate to find their missing cow. Lodging hot complaints with the French that we or somebody had kidnapped him, an innocent Soviet diplomat. They were really most upset. Exceptionally so."

"Why was that?" Kessler asks.

"Oh. Well. It might have been the corporal. That operation, you know, was just instantly blown." This is offered with unmistakable lack of conviction, as though, for anyone dim and ignorant enough to believe that explanation, such credulousness would be its own proper punishment. Kessler senses the warning, but he has no inkling of what explanation might be better.

"Or something else."

"Yes. Oh yes." Sparrow keeps an empty face. "It might have been something else."

"What year is this, Mr. Sparrow?"

"Nineteen sixty-three. January."

Kessler has brought a notebook and a ballpoint, which he set out on the bench within Sparrow's view when he first sat down; since then he hasn't touched them. The sight of a journalist *not* taking notes, he has learned, is sometimes incentive for an interview subject to reach deeper, feeling challenged to impress or to shock. Claude Sparrow is far from succumbing to any such cute manipulation. Nevertheless Kessler has no intention of scribbling a note or a number until he knows better what he is looking for.

"It was before Tronko, then."

"Correct."

"Or before Tronko's own defection, at least. But not before his first contact. Am I remembering that right? Tronko had already made friendly noises?"

"Rome. Summer of 1962. That's correct. This business with Fedorenko was a year before Tronko *announced* his *desire* to defect." The words are chosen pointedly and "desire" is another that comes out, under Sparrow's accent, flat as a praline. "But not before the first of—as you so aptly put it—Tronko's *noises.*"

Difficulties had begun arising before Bogdan Fedorenko was even shipped off from the Frankfurt reception center. In fact that transfer was delayed, over a week passed and Fedorenko still in Germany, because the preliminary debriefing was proceeding so poorly. More accurate to say it wasn't proceeding at all. Fedorenko refused to talk. He had taken a personal dislike to the debriefing officer, he was being intractable, making ridiculous unreasonable demands, possibly he was just a KGB provocation, not a genuine defector after all—each of these notions was floated, sent back by cable to Langley, says Sparrow, where Sparrow himself and others were waiting eagerly to get their first glimpse of the man. Sitting in Langley, they couldn't know what to credit. It was an infuriating, befuddling week and a hard decision—a decision that had to be made quickly but without adequate data. They faced much the same thing a year later with Tronko and managed in that event, Sparrow says parenthetically, from the far corner of his mouth, to be even more befuddled. Bring him to Washington or not? Ever mulish, Bogdan Fedorenko had folded his arms on his broad peasant chest and told the debriefing man, in effect, to go to hell. He wasn't offering any information until certain demands were met.

Well, this was unexpected, Sparrow explains. It simply wasn't the way the game was played.

A defector, especially a Soviet defector and more especially still a KGB man, is generally in poor position to haggle, Sparrow says. He is offering himself for sale on what is distinctly a buyer's market. Misjudging his value, turned down on the first approach, he can be whisked home and tried for treason by his own people. Maybe there won't even be the formality of a trial. He can be counting the trees; he can simply be dead. Very little bidding and no holdouts, generally, in the defection trade. But whether from luck or good planning or his own natural brashness, Fedorenko from the beginning had several advantages. First, he had simply marched into the embassy, rather than making a safer and more discreet approach to an American diplomat or an intelligence officer, so his crossing was a *fait accompli* before anyone back in Washington could deliberate. Secondly, he had documents in his possession, just a few tantalizing samples, that proved his penetration of the Armed Forces Courier Center—though he refused at this point to give the identity of the agent. Obviously Fedorenko wasn't protecting the wretched corporal, Sparrow says; he merely knew how to hold and play his cards. There were some heads at Langley who found this insupportable. They were in fact little short of hysteria. Take the shit-dipped bastard right back to Paris and throw him out of a car in his skivvies, dump him off on a street corner, let the KGB have him, these persons said. Kessler is mildly startled to hear the prim Claude Sparrow go into character, quoting them. It was a taxing week, Sparrow says. Acrimonious discussion. You will understand, Sparrow says, that I prefer to mention no names.

"Mention some names," says Kessler.

"Jed McAttee," says Sparrow.

The Director himself overruled this hysteria, fortunately, and Fedorenko was at last flown to Washington. He still hadn't offered anything for his keep. All Langley had were the cold documents and the warm body. The documents proved—or at least suggested a frightening plausibility to Fedorenko's claim— that there was an artery open somewhere in NATO communications, most likely at the courier center, and that information of the highest sensitivity was not just bleeding away but being pumped. A really disastrous hemorrhage, according to Sparrow. It simply had to be stanched, at once, without excuse or further delay. What were the options? Well, close down the courier center completely, lock the place up and detain every courier and cryptographer and guard who worked there or had recently passed through, put them all under security review and interrogation—which of course would soon leak to the press, cause a panic of distrust among the allies, and make the United States look as though it were staggering around wrathful and blind as Polyphemus. Or else find the particular agent. Whom Bogdan Fedorenko already knew by name. So you see, says Sparrow. For this piece of information, it was a seller's market.

We put Fedorenko into a nice little house with a confined garden, up in the suburbs of Baltimore, a friendly and deceptively relaxed environment, says Sparrow, and one of McAttee's people went up there to talk with him. To find his price. Reach an agreement, get him talking, and for God's sake do it fast, were the instructions to McAttee's fellow. But don't let Fedorenko know just how desperate we are.

"Who was that?" says Kessler. "McAttee's fellow. Was it Lentzer?"

"No. Not this time. Scott Wickes was the man's name. Which I tell you only because he is out of the Agency now. He worked closely with Lentzer though, yes. A bit later." Sparrow sits. He appears to have lost the thread of his thought, although Kessler considers that unlikely. Kessler waits through another full minute before saying:

"I didn't mean to interrupt. Fedorenko in a nice little house with a garden. An open artery at the courier center, blood everywhere."

"Hmm?" says Claude Sparrow. He blinks at Kessler from a great distance.

Kessler is perplexed. Can this be an act?

"You were about to tell me about getting the agent's name. The corporal. From Fedorenko."

Sparrow gapes serenely. "Yes," he says at last. "I was. Well, but you already know the answer to that. The corporal. He was quickly arrested. He had been too stupid to escape east with the help of his friends. And then again maybe they didn't want him. He merely waited a week, dithering, growing more nervous, and finally went AWOL. To Marseille. We found him there, drunk, in a hotel." The momentum seems to be gathering again and Kessler is wary of interfering, but he says:

"Scott Wickes had found the price."

"No. Decidedly not. Wickes was a dreadful failure with Bogdan Fedorenko."

"Who, then?"

"We gave Wickes two days. Nothing. He accomplished nothing. We couldn't afford more delay. So I began going up there myself."

"And he told you about the corporal. While the two of you strolled back and forth in that garden."

"Precisely correct, Mr. Kessler. It was January. Brown grass, bare shrubs and trees, just like this. I remember it quite vividly. Not as cold as this, though. There was mud."

"What was the price?"

Sparrow tightens his lips, letting his head dip through a series of tiny nods. "Fedorenko did require special handling. He had certain demands. I've told you what Frankfurt initially cabled us—that he was making what they called ridiculous and unreasonable demands? Well, Frankfurt was just embarrassed. Difficult demands, yes. Demands that might be beyond our power to satisfy, yes, perhaps. Not necessarily ridiculous. Fedorenko had simply insisted on being debriefed at the highest level."

"He wanted to talk directly to Eames?"

"Oh my, no. That would have been easy enough. He wanted to talk to the President."

Almost a week had passed with the corporal still in place, undetected, and not only Frankfurt but Langley also embarrassed by the fact that their crucial new source refused to deal with them at all, insisting instead with that famous mulish will of his that he would tell what he had to tell only in a private audience with John Fitzgerald Kennedy. Fedorenko knew the "Fitzgerald" and used it unfailingly when repeating his terms; evidently he thought of it as a patronymic.

"Why Kennedy?" says Kessler.

"Why indeed? That's what Wickes, and the others before, had kept asking him. Yet they weren't really asking. They were badgering. All they saw was a pudgy Ukrainian major who still smelled of boiled cabbage, a KGB thug, a *Communist*, demanding to be ushered into the august presence. They were not willing to discuss it as even a conceivable possibility. So they got nowhere with Fedorenko."

"Did he imagine the corporal was that important? Important enough for Kennedy to handle it personally?"

"No. Fedorenko wasn't stupid," Sparrow says brusquely. "It wasn't the corporal he wanted to talk about."

"Something else."

"Something else."

"And John Kennedy was the only person in the U. S. Government that he thought he could trust. For this something else. All right," says Kessler. "I'm following you now."

"Yes," says Claude Sparrow.

It *was* in fact out of the question, as Sparrow himself knew. But nothing was to be gained from sheer negativity. Sparrow had succeeded with Fedorenko, during those walks back and forth in the muddy garden, by offering a reasonable compromise. Fedorenko went for it. Within forty-eight hours Sparrow had delivered up the corporal's name, back-checking was under way to determine what documents and codes had been exposed at Orly during his tour there, damage-control instructions had gone out by cable, and a quiet contingent including French counterintelligence officers, U. S. Army MPs, and a senior case officer from the Agency's Paris station were already converging on Marseille. Three days later a small meeting was held at the Justice Department, in the personal office of the Attorney General. Warm vodka was served—Stolichnaya—and herring. The group consisted of Robert Kennedy, Bogdan Kirilovich Fedorenko, Herbert Eames, and Claude Sparrow. Jedediah McAttee had been pointedly disinvited, on word that came down from the host.

"The meeting went well. A triumph of good chemistry. A triumph for the family traits, imperious authority blended with charm. This was the occasion when we first heard about Dmitri, you see," Sparrow says. "January 17, 1963." He loops a glance out toward Kessler's notebook.

"Dmitri who?" says Kessler.

"Of course 'Dmitri' was not the way Fedorenko referred to him. That was simply a code name we chose in the following weeks."

"Who is Dmitri?"

"Yes." Sparrow offers a dainty smile. "That was precisely the question." Then he hikes his eyebrows like tall Byzantine arches, a pedagogue's coy mug to alert a slow student that some point or other has just been deftly made. "Wasn't it."

"Dmitri was the mole."

"We never used that word. That's a new word," Sparrow quibbles. "It's a spy-novel word."

"You had other terminology for the same thing."

"Yes we did," says Sparrow. "A *penetration.* Less vivid, I'm afraid. But there you are. Truth be known, it isn't always such a vivid profession."

"Your version does have its own sort of vividness," says Kessler. "If you consider the sexual connotation." Which connotation Sparrow shows no inclination to consider. After a queasy silence, Kessler adds: "And Dmitri, he was vivid enough."

"The *notion* of Dmitri, as offered by Fedorenko," says Sparrow, "—yes, it was vivid indeed. All we had so far was the notion. You went over this part with Melvin, I take it. Is that right?"

"I've heard bits and pieces about the penetration," Kessler answers evasively. "I'd like to hear it again. Your version."

"Did Melvin call it a mole?"

"I don't recall," says Kessler.

Now they glare at one another, each refusing to yield. Seconds and more seconds pass. Claude Sparrow, steady and unblinking as a python on a branch, does not seem to be capable of discomfort or impatience during such a prolonged staring contest. Kessler discovers that he himself is capable.

"Besides, Mel was a special case," Kessler says finally. "Sometimes it was hard to distinguish. What was real, versus his own inventions and adornments."

"Yes. True enough, Mr. Kessler." Gracious in his little victory, Sparrow turns easily, bringing his gaze back around to the line of brown treetops. "It sounds as though you knew Melvin Pokorny at least a little well."

"I suppose."

"But then you must have. He went all the way up to New Haven, seeking you out." Sparrow repeats himself, not unconsciously: "Is that right?"

"I knew him some."

"From your earlier work, writing about the Agency?"

"I knew him some," Kessler says again, stubbornly. "I used to live in Washington." This line of questions from Sparrow is coming close to being troublesome. Kessler picks up his pen and notebook, and with hands that have grown clumsy from the cold, almost embarrassingly so, he makes a notation. Then he says: "January 17, 1963." A way of changing the subject. "Fedorenko gets his audience with a Kennedy. In exchange, 'Dmitri.' Only not yet under that name."

"Not yet under any name."

"No. Merely *someone*. A person. Fedorenko has given you your first warning of a high-level penetration. I assume you mean a penetration at the Agency."

"Yes." Immediately again Sparrow is the gracious, artless informant. "Oh yes. At the Agency, yes indeed."

"It must have been an alarming piece of news."

"Most certainly that."

"But Fedorenko couldn't pinpoint Dmitri's identity. Not like with the corporal."

"Not like with the corporal. God knows. No. This was quite different. Fedorenko swore to us on the graves of both grandmothers that there was a penetration. With equal vehemence, he swore that he didn't know just who or just where. But he claimed he could help us figure it out."

"Did the Agency believe him?"

"That's no simple question to answer. It's a long story itself," Sparrow says.

"Don't we have all afternoon?" The sky over Washington is gray and cold like tarnished chrome but the sun, dim and heatless, is still high.

"*I* believed him," Sparrow says.

The mud grew worse, the shrubs and trees broke into leaf, before Fedorenko saw the last of that enclosed garden behind the safe house on the south side of Baltimore. Sparrow had many further strolls with him there—although much more of their time together, over the next three months, was spent at a large round oaken table in the dining room of the house, a room that was otherwise almost entirely bare. Sparrow and Bogdan Kirilovich (as Sparrow, describing the scene to Kessler, now calls him) sat on straight chairs. Littering the table before them, during these sessions, were pens and yellow pads, a teapot in a cozy, cups. Inside the light fixture overhead was a microphone and in the basement was a recorder attended by a technician in headphones, all of which Fedorenko knew nothing about but presumably could have guessed. Sparrow took notes on one pad, yet that was only the thinnest pretense; the main record of this debriefing, they both understood, would be the transcript of the tapes. After each several hours they paused, unbent their legs, made a circuit of the garden or else went to a sideboard in the next room where an elderly woman, Fedorenko's official housekeeper, would have set out plates of herring and caviar and sausage, also a bottle of Stolichnaya and a few small glasses that seemed originally to have held jelly. Bogdan Kirilovich once asked Sparrow, with deep and genuine curiosity, about the figures printed on those glasses. The glasses were symptomatic of Agency parsimoniousness toward the furnishing of safe houses generally, a chronic annoyance for which the trolls in Management and Services were held blameful, and Sparrow had a moment of embarrassment. Well, they were fairy-tale characters, in a sense, he explained to Fedorenko; the glasses were meant for children. Fedorenko looked shocked: children drank vodka in this country? No no, the children would drink their orange juice from such glasses, after the jelly had been all eaten, Sparrow explained. Bogdan Kirilovich now understood. Of course. Orange juice and jelly for children, very good. He pressed to know which fairy-tale characters these might be, adding expansively that he had warm recollections of many Ukrainian fairy tales from his childhood in a village near Krivoy Rog. Ukrainian fairy tales, American fairy tales: maybe they weren't so very different? Well, Sparrow said, this one was called Donald Duck. This other was evidently Snow White. This one, though Sparrow couldn't be sure, was to the best of his imperfect knowledge an individual named Goofy. It is one of Sparrow's most vivid memories from that period, he tells Kessler: Fedorenko, convulsed with laughter over the jelly glasses. In later weeks, when they adjourned to the sideboard, there would often be an elaborate exchange of jocular courtesies as to who should be so favored, that afternoon, as to take his vodka from Goofy. Of course that was on those days, only those, when the sessions were flowing smoothly.

There was a great sense of urgency surrounding the debriefing of Fedorenko, that winter and spring, because of Dmitri. Everyone at Langley felt it. The Attorney General felt it, keeping himself informed by way of phone calls to Herbert Eames. Fedorenko claimed to feel it, this urgency, though for days in a stretch he would seem blithely impervious. Claude Sparrow most certainly felt it. At the Agency they had all imagined they were under egregious pressure of time when the problem had been still merely a treasonous corporal somewhere in NATO communications, but that earlier week of panic now seemed risible, Sparrow says. A grass fire. A lark. Compared to the problem of Dmitri. Sparrow himself went short of meals and sleep. He drove back and forth between Langley and the safe house, virtually every day for three months, coping with Bogdan Kirilovich's imperfect memory on one end and Eames's nervous impatience on the other, just one leg of the drive taking him more than an hour in traffic, and it became rare that he ever saw the front door of his own home before nine at night. He devoted himself entirely to this effort, leaving all other business of the Counterintelligence section in the hands of his chief deputies, Pokorny and Roger Nye. He practically lived on herring and cold tea. When he slept, his mind worked at fitting Fedorenko's material into untried and more promising patterns —most unrestfully, says Sparrow. Everything was Dmitri. We must triangulate on this Dmitri. Find Dmitri. Sink Dmitri. Sparrow gives another of his encrypted smiles. We were all afever, we were frantic, but at least the sense of purpose was quite high, he tells Kessler. In some ways it was an exciting time. There was great urgency. This sounds, to Kessler's ear, like a very odd sort of nostalgia.

"We hardly dreamed, of course, that we'd still be at it ten years later," says Sparrow. "Sniffing around, halfhearted, for Dmitri."

Bogdan Kirilovich had much to tell, much to offer, not only in the matter of Dmitri but also concerning the particular corner of the KGB that had produced a Dmitri—and produced in addition numerous lesser agents on roughly the same pattern. Fedorenko's memory was especially rich with detail regarding these lesser fry, scattered broadly throughout the Western intelligence and security services; and where he lacked detail, he offered deduction and supposition; and sometimes, as events proved, he was startlingly accurate in what he claimed to know about such cases, the lower- and middle-echelon KGB penetrations. His help was just crucial in routing out certain nasty folk.

No one can dispute that, Sparrow says—suggesting to Kessler that someone must have reason to try. Other times Fedorenko was . . . yes, well, faulty. Confused and faulty. Not so very many times, Sparrow says, given all that the man delivered. Kessler makes a mark on his pad and Sparrow's eyes shift, jealously, to watch him do it. But Sparrow doesn't stop talking.

All considered, Bogdan Fedorenko was perhaps the most valuable defector we've ever gotten, he says. Still, any defector is only so precious as what you make of him. A defector, understand, is not a bag of golden coins. A defector is a field of golden wheat, that's more like it—a crop that requires careful harvesting. No. No, my metaphor is not apt, Sparrow says, raising one pinkened hand. It omits the element of art, he says. Carefulness isn't enough. That raw offering, that crop, it needs to be *artfully* harvested—or, oh, choose any analogy you like. Anyway, this is why it had to be myself, or another person of high competence, long experience, driving out there all that dreary spring to lead Bogdan Kirilovich through the maze of his own memory. Not someone like Scott Wickes. Otherwise you do worse than waste time. You squander and ruin the defector himself. Debriefing can only happen properly when those recollections are *fresh*. Otherwise, no. No, it won't do. Kessler has noticed by now that Sparrow's nostrils dilate with each mention of Scott Wickes. He scribbles a note.

Again Sparrow seems too aware of the note taking, so Kessler diverts him with a question: "Which particular corner?"

"Beg your pardon?"

"Of the KGB. Fedorenko helped to illuminate one particular corner, the same corner that had produced a Dmitri. Isn't that what you said?"

"It was Fedorenko's own corner. Yes. That's why he could tell us about it."

"Which was that?"

"Counterintelligence."

Kessler shifts his own long wool coat more tightly around himself, raising the collar and fastening the highest button. Tomorrow, he resolves, I'll come in long johns and an extra sweater.

But not counterintelligence in the same limited and defensive sense we tend to use that term, Sparrow explains. For the Soviets it carries quite a different meaning. Counterintelligence for them is something altogether more aggressive, more preemptive, directed outward and across toward the opponent's intelligence organs rather than inward toward the security of one's own. For the Soviets, in essence, it means penetrations. Fedorenko during his tour in Paris, masquerading as a visa officer while running an agent within the NATO courier center, was engaged in what *they* would call a counterintelligence operation. Us, our side, *we* are obliged to sit properly in our offices, reading debriefing transcripts and surveillance logs and personnel files, waiting patiently for our turn with the occasional defector, says Sparrow, shaping the words with his teeth.

Kessler sees another point of rancor. He suspects that Claude Sparrow and he could devote the whole of an afternoon just to Sparrow's personal peeves and grudges, an excellent way to waste precious time and be drawn all hell away from the matter of interest; and he recalls the domestic wiretap operation that played a large part, supposedly, in getting Sparrow fired. He feels some temptation to ask: "What about listening in on the phones of the NSC staff, Mr. Sparrow? That's not preemptive counterintelligence?" But he forbears. Anyway Kessler knows what the man would say. "Of course it was. Unfortunately I was not permitted to continue it. I was not permitted to continue at all." The official version. Kessler would rather hear about Bogdan Fedorenko. Intuition warns him that Claude Sparrow may be far more percipient and credible when he is talking about Russians, or even Ukrainians, than when he is talking about himself.

Formally it was known, Fedorenko's division, as Special Service Two within the KGB's First Chief Directorate. Sparrow had long nursed a certain curiosity about that particular service, he says, in what Kessler can recognize as gin-dry ironical understatement, Sparrow's closest approximation of humor. It was, Sparrow says, for obvious reasons a pet subject of his, Special Two.

He had collected a whole room's worth of files devoted to it, all of them filled with speculation, outsiders' gossip, guesswork. No real hard facts. Special Two was still, for Langley, just a magic lantern show. Until Fedorenko. Special Service One, they were familiar enough with that, and with its unexceptional role in transmitting intelligence data to Politburo members. Hardly more than a courier agency, Special One was not in fact very special. Not to Claude Sparrow's mind or imagination. Special Two, however—and Kessler watches Sparrow's eyes widen dizzily.

He always had known it was there, because it had to be, and within the First Chief Directorate somewhere; but he had known nothing about it. Not the name, not the identities of the main personnel, nothing of its methods or its operations. These things are generally kept compartmentalized in the KGB just as at Langley; and neither Sparrow nor anyone else in the Agency had ever before laid hold of a warm body fresh from Special Service Two. It was the dark side of the moon. Hence the great preciousness of Fedorenko, when he suddenly came blinking in for a landing, like an Apollo craft back from the far loop, loaded with photos and one scoop of very exotic gravel.

After the NATO business, Fedorenko's first real bit of usefulness—or rather, Sparrow corrects himself, the first *indisputable* bit, and Kessler guesses this hedge to be an allusion involving Dmitri—after the NATO business, Fedorenko's first big contribution was what he told them about Special Service Two. He had enabled them at Langley finally to place KGB counterintelligence on the organizational chart, and to know it by a name. And not only that, but details. Bogdan Kirilovich described the line of command, the chain of bosses' bosses, from his own immediate supervisor to the chief of Special Two and on to the KGB Chairman. He described the suite of offices Special Two occupied, on the third floor of the Lubyanka, in the newer half of the building. The floor number itself was a valuable datum, which Sparrow had evidently received greedily and clutched to his cold little soul—because the third was a prestige floor at the Lubyanka, as they already knew, with the Chairman's big office there near the junction of the old half of the building and the annex. Such proximity, it could be confidently hypothesized, must reflect Special Two's high standing in esteem and power within the full KGB. Also that proximity offered hope for a morsel or two of executive gossip overheard, perhaps, in the Chairman's office down the corridor. Sparrow and Fedorenko spent an entire morning bent over the oaken table just on this matter of office layout, Bogdan Kirilovich drawing floor plans from memory on a yellow pad while Sparrow demanded more detail and the correction of small discrepancies and still more detail until, dreamy-eyed, Sparrow himself could walk in his mind down that corridor, feel the ugly pink and green runner under his feet, then the bare parquet as he turned and entered a large antechamber, strode past the male secretary in blue uniform, passed through the swinging gate of a low wooden railing, another glass door, an inner office, and seated himself at the desk of a man named L. V. Nechaev.

The desk was an old wooden one, Bogdan Kirilovich told him, crude of design but expansive, and in all likelihood utterly bare. To its right, within reach, was a table upon which sat six separate black telephones. Comrade L. V. Nechaev was the chief of Special Service Two.

Fedorenko himself, during the two years he spent in Moscow before being sent out to Paris, had worked in a much smaller office and one with no window onto the courtyard, though furnished otherwise in roughly the same austere style. He had possessed only three telephones. He never dealt directly with Comrade Nechaev, a fact for which he was grateful, and had been called into the chief's office on just a single nerve-jangling occasion, to deliver a short verbal account of some operation passing across his desk that had come to Nechaev's attention; he was questioned fiercely on that occasion, not by Nechaev himself but by a deputy while Nechaev sat silent, and then was dismissed with a curt wave. Fedorenko felt great relief, getting out of the office quickly and with his whole skin. Comrade Nechaev had no reputation for kindliness or approachability. But neither did he (as Fedorenko told Sparrow, who tells Kessler) have a reputation of the opposite sort, for cruel petulance toward his subordinates. No. That sort were common enough, certainly, on a bureaucratic anthill the tone of which had been set by Stalin and Yezhov and Beria; but no, Nechaev wasn't dreaded as another like those. There was no trapdoor beneath the Armenian carpet covering the parquet before his desk, that carpet upon which Fedorenko had briefly stood; no greased chute, either figurative or literal, from there to the basement cells. Not so far as anyone knew, not so far as gossip dared whisper. The problem was that Comrade Nechaev had no reputation whatsoever. Daring or not, gossip seldom whispered his name at all.

He was distant. A deep-water fish, of indeterminate weight and God only knew what manner of jaws. He was a cipher, even to those who worked under him.

Fedorenko had it (though only at second or third hand) that

Comrade Nechaev was elaborately polite in most contact with
his deputies; polite but formal, correct, cold as the steppes. He
wasn't evidently a fellow to whom one could offer the little
friendly bribes—English razors and whiskey, Yugoslav brandy,
French perfume for a wife or a mistress—that one customarily
brought back to boss and colleagues after a trip out to the West.
Unspoken signals from Comrade Nechaev suggested that such
gifts to him would be unnecessary, or worse. And no one except
two or three deputies was close enough to receive even those
signals. Fedorenko himself did not even know the man's first
name or patronymic. It was thought Nechaev preferred to be
addressed by his military-equivalent rank, which was colonel,
or by the quite unmellifluous official title he held as chief of
Special Two, or simply as Comrade Nechaev. But then again,
few of his underlings ever had occasion to address him. All in
the world that Comrade Nechaev demanded from his own staff,
evidently, was performance. Failing that, fulsome loyalty would
never save you. Brandy and razors would never save you. Being
invisible would never save you.

It was testimony to Bogdan Kirilovich's good head and precise memory, Sparrow claims, that, notwithstanding the chilly
climate of Comrade Nechaev's office during that single visit,
Fedorenko had counted the telephones; that he had noticed and
remembered the Armenian carpet.

Fedorenko also provided a physical description of Comrade
Nechaev, of course, though Sparrow had not then foreseen how
this information would be of any particular consequence.
Nechaev as Bogdan Kirilovich painted him was simply a gray
man of medium height and weight, steady intelligent gaze, thinning hair combed back. He wore eyeglasses. The glassess were
of a style then mildly fashionable among opticians to the Soviet
elite: thick silver framing across the brow but only a thin rim
looping down around the lenses. Rather like peering out
through the oxbows of a yoke. Fedorenko could offer no impression of Comrade Nechaev's voice, never having heard it.
Sparrow let the visual description be duly filed in the mug book
they kept on KGB players. He himself was far more interested,
at first, in the operations of which Fedorenko had personal
knowledge.

Kessler, on the other hand, is interested in where Claude
Sparrow got his familiarity with oxbows and yokes.

The Western services were just rotten with KGB penetrations, Fedorenko told Sparrow during their first week at the oaken table. On that point he was vehemently, scornfully dogmatic: rotten with penetrations.

"Like 'bad goat cheese' was the exact phrase Bogdan Kirilovich used," Sparrow tells Kessler. Then Fedorenko simply waved a hand as though fanning away flies and went momentarily silent—a rarity for him—with disgust. Gently, Sparrow said: Tell me. Sparrow had a yellow pad in front of himself, he took up a ballpoint and held it. Tell me about them, Bogdan Kirilovich. That's what we're here for. The stubby hand swung again, fingers like dill pickles. After which Fedorenko did begin telling him, in horrifying detail, of that true and awesome rottenness. "I didn't want him to see how shocked I was," Sparrow says. "He talked and I made notes and my mind commenced reeling, but I concealed that. Not for any operational reason. I just didn't want him to see. I was mortified. Dumbfounded." But Sparrow recognized at once that Bogdan Kirilovich himself was still harboring a confused ambivalence— one part of him proud, even smug, about these successful Special Two penetrations.

Now Kessler is distracted by the goat cheese. Eighteen years have passed, Sparrow recalls a phrase about goat cheese, also not one but three Disney characters on jelly glasses, and the man talks about *Fedorenko's* precision of memory. Of course Sparrow did have the transcripts. Of course. Every word Fedorenko said to him went onto tape, and Sparrow would have studied the transcripts later with rabbinical diligence. Nevertheless.

We have someone at Pullach, Fedorenko told Sparrow, still by habit referring to Special Two with the first person plural. Kessler shakes his head to indicate ignorance, so Sparrow gives him a gloss: Pullach, just outside of Munich, was the site of Reinhard Gehlen's spy fortress. The postwar, Dulles-financed version, Sparrow adds archly, not the Nazi version. Gehlen had made one of those seamless transitions of loyalty and kept himself in business, says Sparrow, so the distinction is necessary.

A man at Pullach, Fedorenko said, and this one has been in place for years. He was with us in Berlin during the early occupation, making himself useful in various ways, a fellow who knew the black market and the sewer tunnels but could also put

on a dinner jacket, and in 1948 we played him back across to
the West. I've read the whole file, Bogdan Kirilovich told Sparrow. He was well connected to General Gehlen, and remotely
to Adenauer. Gehlen himself brought the man into West German intelligence. He is still there. He has done well, made a
good career. And for that he has us to thank, Fedorenko said.
We contrived and delivered most of his biggest successes.
Name: Otto Schratt. I've handled his product myself, when I
was in Moscow, Fedorenko said. Schratt has fantastic access all
throughout the BND. He reports to us through another BND
man, also in reality ours, but this one just a field officer who
finds excuses for frequent trips to Berlin. The field officer sees a
cutout, a woman, who passes Schratt's reports along to our
officer in Karlshorst, on the other side of the Wall. Understand
that all of this came, Sparrow tells Kessler, in Bogdan
Kirilovich's own blunt and slightly mangled version of English.
We had to go quite slowly. I could get every bit of it down on
the pad. Name of the field officer, I demanded. He gave it.
Name of the woman. He gave it. Name of your own man in
Karlshorst. He gave me that. We had them—all but the KGB
man, who was of course beyond reach—we had them shoveled
up and shit-canned within a fortnight. The crudity this time
seems to be Sparrow's own.

"What was Otto Schratt's exact role?" Kessler asks.

"For whom? In what? His role on which level, in which context?" Sparrow throws up his shoulders, pretending a bemused
helplessness. "In the saga of Bogdan Kirilovich Fedorenko?"

"At Pullach. The surface level. His job."

"He was West Germany's chief of counterintelligence."

"Somehow I knew you'd say that. Do I detect a pattern, or is
it just howling coincidence?"

"Wait," Sparrow says.

"Or a character trait."

We have a person in Oslo, Fedorenko told Sparrow—tossing
these claims out now almost impatiently, more concerned to
prove his original point (the one about goat cheese) cumula-
tively than to dwell on any one case. A woman, in Oslo. She is
personal secretary to the cabinet minister in charge of budget-
ing and oversight for Norwegian intelligence. Also she sleeps
with him, this minister. The minister's oversight function is
largely token, but he does know things. He is sixty and a wid-

ower but very sensitive about his situation with the secretary, because of his great reputation for Lutheran rectitude. Probably he is in love with her. Under instructions from us, Bogdan Kirilovich said, she will refuse absolutely to marry him, though so far he hasn't asked her. She coaxes information out of him in response to specific questions from us. Not a hugely important connection, but it is potentially useful for our Baltic fleet, especially the submarines. The secretary for her part is infatuated with a young French businessman, a wine exporter, who comes to Oslo frequently on his worldly travels. She first met him fifteen months ago at an embassy party. He is her case officer, and she devoutly, ignorantly believes he is carrying her information back to the French. But the Frenchman was born in Riga and he is ours, Bogdan Kirilovich said. Her name is Ilse Sjodahl. The minister's name, Sparrow demanded. Fedorenko gave it. The false Frenchman's name, and where can we find him when he isn't in Norway? Fedorenko told him.

"It all checked, of course," says Sparrow. "Within six months Ilse Sjodahl was on trial, and the minister had locked himself in his study to put a bullet through the roof of his mouth."

"Wonderful. Where was the false Frenchman?"

"Moscow, unfortunately. Thanks to a stupid error by the Norwegians."

In London we have at least one that I'm aware of, Bogdan Kirilovich told Sparrow, and probably many more. Everyone in Special Two dreams of someday going to London as a field officer, according to Bogdan Kirilovich. The opportunities for recruitments are always bountiful, the penalties for those not protected with diplomatic status are relatively quite mild, the standard of living is good, the whiskey is good, the English traitors are so friendly and respectful to their case officers and everyone else ignores you totally. Bogdan Kirilovich himself had angled for an assignment to London, though he had been glad enough to get Paris. A long tour in London was the next best thing to defection, Bogdan Kirilovich said. Even those KGB officers responsible for policing the Soviet colony— they're from the Eleventh Department, Bogdan Kirilovich said, and their job is to spy on the rest of us for signs of ideological heresy and decadence and potential defectors—even those bull mastiffs tend to be slightly more lenient in London. At least so

Bogdan Kirilovich had heard, by hopeful rumor. What's the Englishman's name? Sparrow said.

Fedorenko told him: Nigel Willey. A code analyst at MI-6 with very good access. Also a homosexual and a Marxist ideologue, though he had never been anywhere near Oxford or Cambridge. The Englishman served fourteen years in prison, says Sparrow, then was released and the next day took a flight to Moscow. Perfectly legal, believe it or not. Bogdan Kirilovich also—

"I think I get the idea," Kessler says. "How long did this part of the debriefing go on?"

"Weeks. No, wait," says Sparrow. "There was more."

And he drags Kessler onward through the dossiers on a half dozen other agents or alleged agents of Special Service Two, all of whom had at the time of Fedorenko's defection been safely ensconced within the intelligence agencies of Washington's trusted allies. Another Englishman, this one stationed at a listening post in Berlin. A brilliant Canadian mathematician, former academic, lately working in codes. A Frenchwoman, born in Algiers, also brilliant, and underemployed as a personnel officer with her country's service in Paris. A Mexican, under consular cover at his country's embassy in Madrid, with debts. A young Belgian, disgruntled over Washington's nuclear swaggering. An Austrian Jew incensed at the easy rehabilitation of Bonn and, even more, at Gehlen's propensity for hiring former SS. Sparrow recites names, positions, motives, arrangements by which Special Two maintained contact with these people, an outpouring of recollected detail that is astonishing to Kessler for its sheer volume even as it continues and continues, fogging his brain with confusion and impatience, threatening boredom. Overload, he thinks. Too much data. Where is the switch, how do I cut this man off? Simultaneously he is mesmerized by Claude Sparrow's sudden energy, his intensity, his passionately thorough dedication to the recall of facts and near facts associated with all these stale cases. What's happening here? Something is at stake, Kessler senses. Something is on the line to be proved. Sparrow chatters on like a commodity report over morning radio while Kessler squints at him, noting the flush on those two patches of aging and flaccid skin just under the man's cheekbones, wondering whether that color was there earlier, whether it too is only a symptom of the cold. Bogdan Kirilovich kept us quite busy that spring, Sparrow says after a pause for oxygen. And of course I haven't yet even begun, he says, on the Americans.

"All of these accusations checked out?" says Kessler.

Sparrow is silent. His jaw moves. His mouth seems to be dry from the recitation, but he doesn't evade Kessler's eyes.

"Many of them checked out."

Seated on this bench Sparrow has chosen in this park Sparrow has chosen, he and Kessler are facing northeast, toward the Potomac. Also toward Langley, Kessler has realized. The spot could be thought of as an exile's piteous overlook, just too perfectly surveyed to be accidental. Kessler wonders whether Claude Sparrow has been back to CIA headquarters, on even a short visit, since he was sacked.

Probably at least once. Probably they hauled him back out there for some sort of presentation ceremony after six or eight months had passed and the wounds were at least scabbed over, if not healed, Kessler supposes. A brief afternoon event featuring one bottle of domestic champagne and a half dozen congregants, not including Sparrow's wife if he had a wife, during which they would have presented him with a citation for distinguished or maybe exceptionally distinguished service and given him a flash look at the actual ribboned medal in its little box that was then to be snatched back for safekeeping there in a locked cabinet at the Agency. From what Kessler recalls having once thought he knew, that was an important part of the protocol for a CIA dismissal in bad grace. You give the man a medal and he must accept. The more controversial the case, the more delicate the basis of that bad grace, and the more interesting it might possibly be to a congressional committee staff or a newspaper or the general public—that much bigger and shinier did the vanishing medal need to be. Kessler wonders whether this might be one bit of methodology they picked up from the Russians. He suspects that Claude Sparrow on that afternoon, if there was such an afternoon, got a glimpse of a very grand wafer of gold. Jed McAttee himself might have dropped in for the ceremony.

Fortunately the big building in Langley, though they do face it from their bench, is invisible beyond two miles of hillocks and trees.

That would have been eight years ago, the retirement ceremony. Kessler is curious about what Claude Sparrow has done
with his time. Mildly curious, at least. It's part of the human as
opposed to the professional side of the subject, the vivid banali-
ties that can make a story seem real. How would a man such as
this, forced into early retirement, spend his hours days and
weeks? Toward what other conceivable task could that cold
intensity be aimed and discharged? None comes to mind. If
there was or is a Sparrow wife, Kessler pities her. Imagine it,
Judas, this guy around the house with nothing to do. Even now,
when Sparrow's status as a pensioner no longer seems glaringly
premature—he appears to be in his middle or late sixties—how
would he be likely to cope with it? Long afternoon walks
through the local parks? Bench-sitting with or without journalists? Maybe some fiercely intense pastime like building bamboo
fly rods, translating *Gilgamesh,* trying to recapture with stiffen-
ing fingers a youthful competence on the viola? Or has he just
devoted all those hours days and weeks to planning implacably
toward a Restoration? As Pokorny's visit gave Kessler cause to
suspect. If not that, then Kessler can't imagine what. Literally
he tries but can't. He is able to summon no mental picture of
the man's passing time, eight years of idleness or, if not idleness,
at least obscurity. Kessler can only see the man seated on a park
bench, those eight years raveling out, while the old body per-
forms its furious isometric exercise, one hand locked on the
opposite wrist. Otherwise, for Kessler, a blank.

He has opportunity for this idle speculation, though, because
Sparrow is momentarily distracted.

From the naked brown woods two small boys have appeared,
coming down the paved path. Locked in another of his clamlike
silences, Sparrow is watching them.

These kids are about six years old. They are spaced apart
some distance, one behind the other, as though the first has
stalked off poutishly and the second is tagging after. But it isn't
that. They are simply involved in a game, a little adventure
fantasy of the kind Kessler himself remembers well, though in
their case assisted by the latest in solid-state electronic toys:
they are jabbering back and forth, in their own pseudomilitary
double-talk, on a pair of plastic walkie-talkies.

Claude Sparrow gapes at them distrustfully. He waits until
the second little boy, in a knit hat that almost covers his eyes,

has passed beyond earshot; and Kessler, mystified, waits for Sparrow. Yes, God forbid that we should let the Russians or Jed McAttee tap into this conversation by way of two devious urchins playing hooky from kindergarten.

"They gave him a name," Sparrow says at last. "They began calling him Chicken Little."

"Fedorenko."

"Yes of course, Fedorenko."

"This was a code name?"

"No. Nothing like that. It was a nickname. It was ridicule." A schoolyard joke that Claude Sparrow, after eighteen years, like a wounded child become a maimed man, is still not about to dismiss lightly. Chicken Little. But it wasn't Sparrow's own nickname, after all, was it? Only by extension. Kessler begins to sense just how far Sparrow must have committed himself, professionally and emotionally, to the premise of Bogdan Fedorenko's credibility.

Kessler says: "Because of Otto Schratt and all the others. I see. Sure. The 'rotten with penetrations' business. Not everyone at Langley shared your high opinion of Fedorenko."

"No, later. This was a bit later than Schratt. Two or three months, anyway," says Sparrow. "He had started helping us with our own difficulties. Within the Agency."

"Aha," says Kessler. "Dmitri."

"Dmitri was always a large factor, yes. Always. But it didn't stop there. We had other security problems at the same time. Quite a number. Each of them far less egregious than Dmitri, but nevertheless very troubling. You must understand, Mr. Kessler, these things all interlock with each other."

"Interlock. Explain what you mean by that, please."

Instead Sparrow laces together the fingers of his two hands, holds them before Kessler's face, and repeats: "They interlock. What Fedorenko told us about Schratt, about the Norwegian woman, about Dmitri, and all the rest. The pieces of testimony interlock. Inextricably. It's a crucial point. When one decides to give credence to a defector, any defector, well, after that one simply can't pick and choose among his offerings. Believe this, disbelieve that. Ignore the third. No. No, it doesn't work. One must use everything. Or at very least, make sense of everything."

"And you had already made that decision. Giving credence

to Fedorenko." Kessler amends: "You Claude Sparrow, not you the Agency. The Agency overall was divided. Right? Some of the others out there, they remained unconvinced."

"That is correct."

"McAttee, Lentzer, Scott Wickes. The Soviet Bloc Division versus your own."

"Roughly correct."

"Then Bogdan Kirilovich began naming names on this side of the Atlantic. Agency officers. Quite a number, you say. Dingalingaling. Fire alarms, klaxons, a seismic reaction, no doubt. Norwegian secretaries, they were one thing, Mexican diplomats in Spain, but now watch out. Suddenly the disagreement over Fedorenko's credibility grew distinctly more heated. Am I still roughly correct?"

"You are."

"Tell me about it."

"But you're doing very well yourself. I suspect Melvin must have touched on this, didn't he?"

Kessler ignores that. "Were you still at the oaken table in the little house with the garden?"

"Actually it was rather a big house. But what difference where we were? Bogdan Kirilovich was, all this time, dealing directly and solely with me, yes. If that's what you're getting at. We had only moved into a new phase of the debriefing."

"I just want to see it," Kessler says. "The way you wanted to see Comrade Nechaev, seated among his telephones."

Fastidiously, Sparrow covers his knees again with the tails of his coat, taking time. "We were no longer at the house. We were in my office. Better security."

"Not a home office, I assume. You mean at headquarters. Langley."

"Yes of course."

"Were the sessions still being taped?"

"No. At least I devoutly hoped that they weren't. Not at this point," says Sparrow. "And I had very good reasons. So far as I know today, that was the case. No recording."

"You took notes."

"Melvin or Roger Nye did, usually."

"What's our date now, Mr. Sparrow?"

"Early summer of 1963."

"June?"

"May and June. And right on through until autumn, as it turned out."

"Fedorenko had come across in, what, January of that year?"

"Correct."

"By May he was in your office. Inside the great gates. Seventh floor, presumably. Was that the least bit unusual? For a KGB man, freshly defected, to be taken to bosom so quickly?"

"Fedorenko first came through those gates in April, Mr. Kessler. For a polygraph test. Administered on the first floor, by an examiner from the Office of Security. Which test, by the way, he passed. I only brought him in afterward. And being interrogated in my office, by myself and two assistants—it did not, I assure you, constitute being taken to bosom."

"But you see what I mean. You see how it appears. Was that unusual? Bogdan Kirilovich getting a look at your office?"

"Not very," Sparrow says coldly.

"How long was it before Viktor Tronko got invited up there?"

"Never," Sparrow says. "Not during my tenure, at least. What's your point, Mr. Kessler?"

"No point. Just curious." Unctuously, Kessler adds: "Of course I realize that the two cases were very different."

He persuades Sparrow to tell him about the security investigations, the boards of review, the resignations and demotions and outright firings that Fedorenko's seventh-floor testimony led to at Langley, and this occupies them for a rather long time as the sun loses heart and the afternoon grows even colder, Sparrow pausing occasionally to edit in his head, omitting names and details in those cases, he says, where an officer might still be active for the Agency and so have a right to expect that Sparrow will not jeopardize the man's cover, Sparrow in those cases giving only a silhouette version of the individual episode. But the silhouettes are the exceptions. Mainly what Sparrow offers are vivid and particularized facts—or at least vivid and particularized allegations. The names omitted don't seem to be many. Evidently few of those officers who came under scrutiny, during this phase of Fedorenko's debriefing, are still active for the Agency. Few have anything left in the way of career, it appears, that Sparrow could jeopardize. Of course after eighteen years a good number might just be retired. But that's not the impression Kessler gets. The impression he gets is of rolling heads.

"You're telling me that all these people were Soviet agents? Dozens of penetrations, right there at headquarters? Christ, I don't see how the place could have continued to function."

"I am not," Sparrow says. "I'm telling you that these people came under suspicion. As we began tracking backward from what Bogdan Kirilovich could tell us. But you see, he only had fragmentary knowledge of these cases. Stray facts that had come across his desk, back in Moscow, buried within unrelated reports. Passing allusions picked up in office chat. Not the same sort of full and unmistakably damning data he had been able to give us on Schratt. Or on Nigel Willey. No, no. His access hadn't been nearly so good with regard to the American assets. He hadn't handled the files. Comrade Nechaev kept this group to himself."

"How many people were fired?"

"It was like the challenge to a paleontologist, you see. Working out these cases, from the bits he gave us. You have a fossilized tibia. Or maybe it's an ulna. You aren't even sure which. But you've got to extrapolate from it, imagining the whole animal into being."

"How many people were fired? Counting the resignations."

"I suppose it was thirty or forty," Sparrow says.

"How many were convicted of espionage?"

"None, Mr. Kessler. As a matter of fact, none went to trial."

"And you'd have me believe that that was a tactical matter, right? The Agency declined to prosecute. Cutting your losses. You couldn't afford to have more secrets coming out in court."

"You may believe what you wish, but yes: that happens to have been true. In some cases. We didn't dare prosecute. In others, it was merely that we hadn't the evidence."

"Let me make a wild guess. Did any of these suspect people come from the Soviet Bloc Division?"

"Several. Including one analyst, part of a group set up by Lentzer to read the tea leaves and study the garbage of Politburo members. This analyst was from a Russian émigré family, parents who had gotten out in the twenties—same sort of background as Lentzer himself. But you musn't think that Soviet Bloc was in any way specially targeted. That wasn't so. They had their share, merely. Other divisions had their shares. Even Counterintelligence, we had one man who had to go."

"How did McAttee react?"

"Quite childishly, I thought," says Sparrow. "He made a very large issue of it, over that one analyst."

"What eventually happened to him?"

"Jed? Why of course he—"

"No, no. I mean the analyst."

"It was a she," says Sparrow. "Fired. No criminal charges. She may have signed some sort of confession, a form of consent agreement with us and the Justice Department. There were a few of those. With her, I don't precisely recall."

"How old was she?"

A moment has passed before Sparrow says: "What an odd question."

"You said McAttee behaved foolishly. I'm trying to consider all angles. And I'm guessing that female officers at the Agency, however few there may be, find themselves sometimes with an extra set of problems."

"Nonsense." Sparrow is deadpan but he adds: "No, I think you just have a dirty mind."

"A suspicious mind. But that's all right, I withdraw the question." It is interesting to see Sparrow coming, even obliquely, to the defense of Jed McAttee's professional rectitude.

"She was gray, Mr. Kessler. She was put cruelly out to pasture in the twilight of, oh, I suspect, her fifty-eighth year," Sparrow says with brittle irony. "Very much like myself."

"Did Fedorenko identify this woman by name?"

"No. He merely gave us a profile. He pointed us where to look. We found certain damaging patterns in her record, certain congruencies. She matched the profile."

"She was fired on the basis of congruencies?"

"Counterintelligence *is* largely a matter of finding congruencies."

"I thought it was the effort to see through appearances." Sparrow isn't the only one with a memory. "I'm quoting now."

"And to all appearances this woman was a reliable officer. A loyal citizen. Until we looked more closely."

"What did you find then?"

"That her parents had not fled from the Bolsheviks, as previously implied. They were Crimean Jews, and they had fled from

86   *David Quammen*

the Whites. From the Cossack pogroms. Also that she took her vacations, each February, in Mexico City."

Kessler says nothing. He waits. But Sparrow only gawks back at him, so finally: "Is that *all?*"

"No. Mexico City is a notorious lair for KGB officers. You wouldn't know that but we did. It's virtually a free zone for them. The Soviet Embassy alone, it generally harbors upward of sixty under diplomatic status. Almost no room for real diplomats."

"Aren't there about ten million other folk in the town too?"

"Yes. All of them speaking Spanish. This woman, though—she had made eight trips to the city, she claimed it was for the cultural experience, yet she spoke scarcely a word of Spanish. We tested her. She was hopeless. She couldn't have ordered in a restaurant."

"Maybe she liked mariachi music. Maybe she went for the tan but was embarrassed to say so."

"Why are you defending her, Mr. Kessler? This is the ancient case of a woman you never met."

"I don't know. Good question. You seem to be forcing me. Was there anything else against her?"

"Yes of course."

"Any *evidence?*"

"Testimonial evidence."

"From Fedorenko. All right. I'm listening," Kessler says carefully. He has nothing whatever to gain, he reminds himself, from debating with Sparrow. "Please go on."

"From Bogdan Kirilovich, yes. Back in Moscow, he had seen several pages from a file. The file involved still another case, an English traitor who was then serving MI-6 on liaison to Washington. This man was very delicately placed, his product handled by a high deputy in Special Service Two. Bogdan Kirilovich had no knowledge and no reason for knowledge. But because of his responsibilities in the Nigel Willey operation, for which he was desk officer, Fedorenko suddenly one day was permitted to see several pages. These were just excerpts from a report, no beginning or end, and a number of the lines had been blacked out. He was handed these pages, allowed to have them for half an hour, long enough to read and make notes, and then they were fastidiously collected back. Based on that glimpse, Bogdan Kirilovich could tell us of an American woman, émigré family, who reported to Moscow infrequently but quite usefully through a case officer in a South American capital."

"And you filled in the rest."

"We filled in the rest."

"Like a paleontologist. Imagining a whole animal into being." Kessler is assailed by a heavy dull sadness, retroactive and futile. "Mr. Sparrow, didn't anyone point out to you fellows that Mexico is part of *North* America?"

"Latin," Sparrow says quickly. "I misspoke. It was 'a Latin American capital' that Fedorenko talked of. 'Latin American' was what he had seen."

And the verification is there, somewhere at Langley, in a forgotten file, one phrase scribbled down in the shorthand of Pokorny or Roger Nye. Kessler now understands how convenient it might have been, for Claude Sparrow, that from this phase of Fedorenko's debriefing there were no recordings.

"Who coined the name Chicken Little?" he asks wearily. Kessler's neck aches from facing sideways on the bench and he has long since lost touch with his toes.

"Lord. It might have been any number of people. I never knew. Never even paused to wonder," Claude Sparrow claims.

They return to Dmitri. They return to the month of March 1963, to those early spring days before Bogdan Kirilovich's first polygraph test, before the heads began rolling at Langley, back when most Agency officers on the seventh floor still held the touching conviction—as Sparrow puts it—that even *one* penetration was far too many, those days when heartbreakingly fine weather was encouraging Sparrow and Bogdan Kirilovich to take themselves back outside for long afternoons of pacing the muddy garden of the house in suburban Baltimore. Kessler guides the talk in this direction. He wants to know more about Dmitri. He is puzzled by what he has already heard—great sense of urgency, Sparrow losing sleep, phone calls from Bobby Kennedy that were no doubt more peremptory than supportive, find Dmitri, sink Dmitri, then somewhere along the way that frantic search falling into a stalemate that lingered on for ten years—and he has also a broader motive. Kessler senses that Dmitri must be the link between Bogdan Kirilovich's story, offered at such length, and Viktor Tronko's.

Dmitri must be the link, if any exists, between the festering

abscess in Claude Sparrow's memory and whatever piece of
information got Mel Pokorny murdered. What exactly did
Fedorenko tell you about this Dmitri? he asks Sparrow.

Very little, it seems. Sparrow repeats himself: Bogdan
Kirilovich swore on the graves of both grandmothers that there
was such a creature as Dmitri, lurking within the high reaches
at Langley; there had to be, Fedorenko knew it as unshakable
fact, he had worked after all right there in Special Service Two,
only three glass doors and a railing away from the desk of the
chief. But he couldn't, evidently, give Sparrow much more than
that.

Dmitri had no code name, in Moscow, that ever fell upon
Bogdan Kirilovich's ears. Dmitri had been known to him only
from whispers—but whispers of precisely the sort, Fedorenko
insisted, that invariably proved true. Dmitri had been the private project of Comrade Nechaev himself. Dmitri, whoever it
was, must be a genius of the craft and a paragon of cautious
methodical daring. Dmitri was invisible.

That much Fedorenko knew. So far as the ordinary channels
of communication and support within Special Two were concerned—those channels by which all other penetration agents
were serviced, with reports flowing in by way of a case officer in
the field and small payments or interrogatory instructions flowing out—so far as those channels were concerned, Dmitri was
invisible. It had been the case when Bogdan Kirilovich first
arrived at the Lubyanka, and it was still the case when he left
for Paris. Nothing through channels. Not with this source. This
one was Comrade Nechaev's own personal phantom.

"If you were going to *invent* a source, one that didn't really
exist," Kessler observes, "there's much to be said for inventing
a phantom."

"Precisely what McAttee was fond of pointing out."

"How did you answer him?"

"It wasn't easy. I confess to you. Not easily."

For instance the matter of radio. Dmitri absolutely refused to
use radio. Generally the KGB favored UHF radio, Fedorenko
told Sparrow, for communication with agents within the Washington *rezidentura*. That was true for Special Two and its assets
at Langley, equally true for all other assets within the U. S.
State Department or elsewhere as handled by other KGB
branches. But not true for Dmitri. Dmitri would not go on the

air. There was some risk in any contact or communication between an agent and his handlers, always, inherently, Sparrow
explains. The risk attendant in radio transmissions—brief
bursts, heavily encrypted, and usually untraceable—was generally considered less threatening than most alternatives. But
Dmitri, according to Fedorenko, was nonetheless adamant.
Even crankish. No radio. And not only did Dmitri refuse to
broadcast; Dmitri would not even own an innocent short-wave
receiver.

"What did that mean, if it was true?" Kessler asks.

"Two things. It suggested that Dmitri lived in very great fear
of having his home searched. And also, perhaps, that he had no
confidence in the Soviet ciphers." This is the first time, Kessler
notices, that Sparrow has referred to Dmitri with the masculine
pronoun. "Of course he was right. We were having good success
those days on Soviet ciphers, thanks to a few big early IBMs.
We were getting a lot of their radio. As he well knew. He—"
Sparrow starts again and stops. He holds Kessler's eye. "It *was*,
by the way, true."

He also refused live meetings, Dmitri. Another precaution
against being compromised. No face-to-face encounters with a
Soviet case officer. No brush-contacts for passing rolls of film.
No cutouts, no go-betweens, no third parties of any sort were
permitted to see his face or be seen in his presence. Dmitri in
fact *had* no case officer on American soil. Not a single KGB
man in Washington, neither with diplomatic cover nor among
the "illegals," was allowed to know he existed.

"What's left?" says Kessler. "How could an agent even communicate, with so many phobias?"

"Dead drops, we call them," says Sparrow. "Prearranged
hiding places that serve as mail slots. It might be a crevice in
the concrete of a bridge abutment. The ledge behind a girder in
a subway station. Any little place that is highly inconspicuous,
preferably in the most banal way. Dmitri used dead drops ex-
clusively. A well-trusted courier then carried each report back
to Moscow. Directly to Special Two. He was handled from
there."

"Do you *know* that part? Or is it deduction?"

"I know it by deduction."

"Did you ever find one of these dead drops? I mean one of
Dmitri's in particular."

"No. Those were invisible too."

Of course there was a drawback to this extraordinarily cautious arrangement, Sparrow explains: speed. That is, the lack of it. Dead-drop exchanges take time, usually a day or two elapsing from the alert signal that a message is coming, through the actual placement, to the pickup. Separating the two parties in time is precisely what makes that type of transaction safer. And a courier, needless to say, travels to Moscow far slower than a cable or a radio message. In fact Dimitri's chosen method was drastically slow, and quite clumsy. One might even call it old-fashioned. An antique of espionage tradecraft. The year 1963 was itself not *that* long ago, Sparrow says; we had a few missiles by then, after all; so did they; the whole world could have ended in the time Dimitri took to drive out to his latest drop and jam a note into a crack. Operating this way, he could be of no conceivable value to the Soviets in any matter requiring a fast alert and an immediate response.

"But we know that, on the contrary, he was of very great value," Sparrow says. "And we know it not just from Bogdan Kirilovich Fedorenko, by the way. We know it also from the case of your friend."

"My friend? You mean Pokorny?"

"Viktor Tronko." Sparrow has stretched his face down derisively but Kessler lets this sally go by.

Nevertheless, Special Two tolerated the inordinate delay. They let Dimitri choose his own operational methods. They indulged what you are pleased to call his phobias, Sparrow says. Think about it. Here was an agent, an American, telling them that their most guarded channels of internal communication, their own best security measures, were inadequate or worse. Dimitri scorned the Soviets even while helping them, in effect; and he put them to a fat lot of extra trouble. He got his way with the KGB—an exceptional fact in itself, Sparrow says. And this went on for years, while they coddled him and soothed him and continued to use him. There can be only one conclusion. Dimitri was utterly unique and precious to them as a source. His product didn't go stale. What he gave them, whatever he gave them, it more than justified the wait and the scorn and the trouble, Sparrow says, though Kessler is not sure about the soundness of this whole syllogism.

"It's all negative. Negative evidence," says Kessler. "Proof by what *wasn't* there. By what *didn't* happen. Seems to me there is an alternate explanation that fits equally well."

"Which is what, Mr. Kessler?"

"Dmitri was invisible because he didn't exist. Never had."

Sparrow lifts his shoulders and drops them again ostentatiously, sighing with the weary but unrelenting patience of a trainer of sea lions for the circus. "No," he says simply. And now once again, you stupid beast, the song on the bulb horns—and *then* the beach ball. "No, we had other evidence. Just the sort you want."

"Fine, I'd love to hear it."

Kessler waits. Sparrow meets his stare for a few seconds, the same game of silence and frozen glances until, uncharacteristically, the older man drops his eyes. He inspects the blacktop. Suddenly he looks even more tired than Kessler feels. Forlorn and regretful, the fragile old pariah. This man, Kessler believes, is a wonderful actor.

"I told you, at the beginning . . . I said I would speak of two arrivals. You recall?"

"At last. Yes. All right. And the second of those two was Viktor Tronko."

"No, no. Not Tronko. Bogdan Kirilovich was the second. The other was earlier. This one had come to Washington—inconspicuously, for a very short visit—back in March of 1958."

"Who was it?"

"L. V. Nechaev," Sparrow says.

The sun is down into the trees and low buildings beyond Old Dominion Drive and Kessler was too stupid, today, to eat lunch.

IO

The Tabard Inn is full of parlors and the parlors are full of
sofas. There must be three dozen of these, the sofas, all of them
fine fat Victorian monstrosities of claw-foot carven oak and
overstuffed horsehair in faded maroons and olives, shared out
among the various little parlors through which Kessler must
pass on the long labyrinthine climb to his room, five or six sofas
to each parlor, lining the walls, impeding traffic, as though the
hotel's owner had once been offered some desperate low price
on an entire warehouseful and in the dizziness of the moment
was too foolish to resist. Sofas everywhere. Also horsehair love
seats and wing chairs and a great number of tiny precarious
one-legged wooden tables, the sort favored for those maddening
pen-and-ink decorations in *The New Yorker*. Kessler sidles carefully to avoid upsetting the table upon which sit the half-empty
sherry glasses of two Japanese businessmen and a buxom American woman in tweed; these three suspend their conversation
while he passes by. On the next floor are only the two aged
matrons he saw in exactly the same spot yesterday. One of these
ladies nods over her wineglass to Kessler, graciously, a little
daringly, and the other smirks at her friend. Kessler nods back,
wondering who will steady them down the stairs. On his own
landing is another sofa, this one even uglier but probably also
lighter than the rest, otherwise surely it wouldn't have been
carried up three and a half flights to sit empty outside Kessler's
door, flanked by a matched pair of jade-green porcelain ele-
phants the size of young hogs. Kessler immediately takes off his
shoes and his pants, stretching out on the bed to reread his
latest message.

Nora called, it says. *Termite man in New Haven on Wednesday*. The woman downstairs, at the plug switchboard, no doubt
took it for a matter of pest extermination. *She thought you'd*

want to know. Below which, evidently an afterthought on the part of the caller, is written *Nora Walsh* and then the New Haven number, which Kessler has long since committed to memory.

While his feet evaporate dry he ponders all that, each runic bit in its turn. He pictures Nora, full of misgiving, dialing the Tabard and having her say with the switchboard woman. He smiles broadly. He is on his back, comfortable now and exhausted, high in the air above N Street. He is quietly, cautiously excited. For all its obvious hedging, for all its bareness, this message as he reads it represents an important development.

Nora called, he reads again.

And then, goddamn her, she must fall back to: *Nora Walsh.*

Lack of confidence, maybe, or merely another measure of that same fierce upright formality. Kessler has found, rare thing, a woman of modern intelligence and implacable candor who nevertheless would have been quite at home in Victorian England, though she was raised in the mountain pastures of Idaho. Who would look smashing, for that matter, in a high lace collar and a bun. He'd love to see it. A woman who operates at her own pace and rhythm, with her own adamantine sense of proprieties and principles; who refuses to rush or to be rushed, to allow or to take any unseemly familiarity; who refuses even to presume that Kessler could correctly supply her last name. She wouldn't give him credit for having less than a list of Noras in his life. Advance one step and then retreat two —he recognizes again her characteristic pattern. Still, at least she did call. That took initiative and a little nerve. She even traced him here to the Tabard, Kessler knows not how but probably, he supposes, through Fullerton's office. Kessler is impressed. He is grateful. It is the strongest positive signal he has gotten in weeks.

Never mind that she found a plausibly impersonal excuse for the call: *Termite man in town.*

Never mind that. There is face to be kept, dignity to be safeguarded, and by all means—yes—let her exercise a little wile for a change. He likes the notion. As for the precise meaning of this *termite man* business before it got translated through the switchboard, Kessler is puzzled. He has no idea. Not likely that Eugène Marais will be in New Haven on Wednesday, since the man blew his brains out in 1936.

"Michael C. Kessler phoning for Nora Walsh," he says. "Will Miss Walsh speak with Mr. Kessler?"

"Hello? What?" she says. "Is this collect? Yes, I will."

"No, it's me," says Kessler. "I was just being dumb."

"Oh." She isn't humorless or slow, much the contrary; but she is determinedly bad, as if on principle, at patter. "Good. Then it found you. The desk clerk wasn't sure when you might or might not be back."

"Minutes ago." I spent the afternoon hearing tales from an old man in a very cold park, he would like to tell her, but the professional side knows better. "I came down yesterday on business."

"Yes, I heard. Fullerton's office, they told me you'd gotten emergency leave."

"It's nice of them to put it that way. I didn't ask. I just informed them, and left."

"But nothing's wrong? They said emergency, so I wondered if . . ."

Both Kessler and she let that dangle. In the silence he can hear her growing embarrassed, already, at what she takes to be an intrusion; while he thinks again of that garish, angry sight on the floor of Biaggio's grocery. Is anything wrong? For him right now it is a tricky question. Violent death of an old friend, which friendship was long since lapsed, and which death happens also to have kicked open an interesting door—is anything wrong? Kessler doesn't want to lie to her, and he won't. Not explicitly. But he has no doubt that even bending the truth gently will constitute, for Nora Walsh, a matter of consequence.

"No, well," she says, backing away. "No, that's really none of my—"

"It's a story," says Kessler. "Just a story. I'm down here doing research. Something came up suddenly and if I wanted to follow it I had to jump." *A man came to see me and then was murdered. I left without telling you, yes, but not without thinking about you. None of this damn stuff can be talked about over the phone. The truth is all in an escrow account under your name.*

"I'm glad," she says. "They did say you charged out of town, and I was concerned. Never mind. And I won't ask what the story is."

"Spies," he says. "Cloak and dagger."

"Oh," she says merely.

Her former husband was a Washington lawyer, a young hot-dog with a Q clearance and a fierce tennis game, who worked on the staff of the NSC. Evidently the fellow had a talent for discretion and clandestine operations that was applicable, also, to his erotic life. Nora loved him and her mind worked very differently, so she was about two years slow to learn that he was having affairs. Of course the betrayal hurt, the deceit hurt, but the humiliation of that prolonged ignorance hurt especially. When she did finally learn, she not only wanted out of the marriage. She wanted out of that world. Well before the divorce was final she had moved Emily and herself to Boston, just for the distance, just for the new air, and then back down to New Haven when she was readmitted for her music degree at Yale. She told Kessler these things at the Hotel Alfaro, during the same marathon conversation in which he spoke about being finished with Washington himself, cured of his own fascination over the American intelligence community and its fetid secrets. Now here he is again. Recidivist. He knows that the very mention of an espionage story will be reviving in Nora all the worst associations, all the panic and pain and nausea from her last bad adventure, all the flight instinct that Kessler has been trying to overcome. She has already gone silent.

So he changes the subject quickly to Eugène Marais.

That much of the message got through, he tells her. Something about Marais in New Haven on Wednesday.

"Yes. Yes, I saw the poster today," Nora says, coming back alive with enthusiasm, as though it were her own dear demented project, instead of Kessler's. Not Marais himself of course, she says, for she knows the outline of biographical facts from Kessler. No, it's a film. A dramatic film based on the life of Eugène Marais, Afrikaner poet and naturalist they called him, Nora says, and it's showing Wednesday at the Art and Architecture building. Poet and naturalist, in that order. The poster caught her eye, she stopped, she thought at once of Kessler, naturally, and so she copied the information onto a file folder.

Nora sounds proud and thrilled to have performed this service. Here it is, she says. Wednesday at eight, Art and Architecture, yes. The film and the man who made it. *Fugal* or something, she says, I can't read my own scribble. The director, evidently. Whoever it is, he'll be there to discuss the production, afterward, and answer questions.

"*Fugard,*" Kessler says. "Athol Fugard? Isn't that it?"

"That's it. Athol Fugard, yes. Who is he?"

"A playwright and an actor. An Afrikaner, like Marais. He wrote the film, I think, and played the Marais role himself. I suppose it was made right there in South Africa. Four or five years ago. It's mainly concerned with the morphine addiction, from what I recall. Fugard's personal vision of Eugène Marais. Not so much on the scientific ideas. Fugard himself has a special passion about alcoholism, I guess, and that's the part that engaged him. The travails of addiction."

"Oh. Then you've seen it." Her voice is flat with disappointment.

"No, I haven't. Only read a review."

"Do you have any interest?"

"I have enormous interest. I've wanted to see the thing for three years. And I *need* to see it. This is only the second U.S. screening I've heard about. Also it would be nice to talk to Fugard. Find out how much he really knows."

"Will you be back by Wednesday?"

"That's hard to say." But hard in only this sense: he certainly *shouldn't* be in New Haven on Wednesday—not with Claude Sparrow talking as Claude Sparrow has never before talked, and other leads demanding quick pursuit—yet he certainly wants to be. "I won't have finished down here. Not even close."

"Then I'll go to the film and take notes," she says. "I want to see it myself. You can give me some questions for Athol Fugard, if you like."

"No. No, that's no good. Let's not do that," Kessler says. His brain is beginning to try to gauge precise distances between the few important coordinates of his present existence—a park in McLean, an auditorium in New Haven, a big building in Langley, the little house on the end of this phone line, a concrete cell God knows where, oh and yes there's the serviceable drab apartment off Chapel Street, where a two-inch pile of pages anchors down a desk blotter—but of course that's a hopeless cause. As he well knows. Measurements of that sort never come out the same way twice.

"Can you get a baby-sitter for Wednesday?"

"Definitely," Nora says.

II

Kessler's memory for spoken facts is capacious and precise for up to twelve hours so long as inordinate alcohol or further research don't intervene, so he allows himself only one martini and a glass of red wine over his late dinner at the lonely-man's table in a basement steak house not far from the Tabard, and then with a second glass of the bad house burgundy mainly ignored at his elbow he begins scratching at the notebook that remained virtually empty all day, gathering fever as he goes. One thing brings back another and he writes fast to catch it all. The check arrives. The waiter passes by impatiently two or three times, but Kessler doesn't look up. He can't afford to. Get it down on paper now. Lights are turned off in the adjoining room. Here's a plastic card leave me alone. Otto Schratt. Ilse what was her name Sjodahl, yes, Norway. Special Service Two. Third floor, three glass doors and a railing. Bogdan Kirilovich was a Ukrainian. Kessler proceeds in no order but free-associative, with no organizing principle but inclusiveness. Get it down now or lose it forever. The blockhouse at Orly, the corporal. Stolichnaya with Robert Kennedy. Chicken Little. Chicken Little. Claude Sparrow despises Scott Wickes. History is the control of appearances, quotes. Counterintelligence is something else, what, damn, Kessler feels so very tired. He takes a gulp of wine. Counterintelligence is the effort to see through appearances, quotes, good work. Another sip of wine as his little reward. Also, a matter of finding congruencies, quotes. The émigré woman spoke no Spanish, says Sparrow, we tested her. I'll bet you did. Kessler's cerebral cortex, glory, it's coming back from the dead. Dmitri hates radio. Dmitri might or might not exist, but if so he hates radio.

"Sir?"

"Here. Close out your till, I understand. But I'm staying."

"If you would move into the bar?"

"Sure."

Dead-drops, slow but safe. No live meetings, no radio, no evidence. L. V. Nechaev arrived at Idlewild Airport, on a three-month diplomatic visa which was renewable but never renewed, in March of 1958. He was accredited to the UN delegation. Kessler picks up his notebook and his coat and stumbles into the bar. Two minutes afterward the waiter, a saintly middle-aged man, carries in that half-finished glass of wine.

Accredited to the UN, yet the FBI people on permanent vigil up there in New York claimed they never so much as saw his face. Claimed they had never even opened a file on any L. V. Nechaev, Soviet diplomat and possible KGB man, candidate for serious surveillance, under that name or any other. Claimed they showed no record of any new Russians who fitted the arrival time, March of 1958, and who disappeared again within a couple months. Not months, no, it might have been just weeks, Claude Sparrow had explained to J. Edgar Hoover. Possibly only days. Negative, we did not get a look at him, Hoover had said. Are you sure he disembarked in New York? Who was this man? Give me some more information and I might be able to help. Sparrow had thanked the FBI Director delicately and gotten out of his office fast, coming back empty-handed to Langley. Of course Hoover's denial proved nothing either way, Sparrow told Kessler as daylight leaked away into a bleak, bone-chilling dusk.

The temperature was beginning to dive further, they were now again utterly alone in the little park, headlights were flashing by along Old Dominion, yet Sparrow continued talking.

"Because, you see, Hoover hated us," he told Kessler. "Hoover loathed the Agency with a jealous, venal passion that surpassed even his ignorance of our aims and our methods. He wouldn't have warned us of a falling piano—not if there was a chance he could extract gain somehow, from standing aside and watching the accident happen. It proved nothing, his denial of knowledge about Nechaev. If the man *had* shown up in routine FBI surveillance, Hoover was simply withholding that information. Hoarding it, on principle. Thinking this might be something he could eventually put to his own use." Then again there was an equal likelihood, Sparrow said, that Nechaev had *not* let his face be seen on the streets of New York.

In fact it probably made better sense that way, Sparrow said. Having flown into New York in masquerade as a minor diplomatic functionary, maybe even just a translator, L. V. Nechaev could have gone underground at once, disappearing from sight, slipping on down to Washington by train to avoid leaving so much as a false name in the airline records. In Washington, of course, he would have performed his mission solitarily, independent of the KGB *rezidentura,* going nowhere near his own country's embassy, not even letting them know he was here. Independent also of the "illegal" apparatus in town. He was strictly on his own. So far as humanly possible, he had kept the sphere of his activities and the nature of his mission totally secret. From everyone, Sparrow said. From us, and from his own people too.

"His mission," Kessler said.

"Yes."

"He had come over to activate Dmitri. Who had been recruited sometime before, presumably. And was waiting."

"Yes."

"Why would Nechaev do it personally?"

"To establish those fanatically cautious procedures. To circumvent what you call the phobias."

"An invisible case officer for the invisible agent," Kessler said then, and he was about to repeat his cavil about negative evidence when Sparrow replied:

"Not entirely. In this case there was something tangible. Comrade Nechaev did leave one mark."

It was a visa application. A two-page form, little noted at the time and long since forgotten, slumbering innocently in the records section of our embassy in Moscow, Sparrow said. It had been filed in February of 1958, this application, by Nechaev himself or a trusted assistant acting on his behalf. Five years later when we came looking, it was still there, locked in a file cabinet under no very great security, among similar papers of no very great significance. In those days before computerized records the embassy held a backlog, in routine paperwork such as visa applications, covering the previous ten years. After a decade each year's worth was culled, for whatever morsels might seem potentially worth keeping, and those went back to

Washington by diplomatic pouch; the rest were shredded and then carefully burned. The year 1958, by our good fortune, said Sparrow, was still too young for the shredder. But we couldn't just call up the embassy and ask them to take a peek. Go rooting through your visa records, would you, with an eye open for one L. V. Nechaev. Hardly. Not even by highest-security coded cable we couldn't ask that, no.

"Why not?"

"Oh, too many eyes and ears. Good lord. We might just as well have cabled Mr. Nechaev directly: WE'RE COMING, READY OR NOT."

"But Dmitri himself must have known."

"This part of the investigation was *very* closely held, Mr. Kessler. *Very* closely. We knew Dmitri was well placed, yes, we had that from Bogdan Kirilovich. But we didn't yet know just *how* well."

A courier was sent to Moscow. This courier was a senior officer at Langley who had the full confidence (a rather exceptional distinction itself) of both Claude Sparrow and Jedediah McAttee, not to mention of course the Director, Herbert Eames. Sparrow did not offer Kessler the courier's name. Kessler asked for the name and was politely rebuffed, no reason given. The courier went off at a scramble. His cover story was something about important talks with the CIA chief of station, Moscow, concerning new intelligence requirements and the problem of nuclear-test-ban verification; and that cover story was wrapped inside another, a more public offering, which made the man an agricultural economist on contract to the State Department. The courier returned in four days. He hadn't had much sleep. The chief of station, under instructions which did not include even a modicum of explanation, had seen to it that the man got a secure room and all the files he requested, and otherwise had left him alone, though adhering to the pretense that the two of them were holding very private talks. The courier had done his work after hours on the first full day following his arrival in Moscow. He demanded and got a huge, confusing assortment of archival material, including some personnel files on former U. S. Embassy staff, some correspondence received from naturalized American citizens seeking information about missing Russian relatives, and a selection of backdate visa applications. The visa applications were stored in

packets by month and year. The courier ordered up those packets for January and February 1958; for September and October
1958; for March and April 1953, coinciding with the death of
Stalin; for December 1953, coinciding with the execution of
Lavrenti Beria; for February 1955, coinciding with the resignation of Malenkov; for February and March 1956, coinciding
with Khrushchev's anti-Stalin speech to the Twentieth Party
Congress; and for September 1960, coinciding with Khrushchev's own trip to the UN session in New York. All of these,
except January and February of 1958, were simply red herrings.
The courier ignored those other packets. In the packet for February of 1958 he found a visa application from one L. G. Orlov,
chemical engineer and adviser on industrial aid to developing
nations, Ministry of Foreign Affairs. Application granted: three
months, renewable. The attached photograph and the physical
information seemed to fit with the skimpy description Bogdan
Kirilovich had supplied. The courier's intuition was good: later
investigation established that there was no L. G. Orlov, engineer, assigned to the Foreign Ministry in 1958, and probably
never had been. This despite the fact that Orlov is a common
name, Sparrow said—almost like signing yourself as Smith. The
courier made one photocopy of L. G. Orlov's form, replaced the
original, and flew home.

Bogdan Kirilovich confirmed that the face in the bad copy of
the bad passport photo was indeed that of L. G. Nechaev. Furthermore, Sparrow said, the ugly styling of the eyeglasses
matched—though that bit of detail had been intentionally withheld from the courier.

"We were quite excruciatingly careful, you see," Sparrow
said. The planning had been elaborate but fast, and confined to
a very small circle of senior staff. Besides Herbert Eames himself, and the top people within Sparrow's shop, and the top
people within McAttee's, no one at all knew about this interest
in the Nechaev visit five years before. No one else knew that
Bogdan Kirilovich had directed their attention to that visit. No
one else knew what the courier had brought back from Moscow. "But of course," Sparrow added sourly, "with Dmitri
there, our carefulness was all so much piss in the wind. As you
rightly point out."

Kessler waited to see what might follow that. Nothing followed. So he broke the silence with: "Would you like to continue this in a warm and well-lighted restaurant?"

"Certainly not," Sparrow said.

Ugly silver eyeglasses, Kessler writes in the notebook. Like a yoke with oxbows, he writes. Alias L. G. Orlov, he writes. Fedorenko "confirmed" the identification, Kessler's quotes. In effect, Fedorenko countersigning his own I.O.U. Still, the glasses. Trusted courier, name withheld. A short list of people Kessler hopes to find and, with large luck, to question: Fedorenko, Scott Wickes, um, Roger Nye. Very short. Eames is dead. McAttee is beyond the big gate. Kessler is dopey from fatigue. Remember to check with someone about that Smith business. Remember to dress warmly tomorrow. And then Sparrow will probably haul us off to his favorite secret steambath. Kessler discovers that his wineglass has somehow gotten empty. Pushing the notebook away, he orders a whiskey.

Eventually he shuffles back to the Tabard. Behind the desk it is still the same woman, in the same baggy black mohair sweater with pushed-up sleeves, working the late shift again. She seems to work all the shifts, so far as Kessler can tell. Maybe she sleeps right there at the switchboard. Maybe *she* is the owner. A collector of rare old sofas who needed someplace to show them. With her long neck protruding from the sweater, her pale skin and dark hair and wide bloodshot eyes, she reminds Kessler inescapably of a grebe, though it's not nice, he knows, and as desk clerks go she is quite good about messages. A Western grebe. Her nose is shorter, of course. Probably she is a fine intelligent person with many sterling qualities, beloved to those who know her.

"Did he find you?" she says when she sees Kessler.

"Who?"

Stretching her grebelike neck out through the little window, she inspects the lobby's sole sofa, which is mustard-yellow and empty. Before it is a low table covered deep in newspapers, and a standing brass ashtray.

"A man. He waited. Maybe an hour. Then left, evidently."

"What sort of man?"

"He reminded me of a lizard," the woman says. Her eyes dance guiltily. "Wrinkled face. Skinny."

"Did he give his name?"

"No name. If he's a friend of yours, don't tell him I said that, okay?"

"I don't think he is."

"And an accent. He had an accent."

"Southern," Kessler says.

"No. European," she says. "Somewhere east of Zurich, if I'm any judge."

Kessler's pulse is high, not just from the climb, as he swings open the door of his room and snaps on the light. But there is only his bag, and the pile of books and papers.

12

"Who coined the name Chicken Little?"

A question that flopped once, Kessler has learned, can some-times succeed in a fresh context. He springs this one back out abruptly, before any preliminaries, even as he sits down, but Sparrow is not taken off guard, or else genuinely doesn't know the answer or care. With a vague hyperopic expression and a shake of the head, Sparrow passes directly to a subject of his own choice, seemingly remote: seemingly Viktor Tronko. But fine, all right, now at least we're focusing, Kessler thinks. Today they have bright sunlight of the most frigid and hypocritical sort. Sparrow squints toward Langley.

"We knew he was coming before he came. That's the single crucial fact. Everything was known in advance." There is no tone of exaltation; this seems to be, rather, a deeply galling memory.

"Tronko."

"Yes."

"You knew he was going to defect?"

"Yes. Him or someone like him. We were warned."

It was Sparrow's own dear Bogdan Kirilovich, naturally, who warned them. Kessler is surprised, though he shouldn't be, at the insistent centripetalism that drags Claude Sparrow's at-tention back to Fedorenko. Pokorny did not even mention this character. But clearly Bogdan Kirilovich Fedorenko is the hub star, in Sparrow's mind, to the whole whirling galaxy of facts and suppositions and appearances. Tronko is just a quasar blast-ing away out on the cold fringe. Or a pulsar. Kessler as usual can't remember the difference. After me, Fedorenko warned them, will come false and misleading signals.

"The Russians have a term for it. A quite particularized con-

cept, to them. Language tells us a lot about thought, you know.
They call it *dezo.*"

"I don't speak Russian," says Kessler.

"Short for *dezinformatsiya.*"

"Disinformation. Okay, I follow. A fairly particularized concept in this city too, by the way."

"No," Sparrow says, more meticulous than argumentative.
"No, it's not mere obfuscation I'm talking about, Mr. Kessler."

"Or mere lies?"

"Or mere lies either. No. Precisely not."

"Then tell me what."

"A story," Sparrow says. "If I may. I'll tell you a little
story."

One night in the spring of 1958, Sparrow says, a handful of
youngsters kicked over gravestones at a Jewish cemetery in
Düsseldorf, West Germany. Scrawled a few swastikas with
chalk. The boys weren't caught in the act and there was no
proof, but local people knew who they were. Juvenile delinquents merely. Incorrigible and mindless. Still, from Hamburg
to Munich the Jewish community, what was left of it, shuddered. And the incident got into newspapers, both there in Germany and abroad. The British press were especially fierce on
the subject of Nazism's smoldering embers. The American press
slightly less so.

Toward the end of that year came another outbreak of what
seemed the same type of nastiness, only now more widespread
and more sustained, so of course far more disturbing. On
Christmas Eve the doorposts of a synagogue in Cologne were
painted with swastikas and, in crude angry lettering: GERMANS
DEMAND THAT JEWS GET OUT. Germans demand, Sparrow repeats pointedly. A Jewish cenotaph nearby was also toppled, no
small feat of boyish muscle. During just the next several nights
Jewish tombstones were broken and Jewish stores were defaced
in a dozen more West German cities. Jews began receiving
death threats by telephone, a strange hateful voice and then
click, gone. Over the New Year's weekend this epidemic spread
suddenly to Vienna, Paris, Antwerp, Stockholm, even London
and New York. More swastikas. More graveyard desecrations
and obscene slogans. Many further anonymous threats. So far
no one had been killed. Nor had any of the perpetrators been
arrested.

West Germany continued to be the main locus. Into the first
and second week of 1959, every big city and quite a few smaller
towns, even villages, were getting their turns for anti-Semitic
incidents, enacted in all cases under cover of night. Essen and
Münster in the north, Mainz, Würzburg, a little Bavarian town
called Pfronten, in the mountains, where a lawyer's office
caught fire when a tossed rock broke not only a window but an
antique oil lamp; the office, and two adjacent businesses, were
gutted. It all seemed too familiar. Augsburg, then something
else back in Bonn. These occurrences were all clustered closely
in time, you understand, says Sparrow; all just before or just
after the turn of the year. There seemed to be some sort of
interrelation, a consecutive psychic triggering, one event to the
next, one community to the next. Perhaps epidemic is the
wrong metaphor, says Sparrow. It seemed perhaps more like a
chain reaction among unstable nuclei, he says. Leaping carom-
ing neutrons. Fracturing atoms. Good God, when might it go
critical? Naturally that's what people asked themselves. Not
just Jews. Not just Germans, Jewish and otherwise. This was
getting attention, by now, in all the Western newspapers. And
in the East bloc press too, of course. They were howling pi-
ously, over there. You're familiar, I assume, says Sparrow, with
what I mean when I talk about going critical.

"Sure," says Kessler.

It went hard on the Federal Republic's world image, needless
to say. The Western press were screaming, TASS was screaming, British MPs were screaming particularly, even the Japanese
and the Australians for God's sake—everyone was screaming
about the filthy recidivist murdering Huns. As well they might
have been, says Sparrow. They had every reason. It was all
quite convincingly ominous. One headline in the old *Herald
Trib* said, "Bonn Can't Eliminate Nazi Poison," something like
that. Trade agreements were canceled. West German diplomats
were given the sneer. West German businessmen also. And just
inevitably, of course, there began to be loud talk about whether
such a country could be a fit partner to the NATO alliance.

"It was all disinformation," Kessler hazards obligingly.

"No. The early Düsseldorf business, that was exactly what it
seemed to be. Isolated juvenile vandalism," says Sparrow. "The
rest of it, yes. All a *dezo* operation. A classic of the genre.
Entirely concocted in Moscow, by a man named Avvakian. Ex-

ecuted, the West German part, by good German Communists, agents that Avvakian had played back across from the East. And in the other countries, by his own home-grown Soviet KGB thugs. Brushes and paint paid for by the Central Committee."

"Am I supposed to be shocked? Don't you people routinely do the same kind of thing?"

"No. We do not. That's a sentimental fallacy of great comfort to liberals and other moral relativists, but no. Utterly untrue."

"Come on, Mr. Sparrow. Maybe you don't call it *dezo.* Maybe your term is 'black propaganda.' Doesn't that ring a bell? Or maybe it's just 'operations.' "

Sparrow is momentarily mute.

"Guatemala," says Kessler. "Sukarno's Indonesia. Vietnam under Diem. Cuba during the Kennedys. Nasser's Egypt. Sihanouk's Cambodia."

"We've had our excesses and our mistakes, yes. Not that I grant you anything in those particular cases. Our excesses, in fact, have mainly been ones of caution. Our mistakes, of naïveté."

"That's arguable."

"It *is* arguable, certainly, and I would be delighted to argue it with you. But is this the story you're writing, Mr. Kessler? Evil scheming CIA at large in the world?" Sparrow twists his body suddenly to glower across the park and back toward Old Dominion Drive, as though hoping somebody might appear on the scene to interrupt them. No one around. He settles himself again with a sigh of boredom. "Oh, it's so very tired. It has been done and done. You did it yourself, a decade ago in your callow youth, aren't I correct? This week I rather thought you were more interested in the case of Viktor Tronko."

"I'm not writing *any* story right now. Not until I get a pretty full sense of the who and the why," says Kessler. "What I'm doing right now is called researching."

"Admirable. Very well. And here's what I say to you: the who is General Akop Avvakian. The why?—that's a very much more intricate question. But we're getting there."

"Avvakian. He's new."

"General Avvakian is decidedly not new. He has been with us unnoticed from the start. The man himself died in the late sixties, mind you, but his works and pomps, they abide."

"All right. Tell me about him."

"General Avvakian was an Armenian. A faithful Party member and an extremely capable officer. Not much else is known. Except that he became the Henry Ford of *dezinformatsiya*. He didn't invent it. But he brought it forth upon the modern world."

"History is bunk." Kessler is smiling and, unexpectedly, for the first time in their brief acquaintance, Claude Sparrow joins him.

Back they go into the organizational chart of the KGB and the floor plan of the double building on Dzerzhinsky Square, where Sparrow seems to feel as comfortable as if he himself had spent years of his own working life there, which in one sense at least is certainly so. To him the Lubyanka is a very real place, all familiar and vivid and fully furnished in his mind. He gestures before Kessler with his long fluttery hands. He knows the style of the doorknobs. Disinformation campaigns were the province of a small but potent section referred to as Department D, under this fellow Avvakian, says Sparrow. Like Comrade Nechaev's Special Service Two, it was part of the First Chief Directorate, that half of the KGB responsible for all snooping and meddling abroad. Also like Special Two, it had its office space on the third floor. Of course long before Avvakian there had always been efforts at elaborate disinformation; Lenin himself talked about using the tactic, says Sparrow; one could possibly even argue that it has some particular ineffable appeal to the Russian soul, though I won't, says Sparrow. I despise that kind of loose thinking. Anyway Avvakian, as I say, was not Russian but Armenian. And it was by his influence that *dezo* began to be practiced systematically, strategically, and so very goddamn effectively. Only under Avvakian, finally, did the *dezo* function get status as a full department.

That upgrading happened in '58 or '59, we think—just about coincident with the swastika operation. We *think*, Sparrow repeats. But we weren't ever quite sure. Our information in the area was lamentably meager. Patchwork. Calculated guesses, extrapolations. Avvakian ran his shop quietly. And we were never so blessed as to have one of his people come strolling in our door. We never got hold of anyone from Department D. Not a single defector. Not a single significant arrest. Sparrow pauses a moment, lips pinched, shifting his rear on the bench.

At least that's the orthodox view, he adds. That's the view that prevailed when I left the Agency. Never laid our fingers on a man from Department D, says Sparrow, his voice now full of dark irony. That's the view of record.

"What do you mean? It's not your own view?"

"Later," says Sparrow. "We're getting there."

Bogdan Kirilovich didn't so much as mention General Avvakian. Not by name. In fact he never mentioned Department D, says Sparrow—responding presciently to Kessler's next few questions before they can be asked. It is as if Sparrow anticipates a certain line of attack, perhaps having faced it before from the McAttee faction. No, Fedorenko's hard knowledge in regard to Avvakian seemed to be even more meager than their own. But that wasn't especially curious. Simply a measure of successful compartmentalization at the Lubyanka, says Sparrow, and of the general's deftness of hand. No, these few facts they possessed about Avvakian did not come from Bogdan Kirilovich. These were scavenged and stitched together from the debriefings of several later, less significant defectors. In Fedorenko's time, Sparrow and his colleagues had only the barest notions about KGB disinformation. Akop Avvakian was not a name they had ever heard. Department D was just a blank space and a question mark on their charts. What little they ever got, they got later. Not from Bogdan Kirilovich. He simply hadn't had access. He'd had no opportunity to gather gossip about Avvakian. None. Evidently Sparrow feels some compulsion to stress this point redundantly.

Kessler as discreetly as possible scratches a note: *Fedorenko see-no hear-no Avvakian.*

"But he warned you, you say."

"Yes."

"How?"

"In general terms. General yet most insistent. He knew the standard methods—bloody hell yes he did, even if he didn't know one particular man. This was an urgent concern for Bogdan Kirilovich. I had been hearing this from him forever, since those earliest days at the house with the garden. 'They will send false defectors to discredit me,' he said. He was haunted by that thought. 'Others will come. Everything I have told you, they will deny it.' He knew he had to persuade us, make us hear and believe, before that happened."

"Then Viktor Tronko arrived," says Kessler.

"Then Tronko arrived."

"And it was just as Fedorenko had predicted."

Claude Sparrow says nothing. He is breathing heavily through his nose.

"Who *was* Viktor Tronko?" says Kessler.

Sparrow gapes at him with the imploring eyes of an inpatient at a clinic for the bewildered.

Kessler himself begins now to understand one or two small things, thank God. Or at least so he fancies. He is starting to have enough pieces in his grasp to play at the puzzle himself. Try this up here, hmm, no, but juxtapose with this bit over here, leave a little space, ellipsis, add this bit down here, and oh yes very interesting.

Tronko's first contact with the CIA, Kessler recalls from Pokorny's account, was sometime a year or more prior to the actual defection. Rome, that's right. Summer of 1962. That was also before Fedorenko. At which time Tronko had offered himself as an agent in place, Kessler recalls, for motives still unclear but claiming firmly that he had no interest in coming West. Career and family back in Moscow. Kessler wishes now that he'd taken a good set of notes on Mel's every word but amid all that beer and flying bullshit it wasn't hardly likely, and then in the immediate aftermath he lost presence of mind, damn. Year and a half later Tronko popped up again. This time it was in Vienna, and now his tune was drastically different: Take me I'm yours let's go. Meanwhile there had been the defection of Fedorenko. Meanwhile also, of course, the events in Dallas. Tronko dropped the name "Lee Harvey Oswald," and so Langley scooped the Russian in. How could they not? Debriefed him. Didn't like or didn't believe what they heard, or both. Debriefed him some more. Three years' worth. What had they heard that was so dubious or so disagreeable? Pokorny made a big deal—Kessler remembers it now, aha—a big deal of the point that Viktor Tronko arrived saying there was *not* a high-level penetration. There was not any such creature as Dmitri. Did Mel utter the name "Dmitri"? No, that piece was only from Sparrow. Did Mel mention anything about Comrade Nechaev, or the mysterious 1958 visit? No. Why not? Because we ran out of beer and then he was too dead, is why. All of this crackles across Kessler's brain like shorts on a circuit board while Claude Sparrow is hauling his mouth open to make a statement, a disclaimer, a hypothesis, Kessler can't guess what. And then suddenly they are back at the Lubyanka. Sparrow leads the way, Kessler following as he can.

It is late 1963. To be precise, it is the evening of November 23, Moscow time. Not the third floor now, not Special Two or General Avvakian's domain or anywhere in the vicinity of the Chairman's office; for a change they are in a more remote part of the building, far from the seat of power, at the end of a dreary corridor up on five in the newer half. A small office with one window looking down on an empty courtyard. In this office is Viktor Tronko, standing over a desk, along with an older man.

Darkness and two feet of snow outside, already well into serious winter here, but instead of the usual ear-biting cold, Moscow has gotten a little warming spell, right up around freezing, with the double consequence of slush in the streets and a heavy lingering fog. A miserable, anxious day for everyone in all ways. Most of the city's residents, lacking decent boots again this year, have spent their day cursing the slush; Viktor Tronko has had more reason for cursing the fog. Planes out at Vnukovo Airport were landing after long delays, and with white-knuckled passengers, or else not at all. Since sundown most have simply been waved off. Tronko's own flight circled for forty-five minutes, then was allowed down only after a threatening telephone call from the older man, waiting back here at the Lubyanka, who used his name and rank to convince the traffic controller that the more risky of two risky courses would be to say no. Impeding a mission of highest interest to the Central Committee itself, was one phrase that the traffic controller heard. The older man's name is Rybakov, a major general. The plane in question was an Ilyushin-28, a military transport which had been commandeered that morning for a special service, a fast flight to Minsk and back, and this impressive anomaly also influenced the traffic controller. Viktor Tronko was the sole passenger. On the return trip, he was carrying a cardboard file.

The file rests, now, on the desk before Tronko and his boss. It isn't a thick packet of pages. Each sheet has been sewn into the binding with black thread, individually, according to standard procedure. Rybakov slowly turns those pages. Beside him,

Viktor Tronko gawks helplessly, skimming some passages, reading others with great care, his eyes jumping all up and down
every new page as it appears. The two men can hear each other
breathe. They don't talk. Excruciating nervous curiosity and
mortal dread. They know roughly what they are looking for,
and they hope desperately not to find it.

Rybakov is the chief of a small department within the Second
Chief Directorate, a unit that preys upon foreign visitors to the
USSR, tourists, businessmen, scholars, attempting by various
forms of suasion to recruit them for future KGB work. The file
pertains to an American, Lee Oswald—an undesirable and, until yesterday, obscure young man—during the two and a half
years he was tolerated as an expatriate in Minsk. Immediately
upon hearing the news from Dallas, twenty hours earlier,
Rybakov sent Tronko flying to Minsk. Get the file, don't open
it, bring it back. Good lord, Viktor Semyonovich. We must see
how much, if at all, we have gotten ourselves implicated. Do
you pray?

"That's what we were offered," Sparrow says contemptu-
ously. "A tableau. A little moment of high drama, quite vividly
and convincingly rendered from Viktor Tronko's point of view.
There were others in similar vein. I call this one *Two Russians
Contemplating the File of Oswald.* Complete with snow and fog
and a low wooden desk in a dreary office. Everything but the
smell of damp fur. Isn't it marvelous?"

"Which is the marvelous part?" says Kessler.

"The sheer aesthetic fullness. The sense of form and irony.
That 'Do you pray?' touch, for instance."

"Now you're losing me."

"It's all invented, Mr. Kessler. It never happened. Like so
much that Tronko told us—not everything, mind you, but
much—it was a lie. A methodically prefabricated lie."

"Dezo."

"Dezo, yes. Very good. That's my point. That's what Viktor
Tronko was. Not a defector. Not a deputy in Rybakov's department of the Second CD. Nothing like that. No. He was simply
the most intricate *dezo* operation that General Avvakian ever
launched."

"And the most successful?"

"Yes. Certainly. And the most successful, God damn him."

"Do you have any proof?"

"None at all. Not the kind you mean. No scraps of paper or incriminating photos, no. Only logic. Only the internal consistency of what I can tell you."

"All quite vividly rendered in its own right," says Kessler.

Tronko's entire body of testimony over the space of years was nothing else than a great ragged quilt of contradictions and recantations and solecisms and admitted falsehoods, followed by newer falsehoods and then still newer recantations, to hear Claude Sparrow tell it. As a liar, Tronko was more persistent than deft, Sparrow claims. As a liar, he was shameless and indefatigable. An amazing feat of sheer endurance, in fact, that he had caused anyone at all eventually to believe him. But he certainly had. God knows he had. How to explain it? I don't intend to explain it, Sparrow says. I'm not obliged to explain it, since I was not among the believers. Sheer endurance in his clumsy lies, a brute form of superior mental stamina—or who can say what other factors. A victory of endurance, Sparrow says slyly, is the most generous explanation.

The damage had largely been done before we were ever allowed near him, Sparrow claims. November of 1964. Then finally, belatedly, we were given our inning. Kessler understands this new and more narrow use of the first person plural: meaning not Langley but just Sparrow's own fiefdom, the Counterintelligence section, the forces of keen and skeptical vigilance. Maybe it was irreversible by then, Sparrow says. Maybe Viktor Tronko had made himself inevitable. So many lies had already been told, and ineptly challenged, and refined. Until they were acceptable. So many opportunities had been squandered. A pattern had been set. Mental habits had arisen. Commitments formed. Momentum. But I don't think it *was* irreversible, Sparrow says. I tell you that quite frankly, to my own derogation, he says. I think there did still exist a real opportunity for us to undo what had been done, everything—commitments, momentum, everything. What had been done, and what was threatening. But we somehow missed it ourselves.

"November of 1964," Kessler says. He also writes the date on his pad. "You get your inning. This would be what Mel referred to as the second hostile interrogation?"

"No. Wait. Not yet," Sparrow says. "Another story first."

Viktor Tronko was thirty-four years old when the plane carrying him and McAttee landed in Washington, Sparrow says.

He held the rank of colonel within the KGB and had been serving most recently as deputy chief of the Tourist Department, Second Chief Directorate. His immediate superior was Major General T. F. Rybakov, a conscientious man, unusually forthright and fair-minded for a high KGB officer, with whom Tronko worked on good terms. He liked Rybakov, who was a decent boss and who had also to some extent functioned as Tronko's personal mentor. Brought the younger man into his department, under his wing. Trusted Viktor Semyonovich with large responsibilities. In fact Tronko was grieved to contemplate the colossal problems that his own defection was sure to cause Trofim Filippovich. Things always went hard for those left behind in such cases, both the family and the professional connections, and it was T. F. Rybakov who had signed an order approving Tronko as security man for that trade delegation to Vienna. If Rybakov were lucky, if he had enough powerful friends, his career was merely over. Less lucky and he would go to a camp.

Tronko had been born in Moscow, a privileged son of the new Soviet elite, Sparrow says. His father held a comfortable position in the Central Council of Trade Unions, so called, as editor of the—

"Moscow, you say," Kessler interrupts. "But isn't Tronko another Ukrainian name? Just like Fedorenko?"

"The name, yes. Don't make too much of that. Tronko's father was probably half Ukrainian, or a quarter. But with nothing like Fedorenko's sense of ethnic identity. By the time Viktor Semyonovich was born, the family were pure Muscovites."

"Fedorenko, Nosenko, Tronko, Shevchenko," says Kessler. "What is it that turns these Ukrainians into defectors? Gouzenko. And wasn't there also a Levchenko? Don't the Armenians ever defect, or the Uzbekians, or the Russians themselves? Do the Ukrainian mothers put something special in their kids' porridge? Or is it coincidence?"

"Tronko was a Muscovite," Sparrow repeats dryly. "Born there. Assimilated."

—whose father, Sparrow resumes, had a nice job as editor of the house organ of the Trade Unions Council, a newspaper known as *Trud*. Tronko's mother was an anesthesiologist, and the daughter of a diplomat. Tronko himself was an only child, growing up pampered and preened in the Moscow equivalent of a Westchester County childhood. Private music lessons. Private instruction in conversational German, tennis, and gymnastics. His playmates carefully screened, according to their parents' social standing within the great workers' republic and whether recent political developments had left the father in or out of favor. Thanks to family pull and his own decent scores on the qualifying exams, Viktor Semyonovich was admitted to the Institute of International Relations, Moscow's most prestigious university and a virtually failproof ticket to the good life. For six years he studied languages, history, diplomacy, foreign legal and economic systems, military strategy, and a smattering of philosophy and science. He submitted to having the surface of his intelligence buffed up with what was considered polish. He achieved adequate if not remarkable grades. He succeeded in staying out of exactly and only those forms of postadolescent trouble that were not winked at, sating himself with those that were. In other words he pickled his liver in vodka, he chased girls and caught quite a few, but he never was heard giving voice to a heretical or even mildly original thought. Notwithstanding its atmosphere of academic discipline—which was as intense but intermittent as the field of an electromagnet—the Institute of International Relations made a fine playground for young Viktor Semyonovich, future Soviet official, precocious sot and rake. The Institute, six years of it, was his own long Fort Lauderdale weekend. He lived at his parents' high-toned apartment on Kutuzovsky Prospekt and commuted to school by taxi, spending more in a month on those cab fares than the Institute's few poorer students received as their monthly stipend.

He seems to have been quite the little dandy, says Sparrow. Yet throughout this period he also put in his time, prudently, grudgingly, with the school's Komsomol organization, the youth branch of the Party. In another life he would have been president of the local JayCees, says Sparrow; but a cynical, smarmy JayCees president. Kessler doubts there can be any other kind but does not interrupt. The Komsomol meetings were a tedious and demeaning chore, a charade of Marxist-Leninist zeal, to which Tronko subjected himself only in the spirit of leaving nothing undone. If there had been a safe way to circumvent Komsomol, still taking credit for it later by means of a falsified recommendation or some such, he would have done that. He was lazy but ambitious. A pungent combination.

In the winter of 1953, before finishing his last year at the Institute, Tronko was sent off to Prague for a six-month internship at the Soviet Embassy there. This is standard practice, says Sparrow. The Institute is chiefly a breeding farm for the Ministry of Foreign Affairs, the best of its graduates destined for embassy slots eventually, and so the school administration places them out for these little tours of foreign duty before the final coat of shellac is applied. They spend six months in a socialist fleshpot like Warsaw or Hanoi or Yemen. Nothing in the West; it is the first trip out beyond Soviet borders in almost every case, and the idea evidently is that the experience should be instructive, tantalizing but not overwhelming, and above all, closely supervised. Tronko was fortunate to get Prague, says Sparrow. And of course his own cunning foresight back at the Institute was also helpful: he had made a point, quietly but firmly, of not letting them teach him Arabic. No flyblown desert outpost for Viktor Semyonovich. His Czech was just serviceable.

And this is where he first came in contact with Trofim Filippovich Rybakov, says Sparrow.

"Rybakov was on KGB assignment in Prague?"

"No. Rybakov wasn't there at all. He was in Berlin at that time," says Sparrow. "Let's say it was Rybakov's daughter. She was in Prague. Let's say Tronko met her."

At this point Tronko wasn't yet married. That event took place soon after he got back from Czechoslovakia. His wife was a decorative and vacant young woman of good Moscow family, like his own, whom he had met a year earlier at a certain raw party thrown by one of his Institute classmates in the dacha of the classmate's father, a Politburo member. Her name was Tanya. She worked as a clerk-receptionist at the Mariinsky ballet school, having tried and failed several years previously to get into the school as a dancer herself. Though Tanya had a wonderful long ballet body, she lacked something, drive perhaps, or self-confidence. Possibly talent. Kessler is still waiting to hear more about Rybakov's daughter but it's evidently not going to happen, at least not just now. Tanya loved the ballet hopelessly, she loved the very idea of dance and the image of a woman as dancer—herself preferably or failing that just any woman, provided the body was right and the movement was pure, thoughtless, seemingly effortless, light as eiderdown. Yet despite her own vacuousness, or perhaps because of it, she never became bitter. She liked her clerk's job, relatively. She liked watching girls come and go in tights and warmers while she sat at a desk. Better that than sit at a desk in the Ministry of Water Conservation. She was a good simple soul, Tanya, even if she did happen to be beautiful and stupid. Tronko always said that he loved her. Even over here, even after the defection, after he had left her to some variant of the retribution that Rybakov faced, even then he claimed he loved her. Present tense: he still loved her. He didn't volunteer it but that was what he answered under questioning, says Sparrow. They were married in June of 1953. No very gala celebration, says Sparrow: the country was supposedly still in mourning for Stalin. A good joke in itself. For the first year they lived with Tronko's parents, who fortunately had that luxurious three-room apartment.

In December, Tronko was called to the cloth.

Taken aside by the personnel director of the Institute, who was himself known to be a KGB officer, Viktor Semyonovich was handed a piece of paper and told to telephone the number written there. He did. A voice on the line instructed him to appear the next morning at an office on Neglinnaya Street, not far from the Lubyanka, and present himself to a certain comrade, identified to Tronko only by first name and patronymic, both probably false. Still no explanations were offered, but none were necessary; this wasn't catching Tronko entirely by surprise. Next morning he reported. He was received by a man claiming the two names. His career at the Institute had been followed with interest, he was told. His record there had been an outstanding one, he was told, and the other man kept a straight face, though this fellow must have known as well as Viktor Semyonovich did that it was laughably untrue. Outstanding, no, anything but that. The recruiting officer wore a brown suit of East German or Polish cut, not quite so coarse as the Soviet gabardines, and near his elbow rested a glass ashtray that was empty but hadn't lately been washed. The office had no windows. The air was bad, though during their hour's talk the recruiting officer didn't smoke. He sat hunched forward with his hands folded and his brow near the desk lamp, this man, and frowned as he said flattering things but there seemed little

conviction in it either way. He looked old to Viktor Semyonovich that morning. Old and lifeless, like the vapor-sealed corpse
of Lenin. But more lumpy and comic than Lenin. In retrospect,
Tronko put the man's age at about fifty. This was not the first
KGB officer Tronko had met, far from it, so Viktor Semyonovich allowed himself not to be unduly cowed. He was self-as-
sured yet respectful, answering with forced gratitude the man's
forced flatteries. It was all ritual. Undoubtedly Tronko's record
of unblemished mediocrity at the Institute had less to do with
yesterday's summons and today's interview than did whatever
few words Trofim Filippovich Rybakov had spoken to someone
over the telephone. Viktor Semyonovich was "invited" to become an officer of the Organs—as the *Komitet Gosudarstvennoy
Bezopasnosti* was more familiarly known. He was free to ponder
the matter overnight but it would be still better if he could
decide now. Viktor Semyonovich was pleased to accept. He
signed an oath. He never saw the recruiting officer again. He
might have remembered the name and patronymic, Tronko
claimed years later, if he had not been so positive that they were
utterly bogus.

The next twelve months he spent at a KGB training school in
Novosibirsk, Siberia, separated from Tanya by two thousand
miles and experiencing an austere dormitory existence for the
first time in his life. He was part of a class of twenty-eight
trainees, every one male. Early rising, long hours of class and
study, strict discipline, no carousing during the week. It wasn't
all that bad but, given a choice, Tronko would choose other.
Sparrow states this in the present conditional—"Tronko would
choose other"—as though he had it just recently on Viktor
Semyonovich's personal assurance. In all frankness, Claude, I
would choose other. Kessler wonders fleetingly about the circumstances under which that mild antipathy to the spartan regime was originally voiced. Viktor Tronko locked in a concrete
room, maybe, beginning his third year of American incarcera-
tion? It was pure vocational training at Novosibirsk, methods
and tactics, with only passing attention to such tangentially
related subjects as scientific Marxism and the Soviet criminal
code. Much of the learning was rote. They also attended seminars in which analytical problems were set and discussed. They
took roles and acted out agent-recruitment attempts before
their instructors. They were drilled in the finer techniques of

subornation and traducement. They practiced shoe-leather surveillance on each other through the streets of Novosibirsk, sometimes with droll results—though the local militiamen knew better than to fool with them. Counterintelligence measures received heavy emphasis; but then counterintelligence meant nine different things, all nine important to the Organs. The school itself was in a hulky four-story building that loomed in isolation at its end of Krasny Prospekt and for a year Viktor Semyonovich scarcely left it. In evenings he played cards with the others. On payday he got drunk with the others. On the weekends, when the others prowled Novosibirsk for compliant women, he wrote letters to Tanya and read books, I suppose, says Sparrow, about Felix Dzerzhinsky. Do you believe this? says Sparrow.

"Should I?" says Kessler.

"Wait."

It was only a year, fortunately. He scored well on the passing-out exams. Intellectually it had been not nearly so demanding as the Institute, aside from the difficulty of focusing one's attention for so long on such dreary stuff. Then he was back in Moscow, where he and Tanya received as if by a miracle their own apartment—still just a tiny place, hardly more than a furnished room with rights to a communal kitchen shared also by two other couples, but it allowed them their first newlywed privacy away from his parents. Tanya was thrilled. She was flushed with love and admiration for her clever, well-connected husband, and she expressed it in the most genuine way she could: with her body. Tronko had a satisfying home life and good career prospects. His first assignment was to the Ninth Department of the Second CD, that arm responsible for surveillance and recruitment of foreign students at Soviet universities, not a glorious part of the KGB but not a stinking backwater either, and thought of as a place for promising young officers to be allowed to prove their reliability. Tronko became deputy admissions director of Moscow State University, a cover job extracted on his behalf from the legitimate university administration; his overt duties involved housing, medical care, and living stipends for non-Soviet students while his real chore was to spot and befriend those few, especially from Third World countries, who might be recruited to return home as agents. Another officer made the actual recruitment attempts, Viktor Semyonovich merely supplying him names. It was an easy, pleasant assignment that chiefly entailed drinking vast quantities of tea with nice young Africans. An assignment at which Tronko could not possibly fail and could also not possibly distinguish himself. It might have been a comfortable trap that held him for years, while his youth leaked away, but for Viktor Tronko it wasn't. After just one year, a minimal probation, he was whisked out of the Ninth Department and reassigned to the Eleventh. The ostensible reason for this transfer was his fluency in Czech and German. The real reason, he guessed, was Rybakov.

A post in the Eleventh Department represented almost the best thing that Tronko could hope for at that early stage of his career. Certainly it was the best to be found anywhere within the Second (as opposed to the First, which bore the more interesting burden of foreign intelligence) Chief Directorate. One simple fact made the Eleventh Department desirable: regulating and monitoring all foreign travel by any Soviet citizens so lucky as to get out, it gave its officers too the chance for travel abroad.

Most often, true enough, those officers of the Eleventh spent their time in Moscow or some other Soviet city conducting the routine investigations of would-be travelers on the basis of which exit visas would routinely be denied. But occasionally a few citizens were actually granted permission to go, usually diplomats or scientists or Party officials in a group, and when that happened a man from the Eleventh went with them. Any officer in the department could look forward to one foreign trip a year—Belgrade, Geneva, either half of Berlin, Paris or Stockholm if he were especially favored. It was a jealously treasured privilege yet it was also risky; he would be responsible for keeping those other miserable bastards in line, and if one of them fooled him somehow, God forbid if one of them defected, he would be called to account. This explained why there was a single nervous Doberman in every busload of junketing Soviet borzois. At the age of twenty-six, in 1957, Viktor Tronko joined the Dobermans.

He was already a senior lieutenant, and the following year they made him a captain, says Sparrow. Rank is taken seriously in the KGB, says Sparrow, none of this GS-14 sort of silliness, you need to keep that in mind. It was a good age to make captain, twenty-seven.

Life wore a smiling face. Upward mobility for him and Tanya. They were given a larger apartment, a two-room place on Maksim Gorky Embankment, not even sharing a kitchen. As though to fill the new space, they had a child. A boy. In reward for the competent performance of his duties, and also of course for political reliability, Tronko was meanwhile receiving the standard allotment of working junkets. At the end of his first year in the department he had accompanied a delegation of ceramics engineers on a three-week visit to Prague, a logical assignment considering his familiarity with the city and the fact that he could be shown on the trip manifest as a translator. The second year he got to Cairo and Alexandria with a group of linguists from the Ministry of Culture, plus a side trip to Aswan in a spirit of unabashed tourism. The third year they let him see London, in company with five aerospace scientists who were delivering a carefully distorted and disinformational model of Sputnik to an international exhibition there; the London assignment announced eloquently that Tronko was well trusted at home. From each of these journeys he returned laden with (besides decent tweed suits and oxfords and good linen shirts for himself) the whole panoply of exotic gifts that, as he had learned, it was both the privilege and the unwritten duty of a foreign-going comrade to bring back to those less lucky souls stuck in dreary Moscow: silk underwear for Tanya, clever windup toys for the boy, ballpoints and razor blades by the bagful to be dispensed to his departmental colleagues, hardwood carvings and crystal for his parents' apartment, Duke Ellington and Charlie Parker for his one remaining close friend from the Institute, more pairs of shoes for whomever among his in-laws they might fit, ten-year-old scotch for his immediate boss and rather expensive silver jewelry for the boss's wife, a German stereo and an antique jade bowl for the boss's home, brightly colored sweat shirts for the boss's children—it was not possible to be too generous or too transparently sycophantish in this last regard. For his mentor Rybakov he brought, from London, a fine leather-bound edition of *David Copperfield*. From Cairo, for Rybakov, a high-quality Italian watch—and on that occasion Viktor Semyonovich was gently reprimanded for his extravagance. From Prague, the earliest of these trips, he had brought only an account of his visit to a grave. Each of those three gifts was delivered personally in Rybakov's private office.

Meanwhile a pair of important developments had laid their
magic touch upon the course of Viktor Semyonovich's career.

The first of that pair was far beyond his control, played out in
the highest reaches of Party power. Large shapes and momen-
tous forces began moving, rumbling distantly, shifting across
the horizon like summer storm clouds—and in consequence
there was suddenly a new chairman of the KGB Organs. A man
named Serov was out, summarily fired and probably much
worse, says Sparrow, for lapses of vigilance and of foresight
severely damaging to the People's State, as the official announcement would have had it. A bad leak had been discovered
about that time, true enough. We had had an agent there in
Moscow, says Sparrow, a significant penetration. Not right at
the Lubyanka itself, alas, no, but in one of the tangential military committees, and this fellow had been feeding us some very
juicy stuff. They caught the poor man and squashed him. Chairman Serov wasn't directly to blame, he was merely the logical
ultimate goat, so he suffered. He fell. As they all eventually do.
Also Serov had been a Malenkov man; so it was really only a
matter of time, a matter of finding an adequate pretext. Serov
out, and a character named Shelepin was suddenly in. No KGB
experience whatsoever, and only forty-one years old, yet the
Politburo in their infinite wisdom discerned that Aleksandr
Nikolaevich Shelepin would make a fine chairman of the Organs. He had worked his way into favor through two decades of
brilliantly loyal service as a Komsomol administrator. Brilliantly loyal, yes, says Sparrow, I choose my words advisedly: a
uniquely Soviet category of excellence. And by no coincidence,
says Sparrow, Comrade Shelepin was a Khrushchev man.

"*Whose* grave?" Kessler says sharply.

"What?"

"An account of a visit to a grave, you said. Brought back
from Prague. A gift."

"Rybakov's daughter," says Sparrow.

Along with him, upon elevation, Shelepin of course brought
his own network of cronies, says Sparrow, and in that he was
acting no different from how any sensible bureaucrat does, anywhere. Hard Tennessee heel print on the word "anywhere."
You build breastworks around yourself with the stacked bodies
of faithful, unthreatening toadies, isn't that so? asks Sparrow,
and the bite in his voice causes Kessler to wonder which partic-

ular sensible bureaucrat he has most immediately in mind. Not hard to guess. Jed McAttee becomes Director of Central Intelligence, December of 1972. Soviet Bloc triumphant. Counterintelligence decidedly out of favor. We win, you lose. And then, as in the case of the Malenkovian loyalist Comrade Serov, perhaps it was so also with Claude Sparrow: merely a matter of those who had triumphed waiting, hoping, for a pretext to drop the blade. So Shelepin brought in his Komsomol clique, filling the higher positions with his own creatures, people he knew and people those people knew if he didn't, putting them all around to protect his flanks and keep his boots licked to a nice sheen, and don't be fooled for a minute to imagine that because these men were all *Komsomoletchiki* the KGB had become some sort of haven for aging scoutmasters, Sparrow says. Not at all. Shelepin was unlike any scoutmaster you will ever meet, Sparrow says. He was often called, though not to his face, "Iron Aleks." He was ambitious and willful. He was cynical, like all the successful comrades. Maybe more so than most. The youth work, the zealotry for shaping fresh young minds to the mold of glorious ideological orthodoxy, the entire Komsomol apparatus of which he had become supreme leader—that was all merely incidental, the base from which to launch a career, Sparrow says. It might equally well have been industrial procurement, or the political commissariat of the army, or maybe metallurgy, like with Brezhnev. But it wasn't. It was Komsomol. At the Lubyanka, in consequence, a record of Komsomol activity became the new form of holy grace. Latest in a long series.

Career prospects rose and fell accordingly, within a month of Shelepin's accession. Over in the Tourist Department of the Second CD, Trofim Filippovich Rybakov was not and never had been part of this Komsomol gang but he was enough of a wary professional, an experienced wire-walker, to survive in place. Young Viktor Tronko, on the other hand, possessed in his own personnel file an almost grotesquely flattering letter of recommendation from the man who had been Komsomol secretary at the Institute of International Relations, and who now happened to be a protégé of Aleksandr Shelepin's own chief deputy. It was a letter that had cost Tronko no more than a series of evenings endured in tedious meetings, and a thoughtful gift of some excellent imported coffee, two kilos of it, brought back by Tronko's father from a trade unions conference in Nairobi with precisely that purpose in mind. Two kilos of coffee invested presciently for a son's future. Better than savings bonds or a blue-chip trust. The Tronko family knew how to play this game, you see, says Sparrow.

Viktor Semyonovich was therefore, under the new regime, and through no merit of his own, a young man in very good smell. The second important development for him that year, by contrast, derived from his own genuinely fervid efforts.

In the course of a routine visa investigation for the Eleventh Department, for which he had flown up to Archangel and spent two miserable days in the freezing basement of a town registry, he uncovered a case of fraud.

A certain professor of philology at Leningrad State University—Lavrushko, by name—who had applied to be allowed out on a one-week visit to East Berlin, for an academic symposium, turned out to be not quite the person he claimed to be. In fact he was not even Lavrushko; he was Giterman, a half-Jewish impostor. Years earlier, Giterman as a nineteen-year-old infantry private had traded papers with a dead body, a corpse named Lavrushko, during the early hours of the battle of Stalingrad. Apparently it was done to shed the political handicap of his Jewishness. He had been decorated for valor later the same month, for his own deeds, but under Lavrushko's name; and in recognition of his heroic service he was permitted, after the war, to pursue his education in Leningrad, where he earned the philology doctorate, also under Lavrushko's name. Tronko the eager sleuth unraveled this entire hoax. He established that Lavrushko-Giterman had never been anywhere near Archangel during his childhood, contrary to the adopted biography, having made only a short visit there in recent years to fortify his story; and that the man's father had been neither a full-blood Russian nor a horse breeder employed at a collective farm, but rather a Jew who did carpentry in Tashkent. Unmasked, Giterman was denied his visa, while criminal proceedings began concerning his usurpation of Lavrushko's identity and the innumerable false statements to which, over the years, he had sworn. Tronko received an official letter of commendation from the chief of his department, who in real truth was incensed by this kind of showy zeal but could do nothing else about it.

Viktor Semyonovich had served notice of his drive and his

wit. Besides which he was Komsomol. A rising star, says Sparrow. A rising little snot of a star.

Upon formal request, in early summer of 1959, T. F. Rybakov was permitted to bring Tronko into the Tourist Department as his own chief deputy. *Tourist* Department is really a misnomer, it involved far more than that implies, says Sparrow. Rybakov's group devoted itself, for instance, to surveillance and entrapment games against all visiting Americans—diplomats, businessmen, journalists, sightseers, expatriate misfits. The American Embassy itself was a leading target. So this was a delicate post for the bright young man, Viktor Semyonovich. Age twenty-eight now. Soon to be Major Tronko. We can well imagine that the Eleventh might have been glad to be rid of him, can't we? says Sparrow with another ambiguous smirk.

There is a pause for breath, a pause for shifting weight and allowing blood to flow back into buttocks, and Kessler in that moment makes a tactical decision. Purely intuitive. He decides that he will *not* again ask Sparrow, not one further time, to fill in the part about Rybakov's daughter, dead and buried in Prague. Yes he is curious. Yes Sparrow wants him to be curious. But this is judo, wherein balance and leverage count for more than force. Kessler can wait.

"I have a question," he says. "An obvious one."

Sparrow nods demurely.

"If Tronko made the leap to Rybakov's department in '59, and stayed there until his defection," says Kessler, "why was he getting those trade-delegation junkets later? Rome in '62. Vienna. Didn't you just tell me that that sort of thing was a special perquisite of the Eleventh?"

Sparrow displays a congratulatory smile, gleaming and tepid as the sunshine. "Because Viktor Tronko was a fake," he says agreeably.

Again Sparrow is not meeting Kessler's eyes. He is gazing off past Kessler's left ear, off toward the Saturday traffic on Old Dominion, and maybe beyond that. In this case, he doesn't seem to be merely wandering blank-eyed and numbly through the charred wreckage of his own memory. He seems to be looking at something. Kessler turns.

"Don't," Sparrow says with some vehemence, between the teeth of his sunshiny grin, and Kessler turns back obediently.

He finds a hand clamped on his forearm, firmly, like the grip of a terrified baby chimp. The hand withdraws itself almost at once, disappearing into the pocket of Sparrow's overcoat.

"Is it kids with walkie-talkies? Or strange men in fedoras?" says Kessler.

He saw nothing in his own brief glance except a restaurant on the far side of the road, a low building with smoked windows and a cedar roof, the type of place given to nationally franchised avocado sandwiches. Kessler hopes that Claude Sparrow, the famous pathological paranoid, will not begin to hallucinate menacing skulkers and elect to stop talking. Not yet, please. Leave him alone, you demons, you shadows, you threatening six-year-olds, he's had a rough time and what he needs is to open up. If it weren't for the sobering recollection of Pokorny, splayed and drained, Kessler would be fully confident that this over-the-shoulder vigilance was only a matter of abnormal psychology.

"Neither," says Sparrow. "Never mind. Yes, you're quite right, of course."

"I am?" Right about what? Kessler isn't sure he follows. Right about your mental condition, Mr. Sparrow?

"Tronko could not have it both ways," says Sparrow. "Either he was spying on Soviet travelers, in Europe, or on American travelers in Moscow. Either he was an officer of the Eleventh Department or of Rybakov's. Either he had a routine and legitimate reason for those two later trips—the one to Rome, and then finally Vienna. Or he did not."

Either this or that. Choose one. It seems to echo back from something Pokorny said during their conversation that night. Either the biggest beluga ever, or the biggest hoax since Piltdown. Either *Moby Dick* or *The Confidence-Man*. Uncomfortable as he is with such crisp binary thinking as applied to any mystery of human behavior, still Kessler has no grounds at this point for dismissing Sparrow's view, or Pokorny's.

"And you are quite right when you say the question is obvious. We had fastened upon it ourselves, from the beginning."

"The first hostile interrogation?"

"Oh, well before that, even. The beginning, I say. Tronko was barely off the plane. Still the honeymoon phase. We had him sequestered in a pleasant suburban house, secure but comfortable, as we had done with Fedorenko. The debriefing had only just started. There was still a presumption that he would have something to offer the Warren Commission. 'Why were you in Rome?' we asked. 'Why Vienna?' Naturally we did. 'What business did Rybakov have for you out there?' "

"And he answered . . . ?"

"Nonsense. Just a load of nonsense," says Sparrow, as though that were that and Kessler should accept it as an axiom. He spoke nonsense, next question. Restlessly Sparrow swings his little legs back and forth; they hang clear of the ground and move in brisk arcs, like the miniature pendulum of a mantel clock. But Kessler does not accept nonsense as axiomatic. Not even in this affair.

"Specifically."

"Well. By his account, there was no discrepancy. That was the first version, anyway."

Tronko held firmly to the story of having joined Rybakov's shop, Sparrow says. Yes in early summer of 1959. Yes the Tourist Department of the Second CD. Yes his own personal responsibilities included watching—and whenever possible entrapping—Americans. Most adamantly he stuck with that. Meanwhile he tried to persuade us, Sparrow says, that there was no discrepancy. No logical conflict between the Rybakov assignment and what we already knew. We knew he had gone to Rome, because that's where he first approached us. We knew he had gotten out once more, to Vienna—obviously we did, because there he was. Nothing Tronko could do about either of those two facts, Sparrow says. They were there. Period. So he had to make them fit.

"You didn't care for the fit."

Sparrow sneers. "There was no fit."

"What did he say? What did he claim?"

"That down is up. Black is white."

"More specifically."

"That it was common practice. A former officer of the Eleventh Department, now assigned elsewhere, is given one of those junkets. As a courtesy. Another little form of the Soviets' incessant mutual bribery. Like the wristwatches and the jade bowls and the colored sweat shirts. They call it *blat*. Grease. That was Tronko's explanation. The first version."

"What about Rybakov?"

"Rybakov shows his man as being on loan to the Eleventh.

Special duty. And he winks. Or else—if it's a boss who is not so paternally indulgent as Rybakov—the junketeer takes vacation time. Common practice, said Tronko."

"But you didn't find that plausible."

"It was directly in contradiction to other information we held," says Sparrow. "Viktor Tronko was not the first or the last KGB man who ever talked to us, remember. We knew a thing or three about the Eleventh Department. Travel practices, exit permissions. We had help from some *reliable* sources."

"Like Bogdan Kirilovich Fedorenko."

"No." Sparrow's expression is transformed to a gloomy scowl, which quickly softens toward something else, and then the moment has gone. Hello, what was that? Was that sadness? wonders Kessler. "Not in this instance, no. Not Fedorenko. Other reliable sources."

These other little birds—whoever they were, and for some reason not including Claude Sparrow's own favorite chicken— were quite unanimously emphatic, evidently, on the point: Tronko was talking nonsense. No officer from any part of the Second CD would be allowed to step on a flight for Rome without a very damn good reason. And the Eleventh Department was not likely to share out such precious privileges to colleagues up and down the corridor. Nonsense. *Blat* went only so far. There were also jealousy and rivalry and venality to be reckoned.

And there was one other thing, too, to be reckoned, says Sparrow: Tronko's own statements made in Rome, back in August of 1962, during the initial encounter.

At first word that a Soviet officer wanted contact, Jed McAttee had scurried down from Bonn (where, in those days, he was still just a chief of station) and spent a total of five hours in conversation with Tronko, over the course of two separate clandestine meetings. All of it captured on tape. Tronko had described himself then as a senior lieutenant, serving routine duty within the Eleventh Department. He had talked of a wife and a little boy. He had talked of talent spotting for Africans at Moscow State University. He had even talked of a poor Jew who called himself Lavrushko, having tried to shed his identity. But no reference whatever was made, on the Rome tapes, to a person named T. F. Rybakov.

"Mel told me that Tronko's story was full of flaws," Kessler volunteers. Sparrow's body twists around and he is watching Kessler intently, waiting for more. The legs have stopped kicking. Kessler is about to add, "But Mel didn't tell me what they were." He catches himself. Better not to let Sparrow know anything about what Mel *didn't* tell. He says instead: "Like the Rybakov business, I gather. First of the nagging inconsistencies."

"First of the lies," says Sparrow, nodding.

Comrade Rybakov only made his entrance into the story eighteen months later. Tronko never so much as mentioned him until the second set of tapes, the ones that came back up to Langley by car during the early weeks of debriefing, says Sparrow. February and March of 1964.

And now it was Sol Lentzer in charge, yes, says Sparrow. Lentzer was given first turn on the hillside of fresh snow that was Tronko's memory, Tronko's testimony, Tronko's self-conscious legend. For reasons of witless bureaucratic protocol the assignment was McAttee's to give, and he gave it to Lentzer. The earliest debriefing. A period generally known to us, says Sparrow, as the *honeymoon*. Very crucial time. With any defector. Lentzer was chosen as the debriefing officer and he began traveling out each day (just as I had in the case of Fedorenko, says Sparrow) for these long intimate visits with Tronko. "Lentzer," Sparrow repeats, with a mild huff of frustration. "Well, at least he was a damn sight better than Scott Wickes." In Counterintelligence they had a joke about it at the time, Sparrow confesses. They would say, "The Mad Monk is on honeymoon with La Gioconda."

"La Gioconda?"

"Tronko."

"And Lentzer? The Mad Monk was Lentzer?"

"I'm afraid so."

"Were these code names, now, or just nicknames?"

"'Gioconda' was official. 'The Mad Monk' was just a silly nickname. A derivation. Originally, I believe, they had begun calling him 'Rasputin.' Because of his relation to McAttee, I suppose. And of course his Russian blood."

"They is who?"

"Oh." Shake of the head. "Some of my people."

"It sounds like vintage Pokorny," says Kessler.

Claude Sparrow surrenders to a little wince of a smile, as

though perhaps capable, after all, of innocent human embarrassment. "Yes. I think it was Mel, in fact."

So Rybakov made his entrance into the story at this point, during the honeymoon, only then, when Gioconda began telling the Mad Monk of his work in the Tourist Department. His purported work. First anyone had heard about that. Lentzer reported immediately to McAttee, who conferred with Sparrow as well as with Herbert Eames. "Jed and I were still rather civil to each other in those days," Sparrow inserts, almost wistfully. Rybakov's sudden appearance in the tale was of course linked—linked inextricably, says Sparrow—with the noise about Lee Harvey Oswald. The same noise that had been just enough to get Tronko out of Vienna on a fast flight going west. We already knew of this Tourist Department, so called, says Sparrow. We knew it existed, though not its name or its number, nor that a fellow named Rybakov was its chief. But we knew enough about the distribution of chores within the Second Chief Directorate to realize that, if an Osward file had indeed been opened (either for deeply sinister reasons or routine ones), it would have been there, in that department. Likewise if Tronko wanted to pass himself off as the top Russian authority on Oswald, then that's where he had to be. In the Tourist Department. At Rybakov's right hand.

"And presto. He was," says Sparrow. "Despite everything to the contrary we had heard in Rome."

"How did Tronko explain that?"

"The easiest way possible. He said: 'In Rome I am very drunk. Totally schnockered.' An exact quote. That was merely his first version, however."

"And his second?"

" 'In U.S., when I tell you of a man Rybakov, I am totally drunk. Schnockered,' " Sparrow quotes again. "That was true enough, unfortunately. McAttee was letting him run wild at that stage. Drinking his way across the state of Maryland."

"That doesn't make sense. He needed Rybakov in the story, you said. For his access to Oswald's file."

"No, of course not, no sense at all. But you see it didn't matter. Next day he would recant. Again. 'Definitely I am work under Trofim Filippovich Rybakov. Yes, yes. I am deputy, you bet. This good man. So dead now, I think.' And the bugger would break into tears. Melodrama in the grand Russian tradition. Liquor in staggering quantity, then a piteous thumping of his breast. More liquor, then more thumping. He made no sense at all." Sparrow's slightly strained voice appeals, one sane man to another, for retroactive sympathy. Hands in the pockets of his coat, he flaps his elbows, an odd gesture that Kessler takes to represent hopeless barnyard confusion. "There were other versions as well."

"With or without Comrade Rybakov?"

"Oh, with," Sparrow says. "Yes. In all but the most sodden and implausible tellings, Rybakov did appear. Playing roughly the same quiet, crucial role. Patron and mentor. Immediate boss. Surrogate father, to some extent. No matter what variations Tronko put into the rest of it, Rybakov was indispensable, after all."

"Did you see Tronko yourself during this period?"

Sparrow did not. Even McAttee did not. Only Lentzer, the anointed debriefing officer, had any direct contact with Tronko. But the tapes came back to Langley, and Sparrow saw the transcripts, and those transcripts were full of contradictions and falsehoods so glaring that not an ocean of vodka could explain them away. For instance, Tronko had been just a senior lieutenant when—

"Where were they?" Kessler interrupts.

"The transcripts? Why, they—"

"No. I mean Tronko and Lentzer. Where was this honeymoon taking place? A suburban house, I think you said. But where?"

Actually it was a rather elegant Italianate home, in an old neighborhood of Annapolis, Sparrow explains. A safe house, where Tronko was accommodated in lonely splendor, sharing the place with only a couple of men from the Office of Security, who were there to protect him physically and to help him amuse himself but who were under instructions not to discuss anything substantive with him. His past. The Soviet Union. Lee Harvey Oswald. No, absolutely taboo, they should leave the debriefing to Lentzer. Talk to him about baseball or chess or women or the weather or whatever they might like, whatever Tronko might like, except for God's sake they were not to go stumbling into any subject that was remotely significant. There was also a housekeeper, another of the Agency's trusted dowagers, who cooked the meals and was on hand to answer the door whenever a teenager came around selling magazines, and who herself virtually never laid eyes on the guest of honor. The Security men carried trays of her food to him, up on the second floor. They also did the cleaning up there. Not a difficult chore, the cleaning, since Tronko's half of the house was quite sparsely furnished: a good firm bed in Tronko's own little room, one other bed for whichever of the Security men wasn't on watch, a few chairs and a metal desk in the large front room that looked down toward the street. Nothing else. No carpeting, even. Just great expanses of golden hardwood floor, especially in that front room. Upstairs the place was like a vacant house up for sale, all swept and polished and emptied of individuating artifacts, to be trod through only by realtors and whispering married couples from out of town. It was not dreary but it was also not what one would call homey, Sparrow says. It was meant to be functional. And temporary. Downstairs was entirely different, a buffer zone maintained by the dowager in horsehair and doilies. Lentzer drove his own car, customarily, and came and went through the garage.

"You've seen this house," Kessler says.

"I have."

"But not while Tronko was there."

"No. A later occasion. We can't afford to throw them away after one use." Remembering himself, Sparrow adds sourly: "At least in those days we couldn't."

Lentzer and Tronko had their sessions in that large airy front room. It stretched the whole width of the house, Sparrow says, bare and beautiful as a dance studio, with leaded windows on each end and a cupola overhead and a bay window that hung out over the front door, giving a fine view to the street, at least when the maples were not in leaf.

"Was there a garden?"

Kessler asks this in a spirit of mischief, not because he cares. He is intrigued by the degree of particularity Sparrow seems able and willing to offer. Then again, he realizes, there is probably good reason: at one time Claude Sparrow no doubt spent many intense hours in this house, mentally if not physically, just as he spent half his working life on the third floor of the Lubyanka.

"No garden," Sparrow says humorlessly. "A half-acre yard

but they didn't use it, so far as I know. Too open to the neighbors."

In the bay window was a window seat, of which the red leather cushions had been allowed to remain when the rest of the second story's furnishings were scraped away, and during the long sessions with Lentzer, that was where Tronko preferred to settle himself. The window seat, always the window seat, says Sparrow, who presumably has it from Lentzer's reports. Slouching with his feet out and pretending to concentrate, peevishly fanning away the plume from Lentzer's cigarettes; or sprawled horizontally like a Roman at dinner, and playing bored; or else standing, his back to Lentzer even as he delivered his answers, gaping down through the trees. It was February, and then March, says Sparrow. The maples would have been bare.

"I remember," says Kessler.

"On the far side of the street was a bus stop. Tronko liked to watch the buses, we're told. Pulling up, stopping, pulling away. Occasionally taking on one or two passengers."

"Wanderlust?"

"Something like that, evidently." Sparrow says this with all the warm empathy of a forensic pathologist on duty. "So we are told."

Sol Lentzer meanwhile sat at the metal desk, armed abundantly with pads and pens, though of course there were microphones everywhere and a tape machine running in the dowager's back bedroom. Lentzer smoked his unending chain of Chesterfields and asked his unending chain of questions; made notations, flipped back and forth among his yellow sheets, challenged Tronko in a gentle way on certain points of confusion, and then as the weeks passed challenged him in a slightly less gentle way. Asked for clarifications. Demanded repetition. Sought very zealously—I must give him credit, says Sparrow— to make Tronko's story emerge in a form that might not affront the intelligence of any average human being. Failed utterly in that, says Sparrow.

"Lentzer was fluent in Russian," Kessler says. "Am I correct?"

"He was born to Russian. Raised in Russian and French, with four or five other languages added before he was thirty, I think. It might be less misleading to say he was fluent in English."

"What language did this debriefing happen in?"

"English, mainly."

"Though Viktor Tronko was *not* fluent, right?"

"Tronko spoke English as though he were killing snakes with a hoe."

"Then why not debrief him in Russian?"

"That was an administrative decision. Good translations take time. And they are always subject to minute but crucial distortions."

"McAttee had Russian, right?"

Sparrow straightens his spine to its full if diminutive extension, and tucks his chin. "But Herbert Eames did not. Nor did I."

Kessler pauses to make a few pen scratches in the notebook. His notation concerns the bus stop and the bay window in Annapolis, not Claude Sparrow's ignorance of Russian, but the moment seems well chosen for reinforcing Sparrow's obvious defensiveness on that point. The defensiveness itself might somehow prove usable. Then Kessler shifts the focus back: "Tell me about those falsehoods and contradictions."

Well, Tronko had been just a senior lieutenant, for instance, when he made the first contact in Rome. At least that's what he told McAttee at the time. It's on the Rome tapes, Sparrow stresses: a senior lieutenant, thirty-two years old, serving in routine capacity within the Eleventh Department. His responsibilities involved those visa investigations of Soviet citizens—Lavrushko and other unfortunate souls—and once a year he was given a fancy junket. A trip out, escorting some sort of official delegation like this one to Italy, where they would all spend six or eight crushingly tedious days touring factories along the Tiber, and then another two days back in the best shopping districts of Rome, frantically loading up on the products of decadent Western materialism. He was the Doberman among the panting and drooling borzois, nothing more. It was a good job for a KGB man, says Sparrow, but not an especially important one. Not to the Russians, and not to us. Furthermore thirty-two was just a bit old for the rank of senior lieutenant.

"I thought you told me he made captain in his mid-twenties."

"Precisely. Twenty-seven," says Sparrow. "That's what we

heard later. The Annapolis tapes, as opposed to the Rome. That's what Sol Lentzer heard as he sat at his little metal desk. By which time our dear prodigious young Tronko was claiming to be, not just a captain, nor even a major, but a full colonel."

"He'd had a good eighteen months."

"Yes." Sparrow smiles caustically. "Miraculous, I should say. But even an avalanche of promotions would not have explained the discrepancy, you see. He was revising his own earlier story. No, no, not a senior lieutenant. What a terrible slur. A misunderstanding. He had already made *major,* was the new version, when he met with McAttee in Rome."

There was also the issue of his current assignment: to Rybakov's department, not the Eleventh. This new claim entailed several implausibilities, according to Sparrow, the very least of which was that question of why a close deputy to Rybakov, charged with entrapping Westerners in Moscow, should still be wandering out to Vienna on a frivolous junket. Leave that bit aside, Sparrow suggests generously. Consider only the fact that Tronko seemed almost totally ignorant of the department within which he was now claiming membership. He couldn't describe his own daily routine, Sparrow says. He couldn't describe the chain of command or the flow of paper. He was hazy about the layout of the offices. He described incorrectly the view from what is supposed to have been his own window. He described incorrectly the elevator placement in that wing. He described incorrectly the canteen which served that wing. He was unable to give the correct name and patronymic for Comrade A. S. Samoylov, deputy chief of the Second Chief Directorate.

"Who is Samoylov?"

"The next boss up. He would have been the man Rybakov answered to," Sparrow explains. "Deputy chief of the directorate, responsible for Departments One through Seven. Including Rybakov's, which was the Seventh. The Eleventh would have been under a different man."

"Was it really so improbable that Tronko might forget this guy's middle name?"

"It was, Mr. Kessler. Samoylov was part of the Komsomol clique with which Rybakov had to cope, and beyond that, as deputy chief he would have been Rybakov's own personal bugbear. Rybakov would have been accounting himself to this man

—or at least making provision for that accounting—virtually every day. Thinking out loud about what Samoylov might expect, what Samoylov might demand. How Samoylov might react. Except it would not have been 'Samoylov.' Respectful and meticulous as Rybakov no doubt was, it would have been the first name and patronymic. Even in the presence of his own trusted assistant."

"Is that all?"

"No. Samoylov's patronymic was *Semyonovich*."

"Ah." Even Kessler hasn't forgotten that it's the same as Tronko's own. "Okay." He scrawls *A. S. Samoylov,* with a firm underline beneath the S.

Nor could Tronko describe Samoylov's physical appearance. He claimed that he only saw the man a handful of times, and simply couldn't remember anything remarkable. An undistinguished sort of fellow, Tronko maintained. Beetle-browed and imperious, like all the rest of the higher KGB chieftains, and, like all the rest, devoid of individual distinguishing traits. Which was no accident but rather a point of principle among them, Tronko claimed. Well, he was right enough about that, Sparrow concedes. The general proposition. Best to cultivate one's protective sameness. Yes, no question, they are a drab flock of ducks. Andrei Semyonovich Samoylov, however, was the exception that proves the rule. As we knew well from our other sources, Sparrow says with some sudden vehemence. This man Samoylov, Sparrow says, he was both exceptionally short and exceptionally homely. He had been cursed at birth with an unforgettable face. Homely to the point of repellence, Sparrow says. We had it on reliable authority that he looked like a gargoyle off of Notre Dame.

"How short?" Kessler says unthinkingly.

"Very. Five two," says Sparrow, and without a trace of self-consciousness adds: "Shorter even than me."

It has already been another long afternoon, Kessler is getting just a bit punchy, he knows he should know better but alas he cannot resist. "Plus which you don't look all that much like a gargoyle."

To Kessler's considerable surprise, Claude Sparrow responds with a wry, genteel nod. "Thank you, Mr. Kessler. There are some who would argue. But thank you."

Another problem was Tronko's alma mater—his putative

alma mater, Sparrow corrects himself—the Institute of International Relations. Tronko supposedly spent six years at this place, perhaps the six most impressionable years of his life, and by even his own account the Institute had played a pivotal role in his career, as it did truly enough for every student who passed through it, Sparrow says. The contacts made there. The piece of parchment, more valuable than any other single document that a young Russian could carry into adulthood. For that matter, the education itself. And in Tronko's own particular case, according to the legend we were offered, says Sparrow, that fateful opportunity to spend an internship in the city of Prague, where he encountered Rybakov's daughter. Kessler by now lets this slide past as though it were really a given and Sparrow, reading his eyes, moves right along. The Institute had meant everything to Tronko, says Sparrow. So went the legend. Yet at that impressionable age young Viktor Tronko, student, prospective diplomat, had been oddly impervious to impressions.

"He couldn't describe the elevators," Kessler guesses.

"The elevators he had perfectly. The corridors and the lecture halls perfectly. The desks. The views to the river."

"What, then?"

"He couldn't remember anyone who had taught him. He couldn't recall his professors."

"Not any?"

"Not any. Not to our satisfaction. Not a single one. And it had only been ten years for him at that point, bear in mind."

For a moment Kessler himself thinks back, sixteen years, seventeen, seeing certain jowly chins and certain bloodshot eyes, a man who paced like a cougar and broke pointers for comic effect, a man who leaned heavily on the lectern after a bad night; one very fine beard that the callow Kessler had much envied, on a section instructor in French who often failed to appear for class and who would later allude dryly to woman trouble. The bearded man's name comes suddenly into Kessler's head. He remembers a logic professor who wore always the same burgundy corduroy jacket, with a leaking fountain pen clipped into the chest pocket. All of one term, with mute fascination, Kessler and his classmates watched the ink stain grow inexorably larger. The man's name comes unbidden into Kessler's head. "Possible, I suppose. But unlikely."

"Finally he offered us someone," says Sparrow. "Just a name. Another drab duck. This one had supposedly been a lecturer on capitalist economic structures. Or maybe it had been Third World economic development. Tronko wasn't sure. Anyway it didn't check out. We could find no confirmation that any such fellow ever taught at the Institute. Economics or anything else."

"What was the name?"

"Orlov. Professor Blank Blankovich Orlov. The blanks, I'm sure I needn't explain, were—"

"I know. Tronko's memory."

"The Orlov—"

"I know, I follow you," says Kessler. "Professor Smith."

Likewise with the home address he claimed for himself and Tanya and the boy. It was a rather well-kept apartment building on Maksim Gorky Embankment that was reserved for *apparatchiki,* mid-level diplomats, powerful desk men from the Council of Ministers, and high KGB officers of roughly the echelon to which fantasy had lately promoted Viktor Tronko. He couldn't persuade us, Sparrow says, that he had ever so much as seen the lobby. Let alone a two-room apartment with unshared kitchen on the ninth floor. At very grave risk to one of our few precious Moscow assets, we got a vicarious look inside that building, not just the lobby but a two-room flat, though on the second floor admittedly, not the ninth, says Sparrow. No resemblance to what Tronko had described. Where he talked about parquetry, we found straight hardwood slatting. Where he imagined mosaic tile, we found linoleum. And likewise the business of his languages. He had told McAttee in Vienna, he told Lentzer during the first days of the honeymoon, that he was fluent in German and Czech, as well as in English. *Fluent,* Sparrow repeats sharply, hunching forward on the bench as though from a belly cramp. Of *course* he claimed fluency in three non-Soviet languages: the Institute of International Relations would never let a student graduate with less than that. As Tronko would surely have known, if he knew the desks and the windows so well. McAttee never questioned the part about English, nor gave us back in Langley the opportunity to question it, because McAttee was too busy showing off his own Russian. Lentzer learned better, soon enough. Pidgin English. Pidgin German also, Lentzer could testify. Lentzer did not happen to have Czech, so we brought in a man who did, Sparrow says, a native speaker from within McAttee's own division, and gave him an afternoon to probe and assess Tronko's command of that language. After twenty minutes the man was ready to leave. He actually asked Lentzer whether there might have been some misunderstanding—had he confused the assignment, had he come to the wrong safe house? No misunderstanding. Very well; the fellow closed his briefcase and shrugged. This man you are keeping here, the fellow told Lentzer, he does not speak Czech. A few words and phrases he knows, yes, all right. Like a child who is taken to a strange country on a brief vacation, and picks up some sounds. That much, maybe. But this is not speaking a language, he told Lentzer.

"The Czech fellow was on salary, you know," Sparrow confides parenthetically to Kessler. "I never understood why he acted so huffy. In any case, you see the point. You see the pattern."

Kessler is not at all sure he sees the point or the pattern. But he certainly sees the problem in accepting Tronko at face value—the problem in trying to make sense of Tronko and his story, his many stories, one way or the other. Either this or that. Choose one.

Enough, Kessler is thinking. Enough for today. The weary side of him, the lazy and perhaps the sensible side, hopes that Claude Sparrow will hear that thought and take it for his own. Enough. Stand up, stretch, go eat something, by all means get out of each other's presence. Come in from the sunlit cold. Let Kessler find a very quiet private corner somewhere, preferably within the purview of a bartender, and evacuate his memory into the notebook. Before he becomes just totally fuddled and loses track of something, some small detail, a name or a date or a touch of interior decoration, which might prove to have been crucial. That side of Kessler wishes Claude Sparrow had allowed him to tape—though Kessler hardly ever tapes, even with people who would raise no objection. That side of Kessler has an aching ass and a knot in the muscles of his shoulder. Enough for today.

The other side of Kessler is acutely aware that Claude Sparrow has offered him three days only, of which today is the second. This side of Kessler feels pain also but no impatience and, oddly, no discomfort from the cold. The cold has become part of the story. It arrived, seemingly, with the tableau of two

Russians standing over an open file, November slush and fog outside the window, dim afternoon lighting, silence, wet fur; and it has lingered. Quite naturally. Moscow and Vienna in winter. Suburban Annapolis with bare maples. The cold has been helpful to Kessler's concentration. The cold is a mnemonic device.

"In June, Tronko was given a polygraph," Sparrow says jarringly. "At last. After more than three months of this garbled nonsense." His eyes widen from a resurgence of energy and the old man is off again, talking fast, gesturing with the spidery hands, setting an entirely new scene. Kessler allows himself a slow blink. He had only just gotten comfortable in the bay window.

Trained examiners from the Office of Security do all of our polygraphs, Sparrow says. Did, he corrects himself. Ordinarily such a test would be administered at Langley, in the Security wing on the first floor. A routine exam was given to all new personnel at the time of joining the Agency—very exhaustive, covering all aspects of personal background—with additional and more limited tests for everyone every three or four years, or as particular circumstances might seem to warrant. We called it being *fluttered,* Sparrow says. Sparrow himself was fluttered a half dozen times, he attests. Most of those were at his own instigation. Herbert Eames had been fluttered. McAttee. They kept two special rooms with the equipment permanently at ready, the Security people did. But this was no ordinary occasion and Viktor Tronko was not personnel. Not then he wasn't, Sparrow says, fiercely precise. We weren't about to let him have a look inside the gates. Not then. We still at that moment contemplated whisking his sorry soul back to Vienna, pushing him back across to the Russians, just to see what might happen. So Langley was out of bounds. On the other hand Annapolis, the room with the golden floors, scene of so many inept fabrications, was also ruled out. Get him away from there. It was time to start fresh, if possible. Exact a whole new draconian standard of truthfulness. Truthfulness, or else. That was the notion. Make him walk into unfamiliar surroundings, and sit down in a chair, and be hooked up; and then let him tell us the truth. Or else. So we arranged for him to be fluttered, says Sparrow, in a room of a Holiday Inn at Tyson's Corner. Sparrow points a finger over Kessler's right shoulder. "Just across the Beltway from here."

Lentzer was not present, of course. Not in the actual room where the test was administered. No one was present there except Tronko and the polygraph examiner. Tronko had been locked up in Annapolis throughout the previous four days, no bar crawling at night with his bodyguards and not a thimble's worth of liquor in the house. That was at McAttee's order, delivered in a fit of bombastic exasperation, and quite poignantly tardy, Sparrow says. Anyway it was beside the point, Sparrow says. If we could just wring him out sober and make him know we meant business, Jed thought, we might have something. We might get something. That's what Jed believed. The examiner had been given elaborate instructions about this particular test and the possible aftermath; he had been given the list of prescribed questions. And now something else, Sparrow says. He turns aside, giving Kessler his profile. Something else you should know about. Things had progressed so desperately far, with Earl Warren pressing Eames and Eames pressing us, LBJ of course pressing Warren and everyone, that McAttee and Lentzer and I were actually there, right there, in another room. Waiting for the results, Sparrow says. In another room of the same Holiday Inn. We were a floor above and several doors down, sitting on our hands like utter imbeciles. Sparrow stares into the grass with shining eyes. Then he smirks. It was droll, he says.

"Another tableau," says Kessler. *"Three Americans Awaiting Results of a Flutter."*

They enjoy that together for a moment, before Sparrow continues: "He failed, of course. Howlingly. Thunderously."

"The machine said he was lying."

"As badly as ever. Worse. Worse than we had imagined. The machine, as you call it, was quite emphatic. The examiner said in his own report that he had never seen such a mess. Spikes on all the charts for virtually every critical question. Spikes that ran off the charts. Spikes everywhere. Tronko began lying— lying wildly, almost randomly, it seemed—during even just the warm-up questions. The harmless ones. The givens. It was absurd. He started lying almost as soon as the examiner asked him his name."

"Doesn't that throw the whole thing into doubt? Don't some people just react that way? Simply from stress?"

"No," Sparrow says. "No. The nervous reaction is different. They can tell. That's why we have these carefully trained examiners. They interpret. They can tell."

Kessler again remembers the émigré woman, of the Mexican vacations, who spoke no Spanish. We tested her. We tested him. He spoke no Czech. The machine said he lied. Such a very great amount of self-confident testing, in Claude Sparrow's epistemological universe. It makes Kessler uneasy. He has never seen polygraph equipment but he has a vague idea about sensors and graphs for pulse, blood pressure, respiration, maybe galvanic skin response. By disposition, he is skeptical of it. Of both the technology and its carefully trained interpreters. Not a convinced disbeliever, but skeptical. No doubt it works sometimes, on some people. Either or, choose one, and here's the alarm bell if you lie. It might work on that sort of people, yes, certainly. A perfect fit to their Manichaean minds. But can the thing measure seven types of ambiguity? Do galvanic skin response, blood pressure, and pulse in all cases really offer a window to the soul?

Then again, there is no point in arguing that issue with Claude Sparrow. Kessler wants to hear specifics. What were those crucial questions that made the needles jump? What were the harmless ones? He is about to ask, when Sparrow says abruptly:

"That's enough for today."

"Just a minute more." The rhythm is now wrong for Kessler. "I'm curious ab—"

"No. I said enough." This would seem oddly curt for even the likes of Claude Sparrow but Kessler sees the man's eyes flicking away, back, away again toward a point in the distance beyond Kessler's left ear, and it registers upon him that Sparrow has been distracted, the mood shattered, by something or other.

"Stand up."

"What's happening?"

Looking him straight on, Sparrow presses the words out with exaggerated clarity:

"Stand up. We have finished our chat, Mr. Kessler, and you are leaving. You stand, and adjust your coat, turning toward me with a few final words. As you do that, look at the man in the parking lot yonder."

Obediently, and feeling inane, Kessler stands. He faces Sparrow and casts his glance around casually. "Okay. Okay, here I am. What man?"

"Beige car."

Sparrow has good eyes. Kessler locates the man, forty yards off, seated behind the wheel of a beige LTD, one hand up along the side of his face. Kessler is mildly shocked. At the same time he feels tempted to laugh aloud. He resists the temptation.

"All right. I've got him. Was the visor down when you last looked?"

"No. It was up," Sparrow says.

"Down now." Nevertheless Kessler can easily enough recognize the rectilinear jaw and pinched mouth of the young man whom Dexter Lovesong called Buddyboy.

"Do you know him?"

"I never saw him before," Kessler says. Pulse and blood pressure normal.

13

Tonight there are no messages. There are no visitors waiting, which suits Kessler fine, and no mail or courier-delivered packets, a small disappointment. He asks the desk woman if she is sure. She shoves her slack mohair sleeves up above her bony elbows, waves her hands through the air of the little cubicle, pats them around on a few horizontal surfaces—cluttered desk, switchboard, the top of the bank of pigeonholes, upon which rest several disreputable magazines and an empty yogurt carton with a plastic spoon protruding—and then tells Kessler, not uncivilly, that yes she is sure. No mail, no other deliveries. She parks her hands on her hips for emphasis. Despite the casual chaos, he believes her. Still it's frustrating. Yesterday and again today, Kessler has expected to receive a manila envelope containing some interesting scraps of paper, contents of a modest background file on Claude Sparrow. Not the sort of thing anyone would kill for, not the key to the story, but a packet that could save Kessler two days of legwork.

He was promised these scraps on Wednesday evening, during his last phone call before leaving New Haven. The Sparrow file is part of a personal archive kept by balding young lawyer named Barry Koontz, formerly a staff assistant to the Senate intelligence committee and now a professor at Georgetown Law School. Barry Koontz is Kessler's oldest friend in Washington, and still also his closest, though they haven't seen each other five times in the past five years. Chiefly Kessler's fault. Barry was delighted to hear that Kessler would be in the city and very glad to offer help, within certain limitations dictated by his own sense of the security ethics for a congressional staff person, present or former. The limitations did not seem to apply to old file clips of published material about Claude Sparrow, so the failure of those clips to arrive at the Tabard must reflect some other complication, Kessler supposes. Most likely just bad mail service. Barry Koontz as Kessler knows him is not a man given to lapses of memory, or to reneging upon promises. Upstairs in his room, even before freeing himself from his shoes, Kessler dials the Koontz home number out in Rockville.

Saturday evening, and probably just in time to interrupt the family dinner. Nevertheless. Kessler has completed the shift back to his peremptory journalistic metabolism.

Waiting through a few rings, he absently picks up a sheet of notepaper that lies in sight on the little writing desk. A loose sheet from one of his own pads, scribbled upon in ballpoint. File it or throw it away. But at the same moment that he hears Barry's voice, Kessler realizes that the scribble on this sheet is not his own.

"It's me. Kessler. I'm in town now."

"Michael, welcome back. How's it progressing?"

"Hard to say. I've had two fascinating afternoons with your favorite aging spook. He's been trying to get me totally confused. Fairly successful. Those clippings, by the way, seem to have fallen prey to some sort of mail-intercept operation. And you probably thought that sort of thing went out with the sixties."

Barry Koontz laughs. "No, you can't pin this one on the Agency. I only laid my hands on them today. Perils of a pack rat. I thought they would be with my office papers, but no. They were out here in a box in the basement."

"That sounds familiar."

Barry has been collecting information on American intelligence operations since 1973, the year he went to work for a Senate subcommittee that happened to get interested in the CIA's role in Chile. When the full Select Committee on Intelligence Operations was created in 1975, Frank Church brought him onto the staff, and Barry stayed with that committee and its successors for four years, long after Church himself was gone. He ran investigations and became the unofficial chief archivist, knew the whole inventory of skeletons in closets better than anyone, but when they wanted to make him staff director, he quit. Didn't care to be a personnel manager, he told Kessler at the time. Rather be some sort of shambling historian with dust in his lungs. Rather be a private eye in a cheap suit. Rather be anything, Barry said. What he really loved was the quiet excitement of *evidence*—collecting it, making sense of it. Finding patterns in the carpet. For six years his job was to collect and make sense of evidence on behalf of Church and Inouye and the other men who sat at the hearing-room microphones and asked the pointed questions that appeared almost to be of their own devising. Now Barry teaches a course titled " 'National Security' and Constitutional Safeguards," and Kessler suspects he is still collecting. They have known each other since Kessler's single abortive year in law school. Even back then, Barry Koontz was the only twenty-two-year-old of Kessler's acquaintance who owned his own file cabinet.

"It was the last box I looked in," Barry says. "That's always the way, right? Last of about thirty. I've got enough government paper, I think, to keep a shredder going for a long weekend."

"Don't do it."

"There isn't much on Sparrow, though, Michael."

"I'll be grateful for anything at all."

"An article from the *Times* Sunday magazine, four or five years ago. I'm not sure how reliable that one is. Copies of the Joe Delbanco columns that got him fired. And a little profile of Sparrow that evidently ran in the Vanderbilt University *Alumnus*."

"Sparrow the Shy Troll? He let himself be profiled in an alumni rag?"

"Yes and no. It looks like he fed them a lot of misleading stuff. Who knows what the purpose was, if any. I only read to the point where they describe him, on his word, as a mid-level administrator at the National Institutes of Health. Also there's one other interesting document that I'll tell you about when I see you."

"When is that?"

"Come out here tomorrow and have dinner," says Barry.

"No. Thank you but no. I don't want to bring this project anywhere near your home." Kessler didn't mention Pokorny's death when they talked on Wednesday. By now, though, Barry has almost certainly seen a newspaper story and made the obvious connection. "Give my apologies to Patsy and meet me Monday for lunch."

"Patsy and the boys are away." Kessler gathers he means: for the weekend. "I'm batching. Don't be a jerk. I've already bought two T-bones."

So Kessler agrees. He will bring wine. The prospect of having a relaxed and entirely sane conversation, about the phenomenology of the CIA or anything else, seems very inviting after two days with Claude Sparrow. But Kessler hasn't forgotten the piece of notepaper. In fact he hasn't stopped staring at it through the whole talk with Barry.

He sets the phone back and reads again:

> *Roof. Scaffold.*
> *Leave the Light On, Please.*

First Kessler closes the blinds. Buddyboy may still be keeping watch from a cold phone booth or a darkened car somewhere down on N Street. Serves him right if he is. Possibly also Dexter Lovesong, better concealed, armed with his ivory-handled revolver, vigilant and subtle as a middle linebacker. Kessler doesn't really fancy himself worthy of a full-time, two-man surveillance detail, but the author of the note seems to think he is. Shutting the door behind him, Kessler begins climbing a flight of back stairs, having no idea where they might lead.

Half a flight above the fifth floor the stairway comes to a dead end. Ten feet overhead is a skylight, and for a moment Kessler worries that he might be expected to hoist himself up through that. He can't imagine how. Spiderman couldn't do it. Go back to his room and get a chair to stand on? That will be hard to explain if he runs into the proprietress. Wait for someone to lower a rope? He smells cigarette smoke, distinctly, and in a quick reflex he turns, expecting to face some leering stranger who has crept up behind. No one. Relax, don't be so jumpy. Then his eyes adjust to the dark and he sees a metal hatchway just off his right shoulder, a covered opening through the wall, giving out toward the back of the building. He pushes. Hinged across its top edge, the hatch is heavy but under firm pressure it moves, lifting away slightly. On the bottom edge, Kessler notices, it can be locked from inside by a simple hook-and-eye latch. The hook is dangling free. He puts his shoulder to the hatch and leans out into night air.

This feels, as he does it, like somehow a drastic and irreversible act. Kessler rather likes the feeling.

City lights in the middle and far distance, only darkness closer up, like large bulky shapes cut out of black construction paper and pasted down over a gay painting. The air is a little different, stale with the respiration of whole buildings rather than just cars. No tobacco smell discernible now. The sound is different too, muffled and echoic versions of what he would hear on the street. The atmospheric pressure even seems to be different. Through the looking glass, Kessler thinks. Or at least, halfway through. He climbs over the sill, stepping down onto gravel and tar. There. All the way.

The hatch thuds shut when his fingers release it. At once he is tempted to check whether the damn thing has somehow contrived to lock itself. He doesn't. Have a little faith. Journalism of any worth is not a risk-free endeavor, as you well know. Is that what this is, he answers himself: journalism? Kessler is drawn forward less by professional zeal than by a more personal and haphazard curiosity, his eagerness to know who this shy acrobat might be who wants to talk with him. Then he recalls: no one has said that they want to *talk* with you, dumbbell.

"Here's where I get the big bump on the head," Kessler says aloud to the pigeons.

The pigeons don't disagree. In fact they edge away.

He moves carefully, advancing each foot and finding a place for it before he commits his weight. Not knowing where to go, he shuffles toward the back of the building, since there can be no good in showing his head above the eaves that overlook N Street. Along the building's rear margin is a chest-high parapet. Kessler is cautious not to lean on it. He peers over into the deep canyon of an alley, seeing nothing down there but darkened windows, loading bays, a dozen garbage cans and a couple of dumpsters, an empty car that looks far too expensive and sporty to be entrusted to Buddyboy, a Volkswagen camper parked beside an aluminum shed, and an old Vespa scooter up on its kickstand, with a ten-pound wheel lock on the front. Clearly an heirloom, the Vespa. He turns back, still half expectant of that heart-stopping apparition, the stranger with deep eyes and long jaw and awful pockmarks who travels soundlessly and without moving his legs. No one. It's too cold out here to be wasting a lot of time. Kessler gropes along in the direction of

17th Street, up the block, guiding himself with one hand on the parapet until he comes to another wall, this one only reaching his knees. Treacherously low and nearly invisible. Exactly, Kessler thinks. Wonderful. If I had come stumbling blindly out here I would have gone right over, and broken my skull to kibble. He feels a flash of anger toward the author of the note. Tell me to leave the light on, sure, but don't mention anything about the shin-buster wall that could get a person killed. That's just irresponsible.

Scaffold, he remembers. Scaffold.

Kessler glances around freshly. Several buildings away and across the alley he sees it now, finally, though it must have been easily visible by the light on its pale planking since he first stepped out onto the roof: a set of scaffolding, risen around the lower five stories of what is destined to be the tallest new building on 17th. Scaffold, yes, thank you. Kessler is over the low wall, not so dangerous an obstacle as he thought, since on the far side a copper mansard slopes gently down to the roof of the adjacent building, only one story lower. He rides the mansard like a slide. The gutter squawks once, but holds. He crosses two more roofs just as easily, striding and climbing with more confidence before he is stopped by the alley.

The alley pinches down narrow at this end. The scaffolding, built out from the shell of the new building, makes it narrower still. Barely wide enough to get a car through. Across that gap, up here on the fifth story, someone with a dark and disturbed sense of humor has laid a two-piece aluminum ladder.

Kessler stands at the parapet of this unknown building beneath him and wishes that the folk inside, whoever they are, might have heard his footsteps and right now be dialing the police. As far as he knows he is not guilty at this point of a felony; nor of suicidal stupidity, at least not yet. He gapes at the aluminum ladder, and at the cobbled alley five stories below. He is confused. He doesn't quite believe that he will really be foolish enough to do what he knows very well he is probably going to do. He gawks. A plume of cigarette smoke reaches him in the dark.

"It's all right," says a mild voice from somewhere close, though not nearly close enough.

Kessler squints across. He explores the scaffolding with his eyes, picking over every shape and rectilinear shadow, peering

hopelessly into the deeper shadows beyond, the ones that fill
cavernous recesses in the open shell of girders and rough concrete.

"Then you come over here," says Kessler.

He hears what might be a cluck of disgust. Or it might have
been a pigeon. Or it might have been his own ears popping.
Then a slender figure steps forward from the blackness onto the
half-lit scaffold.

The scaffold shifts slightly from the man's weight. Kessler
can see the ember of a cigarette as it glows scarlet from a final
hard draw and then is flicked into the abyss; he goes a little
dizzy watching the butt plummet. For an instant it seems that
the man is indeed going to cross the ladder—good of him, very
accommodating—and Kessler feels a wash of relief, though he
is not sure that he even wants to watch. The man stoops over
the ladder's far end, where it rests barely overlapped onto the
scaffold's planking. He puts his hands on the first aluminum
rung.

"I have it," he says. "Come."

This does not seem to be a negotiable matter.

So Kessler goes. He goes on his hands and knees. The ladder
feels strong; it gives back small tensile bounces of ghoulish fri-
volity against Kessler's shifting weight; nevertheless he
imagines it folding away at the midpoint like a drinking straw,
falling, crashing, tangling itself through his own gnarled meat.
It does not so much as sag. O upright ladder. Halfway across
Kessler sets one hand on the brass fitting that holds the two
sections locked, then realizing what it is he jerks his hand away
fast, as though the brass were hot as a stove burner, nearly
upsetting his balance as he does. Do not touch this brass doo-
hickey. Do not bump. God knows what might happen.
Kessler's heart is now whomping away like a Buddy Rich solo.
He concentrates fiercely on each placement of each sweaty
hand. Meanwhile there is that sadistic little voice in his brain,
already composing the headline: *Man Splats Gruesomely in Fall
from 12-Foot Ladder.* Height of irony. The *National Enquirer*
readers will love it. Distracted by these various mechanical and
journalistic considerations, Kessler has all but forgotten the
stranger, until he dares lift his face.

Six feet away, infinitely distant, the man gazes back noncommittally. Long nose, mouth like a hyphen, eyebrows that seem

to have been drawn with a ruler. It could be Veronica's veil or a wanted poster. The eyes are fixed on Kessler as he crawls—not to encourage him, those eyes, merely to register and assess, to calculate and measure, possibly to judge. To decide. Calculate what? Decide what? It now dawns upon Kessler, heartbreakingly belated like most of his better insights, that he hasn't just *risked* his life, in embarking on this idiotic little meaningless act of daring; he has *presented* his life, wrapped and sealed, into the hands of the strange man, for disposal or otherwise. Here. Do with me as you choose. No one will ever know. One good tug on the ladder from that side and yahoo, Kessler disappears like a Wallenda.

He stops crawling. He has to study those eyes. It's more important, at the moment, for Kessler to know. Worse to go on in suspense, another three or four handholds, and then be nastily surprised. The man gazes back noncommittally, his specialty. But evidently he perceives what has crossed Kessler's mind.

"It's all right," he repeats.

Kessler crawls off the end of the ladder and across the scaffold and into the shell of the building, still crawling, still light-headed, until he braces himself to his feet by leaning against a pallet of drywall. Pride has prevented him from hugging the stranger around the shins. The man has already lit another cigarette.

As he did with Claude Sparrow, Kessler tries to place the man's accent. The woman in mohair said somewhere east of Zurich, if she is any judge, but Kessler is not sure she is. At times, while the stranger speaks, Kessler suspects that he hears Norway. A minute later there comes a whisper of Brooklyn. Then stretches of bland mid-American English again, faultless and idiomatic. Kessler's guess is that this fellow has a firm command of more languages than two, and can sound at will like whoever or whatever he might choose. He has introduced himself as Max Rosen, occupation unspecified, while implying heavy-handedly that he is an emissary to Kessler from no one other than Jedediah McAttee.

"This is my interview with the Director?"

"No," says Max Rosen. And nothing more. He is thin, an inch or two over six feet, and faintly epicene in his fine charcoal tweed suit; he is more delicate, more the mental type, than he seemed by Kessler's first unreliable impression. He wears round-lensed spectacles, the same sort of amber hornrims that Kessler associates ineradicably with John Dean, behind which the eyes are intelligent, quick, and unrevealing.

"What, then?"

"We can have a conversation, if you wish. Here. Now. When the conversation ends, it has never taken place."

"One of those," says Kessler. "The truth is, those kind aren't really much damn good to a person in my line of work."

He is bluffing. Max Rosen calls the bluff, with a wan shrug declaring his indifference to whatever Kessler might decide. Anyone who is quite *that* indifferent, though, doesn't come out on a cold night to climb across rooftops.

"I'd like to talk with you, yes. Sure. But I'm not granting any preconditions."

"No preconditions," says Max Rosen. "Exactly."

"Why do you want to help me? Now, suddenly. What's changed?"

Though Kessler meant *you* in the plural, the answer comes back in the singular: "I do not want to help you." Rosen repeats it, adding then: "And Claude Sparrow also does not want to help you." The other thing those two seem to have in common, Sparrow and Rosen, is a humorless cold portentousness. "It is better that you should grasp that. Neither of us. We don't want to help you." Okay, Kessler believes he has it grasped.

"You just want equal time."

"I offer you an alternative viewpoint," Max Rosen agrees.

Throughout the entire freezing hour, Rosen remains standing. He smokes a dozen cigarettes, each one lit off the butt of the last. Finishing one pack, he crumples it and tosses it out into space through an open wall, producing another pack from his jacket; in the bad light, with Rosen's quickness, Kessler gets no chance to glimpse the label on either pack. Kessler himself sits on the stack of drywall, with his hands under his thighs to keep the fingers warm. Neither man has a coat. The plume of Kessler's breath is nearly as visible as Rosen's smoke.

Unsure how to begin, or where, Kessler asks: "Did you work under McAttee back in the early sixties? At the time Fedorenko and Tron—"

He stops, because Rosen is already flapping his head to and fro. "We won't talk about Max Rosen," says Rosen.

Oh. Very well. Try again.

"I'm interested in the Tronko case," Kessler says simply.

To this, Max Rosen nods.

"And its context. And its consequences."

Rosen nods.

"Up to and including the murder of Mel Pokorny."

Kessler would have thought that he had just made a provocative statement, or at very least a brash deductive leap. Max Rosen neither nods nor argues.

"Sparrow has told me a lot about it. About Tronko, and how he was handled." This doesn't seem, to Kessler, a violation of any promises made or discretion owed to Claude Sparrow, and besides Rosen must certainly know that much, else he wouldn't be here. Presumably the reports made by Lovesong and Buddyboy have had an attentive audience, if a small one, over in Langley. Kessler wonders just how much they do know over there. Merely that Claude Sparrow has been meeting with some journalist? Or have he and Sparrow sat for two days in the cross hairs of a fancy long-distance directional microphone? Sparrow is the one who should have foreseen and coped with that; he, if anyone, should have an informed sense of their capabilities. And it was Sparrow after all who seemed to care desperately, unlike Kessler, about being overheard. "His side of it," Kessler adds. "I'm aware that there must be others."

Rosen does not deign to nod.

"He also told me about Bogdan Kirilovich Fedorenko."

"Fedorenko was insane."

Only that. Rosen folds his arms, leaning back against a naked I-beam just three feet from where the floor drops away and the sky begins, without even any scaffold along this side. Obviously the man is an acrophiliac, Kessler notes. Who is he to call anyone insane?

"Why?"

Rosen squints wearily, raises a hand, drops it. What that seems to mean is: We won't talk about Fedorenko either. Fedorenko has been declared boring or irrelevant—his whole corpus of testimony, evidently, beneath contempt. Kessler is still groping for a start.

"What about Viktor Tronko? Was he insane too?"

"No. Tronko was more complicated," says Max Rosen. "Clearly he was a liar. Also he was very stupid, I think." Just barely enough interest here to lift Rosen's shoulder blades away from the beam.

"Complicated but stupid?"

"Yes. Oh yes, exactly. And then, also, quite often he told the truth. Viktor Tronko. But where did the lies end? Where did the truth begin? What was stupidity, what was cunning?" Rosen puts the cigarette in his mouth and removes it again without having inhaled. Kessler waits. Long seconds. When Kessler has been forced to conclude that the statement is complete, or at least ended, at that point Rosen adds: "Those are the questions to ask yourself."

"I ask you."

Max Rosen, wooden Indian.

This is difficult. Also it is annoying to Kessler, precisely the type of situation that helped turn him to writing about tigers, giant squid, bird-eating Amazon spiders, and other relatively ingenuous creatures. Termites, with their dependable sense of social responsibility. Anything but humans—and least of all, humans of the clandestine bent. He appreciates now how right the man may have been when he said that, after their conversation, no conversation would have happened.

But Kessler persists. Like searching for a screw lost in ten pounds of flour: you make careful strokes with a long thin knife, listening through your fingertips.

"I've heard about the crossing. I've heard the first version of Tronko's story. Sparrow called it the *legend,* I think. Rybakov. The wife and son. Young intelligence goon on the rise," Kessler says. "I've heard about the honeymoon. Early debriefing. Gioconda and the Mad Monk on honeymoon." Kessler waits.

Max Rosen offers nothing, not even the dimmest hint of a smile.

"I've heard that McAttee let Tronko run. That Tronko was indulged. At first. That he was allowed to stay drunk through that whole early period. Drunk or hung over every day."

Max Rosen nods. No secret there, no dispute.

"While Sol Lentzer was debriefing him. I've heard about Lentzer. That he had first chance with Tronko, as McAttee's chosen man. I've heard that Lentzer's effort, that spring, was a total disaster," says Kessler, pressing a little harder. "Worse than useless, according to Claude Sparrow." He watches the other man sedulously.

Rosen nods. "A wasted spring. Yes."

"I've heard they got nothing at all on Lee Harvey Oswald. None of the important information that Tronko had seemed to promise in Vienna. Nothing plausible. Nothing the Warren Commission could use."

He nods.

"Nothing at all to persuade them that Tronko was real."

"No. That's incorrect," Rosen says. "You didn't hear about the microphones, then."

"Microphones?"

And now for a few minutes Max Rosen talks:

In March of 1964 the American ambassador in Moscow held a press conference that grabbed headlines all over the world. He announced that U.S. security officers had uncovered forty-four hidden microphones within the embassy building there. These microphones had been planted within conference rooms, interview rooms, working offices of the political section. The ambassador's own private office had even been bugged, by means of a wireless mike concealed inside a carven replica of the U. S. State Department's official seal, which hung on a wall near the ambassador's desk, and which proved to be not solid cherrywood but hollow. The seal had been a gift from the Soviet government, along with other items of decoration and furniture, presented when the American mission had moved into their new embassy building on Chikovsky Street. Twelve years earlier. Most of the other forty-three bugs had been built into walls or electrical fixtures, and had also presumably been stealing conversations for the past dozen years. They had escaped notice all that time, despite regular housekeeping sweeps by U. S. security teams, because they had been set in place behind alloy shields that made them invisible to electronic detection. The ambassador sent up quite a stink when he learned of them, according to Max Rosen. An indignant official protest was lodged with the Foreign Ministry. And then this dragging it out before the international press—a drastic step for the State Department—with the ambassador himself posing for photos, a pointer aimed on the hollow chamber within that perfidious seal. No one explained how or why, after twelve years, the Americans had only just suddenly discovered these micro-

156

David Quammen

phones. The implication given was that detection technology had improved. The truth was that they were the first fruit of Viktor Tronko's debriefing. Tronko delivered up the microphones as a goodwill offering, according to Max Rosen.

"But Claude Sparrow didn't mention them," Rosen adds. "How interesting."

"It is interesting. Especially since something like that would be so easy to explain away."

Max Rosen gazes back impassively.

"Let me imagine it from Sparrow's side. Just hypothetical," says Kessler. "I imagine him arguing that the microphones were a giveaway. A deliberate sacrifice by the KGB. If Tronko was phony, if he was sent, the microphones were an investment in getting him accepted. By you all. They were his dowry."

Rosen leans. A weary man.

"What do you say to that?"

"Your hypothesis is correct," he answers.

"The microphones were a giveaway?"

Rosen scowls derisively.

"No. All right," says Kessler. "But that's what Sparrow argued."

Face gone smooth again, Rosen nods.

"How do you respond?"

Again Rosen takes his time. "I don't. There is no rebuttal to such reasoning. It is infallibly tautological. It can be followed out endlessly. The larger the sacrifice, that much greater must be the other side's commitment to deception. That much greater must be the stakes. By this ingenious logic anything—everything—can be seen as the opposite of what it seems."

"Did Sparrow follow it out endlessly?"

Rosen blinks, a languid blink that seems to indicate assent. He picks a mote of tobacco off the tip of his tongue and inspects it with the same intensity of attention he has given to Kessler's last few questions.

"Am I boring you?" says Kessler.

Max Rosen shakes his head.

"I've heard about the foreign junkets," Kessler says, trying for a new start. "Rome and Vienna. Very unlikely that a man in Rybakov's department would get those assignments, according to Claude Sparrow."

Rosen doesn't choose to contradict.

"I've heard about the apartment on Maksim Gorky. Tronko's own home, but he couldn't remember what it looked like. Got the woodwork all wrong."

Rosen is silent.

"I've heard about Prague," Kessler says. "Two visits. One a long internship, before he finished university. Then later, under cover as a translator. But Tronko couldn't speak the language."

Nothing.

"I've heard about Rybakov's daughter," Kessler fibs.

Nothing. Patient, disengaged, Rosen only stares at him.

"He lied about his rank, Sparrow told me."

Rosen nods.

"Claimed he was a colonel," Kessler continues. "On the Rome tapes he was only a senior lieutenant."

"Claimed he was a *lieutenant* colonel," Rosen corrects him mildly. "Not a full colonel. Yes. It was a lie. As I told you, there were many."

"And some big ones, I gather. The whole business of his assignment under Rybakov, for instance. The assignment that gave him access to Oswald's file. It may have been a complete hoax. A total invention," Kessler states firmly, as though he were in any position to judge. "That's what Sparrow suggests. Tronko couldn't describe the offices. The elevators were out of place. He couldn't give the first name and patronymic of—" Kessler stops. He tilts his head back, groping for that name. "Rybakov's boss. Something with an S. It's in my no—" He stops again, catching himself when it is already too late; for a moment he is visited with the certain conviction that, while Rosen entertains him out here, others are burgling his room, and that to mention any bit of physical documentation is only to invite its mysterious disappearance. He clutches for the notebook. But it's right there, unmysterious and reassuring, in his back pocket. "—my notes."

"Samoylov," says Max Rosen. "Andrei Semyonovich."

"That's the guy."

"It wasn't really so damning, that Tronko had forgotten him. A man he scarcely ever saw. Of itself, it proved nothing."

"What about as part of a pattern?"

"Exactly. Then and only then," says Rosen. "But there *was* no coherent pattern, you see. That's what made Viktor Tronko so difficult. Lies, contradictions, some verifiable and quite valuable offerings, much human fallibility—but no pattern, no. None could be found. Despite three years of trying. Three years of bitter contention within the Agency."

"Sparrow seems to have seen one."

"Yes. Certainly he did. But Claude Sparrow could find ominous patterns in a bowl of bingo balls."

Kessler asks about those verifiable offerings. Besides the forty-four microphones, what else did Tronko deliver up to them? Rosen seems momentarily reluctant about answering, not in this case from boredom or scornful detachment but as though he is scanning his own memory to determine what might or might not still be sensitive information, mentally sorting the precious from the expendable. Kessler will no doubt receive the expendable. Max Rosen doesn't look much like a man prone to blurting out rash and regrettable revelations.

"There was a certain French journalist. A free lance, but well connected to one of the wire services. In Paris. He was operating as Moscow's agent-of-influence. A convenient outlet for all manner of disinformation."

"Under General Avvakian?"

"Very good. Yes, under Avvakian's gentle guidance. The Agency had long suspected this fellow. Everyone had suspected him. Tronko supplied confirmation. Eventually the French brought the man up on charges."

Kessler waits, while Rosen mates the tips of two cigarettes and then flings the butt out into darkness. There comes an audible exhalation, after which Kessler continues waiting. Rosen's face is broken in half diagonally by a shadow cast from the scaffold.

"Is that all?" Kessler says.

"An FBI agent assigned to the New York office, who had compromised himself disastrously with male prostitutes," says Rosen. His voice is empty of tone. "This fellow was supposed to be catching Russian spies but evidently they had rather more luck catching him. Photographs, embarrassing tapes. The KGB *rezident* in New York had been running him for five or six years. Tronko did not know this agent's name, only that the man was married, formerly an attorney, certain other facts that made identification possible. The Agency took what Tronko could give, cross-checked with other sources, and immediately alerted Hoover."

"I'll bet Hoover loved you for that one."

"For six months Hoover did nothing whatsoever about it. An unconscionable delay. Almost treasonous, you could say. Until Herbert Eames had a word with Lyndon Johnson."

"What else?"

Again silence. Rosen might be holding back lungfuls of smoke or entire dossiers' worth of information. Again his head wags.

"That's all? That's the whole dowry?"

"He was not a bride. He was a defector. He brought what he could."

"A real defector or a phony one, Mr. Rosen?"

"Real. Quite real. But complicated."

"And stupid, you said. And sometimes a liar."

"Often."

"Often a liar. He gives you one French journalist with a weakness for rubles, and one FBI agent with a weakness for boys. Plus forty-four hidden microphones, the investment upon which had already been amortized over twelve years. Period. Almost everything else he tells you is cockamamie, contradictory, or highly implausible, if not manifestly untrue."

"Much. Not all."

"Much is untrue. Some people we both know would say *most.* Some people would even call this a pattern. Nevertheless you chose to believe him on the crucial things. I'm trying to understand why."

"Me personally?"

"Yes, let's be personal here for a minute. You. *Max Rosen.*" Kessler pronounces the name as though it's a friendly joke between them.

"And what are these crucial things, please?"

"The Oswald connection and Dmitri, of course. Neither of which existed, according to Viktor Tronko."

"The Oswald story—that was never believable, no. Not even to me. As to how crucial it might have been, I couldn't say. Perhaps not so very crucial as some people think."

"Dmitri?"

"Dmitri," says Rosen, and from him it sounds almost wistful.

"Okay, very well. Yes. For a time I believed. That there was no Dmitri."

Kessler says: "For a time?"

But, regarding his personal credulity, Max Rosen has no further comment.

"Ask yourself this," says Rosen. "If Tronko was sent by Moscow, on some great mission of disinformation, why was he not given more to offer? Why was his dowry, as you call it, so meager?"

"I have been," says Kessler. "I get nowhere."

"Then ask Claude Sparrow."

"I will. What about you? Do you have an opinion?"

Rosen ignores that. "Ask yourself: how could it serve Moscow's purposes to send a man who lied so poorly? So confusedly. How could it satisfy Moscow for Viktor Tronko to sit three years in a concrete cell?"

"I assume that they wouldn't have planned on that three years. Moscow. If they sent him."

"Three years, abused and disbelieved. Accomplishing nothing but to focus intense scrutiny, within the Agency, on the question of Dmitri's existence. How could such epic futility be of use to Dmitri? Or to anyone else?"

Kessler has no answer.

"Ask yourself why Moscow should have chosen so badly. If they chose Tronko at all."

Kessler asks himself, not for the first time, why Max Rosen should care what he asks himself.

"I've heard about the night Tronko supposedly flew to Minsk," says Kessler. "But probably didn't, according to Claude Sparrow."

Rosen shows no interest in that subject. He lets Kessler work.

"I've heard about Rybakov's patronship. All his help in getting Tronko promoted. Though I have yet to hear *why* Comrade Rybakov was so benevolently concerned."

"You told me you had heard about Rybakov's daughter," Rosen challenges him.

"I lied. I haven't. I just know she existed. Tell me about her."

But Rosen waves that notion away. Not interested in Rybakov's daughter. Kessler seems to be losing him once more;

evidently it's not the right tack. Maybe Kessler is centering on the wrong person. Maybe he has got his brain in the wrong country. "I've heard all about the safe house in Annapolis," he tries. "The room with the golden floors and the bay window."

"What bay window would this be?"

"A window that Tronko liked to sit in, while Sol Lentzer was debriefing him. Outside in front of the house was a bus stop. Tronko would stare at it. Lentzer had a metal desk. Golden hardwood floors of the debriefing room."

"Claude Sparrow told you these details?"

"Yes."

A sarcastic snort. "Then of course they must be accurate." Whenever Rosen shifts forward slightly, the bar of shadow from the scaffold rises across his forehead, disappearing into the general darkness behind; now it lowers itself back to divide his face.

"I've heard about the first polygraph test," says Kessler.

The shadow rises again, gone like a large silent moth. "Ah. What did you hear?"

"Tronko failed it miserably."

"And?"

"They wouldn't let him on the premises at Langley. So they had an examiner set up the equipment in a room of a Holiday Inn. Lentzer was waiting with McAttee and Sparrow, in another room down the hall."

"Nothing more?"

"I think Sparrow skipped over this part," Kessler says cunningly. "I think there was something he didn't want me to know."

The first polygraph was a fraud, says Max Rosen. It was a ruse, a sadistic little charade, contrived not to advance their understanding of Viktor Tronko but to manipulate him, to frighten him. To break him. It was no spontaneous event that brought the honeymoon phase to an end—don't be misled. It was the well-calculated start of what would come next. Rosen makes these pronouncements with a quiet definiteness suggesting intimate knowledge and, at least to Kessler's active mind, some extra hint of passion that is perhaps confessional. For once Rosen grinds a cigarette out underfoot instead of tossing it toward the gaping alley; the gesture's vehement thoroughness, as he twists and scuffs his shoe over shreds of tobacco and torn paper until even Smokey the Bear would approve, seems an unconscious lapse, betraying emotion. The first polygraph, according to Rosen, was merely a tactical stroke designed to begin the destruction of Tronko's legend. If it *was* a legend. And if it wasn't, then of his personality.

Sparrow and McAttee had scripted the whole scene in advance, with the approval of Herbert Eames and the halfhearted but dutiful cooperation of Sol Lentzer. Even the examiner was brought in on it: summoned up to the seventh floor on the afternoon one day before the test, he was informed that certain special procedures would be adopted in this case. Certain irregular measures were called for. If there is any sort of professional code among polygraph examiners—an unlikelihood, Rosen concedes—then that acquiescent man surely broke it. He was instructed to fit the subject with electrodes for an electroencephalogram, as well as attaching the standard leads for pulse and the other parameters. He needn't worry what the EEG measured, if anything, the examiner was told. But he should make a point of informing the subject, preferably in minacious tones, that these particular wires would monitor the subject's brain waves. His very thoughts. And whatever might show on the graph rollers once the test began, the examiner was by all means, in the immediate aftermath, to stick with their prearranged story: that the subject had failed. That the machines declared he was lying—lying continuously, guiltily, badly.

All of this was most crucial, decreed the scenarists on the seventh floor. The subject will have failed. The machines will have detected his lies.

At the motel, according to Rosen, it went by the script.

The examiner carried his results upstairs and ten minutes later Sol Lentzer burst back into the room, screaming wildly. Tronko sat on a straight-backed chair in his American undershirt, still tethered up like Gulliver. Eyes wide with astonishment and a real or feigned expression of injured trust and maybe also already a bit of dread, the look of a driven deer, as Lentzer let loose on him mercilessly. Lentzer called him a lying KGB maggot and six other unflattering things, all at the top of his voice and with the help of every foul adjective available in two languages. The game was over, Lentzer shouted. No more pretense that Tronko was a real defector, and no more pretense that they had any intention of treating him like one. He was lying. Not confused, not drunk, not weak of memory, but lying lying lying. Furthermore they had always known it. Since he first stepped on the plane that brought him over from Frankfurt, they had known it, and there had been no chance that they would be taken in by his fairy tales. They had only gulled him across for their own purposes. He was a total fake, and they were wise to him. He was an operation, but the operation had failed. And now he should understand: he was a prisoner.

Lentzer strode back and forth, raving on angrily, working himself up to a case of the shakes, spitting, waving his arms like a chicken, making just an absolute fool of himself, according to Rosen. It wasn't an easy performance for someone like Lentzer to summon. But it was good enough. Viktor Tronko believed it.

McAttee and Sparrow then appeared. McAttee repeated the main points of all Lentzer's dire hollering, while Sparrow remained silent and still as a snake. McAttee's unfriendly intervention at just this moment was expected—intended—to be an especially discouraging blow for Tronko, in that Jed had been his chief contact, and his chief sponsor, ever since Rome. But Rome was now part of another lifetime. McAttee, like Lentzer, was suddenly a different person. As for Claude Sparrow, this was the first time he had been allowed to set eyes upon Viktor Tronko, as well as vice versa.

Tronko was handcuffed and led roughly to a car. The handcuffs were purely for melodramatic effect, says Rosen, a touch suggested by Claude Sparrow to which Lentzer had objected with particular outrage. Lentzer had been overruled. Jed McAttee's own views on how to cope with the Tronko dilemma were just then in flux, as they would be again later, and Herbert Eames was not the kind of Director who cared to know too many details. As they passed through the corridors and then the parking lot of that Holiday Inn, Lentzer's suit jacket lay across Tronko's bound wrists—though Max Rosen can't say whether Lentzer had draped it there mainly to hide the sight of those handcuffs from nosy tourists and salesmen, or to hide the sight from himself. They made their exit quickly. They could hardly afford to linger, after all that shouting. They could hardly afford to be stopped for kidnap by the Virginia state troopers, says Max Rosen.

They could hardly afford that precisely because it *was*, after all, kidnap. Viktor Tronko's forced detention, from this moment on, was in contravention of U.S. law, according to Rosen. In fact, it would have been hard to justify with even a loose reading of the CIA charter.

Once in the car, Tronko was blindfolded and crushed down onto the floor of the back seat. He was driven to a new place, a place beyond the far fringe of the greater Washington area, more distant than his comfortable Annapolis hideaway though still only an hour from Langley; a place where secure lodgings of a much different sort awaited him. The new place was on a military base, says Rosen, which allowed a higher degree of privacy and more latitude of methods for the next phase. The building itself had been an infirmary, now in disuse, and located in a remote corner of the base's grounds, so that it offered the advantages of being protected by fence and guardhouse yet was still far out of the flow of routine military traffic. The commandant of the base had signed that single building over to the Agency, no questions to be asked. Certain modifications had already been seen to. Windows boarded over, a light switch rewired, new fittings on the door of one room so that it could be locked from the outside, microphones and recorders. The car passed the guardhouse in late afternoon, McAttee or someone showed a badge, and Viktor Tronko did not emerge again for five months.

"The first hostile interrogation," says Kessler.

Rosen doesn't answer at once. He gazes out from his spot near the beam. The bar shadow has disappeared permanently, which must mean that Rosen has shifted a full pace closer. "Exactly. Did Sparrow call it that?"

"No," Kessler says, then makes a little decision. The best approach with Claude Sparrow is not necessarily the best with Max Rosen, and Kessler has never discovered a guiding principle in these matters that works any better than instinct. His instinct tells him to be more forthcoming with Rosen than with Sparrow, less coy. Rosen himself, anyway, is already coy enough for two. "Mel Pokorny called it that."

"Pokorny. He told you about this part?"

"Yes he did," says Kessler. "Some."

Rosen edges forward another pace. Like Sparrow, he seems to be captivated by the thought of Mel Pokorny, before he died, having unloaded a lot of secrets into Kessler's notebook. But at least Rosen doesn't pursue it with Sparrow's prurient insistence.

"Pokorny's version would . . ." His voice is a little quieter. Then Rosen seems to decide against finishing that statement at all, choosing instead a more guarded formulation: "Mine is liable to be rather different from his."

"Good. That's why I want to hear yours."

"It was a travesty. It was cruel and unusual punishment." Another step closer, close enough now to Kessler that Rosen could whisper if that were called for. He does not whisper. "And nothing of value was accomplished. Nothing."

"Mel said this one was milder than the second interrogation. I think he even used the word 'cozy.' Compared to the second."

"No," says Max Rosen. *"Cozy?* No."

In a few sentences Rosen describes vividly the cell-like room where Lentzer, and sometimes also McAttee, now met with Viktor Tronko. A bare dangling bulb, a cot, windows sealed from the inside with unpainted plywood. Failing plaster on the walls, which in one area near the door had crumbled away sufficiently to reveal lath; failing plaster on the ceiling, stained by rain that had leaked through a bad roof and cracking, dropping. Small bits of plaster sifted down intermittently onto the floor, onto the cot, and occasionally a larger hunk would catch a person on top of the skull. You really wanted a helmet even to step into that room, says Max Rosen. An irredeemably shabby place. Little wonder that the commandant had no use for the building. It was past saving. Of course the Agency could have got something in better condition, but no, this was precisely what they wanted. This was the desired ambience: a grim and forgotten hole. End of the line.

There was a folding chair that came in for each session with Lentzer, says Max Rosen, and was taken out again afterward. No other furniture. No sitting for Tronko, except on the floor, or the edge of the cot—and only when he was given specific permission. No metal desk for Lentzer, who now worked from a clipboard—though of course the tapes were always running, says Rosen. Even the cot's factory label had been sliced away with a razor blade.

"Why in the world did they do that?"

"So that Tronko couldn't read it. He was to have nothing to read. Absolutely nothing. Complete mental starvation. That was to be part of the psychological torture."

"Torture," says Kessler. He dips his head in appreciation of Rosen's candor. "First time anybody has used the word."

"Oh of course it was. Even Claude Sparrow, I think, couldn't deny that."

The whole idea, after all, was not simply to incarcerate Tronko while questioning him—not at this stage, not anymore, no—but to demoralize him and break the man's will, says Max Rosen. Breaking the will would also break open the legend. Expose the truth behind all his implausible falsehoods. At least that was the theory, says Rosen. Will to resist was equated with will to lie, by the theory. Will to lie was equated with performance of a mission concocted in Moscow. Break the man's will like an eggshell—and find Moscow's dark purpose inside, *voilà*, like a baby chick.

"Or a baby turtle," says Kessler. "Or maybe a caiman."

"Yes. Or just a ruptured yolk. Except the theory itself was inadequate," says Max Rosen. "In this case, it didn't serve."

"Why not?"

"Because Viktor Tronko was not who we thought."

"Not who *you* thought? Or not who Sparrow and Pokorny thought?"

"Everyone," says Rosen. "Everyone."

14

Kessler sits on the edge of his bed, finally now, at what he imagines to be the end of what he knows to have been an arduous, wearisome, brutally chilling day. He is waiting to thaw. The shivers pass up through him in waves, thrumming his rib cage, jiggling his whole body like a Maytag on spin cycle with an unbalanced load. His hands are useless. The notebook rests beside him but Kessler simply must wait, patiently, until his fingers regain enough touch for him to hold and steer a ballpoint. Then as the thaw begins arriving so does the pain, a pulsing ache that makes his fingertips feel as though they have been slammed in a car door—his ears too, if that were possible. Kessler thinks about it. He has already listened to more than a few revelations that certain folk might strongly prefer he had never heard; continue on this course, stretch his ears much wider and, yes, there might be good chance of getting them slammed in a car door.

Maybe he should buy a watch cap. Definitely he should be careful.

Now his toes also come painfully back to life. And the earache reaches right down his Eustachian tubes from each side to a midpoint behind his eyes, meeting there like a pair of knitting needles. But at least he can write.

Amobarbital is the first word Kessler puts down. Proper names and dates always make the best framework for a set of notes, Kessler has found; the finer details and causal connections that will constitute the real story can be filled in later by metonymical recall. Sedative and hypnotic, short-term depressant, treatment of epileptic seizures, he writes. Overdose, he writes. Weakened resistance. Confusion. Psychological vulnerability. Lowered defenses, hypersensitivity. Sizable intramuscular injections. Ass. But Eames said no, Kessler writes.

He scribbles several more phrases quickly, just whichever
come to him, without yet making the mental effort of systematic
retrieval. Military base, less than an hour, he writes. No exit for
five months, he writes. Label from cot. Complete mental starvation—and Kessler sets that one within quotes. Psychological
torture, also within quotes. Backtracking suddenly, at the top of
this notebook page he squeezes in today's date and Max Rosen's
name.

Then as an afterthought he adds quotation marks, too,
around the name.

Kessler has no trouble recapturing most of what Rosen told
him about that nervous, airless time, June to November of
1964, during which Lentzer played grand inquisitor and Claude
Sparrow squalled and lathered for permission to put Viktor
Tronko through a course of unwholesome drug therapy. For a
half hour Kessler is transported—remembering, writing fast,
remembering. Arrows and insertions, addenda and still more
afterthoughts. Get it now or lose it forever. The single thing he
would prefer not to remember is his own trip back across that
aluminum ladder.

Rosen seemed to be quite an authority on the use of drug
treatments as a concomitant to interrogation. And not merely
amobarbital, but also a couple of other sweet little potions
called chlorpromazine and haloperidol. In an impassioned di-
gression, he described to Kessler the sort of effects that could be
had from regular injections—say, three or four thousand milli-
grams daily—of these things, shot in the buttocks of even a
strong-minded intelligence professional or a trained soldier.

Irresistible drowsiness, to begin with, either in combination
or alternating with ferocious headaches. Disorientation in time
and space, and then a progressive loss of memory—of which the
drugged subject will be acutely, frustratingly aware, but which
he can do nothing about. The mental functions generally will
become slowed and muddled, Rosen said. Emotions, on the
other hand, will become more intense and more volatile. Paranoia. Crying fits, and in some cases mild convulsive seizures.
Tremors, constant dizziness, fainting, uncontrollable muscular
spasms or extreme muscular rigidity, drooling, involuntary jaw
and mouth and tongue movements that may go on for hours.
The subject will lose control of his face. He will puff out his

cheeks, he will grimace and yawn and hoot, barely conscious he is doing it. The psychological sense of security will be very fragile. He will be quite positive that horrible offenses are being committed against his body, against his whole selfhood, Rosen said; and as far as that goes, Rosen said, he will be right. He will believe that he is losing his mind. These drugs can actually induce fear and stupidity, in direct correlation to dosage, Rosen said. With them you can destroy the humanness of a human being. Eventually, as the treatments continue, the subject's skin will turn dirty gray, the shade of smeared newsprint. Painful nodes, like gravel, will appear in his muscles. The lenses of his eyes will fog over with little star-shaped cataracts. Blind and alone. Probably by now, too, he will be utterly incontinent. No question, then, he is in your power, Rosen said. For whatever that may be worth. He is a cracked egg.

"Whose power?" Kessler asked.

"Whoever holds the needle."

"It doesn't make any sense. Destroying the memory, muddling the mental processes. Why do that to a man you're still trying to debrief?"

"Exactly. Of course it makes no sense at all. Except now they were *not* chiefly concerned with debriefing Tronko. As I told you. They were concerned with breaking him. For that, the drug tortures can be quite useful."

"But you say Herbert Eames wouldn't allow it."

"No. A small blessing for Viktor Tronko. Eames would not allow drugs. Not any. No physical abuse of any kind, Eames decreed. That was to be the way."

"Despite pressure, I suppose."

"There was just enormous pressure during this time," Rosen agreed emphatically. "Just incredible pressure, you wouldn't believe. Lyndon Johnson himself, for a start. And everyone else. They wanted Tronko to testify before the Warren Commission. By the end of August, no later. They wanted him ready—talking, being believable. Not the confused drunken lies."

"Wasn't he already saying just what they wanted to hear? 'Oswald was only a crank. A demented loner. Not even the KGB would have anything to do with him.' Wasn't that Tronko's line?"

"It was exactly Tronko's line, as you say. And the Commission's line too, yes. Precisely that is why they couldn't use him.

Couldn't take his testimony. Not yet. Not until he had been broken and then patched back together. Otherwise people would say: 'The Warren Commission was fooled. They were fooled by that Russian, that lying Viktor Tronko.' Do you see? The Commission was very afraid. They were afraid to let Viktor Tronko tell them the one thing that they desperately wanted to believe."

"It's nice to know they were so careful about something," Kessler said. "Meanwhile, what was Eames telling LBJ?"

" 'We are working on him. But we cannot vouch that he is real.' "

"What about the drug option? Didn't Johnson try bullying Eames into that?"

"The President didn't know that there was a drug option. It was not his business, Eames would have said. It was an operational detail. A means. Presidents should be answered to in the matters of goals and results, he would have said. They were to be protected from knowledge of means."

Kessler was gaining a new respect for the late Herbert Eames, who had always before seemed just a slightly befuddled Colonel Blimp. And the pressure upon Eames, as Rosen made very clear, had come not only from Lyndon Johnson but from inside the Agency as well: namely Claude Sparrow. Sparrow argued perfervidly, all through the summer of 1964, that Tronko was still being coddled. That McAttee and his Soviet Bloc Division were botching the job. Squandering time, and worse. Sparrow argued for the dismantling of Tronko's personality by pharmaceutical means.

"But Sparrow was voted down."

"Yes. By Herbert Eames. One vote to zero," said Rosen.

"McAttee was opposed also, I assume."

"McAttee was mainly opposed. Usually. Sometimes he wobbled. Sometimes, I think, he was tempted. He felt all this very enormous pressure himself. If it had not been for Eames's attitude . . . who knows?"

"You were opposed?"

Max Rosen opened his mouth to speak, and then before doing so smiled slyly back at Kessler. "I was not among those consulted."

"Lentzer was opposed?"

"Adamantly. I think," said Rosen.

"And it didn't happen. No circumvention of Eames's order. Is that right? You're telling me that, from the moment he set foot on American soil, Tronko was never drugged?"

"Only with vodka," said Rosen, pleased at his own wit.

But vodka, at least in Kessler's experience, does not turn skin gray or cause star-shaped cataracts. If drug tortures were really forbidden by order of the Director, Kessler wonders, why should Max Rosen know so much about them?

After forty-five minutes Kessler has recorded every fact and nuance he can recall from the hour with Max Rosen. The afternoon's session with Sparrow is still to be done, but Sparrow will just have to wait; Kessler needs food. He needs a little respite. Liquor he needs, followed eventually by coffee, a shower, then perhaps more remembering. And there is one other chore he wants to get done, back out in that alley beneath the scaffold, while the spoor is still fresh. He lifts the bedspread and slides his notebook (the first one, now almost full thanks to Sparrow and Rosen) in between the mattress and the box spring, a precaution that seems ludicrous and amateurish even to Kessler, but nonetheless worth taking. Then he goes downstairs to the Tabard's restaurant, a modest room that owns a small half-secret renown for its duck and its desserts, unfortunately, and is therefore crammed to capacity with sleek young lawyers and their husbands and boyfriends at this hour on a Saturday night. Kessler puts in his name.

He fetches himself a martini. He stands for a few minutes in the doorway of the bar, staring into the dining room. Watching pairs of heads lean together over white damask, for the passing of little confidences that more likely involve power than romance, though most likely a synergy of both. He hears the quiet laughter, sees the savvy smiles. Large globes of Cabernet are raised. Not a sole human within Kessler's view seems to be younger than twenty-six or older than, oh, fifty; there is also a dire uniformity of good clothes, good looks, good haircuts. The restaurant has never been his favorite part of the Tabard. Most of the people seated in there are Washington professionals who would never dream of taking a room in the old fleabag if, God forbid, they found themselves somehow transformed to out-of-towners; and the hotel guests, reciprocally, seem to find their food elsewhere. Kessler himself has no energy and no time, tonight, for prowling out across town for his dinner. So instead he gawks, still funky from the day's exertions and wearing no tie.

Nora would loathe this roomful of people, he thinks suddenly. Her lips would go white. He isn't sure how he feels about the scene himself. Everyone in this city has his or her precious little secrets to broker—but then who is he, at the moment, to look down upon that?

Flagging for another martini, he asks the bartender whether the patio door is locked.

"Patio is closed," says the bartender, instead of answering the question. The bartender seems to be a male model fallen on lean times, who wears a ruffled linen shirt and a gold ear stud and believes himself to be very busy. "Lunch only."

"Fine. All I want is air," Kessler says aloud to no one, turning away.

He moves deliberately, like any innocent tourist wandering where he shouldn't. He slides out the door onto the red brick patio, threading among the wrought-iron chairs and umbrella tables until he is beyond sight from the bar window. He carries his drink. He strolls, but quickly and purposefully. At the rear of this little interior courtyard he sees that the iron gate out to the alley is held by a heavy padlock; on the other hand, the wall is only chest-high. Kessler rests his elbows over it, sipping gin, gazing down at the same view he had from far above: cobbles, a few vehicles, loading docks, garbage. He glances back toward the bar window, to confirm that he is safely eclipsed. He drinks. Beautiful night, though cold. No stars, no moon, but beautiful. Kessler is posing himself, the lonesome traveler taking air on a patio. All right, enough, let's get this done fast. He sets his glass on a table. If Lovesong and Buddyboy are watching at all, Kessler figures, they are watching the front. He swings one leg then the other over the wall, hangs, and drops six feet to the alley.

He is looking for that crumpled cigarette pack.

He is keen to see what brand Max Rosen smokes because he wants to know who Max Rosen is. Lentzer, he remembers, was addicted to Chesterfields. Do they still even make Chesterfields? If not, what is the modern equivalent? Would an aging Sol Lentzer be the right man, this many years later, to run delicate errands for Jed McAttee—errands that might include meeting with journalists on rooftops? Kessler is inclined to think so.

No sign of the pack where it should have fallen, in the alley near the base of the building shell. No sign of it there or anywhere. Kessler goes down on hands and knees to peer underneath the Volkswagen camper. He inspects the top of a dumpster, then behind it and under it, finally opens the dumpster lid to frown in at the contents for several minutes. Sees no cigarette pack in there, and he hasn't the heart, not yet, to climb in and grovel around. He stands on the Volkswagen's bumper and cranes for a view of the roof of the shed. The shed roof is a long shot, seemingly out of range, but Kessler knows that this sort of thing can sometimes defy reason and probability. Sure enough, the roof is bare. He searches behind garbage cans and in them. Nothing. An immaculate alley, this is, except for all the other and less meaningful trash.

Now Kessler wants that pack more than ever; the longer he hunts, the more tantalizing it seems. He knows he has not misremembered the act—Rosen crumpling a cigarette pack, tossing it over the edge—because Kessler noted it consciously at the time, forming a mental resolution to come back. In fact his attention had lurched out into space, diving after the pack, and Kessler had covered his twitch with a shift of position so that Max Rosen wouldn't notice. But maybe he did notice. Maybe Rosen has already been down here, policing up after himself.

Kessler gazes up again toward the fifth floor of the building shell, estimating positions and distances. Probable trajectories, with a breeze and without. This time he registers the fact that the ladder is gone. Pulled in out of sight, evidently, after Rosen had steadied it for Kessler's passage back across. Well, that's not surprising. More foolish would be to have left the ladder in place, inviting troublesome curiosity when the workers returned by daylight. But if Rosen managed that chore alone and without a great clatter of noisy aluminum—lifting the ladder from one end, bringing it in off the alley—he must be stronger than Kessler would have judged him. The alternative, of course, is that he had assistance. A second pair of hands. The alternative is not to be contemplated, since Kessler has enough to worry over already. Neck bent, staring up, Kessler suddenly realizes where the cigarette pack has gone. Possibly. Oh dear.

It never fell more than one story. Or two. It was blown back into the building shell, somewhere not far below where Kessler and Rosen stood talking. Just the faintest breeze would have

been sufficient for that, much less breeze than what Kessler was
willing to postulate for getting the damn thing onto the roof of
the shed. Tumbling unevenly in the air, nudged by a little gust,
it could have stalled back on itself and come to rest on one of
those naked ledges. Up on the third or fourth floor. Yes, obviously it had. It must have. Sure proof of the cogency of this new
hypothesis is that, having reached it, Kessler discovers that his
poor frostbitten body is now leaking sweat. He is hot and
queasy with dread, knowing that he has got to go back up there.

He picks his way through the dark, among pallets of decorative block and mixers and scrap wood and bags of cement, in
search of a fire stairway. Naturally there is no fire stairway. Not
even a rough framing of one. The crew hasn't yet got around to
putting in a fire stairway because as everyone knows construction workers, like little boys, enjoy climbing up and down scaffolding; part of their professional sense of adventurous competence, no doubt. Kessler himself, personally, has had more than
his fill of adventurous competence for tonight. Also, if he were
in the building trades it would be as a cement finisher, specializing in sidewalks. He most emphatically does not enjoy climbing,
not ladders, not scaffolding, not mountains, not even overly
steep sets of stairs. Gravity is one of the last absolutes he believes in. Still, he will climb if he must. Under silent protest,
with grave misgivings, feeling like a lunatic, he will climb.

He climbs.

Hauling himself up to the second story isn't difficult, with the
cold iron piping of the scaffold frame offering plenty of footholds. Thereafter, harder, because the footholds are merely the
same, the reaches and pulls seem longer, and the ground is
farther away. In fact the ground has become an enemy again, a
distant menace. Kessler clambers. He jams his feet into notches,
he hoists, he lays his belly over the coarse planking of another
level and huffs, grateful. He is not good at this. His mouth is
wide open, his eyes too. He fills one hand with wood splinters.
His blood thumps metronomically in his ears. He climbs high—
no real great altitude, but sufficient to focus his mind on the
dull reality that only his own grip separates him from a splat-
tered skull. At one point the whole scaffold shifts a small bit
and he clutches desperately, feeling panic like a jolt of pain,
preparing to topple. But he doesn't and the scaffold doesn't
topple. So when his breath is back he has no excuse but to go

higher. In his terror, Kessler is methodical. He places each hand and each foot with individual conscious acts of mad concentration, assuring himself of the grip before he commits weight and life. He ascends this way to the fourth floor of the building shell and sprawls there on the boards like a shipwreck survivor coughed up on a beach. He pants—from exertion and fear in about equal measure. Before the panting has quieted, before his heartbeat steadies, he has begun again to shiver. From cold and fear in about equal measure.

Now that he has gotten where he wanted to get, Kessler senses more vividly the stupidity of this whole idea. Cigarette pack or no. It just cannot be so crucial to know Max Rosen's brand of tobacco, or Max Rosen's true identity, or for that matter even Max Rosen's innermost secrets and motives, whatever the devil those might be. Not nearly so crucial as to be worth risking a broken neck. Screw it. Kessler is not concerned about Max Rosen right now. Nor even about Mel Pokorny. He is concerned about young Michael Kessler.

He raises himself to his feet: carefully. He steps across from the scaffold into the building. There is scarcely any light and the floor here is as cluttered as the one above, a confusion of dim irregular shadows, so he scuffs along with small strides, wary of tripping over a pallet or a stray block or a two-by-four toothed with gleaming nails. He steadies himself with hands fanned out, palms down. Methodical. Don't hurry now. Every precaution. Kessler takes another two steps and part of a third and then is hit on his right hip by a shocking thick low animal force that drives him right off his feet, sideways, into darkness and air.

He paddles his arms hopelessly.

15

Dexter Lovesong can hear Buddyboy coming from halfway down the block. *Trotting,* for Christ sake, then skidding and changing course, flapping his shoe leather like castanets. The blood rises in Lovesong's neck and at once his shirt collar is as tight as a tourniquet. But he does not shift position, does not raise his eyes above the car seat; there is no need to look up, since Lovesong can so clearly imagine it. More noisy footfalls, coming closer, then abruptly crossing back to the far side of N Street. He's hunting for the right car, Lovesong knows. He has already forgotten the make and color. Hunting for me. All urgent and earnest and breathless—as Lovesong pictures him—running wildly up the pavement, dodging from one parked car to another, with some very hot fat message that demands announcing his presence and Lovesong's also to anyone who might care enough to open an ear or an eye. Lovesong may just as well sit up now, because his painstakingly devised invisibleness has been squandered, his cover is a joke. But he does not sit up. Instead, for his own satisfaction, he imagines Buddyboy taking a round of .270 magnum in the forehead. Right there in the middle of N Street, picked off his feet and laid flat, nothing but daylight and bone stubble left from the eyebrows up. Now that is precisely what would happen, Lovesong imagines, if God were just, and a sniper.

The right rear door of the Audi is jerked open. Lovesong, supine on the floor of the back seat, rolls over disgustedly onto one elbow. Near his knees is the door panel from the left rear door, which he pried off with the same screwdriver that he then used to punch three holes through the Audi's thin sheet metal. The holes are in a tight cluster, low on the door, just beneath the spot where Lovesong's head now rests at a crimped angle. His shoulders are twisted. His suit is filthy. The three holes have given him an excellent if uncomfortable view of the front door and upper windows of the Tabard Inn. Buddyboy gapes from the curb, his shiny young face gone suddenly slack. Buddyboy seems to have forgotten, for an instant, whatever hot fat message he came running to deliver.

"Does Motor Pool know you did that?"

"Shut up," says Dexter Lovesong. "What? What is it?"

"I heard a noise."

"You heard a noise." Lovesong closes his eyelids and begins counting slowly to twenty, with measured breathing, as his idiot of a doctor has recommended. He imagines himself poking holes in Buddyboy with a screwdriver.

"Loud. Back in the alley."

Seven, eight, nine, he opens them early, as usual. "A loud noise. Okay. A shot?"

"No," says Buddyboy. "No. I don't know. More like a swivel chair thrown through a plate-glass window."

16

Kessler has a terror of not finishing. It is a recurrent fear, quiet and corrosive each time it visits, arriving at some awful moment in the course of every long difficult investigative article and every book he has ever written or tried to write: the mutter of doubt, the loss of single-mindedness, the loss of focus, the loss of momentum; the almost audible creak and groan of an edifice on the verge of collapse. The loss of authorial nerve. The loss of energy. Nothing is worse. No other sort of trauma has the power to leave Kessler more depressed, more fuddled and terrified, than that moment of failing faith when he senses that whatever this thing is he has been trying to write is not, after all, going to get written. He panics, wanders the neighborhood, sometimes for days. Hides out in afternoon bar-and-grill places. Feels his identity leaking away like the oxygen pressure in a submarine. And this is not an illusory phobia; he has in fact lost whole months, whole years of work, entire two-inch piles of half-complete, unsalvageable manuscript. Gone: patient turned cold on the operating table. All right, no point in any more suturing, wrap it up and take it away. Mark it for the morgue.

Kessler glances again at this young emergency-room doctor, with his crooked glasses and his shaggy curly hair, and thinks: No, it's much more traumatic than that. For them, there is always another patient.

Death from cerebral hemorrhage or spleen rupture as result of a fall is one way of not finishing, Kessler thinks. But there are others, too, which may be just as painful and just as certain. Loss of momentum. Loss of nerve. He thinks of Mel Pokorny and of Viktor Tronko, and then of the late Afrikaner naturalist Eugène Marais, subject of a certain two-inch pile on the desk back in Kessler's New Haven apartment. Who *is* the patient on the table? Kessler can't at the moment see the face very clearly.

He can't even tell whether the body is cold or warm. He is very confused. Maybe that's a symptom of concussion. He says nothing about it to the young doctor, who is still amusing himself with a rubber hammer and the bottoms of Kessler's feet.

"Who called the ambulance?" This is the doctor's forty-ninth question, roughly, in fifteen minutes.

"Friends of mine," Kessler lies. He remembers listening to Lovesong and Buddyboy discuss the security and medical considerations, in that order, bearing upon whether they should move him themselves or just find a telephone. They chose the telephone, but it was better than deserting him entirely. Kessler still thought at that point that his back might be broken, and he was also a little concerned lest the Volkswagen's owner come along before he could get himself up. There was ragged fiberglass everywhere.

"Where are they, these friends?" says the doctor.

"They went home. When they saw I was okay."

"You're not okay. No one *knows* whether you're okay. I don't want to alarm you, but it's perfectly possible you could still die from this fall, Mr. Kessler."

"Thanks for not alarming me."

"If you aren't properly cared for. Observed. Can you stay with those friends tonight?"

"No. I'm at a hotel."

"*Can* you stay with them? You need to be waked up and checked on every two hours."

"No. They're just acquaintances actually. No."

"Then you aren't leaving this hospital."

"Sure I am."

"Not tonight, no. We'll get you admitted to a ward. Right after the spinal X ray."

"I feel okay. I was lucky." For instance, it could have been the bare cobbles of the alley that he landed on. Or, worse still, the heirloom Vespa. "Of course I'm leaving."

"No. No, you're staying."

"Wrong."

"Observation. This is standard in any head-trauma situation. Just for tonight."

"No."

"Listen carefully: yes."

"Screw you, Doc."

"Fine. 'Screw you, Doc,' is fine. All right. But before you leave this building tonight, if you do, you'll have to sign yourself out 'against medical advice.' That's a category we reserve for stupid people who may also be sick." No more bedside manner. The doctor's voice has gone hard, and he now begins swatting his own palm with the hammer, snapping his fist closed on the rubber head with each stroke. His reflexes seem to be good. "After that, you can die in a taxi or at a hotel or in an all-night laundromat, if you insist on it."

"Don't be so touchy," says Kessler. "You're not the only one who's had a hard night. How would *you* like to fall four stories and go through the roof of a Volkswagen camper?"

The doctor flattens his lips together, saying nothing. Then: "I apologize." He looks down at his penny loafers.

"All right. So. Okay, I'll stay."

Kessler doesn't care much for the idea of being stupid and sick at the same time, it's bad enough to endure them consecutively. He allows himself to be booked into a room upstairs, on the far side of a white curtain from a man who is either snoring ecstatically or dying of emphysema, where it is promised that a nurse will come in every two hours to wake Kessler up, gaze into his pupils, ask him a few questions, and ascertain whether he has a brain cavity full of blood or spinal fluid dripping out of his ears. Kessler has decided to be a good patient. He doesn't even ask what it's all going to cost him. But if they were truly concerned for my health, he thinks, they would wake me every two hours just to say this: "Forget about Viktor Tronko. Get out of Washington."

Which is precisely what Nora would be saying also, for her own reasons, if he gave her the chance.

Nora's reasons happen to derive from concern for his literary soul, not his physical welfare (though if she knew about unseen strangers throwing him off high buildings that too would certainly find a place in her arguments). She would tell him, he knows, that he should go home and get back to work on the book. Nora retains a fierce hatred for the city of Washington. She despises what she calls the adolescent fascination with power and secrecy. Her own bad experience only exacerbated this feeling—she has told Kessler that she despised the very same things about the city even back when she thought she was happily married. She considers espionage a game for small boys. She seems to have forgiven Kessler, grudgingly, for having once lived in this place and devoted himself to the spy beat. On the other hand, from the first moment she heard about the Marais project, she professed to believe—bless her heart, one in a thousand—that writing a book about this holy lunatic could be extremely goddamn worthwhile.

In fact she did not even use the word "worthwhile"; she used the word "important." The very thing that makes Nora's set of attitudes so troublesome, so unanswerable, is that they coincide closely with some of Kessler's own.

Kessler can remember his own first response to the stark outline of the Marais story—though for Kessler that was more than five years ago now. He was in Kenya, over Christmas of 1975. He was alone, and with no premeditated itinerary. The Church Committee had just issued its interim report, the newspapers and magazines were full of stories about CIA assassination planning—Lumumba, Trujillo, Diem, Allende—but Kessler himself was already withdrawn from all that. He felt distant and cynical. He had written his last CIA story a year before. He had run into Pokorny at the Capitol, and made excuses to slip away quickly, which was itself quite a departure from old patterns. Now he was on a vacation, a suitably drastic escape from Washington and his recent life and work there; at the same time, Kessler thought he might drop down for a tour of the Serengeti while he was in the neighborhood, hoping maybe to find something to write about. Big animals, or something. Lions interested him mildly. Possibly there was a situation about poaching, tourism, and the politics of *uhuru.* He would see. The notion of finding a story was really for the sake of the IRS as much as anything. Mainly he had come to bake his sinuses dry, and walk some dirt roads, and surround himself with the sound of a language he didn't speak. He could have chosen better for that last, since there was already a Colonel Sanders franchise in downtown Nairobi and plenty of white English faces, some newly arrived, some having never left. But he stayed away from the patio cafe at the New Stanley Hotel and got on out of Nairobi as fast as possible. When his bus stopped in Mombasa, down on the sweaty coast, he went into a drugstore and bought four or five paperback books from the small but eclectic selection on a metal rack. One was a Penguin that caught his eye with its cover: a garish painting in oranges and creams of a grotesquely gravid queen termite. She was swollen like a fatty sausage, attended by workers and soldiers just a tiny fraction of her size. Kessler stared briefly, then added this paperback to his pile. He had never heard of the author. The book cost him less than a pound Kenyan. Its title was *The Soul of the White Ant*.

It was the masterwork of Eugène Marais, published posthumously under weird circumstances. At that time, of course, Kessler knew nothing about the circumstances. It was just something to read in English, a book with a gaudy cover and a nice title.

He took the book with him up the coast to Malindi, a bizarre little settlement that seemed to fancy itself the Palm Springs of post-independence Kenya, where Kessler got an intestinal bug and spent a comically miserable Christmas confined to his own luxurious beach hut, surrounded at not great enough distance by German and Irish skin divers and their loud bad music. Fortunately the hut had plumbing. All day on the twenty-fifth Kessler did not walk any farther than thirty yards to the main lodge, and even that he did only to carry back more mineral water. Mostly he lay on the bed, beneath a mosquito net, while a half dozen geckos belayed from the various walls and watched him for vital signs. He drank his water. He read about termites, and about a man who had studied them.

The name Eugène N. Marais is known to all Afrikaans-speaking South Africans as a writer of short stories and verse, according to a short preface at the front of the paperback, contributed to the original edition by the book's translator. *He himself, however, would wish to be remembered for his lifelong study of termites and apes.*

The preface was less than two pages long. When he had finished reading it, Kessler read it again. Having finished the whole book, five hours later, he read the preface once more. It gave just a bare outline of Marais's early adult life, from the time he came out of college and began work as a journalist in Pretoria, through the years he spent in London during the Boer War, studying medicine until he was nearly a doctor and then switching suddenly into law, up to his return to South Africa as a practicing lawyer. Evidently Eugène Marais loathed or was bored by the legal profession; Kessler liked him already. Losing patience quickly, Marais had abandoned his law practice and gone north into the Transvaal. *A scholar and a man of culture,* said the translator's preface, *he chose nevertheless to live for a period extending over many years in a "rondhavel" or hut in the lonely Waterberg mountains, learning to know and make friends with a troop of wild baboons, whose behavior he wished to study. He tamed them to such a degree that he could move among them and handle them with impunity. At the same time he busied himself with the other end of the chain and studied termite life, a study which often meant tremendous drudgery and needed endless patience.*

During those years of lonely drudgery, Kessler read, Marais made no attempt to publish his observations on animal behavior —neither those from the baboon study nor from what his translator termed the other end of the chain. But finally a friend talked him into writing one article, for an Afrikaans periodical called *Die Huisgenoot.* That article was well received, and so over the next several years he was persuaded to write more, entertaining the readers of *Die Huisgenoot* with a series of odd facts and even odder ideas derived from his termite investigations.

His years of unceasing work on the veld, said the translator's preface, *led Eugène Marais to formulate his theory that the individual nest of the termites is similar in every respect to the organism of an animal, workers and soldiers resembling red and white blood corpuscles, the fungus gardens the digestive organs, the queen functioning as the brain, and the sexual flight being in every aspect analogous to the escape of spermatozoa and ova.* Well.

Not long after those articles appeared in *Die Huisgenoot,* Kessler read, they were plagiarized in a book published by Maurice Maeterlinck.

Kessler knew of Maeterlinck as a playwright, a Belgian who had won the Nobel and scored great European successes with his verse dramas, but evidently he had dabbled in natural-history writing also. An earlier book by Maeterlinck, about the life of the honey bee, had been a best-seller all over the Continent. Then in 1926 he gave forth with *The Life of the White Ant,* in which Maeterlinck described how a termitary with its elaborate organic integration was an uncanny analogue to the human body. *This theory aroused great interest at the time,* according to Eugène Marais's translator, *and was generally accepted as an original one formulated by Maeterlinck. The fact that an un-*

*known South African observer had developed the theory after
many years of indefatigable labour was not generally known in
Europe. Excerpts from Marais's articles had, however, appeared
in both the Belgian and the French press at the time of their
publication in South Africa. Indeed, the original Afrikaans articles would have been intelligible to any Fleming, for Afrikaans
and Flemish are very similar.*

The book in Kessler's hands was assembled from those *Huisgenoot* articles, which had been originally published during the
six years in advance of Maeterlinck's act of piracy. Anyone who
read the earlier versions, the Marais versions, could not hesitate
to grant Marais the credit that justice and Maurice Maeterlinck
owed him—at least, so said the translator. Then the preface
ended: *Eugène Marais intended writing a fuller and more scientific volume, but this intention was frustrated by his untimely
death a few months ago.*

The translator's preface had been written in 1936. *The Soul
of the White Ant* was first published in London the following
year. That much Kessler gleaned from the copyright information at the front of his Penguin. He recovered from the intestinal bug, he escaped Malindi as gratefully as he had escaped
Washington, and the Serengeti lion gave him no story. For five
weeks Kessler thought intermittently about Eugène Marais.
Then he flew back to the United States and began a casual
search in used bookstores. For another half year all he knew
about the man was what came from that preface, and from the
thin book it introduced: "untimely death," plagiarism, and a
fevered vision of termites. Kessler was curious. But nothing
happened quickly.

Throughout the next two years, some part of his brain always
told Kessler to stay away, to think again and better—to recognize that this Marais fancy of his was a very bad and impracti-
cable idea. A nonsensical waste of time, at best. At worst, a cold
blind alley. He was wary of ever really starting. He recalls vividly how wary he was. At 4 A.M., when the nurse comes in to
wake him and compare the size of his pupils, Kessler is already
wide awake, thinking.

If he leaves in the morning, as soon as the hospital will release him, and stops at the Tabard for just long enough to check
out, he can be back in New Haven by early evening. He can
have the Marais typescript in his hands, and a cup of decent

coffee at his elbow. He can write just two or three sentences, half a page maybe, reestablishing contact and just the tiniest bit of momentum, then begin again earnestly on Monday morning. He can call Nora and tell her. The Washington thing was a bad idea, he can say. A false start. I'm back with the termite man.

Kessler knows that he is not going to do any of this and only suspects that he should.

He doesn't want to bleed to death. Not the quiet way, alone in a hotel room and leaking blood into his cranium until the pressure squashes away consciousness—and not Mel Pokorny's way either. But he has a greater terror of not finishing. It's confusing now because Viktor Tronko, like Eugène Marais, is something that he has begun.

17

Late Sunday afternoon he drives out to Rockville and finds Barry Koontz, the congenital pack rat, living without furniture.

The house is an empty shell. Nothing left from the way it was when Kessler last saw it except the rich cream carpeting, now badly in need of a professional shampoo. Kessler can still make out marks in the pile from where the piano sat. Naked picture hooks poke forth from the walls. There are no lamps. No curtains. Even the ladybug magnets that crawled up and down the refrigerator door are gone, and through the kitchen window Kessler notices two scuffed patches of bare dirt paired together in the middle of the lawn, but the swing set itself has disappeared. To take curtains and swing set, Kessler thinks, is the act of a vehement person. Barry has carried a few file boxes of government paper up from the basement to function as chairs and ottomans. He has brought a card table home from Montgomery Ward. He serves Kessler's gin and his own scotch in fine crystal lowball glasses, which seem to be almost all she has left him. The odd thing is that Barry looks not much worse than ever. He always wore wrinkled suits, he was always half bald (since adolescence, for all Kessler knows), and the gray crescents under his eyes have always come and gone routinely in conjunction with cycles of compulsive overwork. He raises his glass at Kessler with a grin that is genuine, though perhaps a little pinched.

Kessler feels sad and embarrassed. "When did she go?" he says.

"Four or five months ago. I think about four months, yeah."

"You think?"

"I was teaching two new courses, plus trying to finish an article. And then I got stuck on this committee to redesign the curriculum. It was a crazy time. Just brutal."

"Christ, Barry."

"She had a professional mover pack it all up. Took them less than a day, you know? Very fast, very efficient. Not that expensive. I spent a night on the floor at my office, because it was already hard enough on her."

"On her."

"Yeah, that seemed best. I stayed away. No scenes, no screaming. You could see, it was taking its toll on Patsy, inside. Not an easy thing for her to do. I suppose I've got to admit it was brave. Four months at least, yeah, because that was before Halloween. Otherwise I would have had Matthew out around the neighborhood, in his Garfield costume."

"Barry, it's me, Kessler. Stop this bullshit."

"Adam's too old now. So he says. Eleven in July and he's too old for Halloween, can you imagine? My God. How old were you when you got too old for Halloween, Michael? I was about twenty-three, still going out at least to steal pumpkins and throw cherry bombs at cars."

"*Barry.* Are you all *right?*"

Barry Koontz stares at his ice cubes, fused, circling in the glass like a cam.

"Agh. Yeah, I am, Michael. Yes."

"She took them back to Colorado?"

"Right."

"Is this permanent?"

"Oh, I suppose. I think so, yeah."

"Were you screwing around?" Kessler knows the answer to that one already, if he knows anything at all about human nature: not Barry. Why he nevertheless felt the need to ask, he isn't sure. Generalized crisis of confidence, maybe.

"No, of course not," says Barry. "Nothing like that. It was just a thing between us. Patsy and me. Just a thing she felt she needed to do, apparently. You know?"

It was just a thing. No, Kessler doesn't know. He has never been married, and he has never been Barry Koontz. He is silent. He has no more questions, for once.

"Damn, though." Barry sips his scotch, and then faces Kessler directly with a flinty smile. "I mean damn."

They eat their steaks and drink their bottle of red, seated upon file boxes with the surface of the card table not far below their chins. Kessler does not mention Colorado again, or raise the subject of Viktor Tronko. He is in no particular hurry; in fact he is enjoying himself for the first time all week. Most of what they talk about involves people and events from their shared past, relatively harmless memories, ranging backward through the heyday of Senator Frank Church and Kessler's last gambits in political journalism all the way to their loathsome first term at Chicago Law School. You were right to get out when you did, Barry says, and at first Kessler, with some help from the gin and the wine, misunderstands him to mean: out of Washington. No, no, out of law school, of course. I've never doubted that for a minute, Kessler says. He adds, then, that Barry seems to have no reason for regretting he stayed. Barry shrugs. The subject passes, leaving Kessler with the impression that perhaps it is another tender area that shouldn't be probed further tonight. Barry asks him about his "personal life," by which prim formulation Barry means women, and Kessler describes the situation with Nora in two or three reticent sentences, trying not to seem coy but also hoping not to jinx himself. Barry knows him well enough to recognize that those couple sentences are sounding, for Kessler, a fundamentally new tone. So, Nora Walsh, Barry repeats. A music teacher with a young daughter. He is pronouncing the words out loud as though to test their feel on his own tongue, to grant his approval, to commit the important facts to memory. Well well, Barry says.

Oh shut up, Kessler says, but can't suppress a grin.

They carry dishes out to the kitchen and dump them. They each carry back a scotch. Barry recounts an old story that they both know by heart and both consider hilarious, about the distempered man who taught them torts and later died in a tram accident at Knott's Berry Farm. By now this particular tale is almost a ritualistic recitation, like Homer, and they cackle together on cue in boozy falsettos. Kessler tells a funny story about being chased by a rhino, in a forest in the Nepalese lowlands, while he was doing the early research for what became his tiger book: how he ended up stuck to his hips in the mud of a small oxbow pond, into which the rhino was too smart to follow, and his Nepalese hosts pulled him out with a long rope because they themselves were more wary of crocodiles than of rhino. Mud over every inch of me, says Kessler, I had to be dragged across twenty feet of it on my belly, and those khakis

still smell like a sulfur swamp. The particular species of crocodile in question, says Kessler, is called a marsh mugger, though
they didn't tell me that part of it until we were back at the
lodge. Barry tilts his chin up and laughs, deeply, silently. Then
he says a few flattering things to Kessler about the tiger book.
And then he goes back to the kitchen for the scotch bottle.

They sink deeper into the squashed-down tops of their file
boxes. Barry tells a story about Senator Howard Baker, not
from the Church Committee period but from Watergate, a story
told to him by another staff counsel and illustrative of the subtle
truth, says Barry, that you can't believe everything you see on
TV. He tells another in roughly the same vein, from his own
experience, about the day Frank Church held up the poison-
dart gun for a photographer and appeared thusly posed in
newspapers all over the world. He tells one about the elaborate
negotiations that preceded Jed McAttee's consent to testify;
among the critical issues, says Barry, was the question of where
the network news cameramen would be allowed to place their
lights. McAttee was all in favor of good lighting, as long as the
floods would not be so positioned as to make him appear old or
sinister. In that order, says Barry. He tells of calling on McAttee at Langley during the course of those negotiations, getting
to ride the Director's private elevator and see (but not eat in)
the Director's private dining room, and of then forgetting to
turn in his visitor's badge when he left the building. Six months
passed, one night there came a panicked phone call, and they
sent a man out here to the house, says Barry, at ten o'clock the
same evening to pick the silly thing up. Six months, ten in the
evening, *you* figure that one. Fortunately the badge was still in
my side jacket pocket, says Barry. Thank God I hadn't had the
suit Martinized. Kessler laughs. Barry begins telling then of a
bizarre trip he made to New Orleans in early 1976, and before
the story has gone five sentences Kessler realizes that this is not
going to be one of the funny ones.

Barry had gone down there to interview a man named Alex
Djevdjevich, who as it turned out died suddenly.

Nobody had ever heard of Alex Djevdjevich until the late
sixties, Barry says, long after the Warren Commission had completed and published its report. Practically nobody, he corrects
himself. Djevdjevich had never gotten into the headlines. If you

had sat down and actually read the Warren Report, you would
have known a little about him, only a little, most of it not very
interesting. Anyway, how many people ever did that? But he
was there, he was in the record, Djevdjevich, having testified for
two solid days before an assistant staff counsel to the Commission and one stenographer, in a hearing room somewhere in
Washington. Also the FBI was well aware of him; they had
been carrying a dossier on the guy since at least 1942. Almost
three hundred pages by the time I saw it, says Barry. Otherwise,
though, he was obscure. A tertiary figure. Until 1967, when
everyone suddenly got so interested in the famous photograph
of Oswald with the rifle. Until then, Djevdjevich had kept a
very low profile.

He had been off in Japan and Indonesia for most of that time,
since even a half year *before* the assassination—or at least so he
told me, says Barry. Came back especially to testify for the
Commission, in early '64, then left again quickly. He had business interests out there, evidently. Hotels or something, or
travel services, some sort of government contracts involving
tourism. It was vague. Like so much of the rest, with
Djevdjevich. The FBI found one source claiming that
Djevdjevich had never set foot in Indonesia, for instance. *Korea.*
Korea, that's where he really had been. North or South? asked
Barry. Nobody knew. The Bureau had never thought to inquire,
and that souce was no longer in contact. Very typical. With
Alex Djevdjevich, says Barry, reality always seemed to be just
an arcade of shimmering epistemological possibilities.

But he was not slimy, says Barry. He was a rather likable
man. He had a good wit, and he had charm. Almost every
source who talked about Djevdjevich, in fact, mentioned that
one point: charm. He was one of those guys the word was invented for. Charming Alex. He listened well, and he enjoyed
talking. An old-style conversationalist. Very fluent and gracious, even in English, which was his fifth or sixth language, I
think, says Barry. It was no wonder that Lee Oswald should
have been infatuated. If that's what it was. On a form he filled
out for the Texas Employment Commission, Oswald had listed
Djevdjevich as a reference and then described the relationship
as *closest friend,* that's a quote, says Barry. This was in August
or September of '63. Closest friend, despite the fact that

Djevdjevich had disappeared from his life five months earlier. Supposedly gone off to do business in Jakarta.

And there was one other factor besides charm, says Barry. Oswald was glad to have someone he could talk to in Russian. He was hungry to practice the language, didn't want to lose it. His fluency in Russian was one of the few things, so very few, that made him special. That's why he wouldn't let Marina learn English, and that's why he glommed onto Alex Djevdjevich. Or at least so we are told, in the official understanding, says Barry.

Kessler says nothing. He sits on his box, back to the wall, legs out, and sips scotch.

"I read everything we had on Djevdjevich before I went down there, of course," says Barry. "Two or three times. Studied it."

"What did you have on him?"

"Not that much. The FBI file, which was fat but very rough. Confusing. Transcripts of previous interrogations of Djevdjevich himself, plus a lot of unchecked and uncheckable hearsay from other sources. And then we had the transcript of his Warren Commission testimony. And a bit more—a few scraps that had been gathered by our own staff investigators. Not so much, altogether, that I couldn't memorize practically every fact."

"You always do that?"

"No. But with Djevdjevich it seemed like a good idea."

Barry flew to New Orleans in February of 1976 and got a day and a half with Djevdjevich before the interviews were abruptly terminated.

Djevdjevich showed no apparent reluctance about talking into Barry's recorder. They held their sessions in Barry's room at the Marriott, and on the second day Djevdjevich announced quite cheerfully that he would like to adjourn long enough for lunch and a couple of errands, but that he would meet Barry again in two hours. Fine, Barry said. At that point, Barry tells Kessler, they had covered much of Djevdjevich's adult life, up to and including his early acquaintance with Lee Oswald. But they had only just begun discussing the photograph.

"Did Djevdjevich take that photograph?" Kessler asks idly.

"No. Marina. According to the official understanding. The less official understanding, as you well know, makes it a clumsy composite."

"Oswald's head on the body of John Wilkes Booth. Amelia Earhart's arm. Jimmy Hoffa's chin."

"Exactly."

"A sundial in the background reading thirteen o'clock."

"Yes. All of that."

"What's *your* understanding?"

"That it was a genuine photo," says Barry. "I saw Djevdjevich's personally inscribed print."

"Before he died?"

"After," says Barry. "That was supposed to have been one of the errands."

"Was it your interest in the photo that upset him?"

"*If* he was upset. Maybe," says Barry. "Possibly. We'll never know."

What Barry had heard from Djevdjevich during their day and a half of talk jibed roughly with what he had read in the FBI file and the Warren Commission testimony—roughly, but not perfectly. It jibed only as well, Barry says, as the two other versions jibed with each other. The problem was not simply that third-party informants contradicted Djevdjevich's stories; Djevdjevich also contradicted himself. According to Barry, the autobiography of Alex Djevdjevich seemed to change slightly, to evolve slightly, with each repetition.

Like the song of the humpback whale, Kessler thinks, but he does not interrupt. By now he is half drunk.

Djevdjevich was born in 1913, or possibly 1916, in a town called Kishinev on the western fringe of Soviet Moldavia, not far from the Dniester River. The lunatic Balkans, says Barry. Moldavia itself was one of those rich and contested borderland zones, like Alsace-Lorraine, that had been wrenched back and forth over the centuries between two suzerainties, depending on whose empire was in ascendancy. Evidently Peter the Great fought over it, says Barry, then for a hundred years or so it belonged to Romania, then the tsars got it back for a while, then Romania again, then the Soviets. The international border had been yo-yoing to and fro, charted on one side of the town of Kishinev and then on the other, for as long as history could remember. The hills around Kishinev were fertile and the climate was mild, a region of orchards and vineyards, which was apparently what caused the place to be fought over. Wine and brandy. Djevdjevich's father was a thriving middle-class vintner, not a producer but a wholesaler, who bought by the barrel and exported through Odessa, according to one version. According to another, he was a fallen-away Orthodox priest who worked as a day laborer and proselytized socialist revolution. Take your pick, says Barry. Alex had half a dozen older siblings of whom one, a brother, may or may not have preceded him to the United States. If so, the brother changed his name and the family lost touch with him. Alex never knew for sure whether the brother had really made it to America. Or so he said. Anyway, for Alex himself that journey came much later. At the time he was born—whether you took 1913 as the date or 1916 —Moldavia was definitely part of the Russian Empire, and Alex learned Russian as his first language. But as the Revolution began in Moscow and everything got crazy, Moldavia declared itself independent, with a call for land reform and the reestablishment of the Romanian language. The Bolsheviks invaded in early winter of 1918 and held Kishinev for precisely eight days—until a division of Romanian Regular Army booted them out. Why am I telling you all this? asks Barry. Good question. Because it's the perfect analogue to everything else you'll hear about Alex Djevdjevich, is why. Was he a Russian or a Romanian? Was he a wave or was he a particle? The answer is yes.

He gave me the whole history-and-geography-of-Moldavia spiel himself, Barry says, and I've never been able to forget it, though for all I know he was actually born in Minsk.

During that week when the Bolsheviks held Kishinev, Barry says, his father was executed. According to one of the versions. Put up against a stone wall and shot. Very unceremoniously. For being a kulak—which was not even accurate. Case of mistaken identity. That's what the FBI heard from Djevdjevich, as I remember. To the Warren Commission, who had his FBI file right there in front of them for reference, he claimed that his father lived to a happy old age in Bucharest. To me, Barry says, he explained that his father had *almost* been shot in 1918 but was saved at the last minute by a friendly commissar the old man had known in Odessa.

"Jesus," says Kessler.

"Right. And he knew perfectly well that we were helpless to verify or refute this stuff. He just kept talking. Inventing or remembering, who knows. Maybe it was some sort of game."

If you accept the commissar part, says Barry, then the next
bit follows rather plausibly: the young Alex was sent off to Kiev
for his secondary education, showed promise in math and mechanics, and graduated to a cadetship in the Red Army Engineers. After a year he was transferred to the Academy of the
Air Fleet, in Moscow, an elite school and a rare opportunity for
a Moldavian kid (some would say, a *highly unlikely* opportunity, Barry inserts), where they taught him among other things
how to fly. The trainer he learned on was an old Sopwith Pup,
captured on the ground during the Civil War and still in good
repair, notwithstanding the difficulty of getting spare parts. He
was assigned to a reconnaissance aviation squadron; he got further training, a little, in aerial photography. Then he logged a
good many hours over the Polish border, in a newer Soviet
biplane that was more powerful but more stupid to the touch—
so he described it, says Barry—than that old Sopwith. I don't
recall the name of the Soviet plane, says Barry.

"Don't apologize," says Kessler.

That version was in the FBI file, Barry explains. It came not
from Djevdjevich himself, but from a friend he made in Newport soon after arriving in this country, who claimed that
Djevdjevich had told him the story one night over dinner. The
leading alternative version was that he had learned to fly from a
British instructor in Greece, during the early 1930s. On an old
Sopwith Pup.

The FBI asked him about this particular discrepancy during
one of their many follow-ups. Djevdjevich asserted with no loss
of aplomb that the Newport friend's memory was simply mistaken. He had never been near any flying school in Moscow, he
told the Bureau. The Warren Commission, in their turn, never
asked. When I asked, says Barry, he told me that the Kiev-
Moscow version was quite correct, yes, he had most certainly
attended the Academy of the Air Fleet and was proud of it—
but that in 1942, as a recent immigrant, confused by his situation, he had been afraid to admit those facts to the FBI. The
Greece business had been a lie, was what he told me. The foolish lie of a scared young man.

"How old was he then? When the FBI was grilling him."

"The first time?"

"The first time."

"Twenty-nine," says Barry. "Or twenty-six. Depending on which birth date you use."

From Greece—according to the lie as recorded in FBI records—from Greece he had gone to Spain in 1936, and flew as a reconnaissance pilot for the Loyalist forces during the siege of Madrid. Another of the FBI's third-party informants had disputed that. No, if he flew in the Spanish war at all, said this unnamed source, it would almost certainly have been for the Fascists—an allegation that may have been founded merely in casual spite, but which cost Djevdjevich some trouble and put the Bureau to considerable extra work, since the point of the whole inquiry at that time was to check on suspicions that Djevdjevich might have Nazi contacts. The FBI decided no, that he wasn't a Nazi agent. At least, probably not.

On the other hand what he told *me,* says Barry, was that he had learned all of his Spanish in South America. That he had never fought at Madrid nor had anything to do with the Spanish war. "In those days, Mr. Koontz . . ."—it was a measure of the charm again, Barry explains, that he could say this kind of thing without sounding crass or cynical—"in those days, as in these, I was less interested in politics than in making a little money." Then a smile. I believed him, God help me, says Barry. A limited belief, in the verity of that particular statement. He dressed well, he drove a Chrysler. You could see he enjoyed having money. That wasn't in question. But I wanted to know a lot more, says Barry, about his particular brand of private enterprise.

"Wait a minute. We're in Spain, we're in Greece, now we're in South America," says Kessler. "How did he get out of Russia?"

"He walked."

"From Moscow? That's quite a feat. Even for a man with charm."

"No, of course not. From Moldavia."

"Ah, Moldavia. Land of mystery. All right, tell me about it, please."

"He was home in Kishinev on leave, so goes the story. The purges had begun. He was terrified by what Stalin was doing to the officer corps of the Army. He decided he wouldn't go back."

"A deserter. He would have been shot if they'd caught him, right?"

"It seems like he would have, yes. But he expected that or worse if he stayed. So goes the story. He walked west to the Prut River and hitched a ride on a barge. Got off on the Romanian bank, then hiked again, over the mountains. It was he and his father together, actually. The old man was a physical specimen, matching him stride for stride over a pass through the Carpathians. Fortunately it was summer. So goes the story."

"I thought his father had been shot."

"Not in this version," says Barry. "That's the other version. This is the version where his father winds up in Bucharest, chasing rich widows."

There is a little gap now, Barry warns. In all of the versions. Somehow 1936 becomes 1938. Somehow an ocean gets crossed. In autumn of 1938 we find him in Bogotá and Barranquilla, bouncing between the two cities, first as a pilot and then as deputy managing director of a down-at-heels Colombian airline known as SCADTA. At least, on the surface it was Colombian. The company was registered in Bogotá. Actually by then, though, it was owned mainly by Juan Trippe of Pan Am, and run for him by a bunch of Germans.

"Scatta?" Kessler says.

"SCAD-TA," Barry corrects him. "An acronym. Standing for, let me see, *Sociedad Colombo-Alemana de Transportes Aéreos.* It had the mail contract from the Colombian government, plus a bit of passenger traffic. How's your drink?"

Kessler looks. "Empty," he says.

Barry raises himself, teetering across the room to pour Kessler a refill. Neither of them bothers to mention ice.

"Alemana," says Kessler. "Nineteen thirty-eight."

"Right. Very good. That was part of the problem Djevdjevich had to face later on. This SCADTA outfit was practically a training academy for the Luftwaffe. It was run by a man named Peter Paul von Bauer, an Austrian, who had gotten himself into hock to Berlin before Pan American bought controlling interest. The planes were German. Most of the pilots were German. The airport managers, the mechanics, the radio men were German. Our State Department was working up to a case of serious bad nerves over the whole situation. They realized how easy it would be for a few SCADTA pilots one day to fly a surprise bombing raid on the Panama Canal. Or on the big Shell refineries on the island of Curaçao. Meanwhile, amid all those Germans were a Colombian figurehead president to satisfy the regulations in Bogotá, and one guy on a Yugoslav passport, named Alex Djevdjevich."

"What was his story this time?"

"That he had come in, all innocent, by way of Pan Am. That his presence there in the late 1930s represented one step toward de-Germanizing the SCADTA staff, which was precisely what the State Department had been whining for. In fact he made a very persuasive argument along those lines. Then in a reckless moment he went too far, telling the FBI that he had known Juan Trippe at Yale. But the dates didn't work on that one. Furthermore, Trippe denied it. No, no, Djevdjevich said a bit later, the FBI fellow had misunderstood him. It was his older brother who had been acquainted with Mr. Trippe—and with Henry Luce too, by the way—during their years at Yale. Alex himself had merely met Trippe one time, at a lawn party in Newport. Turned out that Juan Trippe remembered the party, or such a party, if not his encounter with Djevdjevich. And so the story held, more or less."

Kessler smiles crookedly. "Here's to charm."

Barry raises his glass also.

Whether or not he knew Trippe socially, whether or not he lied about it, didn't seem to matter back then in the thirties, says Barry. Djevdjevich was on the rise regardless. By 1939 he was clear of SCADTA and working for Pan Am itself, out of the Mexico City office.

"As a pilot?"

"No. Not a pilot. Some sort of management or promotional job. He traveled a lot to other capitals in Latin America. Met with government officials. Pan Am was still trying to win the concessions for some new South American routes. Mail and passenger. That was Djevdjevich's role, evidently."

"Grease. Bagman."

"No. I don't know. But there was never a hint of scandal over whatever he did down there for Pan Am."

"Never a hint, Judas. How boring for poor Alex."

In July of 1940 he made his first landfall in the United States, Barry says. Traveling still on the Yugoslav passport, he arrived by plane at New York and was granted resident alien status, as an employee of Pan American. He continued to make trips down to South America, apparently doing the same sort of work as before. For a year, he continued. Then he quit or was fired or—

"Hold on, Barry," says Kessler. "I'm getting too drunk, I missed something somewhere. Yugoslav passport, you said."

"Yugoslav."

"When was Moldavia annexed by Yugoslavia?"

"Never. Nowhere near."

"Then where did he get the passport?"

"At the Yugoslav Embassy in Amsterdam," Barry says. Kessler only stares at him. Barry repeats: "It was issued in Amsterdam. Sometime in 1937."

"Explain."

"I can't," says Barry. He shakes his head. "That was one of the things I planned to ask him about on the second afternoon."

He was fired or quit or for some reason parted ways with Pan Am, and now begins what I suppose you could think of as the gigolo period, says Barry. He had no job. He had no personal savings to speak of. He had no other source of income—none that he was ever willing to talk about, anyway. He spent the summer season of 1941 in Newport and most of the winter either in New York or down on Cape Hatteras, where some friends of his had an extra house. That's exactly the way he phrased it to the FBI, by the way, Barry says: Some friends of his had an extra house. I wonder what the Romanian word is for chutzpah. In any case, unemployment seems to have been no very great hardship. He worked on his tan. He dined out on his accent. He cultivated his poolside manner, we can assume. Later on he would claim that in the year following Pearl Harbor—this is roughly a quote, Barry says—he began "investigating investment opportunities in the travel business." For that, Barry says, you could read: "Found an heiress, and married her." She was eighteen years old and came from one of the most formidable new families in Charleston, South Carolina, only daughter of a man who owned hotels in Charleston, St. Simons, St. Augustine, and Palm Beach. Her old man was a parvenu then but I suspect the family name would sound resonant by now, Barry says, if you knew Charleston society. Djevdjevich referred to her as Sissy. Sissy's hosteler father was a great fan of the new son-in-law, evidently—while the marriage lasted, at least—having been won over by Djevdjevich's nice European style and the fact that he knew wines and forks and allowed the old man to beat him, narrowly, at golf.

"Golf?" says Kessler. "Where did the son of a bitch learn to play *golf?*"

Also Djevdjevich may have concocted a phony Romanian barony, Barry says. Told me he just couldn't remember, honestly, whether it was this father-in-law or the next one on whose behalf he had awarded himself a modest notional title. The marriage to Sissy lasted ten months. She divorced him. There were no children. Our Alex does not seem to have been especially heartsick over the split, though no doubt he regretted losing custody of those hotels.

"He told me: 'Sissy was a troubled girl. Very gorgeous. Sweet, sometimes. But hysterical.' That was all," Barry says. "Who knows what it meant."

Kessler nods. Who, indeed.

In June of 1942 he was arrested for the first time.

This was the incident that got the FBI interested, Barry says. He was detained by Army MPs outside of Dayton, Ohio, for taking photographs near a perimeter fence of Wright Field at the very moment a B-29 Superfortress had been taxiing for takeoff in the background. The B-29 was not yet an operational plane, this was only a prototype being tested at Wright, and the Army Air Force was sensitive. Djevdjevich claimed that it had been an innocent misunderstanding. His camera was just a cheap Kodak. He had made no effort to conceal himself. In the foreground of all his snapshots was an attractive seventeen-year-old girl whom he had met in a Dayton restaurant three days before. She was wearing a sun dress in the photographs, posing gaily; the B-29 was only distantly visible beyond her bare shoulder, hardly more than a gray shape, and not in every frame. Djevdjevich apologized for alarming the U. S. Army but stood firmly upon his innocence. They had been having a picnic, he explained. In a cattail swamp? asked the FBI. No, no, it had been damp perhaps, but certainly no swamp, according to Djevdjevich. He was held for two days at the county jail before being released. Part of his difficulty in getting the FBI to believe him stemmed from the fact that he had been carrying two wallets, with two distinct sets of identification. In his hip pocket was "Alex Djevdjevich," a twenty-nine-year-old Yugoslav with resident alien status. In his jacket pocket was "George Hadas,"

a naturalized Greek-American whose physical description also
matched the bearer perfectly. But George Hadas was simply a
friend of his, Djevdjevich explained, who had mislaid his wallet
in Djevdjevich's car. He was carrying it until it could be returned safely to George.

After his release in Dayton, Barry says, the FBI did a full
investigation of Djevdjevich's background and current activities
that went on for most of six months. Djevdjevich had two other
sessions with them himself, in New York, answering questions
about SCADTA and Peter Paul von Bauer and the siege of
Madrid. During one of those sessions Djevdjevich declared that
he was not only pure of Nazi taint but rabidly anti-Nazi, owing
partly to the fact that he himself had some Jewish blood. This
was news to everyone else whom the FBI visited.

Nevertheless his former father-in-law gave a supportive account of his character. Various acquaintances from Newport
society spoke glowingly of him, evidently under the misappre-
hension that this FBI check must be preliminary to some sort of
high diplomatic appointment. Officials at Pan Am had nothing
bad to say. No charges were filed.

God knows why a draft board hadn't nailed him by this time,
Barry says. As a resident alien, healthy and male, he was certainly eligible. Just more of that magical Djevdjevich immunity,
evidently.

In 1943 he applied to the OSS, through their Washington
headquarters, as a prospective liaison agent to the Yugoslav
resistance. He was willing to parachute in or be infiltrated by
submarine. Or if it were more convenient, he told them, he
could walk in from Romania. He had come to the OSS on a
referral by one of the Newport crowd, who knew General Don-
ovan from having been a client of his law firm, so the recruiters
listened carefully to Alex Djevdjevich, and they were tempted
by what they heard. He could fly any sort of plane. He spoke
fluent Serbian, as well as German. He also happened to be an
excellent marksman, having won several European trapshooting competitions.

"Oh come on," says Kessler.

He was young and fit and single. He was a patriotic American—though admittedly not yet a citizen—and eager to be part
of the war effort. Equally important, he declared himself apolit-
ical with regard to the internal Yugoslav factions: he had no

prior association either with Mijailović's group of guerrillas or with Tito's. He didn't care which of them controlled a postwar Yugoslavia, Djevdjevich said; he merely wanted the Nazis out. That was the right thing to say. Gears had already meshed and begun turning, toward his formal recruitment and a crash program of training that would have put him in the sky over Yugoslavia within three months, when the OSS screeners received his FBI file. He was rejected. Politely but unambivalently.

Later the same year he applied to the OSS again, this time through their station in Cairo, which served as field headquarters for all operations into southern Europe.

"Cairo."

"Cairo," Barry confirms.

"Nineteen forty-three, and he just happened to be in Cairo?"

"No. He admitted to me that he went out there, specifically, to take another run at the OSS."

"Wouldn't it be damned hard just to *get* to Cairo in 1943? For a civilian. Even one starting from Newport."

"Sure. I'd say it would have."

"How did he do it?"

"Another mystery."

"Why would he imagine that OSS-Cairo might want him, if Washington had already said no? Didn't they talk to each other by cable?"

"Because he was using a different name," Barry says.

For the sake of the Cairo station he had become Ari Delevoreas, another Greek-American, who had supposedly spent the last several years making bales of money as a cloth exporter in Algiers and Tunis, and who now finally felt he should do something for the Allied cause, preferably in conjunction with the liberation of Greece. This time he said nothing about his flying skills. Nor about his Serbian, nor his trapshooting, Barry adds. Yes he would gladly learn to parachute. Yes he was sure he could master the radio work. Yes of course he could pass for a Greek farmer: wasn't that precisely what he had been until the age of eighteen? Furthermore he professed his willingness to accept any mission, no matter how great the risk, no matter how slim the chances that he could accomplish it and be gotten safely back out. Again he had said just the right thing. OSS-Cairo had need just then of someone reckless but steady to be sent into Greece, on a mission that was figured at

chances no better than one in five for survival. They wanted
someone to steal a sample of the new German glider bomb from
the Luftwaffe airport outside Athens. Good possibility of being
betrayed to the Nazis by the first villager who saw his parachute; good possibility of being caught red-handed at the airport, or before he could wagon this unwieldy thing down to the
coast and meet his pickup; excellent prospect of torture and
death. Yes I would do that, Ari Delevoreas told them. Evidently
he projected just the right quiet tone, because the OSS—wary as
they were of hot-blooded Mediterranean daring in its more ex-
cessive forms—snatched him up for the job. He got five weeks
of intensive training there in the desert. He studied the file on
these glider bombs and the intelligence reports on the Athens
airport. He was ready to jump—waiting only for the completion
of support arrangements with Greek resistance. At that point a
deputy director of the OSS arrived from Washington on administrative business, and the Cairo chief insisted proudly on intro-
ducing him to this man Delevoreas. The deputy director had
spent thirty minutes of one staff meeting arguing over the
Djevdjevich case, less than a year before, and he had a good
memory for faces. Highly embarrassing situation for all concerned, since Delevoreas-Djevdjevich had already been so thoroughly briefed. He was not only dumped by the OSS. He was
almost denied reentry to the United States.

Djevdjevich's own explanation, of course, portrayed him as
just a foolishly overeager patriot who would tell any fib in order
to be allowed to fight Nazis. Like the underage kid lying about
his birth date to get into the Army. Fine, a reasonable premise
—except that, in two years since Pearl Harbor, Djevdjevich had
made no effort that anyone was aware of to get into the Army
itself. Only the OSS. He wanted to be a spy.

"Wanted to be."

"Sure," Barry says, agreeing with Kessler's innuendo. "Oh,
definitely, yes: there were plenty of reasons for suspecting, by
this point, that maybe he already was one. Acting for the Nazis,
perhaps. Or for the Russians. One source later claimed that he
had been on retainer to the Free French."

"What about you?"

"I was on retainer only to the U. S. Senate."

"You know what I mean."

"Sure. I couldn't say, Michael. Maybe the Russians. Maybe.

During the war—not necessarily later. It was just so hard to know."

"I heard once that the KGB has a training module in golf. Their own links and everything. All these future agents out there, soon as the snow is gone, hacking away."

"Seriously?"

"No. Yes." Kessler smiles.

After Cairo the FBI reopened its Djevdjevich investigation, which yielded an increasingly thick sheaf of contradictory data, slanders and testimonials, suspicious coincidences, unverifiable claims and accusations but, again, no criminal charges. The Bureau sent a report across to the Immigration and Naturalization Service, but that report had been coyly edited by Hoover himself so as not to give away any precious FBI secrets; the INS, consequently, took no action. Djevdjevich might well have been deported just on the basis of the Wright Field and OSS incidents. But he wasn't.

Now we jump ahead, says Barry. Slide that bottle over here, says Barry. With clumsy movements Kessler tightens the top and complies.

Now we jump ahead again, Barry repeats eventually. Next nine or ten years, our Alex has no visible occupation, unless you want to count matrimony or drinking cocktails. He travels the circuit from Newport to New York to Palm Beach. Doesn't appear to lack for cash or for friends. Marries twice more in that period, each time to a girl under twenty from a rich family. Each time the marriage lasts less than three years. During the first of these two—that's the second marriage overall, Barry says with the exaggerated concern for clarity of a man who is well pickled—during that second one, he and the girl live in a forty-room mansion, full of butlers and maids and cooks. They throw quite a few parties. Djevdjevich liked it, he told me, says Barry. But the wife was a manic-depressive and a drunk, poor girl. Somewhere along through here he picked up his U.S. citizenship. Also he picked up a daughter—from the third marriage, I think, says Barry. They named her Tatiana. Born around 1949. She was fourteen in 1963, I remember that, says Barry. What's fourteen from sixty-three? says Barry.

A moment of silence.

"Roughly forty-nine," Kessler says at last.

Tatiana even had a nurse. There was more travel to Mexico

City and Bogotá again now, Rio, Havana, who knows where else. Generally he went alone but on a couple occasions the third wife was with him, no doubt partly because it was her money that bought the tickets. He would say later that these trips involved "hotel investments in Latin America," close quotes. But according to the third wife—when she was an ex-wife, discussing it with the FBI—that was a joke, ha ha. The only sort of hotel investments in question, she claimed, were the room bills that her accountant paid. The third wife also mentioned a long autobiographical manuscript that Alex somehow found time to write, between the travel and the parties: an account of his youth in Romania and his early flying adventures, evidently. Pages upon hundreds of pages of his creaky grandiloquent English, according to the wife. He had begun to imagine himself as some sort of international adventurer and photojournalist, she said; he took snapshots constantly and kept diaries during his trips; sent a letter to *National Geographic* once, but never heard back. The autobiography also failed to find a publisher, though he mailed it to six or seven, she said. Djevdjevich himself never mentioned such a manuscript to either the FBI or the Warren Commission. To me he admitted that it had existed, says Barry. The wife was wrong, though: he had only tried three publishers. One was interested but wanted too many idiotic changes, so he had let the project drop. In 1953 he was arrested again.

This time they laid hands on him near Edwards Air Force Base, in the desert west of Barstow, California, on a day when a test pilot named Scott Crossfield had been scheduled to fly a rocket plane known as the D-558-2, predecessor of the X-15. The flight had been scrubbed that morning because Crossfield had a case of mumps. Djevdjevich of course was just on a picnic. Another inconvenient coincidence. He liked to get out sometimes and watch the planes roar off, yes, admittedly. He loved the outdoors. He was an avid amateur photographer, yes. The young woman who graced his latest set of Brownie snapshots, posing merrily beside Joshua trees in her strapless cantina blouse, was of legal age, barely. Djevdjevich was interrogated, and released the next morning. He was very lucky—though the FBI didn't tell him so—that Crossfield had been sick.

Deportation proceedings began but were suspended after one

hearing, to which Alex Djevdjevich had been accompanied by an extremely eminent Washington lawyer whom he had known for years from Palm Beach.

By 1956 Djevdjevich was married again and living in New Orleans. This one, the fourth wife, was all of thirty years old, a Greek immigrant from a middle-class Athens family. She had a classical education but no money, no hotels or maids. Her name was Irene. Djevdjevich told Barry: "Irene, this was my true love. At last. A spectacular woman. We were very happily married." In New Orleans they lived modestly, working elbow to elbow to build up a small travel agency. That was according to the Warren Commission testimony. By another version, in the FBI file, it was "a small flying service" they owned, Djevdjevich as sole pilot and Irene as office manager. Which of those versions was true? Barry asked him. Djevdjevich explained that it was really all the same thing, a semantic distinction merely; and then he slalomed off on another subject.

"Did Irene talk to the Warren Commission herself?" says Kessler.

"No. She died of liver cancer in 1962. One of the few indisputable facts."

But before that cruel stroke had fallen, as Djevdjevich told it to Barry, he and Irene had been fortunate enough, at least, to have taken their big trip.

The trip was Alex's idea. It had been "the dream of a lifetime," he told Barry—same phrase exactly that appeared in his Warren Commission testimony. The dream of a lifetime. Since even before his first experience in South America, his first view of the jungle canopy as he flew that route between Bogotá and the Colombian coast, he had envisioned this grand adventure, he claimed. Something he had promised himself, something he had vowed. And in Irene he had found the perfect accomplice: she was hardy, she was game, she loved travel and cared minimally about physical comfort, plus she spoke a little Portuguese, which he lacked. Alex himself was not getting younger, he confided to Barry. Already at the time of the trip, in fact, he had been forty-seven. (Or else forty-four, depending, Barry notes.) So why not? Their friends back in Newport and New York began hearing about this scheme, by letter and telephone, about three months before the departure date. Certain arrangements had to be made, good-byes had to be said, because Alex

and Irene intended to be gone for most of a year. If anything
happened to them, God forbid, there should be some provision
for Tatiana, his daughter. They planned to fly to Lima and
spend three weeks assembling equipment and supplies, dealing
with visa questions, possibly securing a guide or a crewman.
Then a train connection to the highlands, an overland portage
with the aid of llamas, and they would launch the real journey:
a descent of the Amazon River, from very near its headwaters
all the way to the mouth at Belém, by raft and small motorized
boat. The dream of a lifetime, Barry repeats. Don't ask me how
many other Romanian kids dream of running the Amazon, he
says. Djevdjevich was one of a kind.

"One of several kinds, I'd say," Kessler offers.

They were gone for the full year. The New Orleans travel
agency had been left in the hands of a salaried manager. Tatiana
and some of the friends received letters—only a few—post-
marked exotically. Most of these letters were eventually borrowed and returned by the FBI. In one, Alex described how
they had lost their beloved German shepherd, who as it turned
out was their sole companion on the raft and then later on the
boat; the dog went for a swim at dusk one day and was am-
bushed by an anaconda. In another letter Irene recounted buying a smoked monkey from a woman in a riverside village, first
meat they had had in a week and surprisingly palatable. They
spent all of one night being swept around in a very large eddy, a
whirlpool really, and nearly sank, but were pulled out at dawn
by a native man on the bank with a rope and a brace of mules.
They ate much fish. Alex was stung nastily on the calf by a
fresh-water ray. Both of them suffered severe dysentery, as well
as a whole menagerie of repulsive parasites. Having exhausted
their own first-aid supplies, they were forced to rely on native
pharmaceuticals. But the letters were always cheerful and bully.
Then after so many months they were in Belém and, at last,
home. An astounding experience, they told everyone. An absolute miserable bitter ordeal, intermittently terrifying and tedious, often disgusting—and yet they professed to count it a
glorious success. They wouldn't have missed it for a fortune;
they wouldn't repeat it for a fortune. Djevdjevich immediately
began composing, from his diaries, a long travelogue manuscript. That opus was published the following year, by a vanity
publisher who charged him less than a thousand dollars. Every

friend and acquaintance on their Christmas-card list received a copy.

"But it probably never happened," Barry says.

"Never happened? What didn't?"

"None of it. Smoked monkeys and dog-eating snakes and giant whirlpools. None of it."

"He embellished."

"No. He invented. From scratch. This isn't positive, though. Just one theory."

"What are you telling me, Barry?"

"That the trip didn't happen. It was a hoax. Two separate sources gave the FBI to believe that Djevdjevich and Irene spent the whole year in Colombia. Living quite comfortably, at a borrowed villa near Barranquilla. Like I say, though, that's just a theory. Call it the skeptic's view."

"What did Djevdjevich say?"

"He got very indignant when I raised this. The only such time, in my sessions with him. He was furious at being doubted."

"That was hardly a new experience for him."

"Furious. Really convincingly angry. He started ranting about his famous ray injury—a hole, big as a grapefruit, rotting out of his calf. About these little bugs that lay eggs under your fingernails. Gruesome stuff. I tell you, Michael, you'd never get me to the Amazon."

"But he was making it up."

"Maybe, I said. A distinct possibility. If so, he did a good job."

"And Irene was long since dead. So she couldn't confirm his story. Or refute it."

"Exactly. She died in 1962," Barry says. "At Parkland Hospital, actually."

"Parkland?"

"Right. When they came back from Brazil, or Colombia, or wherever it was," Barry says, "they had decided to resettle in Dallas."

He told the Warren Commission that he never gave Oswald any money, Barry says. The testimony was under oath, of course—for whatever difference that might conceivably have made. Probably none. Anyway, whether it was true or not, significant or not, Djevdjevich sounded the point rather emphatically: No, he never gave Lee Oswald a cent.

Nor was there ever a loan, no. Toys for the baby, yes; he did occasionally bring small toys. They were so dreadfully poor, Lee and Marina, and the infant had almost nothing. Groceries, yes; on at least one occasion he had brought a bag of groceries, including some beer and a few jars of baby food, for which Oswald seemed grudgingly grateful. But the man was too proud to accept anything more, Djevdjevich testified. Lee's stubborn pride alone would have made the giving of money impossible, unthinkable—though Djevdjevich himself confessed (as he put it) that for his own part he felt no great desire to subsidize the Oswalds financially. He had rather liked Lee, yes, he would admit that. Damaging as it might seem now, in the circumstances, he would not deny that. This was April of 1964, remember, Barry inserts, so it was in fact a reasonably courageous, or foolhardy, thing to say. Or maybe just very cunning. Yes, he had liked Lee Oswald, Djevdjevich told them, and had enjoyed his company, sometimes. No question, this angry young fellow had a very good brain. He could be either quite pleasant in conversation, stimulating even—or else utterly obnoxious, boorish. Sometimes *very* boorish. But in their chats about politics and world travel and foreign cultures—chats that were generally conducted in Russian, though at times too in English—Djevdjevich himself seemed to bring out the better side of the man, if he might be allowed to say so. Politics was boring to Djevdjevich, so he claimed, but good conversation on any subject at all, even politics, was a rarity to be savored. Also —Djevdjevich added this as an afterthought—like all autodidacts, Oswald was sometimes pompous. Confused and pompous. He would use large words, which one could tell he had taken from his lonely reading but never quite digested, and often as not he would mispronounce them. In English and Russian both, one encountered this trait in Oswald. But he did have a good mind. No, Djevdjevich would never have tried to give the man money, positively not. Djevdjevich had no desire to insult Lee. Nor to be insulted back, as thanks for his good intentions. It was bad enough, Lee's reaction, when Djevdjevich performed those few small kindnesses for Marina and the baby. That's what he told the Commission, Barry says.

One other Dallas samaritan who had helped Marina, though, remembered it differently.

This woman's name was Jane Chestnoy. She was a middle-aged American, recently widowed, whose husband had been part of the same circle of Russian émigrés, there in Dallas, among whom Alex Djevdjevich spent much of his time. The émigré group was a loose collection of couples who gathered regularly to speak the language, drink vodka, and trade turns hosting each other to dinners of authentic old-country food. The group's essence was social, certainly not political, though some of the older members *were* rather rabidly anti-Soviet. They all clung together with a certain clannishness. Sometimes they joined in doing what Jane Chestnoy described unself-consciously as "good deeds," small acts of consideration for other Russian émigré families, poorer and less educated people, in the Dallas area. Like an informal benevolent society. Their generosity stemmed from a sense of shared exile and from the large Russian heart, Jane Chestnoy thought. Mrs. Chestnoy was on the fringe of this group, since her husband was now gone and she herself spoke only a little Russian. Chestnoy and she had married late, and she had just begun studying the language when he died. She wanted to continue. She also hoped to remain in touch with the other émigrés. She was a Christian Scientist. It was she who had accompanied Alex Djevdjevich to the Oswald apartment on Neely Street, in March of 1963, after Marina had complained that Lee was beating her.

The idea was that Marina and the child would come to live with Mrs. Chestnoy, who welcomed the company and the chance to practice her Russian. They would use Djevdjevich's car for moving the crib and what few other items Marina had. On the afternoon when Djevdjevich and Mrs. Chestnoy arrived, Lee was gone and Marina was nursing a black eye. Mrs. Chestnoy remembered vividly this one particular thing that Marina had said—as Mrs. Chestnoy, later, told the Warren Commission—because at the time she had congratulated herself, privately, on her improving ear for spoken Russian. The remark had passed quickly from Marina to Djevdjevich. It gave her a small shock of satisfaction, said Mrs. Chestnoy, that she had caught the statement at all. One of those breakthrough moments that anyone experiences in the course of learning a

language. So she remembered vividly, she swore. According to
Mrs. Chestnoy, Marina had said to Djevdjevich:

"My fool of a husband spent that money you gave him on a
rifle."

The translation was Mrs. Chestnoy's, Barry says. But she
also recited it into the record in Russian, exactly as she claimed
to have heard it, and the Commission's interpreter (the same
one who had worked Marina's testimony) later verified the
translation.

Barry repeats: " 'My fool of a husband spent that money you
gave him on a rifle.' "

In her own testimony to the Warren Commission, Marina
neither confirmed this nor denied it. She couldn't recall. She
seemed to be very confused, and frightened. She contradicted
herself on a number of points. It was possible, yes, that she had
said such a thing. What money, then? the Commission demanded. When exactly had Djevdjevich given it? How much?
Was she present at the time it changed hands? What had been
said between Alex Djevdjevich and Lee Oswald? Marina didn't
seem to know. She couldn't answer. She couldn't remember.

But Djevdjevich, Barry says, was adamant. No, he told the
Commission. No, Mrs. Chestnoy is a very nice woman but she
no more speaks Russian than a parrot does. Such a statement
was never made. Nothing remotely like that. Mrs. Chestnoy
was mistaken.

"All right now," Barry says. "Here's where it gets interesting."

By this point he and Kessler are both seated on the floor, at
opposite sides of the room, the scotch bottle having rolled to a
dead empty stop on the carpet halfway between them. Sometime in the past hour Kessler has removed his left shoe, evidently. He wiggles his toes and observes with fascination that
they respond almost perfectly to the neural signals. The shoe is
nowhere visible, but it can't have gone far.

"All right now," Kessler agrees.

"In the first week of April 1963, Oswald was fired from his
job. Latest in a long sorry series. This particular job had been at
a printing company called Jaggars-Chiles-Stovall."

"Chiggers-Chives-Stovall," Kessler repeats.

"But that's not important," says Barry. "The name."

"Oh."

"He takes a bus to New Orleans and disappears for two weeks."

"He disappears," says Kessler. "The son of a gun."

"First three days of that time he was registered at a YMCA. Supposedly looking for work. According to the official understanding. Then gone. His movements, his whereabouts, his associations, and his activities all unaccounted for. Presumably, but not certainly, he was still somewhere in the New Orleans area. Then at the beginning of May he turned up again, hired on as a shipper in the warehouse of a coffee company. From that point until November, most of his movements are traceable. Pretty strange, some of them—his wildcat excursion to Mexico City, for instance, raising hell at the Cuban consulate there when they wouldn't give him a visa—but at least traceable."

"Oswald in Mexico. Cuban consulate. This stuff is all so morbidly, inexhaustibly intriguing," Kessler says disconnectedly. "Isn't it? And we'll never come to the end of it all, will we? A century from now it'll be only more muddled. Twelve million people will each have a great-grandparent who was in Dealey Plaza that day and heard machine-gun fire from the grassy knoll."

Barry ignores him. Barry, for some reason, is slightly more sober. "Meanwhile Alex Djevdjevich had left on his trip to Jakarta. According to the official understanding."

As he and Irene did before the Amazon adventure, Djevdjevich had again said his good-byes and made careful arrangements for the handling of his business and personal affairs. It was expected to be a lengthy absence. He might have to stay out there well over a year, he told friends, establishing trade compacts with the Sukarno regime and founding a new airline, then dealing with the problem of landing rights throughout Southeast Asia. And this time, he told the friends, he would be taking his daughter Tatiana along with him. Her mother had been committed to an expensive sanitarium two years before, Barry explains, and since then Tatty had been living with an aunt. A maternal aunt, who was also now the girl's legal guardian. But the aunt had agreed with this idea, that Tatty should accompany her father. At least that's what Djevdjevich told the Warren Commission, Barry says.

"Nineteen sixty-three. Tatty was fourteen," says Kessler. "Sixty-three minus forty-nine."

"Correct. Seventh grade. He knew of an excellent school in Singapore, run by British nuns. He could see her on every holiday. It would give her some rich polyglot experience, like his own."

"British nuns? There *are* no British nuns," says Kessler.

"French nuns, then."

"Better."

"Or Chinese nuns."

"Make it French. I think French is what you want."

So Djevdjevich went off on his trip, Barry says. April of 1963, he closed up his house in Dallas and left. Almost exactly the same time that Oswald, having booted the last Dallas job, made his temporary move to New Orleans. They never saw each other again—so we're told. And as Djevdjevich had predicted, his sojourn in Indonesia was a long one. Much water meanwhile passing over the dam. By the time he came back Lee Oswald was infamous and dead. The Warren Commission had evidently reached Djevdjevich in Jakarta, through our embassy there, and requested firmly that he get his ass back to testify. He was an American citizen by then, on an American passport, so there was hardly a choice. But he told the Commission's assistant staff counsel, when they met here in Washington for their official sessions, that this attention threatened to destroy his business position. Mr. Sukarno was very nervous about assassinations, assassination plots, coups, the whole dreary subject. The Diem brothers had just been dispatched too, remember, Barry says. Sukarno was seeing shadows in every archway, according to Djevdjevich. Djevdjevich himself was just heartbreakingly innocent of anything but the most trivial, accidental connection with Lee Oswald, of course, yet the Commission's very interest in him as a witness might seem to cast Djevdjevich in a damaging light. It's all in the record, Barry says, volume something of the Warren Commission hearings: Alex Djevdjevich's entire testimony. With fully three pages at the start devoted to his complaints, Barry says, about how his good reputation might be darkened in the paranoid mind of Sukarno. He put the staff lawyer right on the defensive—got the man making all manner of ridiculous placative statements. Now of course no one doubts your own character, Mr. Djevdjevich, we will exercise every precaution, Mr. Djevdjevich, et cetera. I can assure you that this Commission has no desire blah blah blah. You can read it, Barry says. Bad technique. But the Warren Commission wanted order, neatness, politeness, reassurance; most of all, closure. You can get that right out of the published record, you can taste it and smell it, Barry says vehemently. They did not want to dig into some endless rat hole of troubling possibilities. They did not want to discover, for instance, that Alex Djevdjevich was lying.

"Was he?" says Kessler.

"He *always* was. At least a little. That's the whole point with Djevdjevich, for God's sake. How could they miss it?"

"But about Oswald?"

"I don't know, Michael. Very possible. There were a couple problems with this Indonesia story."

"Let me guess. For starters, none of it happened."

"No. No, some of it definitely happened," Barry says. "They definitely traced him to Jakarta in early '64. But the girl Tatiana wasn't with him. And she wasn't in Singapore. She had spent the year at a boarding school in Massachusetts, according to what I was told."

"No doubt a rich polyglot experience in its own right."

"I couldn't say."

"Did you get that from her directly?"

"No. I never found her. She had long since changed her name, by the time I came along. Distancing herself from the whole deal. Which was understandable, I suppose. Even Djevdjevich himself hadn't heard from her in five years. So he said."

"Maybe he didn't want you to find her."

"Maybe indeed. It occurred to me."

"What else?"

"A certain hotel registration ledger," Barry says. "A piece of phantom evidence that bedeviled me for an entire year."

He never actually saw this hotel ledger himself, Barry explains. He heard about it from other people—most of whom had likewise never seen it themselves, the difference being their general inclination to believe in it, nevertheless, like a theological axiom. The ledger from the Hotel Chantilly: aha, yes of course. These people from whom he heard of it were assassination-conspiracy buffs, full-time amateur sleuths, obsessive about the subject and ecstatically paranoid, a whole weird subculture of folk in the grip of a dementia that is possibly only an acute version, Barry says, of what you mentioned. What we all suffer from chronically. The morbid and inexhaustible fascination. But chronic is not acute. There's a line worth drawing. These buffs, so called, they are just way out there beyond healthy skepticism, beyond cynicism, beyond wild suspicion, Barry says. They are liberated from reality and common logic, many of them anyway, into an exquisitely cabalistic evermore. They hold conventions, you know. They gather to trade theories and give presentations of what passes for new evidence, and to hoot chorally at the official understanding—which, bad as it is, comes closer to plausibility than much of what they offer, Barry says. They refer to each other as *independent researchers*. Little old ladies, emeritus acid-heads, many many varieties of crank. I met a retired newspaper editor, otherwise quite sane and intelligent, who had bought Jack Ruby's can opener at an auction, Barry says. Not for any evidential value, God knows, but just as a ghoulish sort of souvenir. He showed it to me. A rusty can opener. He carried it wrapped in a piece of chamois. I mean yipe, Barry says. Of course they can talk about the Zapruder film for hours, citing the various frame numbers from memory. Muzzle velocities of a Mannlicher-Carcano, Oswald's riflery rating from the Marines. The forty-three material witnesses who had died oddly or violently by November of 1966, despite ten-million-to-one statistical odds against that, as supposedly certified by one of London's top actuarial firms. Who had made a mistake in math, by the way, Barry says. Never mind that. Never mind the more banal forms of good sense. Every coincidence is sinister, for these people. Every loose thread in even the woolliest snarl of random and contradictory data makes them smirk knowingly, not to be fooled. Meanwhile, they themselves float free of rational tethering, riding all the more strangely ionized breezes. Gnostics. They know what they know. And that is: that an elaborate, inept, and uneconomical conspiracy culminated successfully at Dallas and then was followed by the most enviably efficient cover-up. And Alex Djevdjevich, by no great surprise, ranks high among their favorite topics.

I went to one of their gatherings, in Ann Arbor, Barry says, and a half dozen of them told me about the Hotel Chantilly ledger. But none of them had actually seen it. In private ownership, I was told. In the collection of still another buff. A strange soul who kept his distance from the others. If *they* called him a strange soul I knew he had to be something, Barry says. If he existed at all. Later I did find one guy who claimed to have seen the ledger first hand: a drunk in a fly-ridden motel room outside of Pensacola, with a four-day beard and darting eyes. Yes he could tell me about the Chantilly ledger did I bring whiskey, was what he said, no pause for breath. That was another false lead. I'd wasted a day on the road, driving over from Jacksonville. The FBI even had a file on this man, I found out, for a whole history of trying to sell—

"The ledger," says Kessler impatiently.

"Right. The ledger. Now even if it did exist, of course, in the hands of some gnome, that would prove nothing. You'd want to bring in a handwriting expert, an ink and paper expert, run the thing under every sort of scanner. It could easily be faked."

"Suppose it wasn't."

Then you had an interesting piece of neglected evidence, maybe, says Barry.

The Hotel Chantilly was in New Orleans, just five or six blocks from the building on Camp Street where Oswald briefly rented an office, that summer, for the pro-Castro organization of whose New Orleans chapter he seems to have been the sole member. The Chantilly was a dive, Barry says, crumbling, robustly disreputable. Long since torn down for urban renewal. No one knows where the owner went. No one knows where the records went, if there were any records. But the mythology tells of a registration ledger, the old-fashioned type, folio size—a sacred relic, to the conspiracy buffs—in which, during those two lost weeks after Oswald first arrived in New Orleans, someone signed in as "A. J. Hidell."

"A. J. Hidell," Kessler repeats, trying it for the feel. "Means nothing to me."

"Oswald's favorite alias, at that time. It's the one he used when he ordered the rifle. Also for some of his P.O. boxes."

"Is that all?"

"No. Another name turned up on the same ledger page. So they say. A different room on a different floor. But overlapping with A. J. Hidell's stay at the Chantilly during two nights of the first week."

"Lamont Cranston."

"No, but you're close."

"Harry Houdini."

"Ari Delevoreas," Barry says.

Kessler sucks at the dry sticky rim of his whiskey glass, struggling to concentrate, struggling to focus. It seems as though this phantom ledger might be as significant as Barry implies, yes, though he can't be sure. He can't quite see the pattern. He is so very plastered he can barely sit up.

"Now let's think about this carefully," Barry says.

Kessler is all for that, in principle. He tries to do his part. He exerts himself on some eyebrow isometrics.

"Let's think about it in these terms," Barry says. "Let's attempt to interpret Alex Djevdjevich's behavior in the light of his connection with Lee Oswald. Rather than vice versa, as the others have all tried to do." Barry seems to be getting only more lucid, which Kessler takes for an altogether bad sign in a man with a head full of Cutty Sark and a missing wife and swing set. The inability to be drunk, despite high intake, being perhaps a symptom of some sort of emotional aridity. "Let's pretend that Alex Djevdjevich—and not Lee Oswald—is the object of our primary interest."

"Good idea," says Kessler.

"Fine. All right. Now. It's December of 1963. Here you are: Alex D. Roughly a year before, you loaned or gave Lee Harvey Oswald—as he is suddenly so famously remembered, though the middle name is new to you—a year before, you gave this man some money. With which he bought a cheap rifle. Maybe that was precisely the purpose for which the money was offered; maybe not. Leave that question aside, for the moment. No one knows about the small grant-in-aid, not yet anyway, besides you and his widow and perhaps a few others. Okay. What would you do?"

"Where am I?" says Kessler.

"Oh, say you're in New Orleans. Some quiet retreat there. A cheap hotel."

"December of '63?"

"December."

"I'd get on the first plane for Indonesia," says Kessler.

"Good. All right. Thank you, Michael. Now: now you're in Indonesia. Several months have passed. One morning you receive a telegram, delivered personally by a second secretary from the U. S. Embassy, stating that the Warren Commission wants to talk to you. In Washington, D.C."

Kessler ponders for a moment. "I wouldn't go."

"Your passport is at stake."

"So what? Passports are expendable, for a charming guy like me. I'd fly to Amsterdam and get a new one from the Yugoslavs."

"Okay. You wouldn't go. Preferring to expatriate. Fair enough. But can you imagine any circumstances under which you *might* fly back to testify?"

Kessler labors at that one like a cub bear trying to unscrew the lid on a jar of mayonnaise. Barry waits.

"If I was innocent and cocky," says Kessler. Barry nods but does not smile. "Or if I was guilty of something, and under orders to keep it covered up."

Barry smiles.

Back in February of 1976, at the New Orleans Marriott, Barry asked Alex Djevdjevich about the Hotel Chantilly. Djevdjevich frowned. He wagged his head side to side in what seemed like soul-weary disgust. Yes, he knew all about that story, he told Barry. He had gotten calls about it even, from strangers, bizarre individuals, in some cases at alarming hours of the night. One of these callers had even offered to sell Djevdjevich the original Chantilly ledger. Sell it to him, Djevdjevich repeated indignantly. Blackmail and harassment. But Djevdjevich had done nothing for which to be blackmailed. It was all pure concoction, a brain-sick lie launched by someone who wished to destroy Alex Djevdjevich's reputation, ruin his life totally—and who nearly had. Yes of course he had used the name Ari Delevoreas, in Cairo during the war, for the very good reason that Barry had already heard explained. No he had never registered at the Hotel Chantilly—not in spring of 1963 while Oswald was there, nor at any other time. No. Issuing these denials, Djevdjevich grew gradually quieter, more subdued, finally his voice sank to a whisper, as though his energy were running down. The very mention of the Hotel Chantilly seemed to sap and sadden him. No, he said. No. Shook his head again. No, it just wasn't true. This was late in the morning of the second day. Barry then asked him about the photograph.

The photograph, by all means, said Djevdjevich with slightly
more animation. He could tell Barry a little something about
that, yes, and he would be glad to.

The photograph was no fake. On the contrary, it was just too
pathetically real. Yes, Djevdjevich had come forward on his
own initiative back in 1967, when all the silliness began to be
spoken and published (and to be taken seriously by so many
people who should have known better, Djevdjevich said) about
that notorious photograph. About how it had been manufac-
tured. Pasted together clumsily, toward the purpose of framing
Lee Oswald for a crime of which he was innocent. Such nonsense, Djevdjevich clucked. Such perniciously futile silliness.
Certainly the photo was genuine, it was *self-evidently* genuine,
and anyone who had known Lee at all would never bother to
doubt that. The belligerent bantam-rooster stance, pistol on hip,
of the young man in the picture. The Marxist newspapers defi-
antly displayed, as though to prove God knows what. The
shabby little backyard of the Neely Street place. And the rifle
too, yes, definitely. No one would need to invent a photo like
that in order to frame Lee Oswald: it was too perfectly characteristic of the real man, as Djevdjevich knew him. In fact,
Djevdjevich thought, no one else *could* have composed a photo
that so perfectly captured Lee's self-image. Besides which,
Djevdjevich *knew* it to be genuine—knew that and wished for-
evermore he could forget it—having kept his own copy of the
thing, hidden, in a phonograph-record jacket, for four years. He
had been afraid to destroy it and afraid to show it. Until the real
lunacy began, in 1967. At which time he came forward with the
evidence—as he was pleased to remind Barry—on his own initiative.

"Did Oswald give it to you in person?" Barry asked.

"No. Not in person. He enclosed it in the record jacket where
it later remained. I had loaned Lee the recording, you see. Mussorgsky. He was trying to improve himself, as always." Alex
Djevdjevich sat very straight in one of those half-comfortable
vinyl hotel chairs not made for sitting, Barry opposite him in
another just like it. The curtains to the terrace were closed, at
Djevdjevich's request; all the room lights on. Djevdjevich wore
a white linen suit that was clean but not new. He was tan.
Roughly six foot three, by Barry's guess, and reasonably trim: a
handsome fit white-haired man of sixty-three. Or just sixty, de-

pending. "The photo was a surprise. Lee's underbred notion of a dashing gesture, you know. Between two men of the world. He said nothing about it. I did not even discover it there until months later, afterward—after everything. When I happened to be in a mood for Mussorgsky."

"Tell me the exact inscription," Barry said.

"I don't listen to Mussorgsky anymore," said Djevdjevich. "Another thing ruined."

"Tell me the exact inscription."

Djevdjevich lowered his eyelids. He had been over this often before, Barry knew, yet it still took him a moment. He said: *"To my good friend Alex, with thanks, from Lee."*

"Thanks for what?" Barry said harshly.

"I don't know," said Djevdjevich. "I suppose he thought I had been kind to him."

They adjourned then, Barry says, with the understanding that Djevdjevich would see to his errands and be back in two hours, bringing with him this time the inscribed Oswald photo. He had already agreed that Barry could take the print back to Washington. He was giving Barry the impression that he wanted to trust someone and that Barry perhaps had been chosen. Definitely he seemed more unguarded than he had to the Warren Commission or, ever, the FBI. Barry for his part had made none of the promises and placations that the Commission's assistant staff counsel had—though he had also made no threats, except regarding the possibility of a Senate subpoena—and wasn't at all sure that he wanted to be graced with Djevdjevich's real or feigned trust. He himself didn't trust Djevdjevich, not in the least. Even less so when, at four o'clock that afternoon, he was still sitting alone at the Marriott, abandoned.

"I had a rental car," Barry tells Kessler. "I knew his home address but not how to find it. I used an Avis map and got caught in the midst of the rush-hour feed to the Causeway. When I finally got to his house, it was after dark. An old place with a porch behind wood lattice, straight out of Tennessee Williams. There were two police cars and a lab van."

Kessler is suddenly having less trouble with his concentration. He sits straight.

"No one heard the shot," Barry says. "A paper boy came around at about five, doing his monthly collection. I'm not sure what made the paper boy so bold as to let himself in. Maybe he knew Djevdjevich pretty well. The front door was open. Maybe he got tempted to steal something. Maybe there was a strong smell of blood. Does blood smell, Michael? Human blood, in largish quantities?"

Kessler nods his head stiffly. Yes it does. A strong odor like freshly ground hamburger, he thinks, remembering Biaggio's grocery.

"Anyway there wasn't what you'd call a largish quantity, I suppose. It was all too neat. One bullet from a .22 pistol, through the soft palate and out the top of his skull. The body was still seated in a leather chair in the study. The bullet was in the ceiling. The pistol was legally registered to Djevdjevich."

He had sat himself down and bit on the muzzle and fired, Barry says. At least that was the official understanding. The coroner's jury ruled it a suicide.

Barry checked out of the Marriott and came home.

"You shouldn't drive," says Barry, hand on the doorknob.

"I know. But I'm going to," says Kessler. "So wish me luck."

"Stay here. God knows I've got plenty of room. Drive back in the morning."

"No, Barry. Thank you. I've really got to be back there to-night. I'm, uh, there's supposed to be a message left for me," Kessler lies, not knowing how guilty he will feel, later, about this particular one. "Time and place of an appointment, for first thing tomorrow." The craven truth is that, in its hollowed condition, Barry's house is just too depressing for Kessler and, if at all politely possible, he wants now to get clear of it.

"That's stupid. Call them from here and get the message."

"Their switchboard closes at ten." Never before has he lied quite so shamelessly and badly to Barry. Kessler himself is surprised.

"Well. Then at least drink some coffee."

"Do you have fresh beans? Just give me some beans to chew."

Barry disappears back toward the kitchen and then is gone for more time than it would seem to take. Kessler, where he leans woozily, becomes slowly aware of not having heard the refrigerator smack open. Finally Barry returns from a different side of the house, handing to Kessler not coffee beans but a manila envelope.

"We almost forgot. Claude Sparrow and company."

"Thank you, Barry. Thank you, I mean it. I'll call you tomorrow."

"Call me tomorrow. There's one other piece you should see. It's in my safe deposit box, downtown. We'll meet for a sandwich and go pick it up."

"I'll call you tomorrow."

"Drive carefully, Michael. God damn it."

"Give my—" Kessler stops himself jarringly, mashing his molars together. Give my love to Patsy, he would have said.

"Give my eyes to science if I don't make it," he says.

18

Monday morning is open, Lord be praised. Kessler spends it in the dining room of the Tabard, drinking large doses of tomato juice and coffee, doing all within his power to avoid loud noises, sudden movements, and daunting thoughts. He feels sure that the evening with Barry must have taken five or ten points off his IQ, possibly inflicted some other permanent physical damage as well. His stomach is not good and his head is worse. It wasn't worth it, not even for Barry. Certainly not for Alex Djevdjevich. Kessler should know better by now. He vows silently, as his trembling hand clatters cup against saucer, that he is positively not going to take another drink of alcohol until, um, well, until he truly regains a yearning for the taste of the stuff. Or, say, tomorrow evening. Whichever comes first. Never mind, this is bitching hard work, this particular project, and he finds himself in a weakened state today, so it's no time to try to deal with what Nora is pleased to call his "incipient problem." The intractability of the Viktor Tronko story, compounded by certain people who throw other people off tall buildings, is his real incipient problem, thanks. Meanwhile, fluids. More fluids, waiter. Kessler concentrates in his quiet maimed shaky way on the intake of copious amounts of innocent liquid, hoping to rinse himself clean of poison and stupidity; and he reads. A restorative, meditative morning. He does not plan to leave this wonderful little white-damask-covered table for hours, by God. He reads the *Post* with maniacal thoroughness, even the editorials. Then after three cups of coffee and a pitcher or so of ice water he is capable of addressing the contents of Barry's envelope.

Barry spoke truth: there isn't much. Clips of the two Joe Delbanco columns that provided occasion (if not necessarily cause) for Claude Sparrow's firing, eight years ago. A photo-

THE SOUL OF VIKTOR TRONKO 223

copy of a longish article from the New York *Times Magazine,*
dated almost four years ago itself, on the subject of a supposed
Soviet penetration agent somewhere in the higher echelons of
the CIA, and the fevered search for that agent, which had "rent
the Agency in half for much of a decade," according to what
Kessler reads in the article's breathy subtitle. And, as promised,
an intact copy of the Vanderbilt University *Alumnus,* this one
ten years old, with a paper clip guiding Kessler to the short
feature on an alum named Claude Sparrow, former undergraduate poet and self-confessed government bureaucrat.

Government bureaucrat, who are you kidding? thinks Kessler, smiling despite himself.

Of the four stories, only the one from the *Times Magazine*
includes a photograph of Claude Sparrow, and even that is
grainy and bad, evidently taken with a long lens while Sparrow
in his familiar camel-hair coat was ducking into a car. But
Kessler already knows what the man looks like. He also knows
a little something about Sparrow's notorious phone-tapping operation, against "high U.S. officials, within the National Security Council staff and elsewhere," as the first of the two
Delbanco columns puts it. Glancing over the columns again
now, Kessler notices that Joe Delbanco seems to have missed a
crucial fact: the "elsewhere" in question had included the CIA
itself, and among those "high U.S. officials" were a few of what
Pokorny had called the "big boys" of the Agency, possibly even
including Jedediah McAttee. All of which presently makes better sense, to Kessler, in light of what he has heard about the
search for Dmitri. Sparrow on his last paranoid rampage. Sparrow listening in on everyone, suspecting everyone. The
Counterintelligence chief tapping his own DCI. What a mad-
house it must have been.

Kessler sets the columns aside. He can come back to them.
For the moment he is interested, rather, in Claude Sparrow's
more distant history.

History, Kessler remembers. The control of appearances.
Well, the Vanderbilt magazine and its literate but too trusting
undergraduate correspondent, the young fellow who interviewed Claude Sparrow, class of '35, seem to have offered Sparrow exactly that: control of the appearances. This was back
before Joe Delbanco made him infamous, America's most re-
nowned unemployed spymaster. Several years before the great

publicized purge. It happened in 1970, Kessler gathers, when Sparrow was back for a brief visit in Nashville, ostensibly on the occasion of his thirty-fifth college reunion. Only a small privy circle of folk, back then, knew anything of Claude Sparrow and his role at the CIA. And that was by no accident, Sparrow having always guarded his privacy (or call it his cover) sedulously. His public reputation was still a bare slate. Then the Vanderbilt *Alumnus,* accommodatingly, invited Sparrow himself to chalk a few things on it. He was interviewed over dinner by the author of this article, a young man from the class of '70, identified in his by-line as a philosophy major and an aspiring poet. As Kessler reads through the piece he understands that it was those two subjects—philosophy and poetry—and only those that would have seemed to justify any attention at all to this dusty alumnus, Mr. Sparrow, who had risen to be "a mid-level administrator at the National Institutes of Health."

The profile is full of lies. Kessler can see that much at a glance. The dinner interview in Nashville was itself a small disinformation campaign conducted by Claude Sparrow, with the collaboration of one unwitting undergraduate who had no way of checking—and no reason to suspect that he should check—these things Mr. Sparrow was telling him. Some of the "facts" are so wide of truth as to be comic. And some are not so far wide. Some read like gentle parables, though Kessler can't imagine whom Sparrow felt he was addressing. Also, as in any adept campaign of disinformation (Kessler having lately learned this principle from an expert), there seems to be a fair portion of real facts marbled in. Sitting over his coffee, ignorant as he is of Sparrow's earlier life, Kessler has no better means of sorting fact from lie than that Vanderbilt senior did. Merely a somewhat more skeptical predisposition. Still, he can only read and guess.

The focus of the piece is not Sparrow himself but his famous teacher Ludwig Wittgenstein. Sparrow appears in the role of acolyte to the historic personage, and as survivor, grave-tender, offering his reverent recollections. There is much talk about Cambridge and Vienna in the 1930s. Sparrow was there, yes. He sat on a folding chair in Wittgenstein's small crowded room at Trinity College, yes, and struggled to follow while the century's most original philosopher conducted his seminars. Yes, an incredible privilege, an incredible opportunity, Sparrow told the undergraduate interviewer; of course I had only half an idea, at the time, just how fortunate I was. Otherwise I might not have wasted so much, Sparrow said. I might have struggled harder. Used my brain, such as it was, to better effect. But no, Sparrow said, no, I wouldn't have stayed with philosophy in any case. No. Wittgenstein was too persuasive on that point. Get out of it, he had told the young Sparrow. Get out. Do something worthwhile. Something real. Become a physician or a cabinetmaker or some such. It wasn't intended as an insult; it was heartfelt and I suppose loving advice, Sparrow said. He told all of us that—all those of us students who were reasonably close to him, and for whom he seemed to have some modicum of respect. Get out of academic philosophy. Do something useful. "And so finally I took him at his word," the *Alumnus* quotes Sparrow as having said. "I went back into microbiology."

Kessler smiles again at that one. He can picture Sparrow delivering it, with a face bald of all shame or irony.

Mind you, biology had never been really a passion for him, Sparrow explained. It had never been an obsession, a sheer transporting obsession, in the way that poetry was, and then later, for its time, philosophy. Nothing like that. Biology was merely an interest, call it. A reasonably stimulating intellectual discipline which happened also, eventually, to offer him a career that fitted the specifications Wittgenstein was urging. Originally he came to it in a rather haphazard way. When he had first arrived at Vanderbilt as a callow sixteen-year-old, Sparrow said, he had seized on biology as a major, though even then his head had been full of poetry, and of dreams of the life of a poet, whatever in God's name that might have been. He certainly didn't know. Subsisting on dry bread and rough wine in some Parisian cold-water garret, perpetually dizzy with inspiration and malnourishment, he supposed. But his father back in coastal Georgia was a sternly practical man, an important figure in Savannah law and Tattnall County rice, who had a balance-sheet approach to any enterprise in which he invested money, including his younger son's education. Therefore poetry could be only a stolen pleasure, Sparrow said, which is what best suits it anyway; and law also was excluded as a profession, based on the coppery bitter taste left in young Claude's mouth by negative example of the father. Therefore biology. Biology

because—if there was any real reason at all—his favorite maternal uncle was a medical doctor. Anyway I was five years too
late to be a poet at Vanderbilt, Sparrow said. The Fugitives were
all gone. Graduated, dispersed, moved on to teaching positions
in other universities. I had missed the golden age, barely. I did
have one course from John Crowe Ransom, my freshman year,
Sparrow said; but Mr. Ransom was distant, he did not seem to
care for me personally; or else he thought my poems were just
rotten, a distinct possibility, and he was too polite to bring
himself to tell me. There was no magical circle of gifted poets,
in any case, not anymore then, not when I arrived, Sparrow
said. Kessler wonders whether Claude Sparrow, in truth, ever
spent a day of his life studying biology.

The poetry part he does not doubt. The *Alumnus'* correspondent has even quoted some lines from a Claude Sparrow lyric,
ferreted out from the 1935 Vanderbilt yearbook. The subjects of
the poem are love and early death, the principal figures are
Harlequin and Pierrot. Kessler is inclined to agree with Mr.
Ransom.

By the time he left Nashville in '35, Sparrow told the *Alumnus,* his father the rice planter was dead and so he had a bit of
inherited money. By then also he had read himself deep into
philosophy and all through the Western canon, from Heraclitus
right up through Hegel, which seemed at that time to be the end
of the line. Hegel seemed to me then, Sparrow said, smirk if you
like, the ultimate modernity. Nietzsche and Schopenhauer I
didn't care for. So, Sparrow said. I had this bit of money. Naturally therefore I took off on the first ship for Europe, which is
what a young man did in those days. Maybe these days also, I
wouldn't know. But I wasn't going just to hitchhike up and
down through the wine valleys wearing an orange backpack,
Sparrow said. Not that there's anything necessarily so bad
about that, for a young man. But I had an agenda. I had been
admitted to read philosophy at Trinity College, Cambridge. It
was just a happy accident, almost, Sparrow told the *Alumnus.* I
knew something about Russell and G. E. Moore and the tradition at Trinity. I had barely heard the name, though, of Ludwig
Wittgenstein.

Quickly enough I was a convert, Sparrow said, to this very
new way of doing and talking about philosophy. To the man
himself. I was at his feet, I was hanging upon his words, I was

half-consciously adopting his quirky personal mannerisms, copying him, mesmerized and terrified by him, as were a dozen others my age and older, with my share of wits and considerably better. His personal intensity, the force of his presence let alone his intelligence, Wittgenstein's, were simply startling, Sparrow said. Electric is the only word I can use. A cliché, I suppose, but there you are. All of his students and colleagues have said roughly the same thing. His electrified presence. The *Alumnus*' correspondent was getting it all on his little pad or else he had brought a recorder, Kessler thinks; this was what he had come for. These recollections were what made Claude Sparrow, class of '35, newsworthy. Then after I had been attending his lectures just two terms, Sparrow said—after I had gotten to know him a bit, spending hours during the week on walks with him across Midsummer Common and along the river, talking about whatever he fancied to talk about and struggling just like a young bride to make him good company, listening mostly, going with him often to the cowboy films he loved so well—when I was under his sway utterly, Wittgenstein announced that he planned to leave Cambridge. For a year at least, possibly more. Needed to do some serious thinking, was the way he put it, typically. As though all his brain-spraining efforts there at Trinity were just casual daydreaming; as though all those electrified lectures were just chat. He had to think seriously now, for a while. So he was going to Norway, to live in a hut he had built with his own hands, on the coast above Stavanger. Later I would envision him there, in his mud hut—or his whatever sort of hut. Eating raw chickens he'd killed with his teeth, perhaps. And thinking. I couldn't tag along to Norway of course, Sparrow said. So I did what I felt was the next best thing. I left Cambridge and went to Vienna, from which Wittgenstein had originally come. It's fashionable now to say that one can't understand Wittgenstein's work without understanding late Hapsburg Vienna, the cultural milieu in which his sensibility and his moral concerns were shaped, Sparrow said. Maybe that's right. I don't really think many people—not more than a handful in the world, I mean—understand his work anyway. With or without the Vienna context. Certainly I don't claim to. But back then in '36 I hit on the very same notion, intuitively, you see. I'll take some credit on that ac-

228 *David Quammen*

count. Wittgenstein was hiding out in Norway so I went looking for him, for his meaning, in Vienna.

Eating raw chickens he'd killed with his teeth: Kessler enjoys
imagining a hesitation, when that phrase fell, in the earnest
note-taking of the philosophy major.

It was the start of his life's third great passion, Sparrow
claimed. His passion for the city of Vienna. And this one out-
lasted the others, long surviving his delusions that he could ever
write decent poetry, or make so much as a spear carrier's contribution to the modern revolution in philosophy—surviving
even his infatuation with Wittgenstein the person. Vienna became an important character for him, very much like a person
herself. Vienna was the older mistress, gently initiating the
young man into certain purpled mysteries, letting him cash his
energy and his innocence for a little pleasure and wisdom, at
steep but not unfair rates of exchange; the older mistress to
whom the young man will later sometime return, loyally, nos-
talgically, condescendingly. I myself returned after the war and
then again in the early 1950s, Sparrow said. Both times under
very different circumstances than during that first enchanted
stay, when I was young and moon-eyed. That first stay, I spent
most of my time in cafes. Demel's was too fine for me then, but
I had a regular table at the Sperl. Where I met my few Viennese
friends and did my reading—philosophy and German newspapers and Ezra Pound—and consumed enough dark wonderful
coffee to rot out my guts permanently, if it hadn't been for the
magic immunity of youth. I lived with a middle-class family in
their apartment just off the Lassallestrasse. The father was a
businessman whom I addressed unfailingly as Herr Direktor for
the fifteen months I spent under his roof. Having come to him
with a reference from Wittgenstein, whose family name was
eminent in the city, I was treated always with reciprocal respect, even when it became clear that I was just a philosophy-
drunk American layabout. My room at the family's place was a
deep cave in back, dark but perfectly satisfactory to me, furnished with a wooden table and a chair and a cot and a lan-
guishing aspidistra planted in a chamber pot. To which decor I
added a life-size bronze stork, acquired from a painter friend
who was leaving town, Sparrow said. After quoting this outpouring for its color value, the *Alumnus*' correspondent begins
circling his material back. Too soon, damn it, for Kessler's

wants. No, I didn't find the meaning of Wittgenstein in Vienna, not on this stay or later, Sparrow is quoted. I found everything *but* that. What did you find? is the question hollered in Kessler's brain, but the *Alumnus* doesn't bother to ask. Yes, I left and went back to Cambridge in early '38, just before Hitler's triumphal welcome by the Viennese. We practically passed at the city limits, he and I. Very glad I missed that occasion, actually, Sparrow said. Yes, Wittgenstein was back in England also. Get out, he told me. Find something useful to do. By then I was capable of hearing him, so I returned to the States, and to another stint of graduate school. Kessler frowns, frustrated. The profile is winding down to a finish. The philosophy major has been writing about an unexceptional man, a microbiologist and government drone, who once knew the great Wittgenstein. Kessler on the other hand wants to hear about Claude Sparrow in Vienna. He suddenly has a strong feeling about Claude Sparrow in Vienna.

"I was there briefly after the war," Sparrow told the *Alumnus*. "Then eventually I went over again, in 1952, and stayed on until the joint occupation ended in '55. I was attached as a consultant to the Allied Council, more or less, advising them on technical matters of waste-water management and hygiene. The city's utilities had been very badly damaged. And there was a cholera scare, several years earlier."

Kessler shakes his head. The cholera scare is one of those nice allegorical touches, presumably. He can imagine for himself what sort of work Claude Sparrow was really doing in Vienna, if in fact he was there at all; still, extrapolation goes only so far and Kessler would like to *know* more. But by 1952, as even Kessler happens to be aware, Ludwig Wittgenstein was dead. Thank you very much, Mr. Sparrow, and Kessler can hear the philosophy major slapping his pad closed.

Thanks a million, Mr. Sparrow. And we'll forward a copy of this story, when it runs, to your office at the National Institutes of Health.

For the second time this morning Kessler waddles out to use the pay phone on the wall halfway between the bar and the lobby. He could use his room phone upstairs, of course, but the very thought of that climb makes his stomach lift like a boat deck and besides there is no need for any great amount of pri-

vacy. He is only trying to reach Barry, who again does not
answer at home, and again also does not answer at his office at
Georgetown.

This time Kessler lets the second call ring on until a switchboard receptionist returns, stating the obvious impatiently: Professor Koontz does not seem to be in his office, sir. Kessler asks
whether Barry has been in at all yet today. She doesn't know,
says the receptionist, implying also by her tone that if there
might be any way for her to find out she is determined not to
discover it. What she does is ring extensions. Kessler leaves the
simple message that he has been calling and will call again.
There is still more than an hour before Kessler needs to leave
the hotel. Maybe it will reach Barry, the message, maybe not.
Maybe Barry's odd immunity to alcohol last night did not apply
to the hangover phase, and he is resting in darkness under a
cold washcloth right now, with the telephone unplugged, as
Kessler himself would very much like to be. Three hours after
having gotten himself vertical, notwithstanding the fluids, Kessler only feels worse. He shuffles back to his table. His coffee cup
has been scooped away, a hint of overstayed welcome, and it's
necessary to ignore the hint and order another. Nothing wants
to go right today.

He continues reading.

The article Barry saved from the New York *Times Magazine*
is titled "Digging After the Mole." It ran in the issue for May 8,
1977, flanked by the usual complement of imperious underwear
ads.

It was written by P. J. Bainton—only a name to Kessler,
though a vaguely familiar one. Over the past four or five years
Kessler has noticed a handful of CIA stories under the by-line
of this P. J. Bainton, mainly in *Harper's* or the *Atlantic,* possibly
one also in *Esquire* if his memory is correct, all of which looked
to be very much the same sort of piece Kessler himself used to
write. And none of which he bothered to read. Now he finds
that P. J. Bainton has preceded him on the trail toward Dmitri.
That might be a good thing, for Kessler's purposes, or possibly
not.

*In January of 1963 a Russian defector arrived in Washington
bearing a very strange message,* the Bainton story begins. Kessler pauses. He can imagine himself writing exactly the same
sentence. This defector will be Fedorenko, Bogdan Kirilovich.

The message is Dmitri. Kessler sits forward and allows himself one sip of coffee, his professional antennae all fully deployed. He hopes half-consciously that P. J. Bainton will prove to be helpful but not *too* helpful; besides curiosity and of course the quest for justice and truth, there is some sense of competition involved. He would not like to discover at this point that the article for which he has been stretching his neck, squandering his time and his piece of mind, has already been written. Then he remembers the tableau at Biaggio's grocery and feels, shamelessly, a caress of relief. Never mind the competition. This is a breaking story and Pokorny's murder is one thing at least that cannot very well be redundant. *The defector was Bogdan Fedorenko, a KGB officer who had been on assignment to Paris. Fedorenko had thrown himself into American hands just a week earlier. The message he carried,* according to P. J. Bainton, *was that a Soviet mole had penetrated high up within the Central Intelligence Agency.*

Yes, thanks, Kessler knows that much himself. The question of the moment is: how high did P. J. Bainton penetrate? Was it high enough to discover Dmitri's identity?

No. Kessler reads quickly to the end of the article. He skims across those parts that match his own information (Fedorenko's initial uncooperativeness, the meeting with Robert Kennedy that opened him up, the big announcement about a mole, the reaction of controlled hysteria at Langley, the arrival of Viktor Tronko to make matters even more confused, the ensuing upheaval and schism, McAttee and the Tronkovians versus Sparrow and the Fedorenkovites), giving closer attention to the rest but rushing ahead impatiently toward the answer to that pressing question. The answer is no: Bainton did not solve the big mystery. Dmitri was not unmasked—not in this magazine piece, anyway. The title turns out to be nicely precise, in that P. J. Bainton was writing as much about the process of *chasing* Dmitri—Claude Sparrow's ten years of relentless spadework, digging after the mole—as about Dmitri himself. Digging *after,* as distinct from digging *up.* Kessler is pleased by Bainton's failure, though he realizes that that is foolish and petty, and can sympathize with the frustrations. He wants Dmitri for himself. He wants his own fair chance with the shovel. You want a hernia or a cave-in is what you want, dimhead. Nevertheless Kessler feels another touch of relief when the Bainton story ends inconclusively, with just a last wild fillip of accusation, rather than anything solid.

Finally, some evidence in Agency hands suggests that Dmitri, all along, was positioned within the Counterintelligence section itself, a classic case of the fox guarding the henhouse, according to Bainton. *A dozen years later, with Claude Sparrow now in forced retirement, the rumor even persists that . . .* et cetera. Kessler recognizes these symptoms. Months of research had yielded a great junk pile of disconnected facts and intriguing suppositions, but no pattern, no single well-supported hypothesis, yet eventually it all had to be shaped into some sort of story. Deadlines had been set. Space had been allotted, investments of time and cash made. Poor P. J. Bainton must have been desperate, turning to lame formulations like "some evidence suggests" and "the rumor even persists." Kessler has been in the same miserable spot. He knows the panic, the code phrases that serve for self-extrication, the feeling that vultures are circling over your typewriter, drawn there by the smell of dead writing and dead hopes.

He goes back at once to comb the piece more thoroughly. What he is looking for now are new names, new details, new fragments, new possibilities—or any versions of reality that do *not* match with what he has already been told. Of this type of minor discovery there are several.

One concerns Sparrow's return to Vienna in the 1950s. Forget waste-water management, forget microbiology. Bainton confirms what Kessler suspected: Sparrow went back to that city for the CIA. In fact, according to Bainton, by 1952 he was the chief of station. And though Sparrow was already then on the rise, Vienna made all the difference to his career, as Bainton tells it. Sparrow's three years there at the end of the joint occupation were something of a triumphal march, evidently, which transformed him from just another bright young field officer, one among many, into a minor legend. The Vienna station under Sparrow became the Agency's best channel of intelligence from eastern Europe. Its productivity—both the number of agents recruited and the consistent quality of their information —surpassed even the larger base up in Berlin. More important, Sparrow himself received almost sole credit for detecting and foiling two major KGB gambits, two nearly successful penetrations of Western services—one of those against the British, one against his own shop. In the first case, he helped the Brits blast open their Soviet cell and salvage what they could in publicity. In the second, Sparrow personally turned back an agent who had been doubling against one of his officers, and that agent eventually furnished dossiers on half the KGB personnel in occupied Austria. These two coups, according to Bainton, gave a new order of momentum to Claude Sparrow's career. In 1955 he was called back to Washington and anointed chief of Counterintelligence. As customary, he brought a few of his own people back with him; but the refurbished Counterintelligence section did not dawdle along in any customary manner. It changed drastically. Some would say, it mutated. Formerly a sober enterprise devoted simply to watching and countering the opposition's more egregious gambits, and conducted in an almost bemused spirit by a clique of Ivy Leaguers, CI under Sparrow became a stronghold of zealotry, pathological vigilance, intellectual brilliance, personal eccentricity, and a complex exegetic view of international relations that would have done justice to a literary scholar at work on *Finnegans Wake*. For instance the Sino-Soviet rift, as seen from Claude Sparrow's office, was a disinformation hoax. The autonomy of Yugoslavia was a hoax. Khrushchev's de-Stalinization campaign was a hoax, and so was the persecution of Solzhenitsyn. Viktor Tronko of course was a hoax. Two of the young officers who followed Sparrow home from Vienna and helped set this tone, according to Bainton, were Melvin Pokorny and Roger Nye. Counterintelligence as run by Sparrow and these protégés very soon earned a mixed renown.

Mixed renown, that's a safe statement, thinks Kessler. Typhoid Mary had a mixed renown and the cold Moscow winters, no doubt, are a hoax—though Napoleon and Hitler were fooled. Kessler never realized that Claude Sparrow in power had been quite so demented. Pokorny had always seemed sane as a fox.

Kessler culls two other tidbits from the Bainton article. Both of these are interesting enough to go into his notebook as well as his memory, though they evidently held no special importance for P. J. Bainton, who let them drop offhandedly in the space of a single paragraph. The first is merely a phrase, a name, and a seemingly frivolous one—"the Schnitzel Group." Kessler guesses that for a Mel Pokorny coinage, the style is recognizable, and he wants to know more about it. The second fact of interest is a death: Fedorenko's. How curious that Sparrow failed to mention this, the demise of his own favorite defector, happening as it did with such unfortunate timing.

The paragraph containing both these small gems appears near the end of a perfunctory summary of the Viktor Tronko case. Bainton wrote: —*makes another bizarre story all to itself. The Tronko interrogation dragged on for more than three years, adding no useful clues to the search for Dmitri. Sparrow had set one of his most experienced and hardheaded deputies, Pokorny, to the chore of this prolonged debriefing. Still, all that could be established beyond dispute was that (a) Viktor Tronko was a liar, and that (b) he claimed Dmitri did not exist. Tronko's testimony about other aspects of KGB operations also differed materially from what Bogdan Fedorenko had said. A committee of analysts had been assigned to the Tronko case (they were known informally as the Schnitzel Group, because Tronko had defected in Vienna) and this group eventually recommended that Tronko and Fedorenko be brought together. Interviewing both Russians jointly in a confrontational context might resolve those discrepancies, it was thought. Before this idea could be acted on, though, Bogdan Fedorenko had died in an accident. He had been granted a CIA pension, after his own long debriefing, and resettled somewhere in New England under a fresh and well-guarded identity. On the morning of February 16, 1965, his body was found near Poughkeepsie. His car had gone off an icy road, landing upside down in a shallow, frozen lagoon.* It wasn't an accident and he wasn't a Russian, Kessler thinks.

He wasn't a Russian, Fedorenko. Not even an assimilated Muscovite. He was a Ukrainian. What else has Bainton gotten just slightly jumbled? No way to know. Kessler records the date, and Poughkeepsie, in his notes. He circles the entire paragraph on Barry's file copy. An accident? Come on, P. J., you can't really have believed that.

The lunch crowd has begun drifting into the Tabard. The waiter has now absolutely cut off Kessler's supply of coffee, averting his eyes on each zooming trip by. All right all right, you can have your table. Time to try Barry again, anyway, and then over the river to meet Sparrow. Kessler sets out a large tip. Then he sits, stubborn goat that he is, long enough to reread that closing passage of the Bainton story:

Finally, some evidence in Agency hands suggests that Dmitri, all along, was positioned within the Counterintelligence section itself, a classic case of the fox guarding the henhouse. Or to stay with our original metaphor: a case of the mole guarding the lawn. For Dmitri, what could have been more perfect? For the CIA, what could have been more disastrous? It isn't proven fact, by any means, but certain officials at Langley imply archly that this is their own view: Dmitri eluded Claude Sparrow's relentless search precisely because he was right there among the searchers. If that is true, the entire decade-long upheaval resulting from Sparrow's great hunt—the paralysis of operations, the dismissals and resignations, the spectacle of an intelligence service turned inward in disarray—can itself be seen as Dmitri's biggest victory. And Sparrow can be seen as his first and last victim.

There is also one other possibility. A dozen years later, with Claude Sparrow now in forced retirement, the rumor even persists that Sparrow himself was Dmitri. Does that notion seem dizzying, outlandish, paranoid in the extreme? Almost too clever and too devious for belief? It does indeed. In other words, it is exactly the kind of idea that might come from the brain of Claude Sparrow.

19

"The next phase lasted three years," says Claude Sparrow.

"The second hostile interrogation."

"So called. I prefer to think of it as the first *serious* debriefing."

"A debriefing conducted in a concrete cell. Under conditions approximating torture. Psychological torture, if not physical."

"Precisely," says Claude Sparrow.

"Tell me about it."

But Sparrow does not seem to be sure that he wants to. For a long time he stares off toward the naked trees, giving Kessler the left half of his face and showing, apart from the ruddy flush brought out already again by the cold air on his otherwise waxy cheek, no more animation than the profile on a buffed Roman coin. His left ear has also gone red. He must have been out for a long luncheon walk, killing time until Kessler arrived, or maybe sweeping the woods and the parking lots himself to make sure there is no Buddyboy watching today.

"Surely Mel did that," he says finally.

"Some."

"Mel would have known all the details. It was his debriefing."

"He was your deputy. It was your operation now. Tronko had been put in your hands. I assume you supervised pretty closely."

Sparrow turns. "Yes. That's correct. I was fully responsible."

"I heard Mel's version," says Kessler, stretching the truth. "Then he was murdered. I'd like to hear your version. Are you concerned about being murdered?"

"Of course not," Sparrow says and again shifts his attention away.

Kessler has noticed that the hazel eyes look faintly aqueous, like a failed gelatin. Sparrow seems to be in a state of emotion but the emotion, true enough, does not seem to be fear. Maybe it's grief over Mel. Maybe Claude Sparrow felt a great deal more strongly about Mel Pokorny than the mere professional relationship would suggest. They had been together since Vienna, after all. Mel was one of his protégés. Sparrow appears to carry some specially paining burden of guilt or regret over the way things have fallen out. And now he is not gazing off with the look of a spurned lover toward distant Langley; he is simply staring at a stand of bare elms, property of the city of McLean and in want of attention from the pruning crew. Litter of foam hamburger coffins and burrito papers on the intervening brown grass. Old man in a park on a dreary winter Monday, no place to go but home.

"Then tell me about it."

"Very simple. We had a complete set of lies, thanks to Jed and Sol Lentzer. Tronko's *legend*. The whole false story he had been programmed to tell." Invocation of Jed McAttee always seems to help Sparrow focus. "Now we wanted the truth."

November of 1964, Sparrow says. McAttee and Lentzer had been given their chance and botched it. All the peremptory presidential deadlines had come and gone, the Warren Report had been issued. The pressures of time and politics had somewhat abated. Though of course there were still other and very grave pressures. The task of Tronko's debriefing was charged over, finally, to the Counterintelligence staff. Tronko himself was not "in the hands of" the CI staff, however, not in the sense that Kessler seems to assume. No, Sparrow wants to make this small but important distinction: Tronko's actual physical custody—his care and feeding, his safety, guard details, the arrangement of living conditions—all that was still a matter for the Office of Security, just as it had been during McAttee's turn. Counterintelligence had no autonomy in that area. None whatsoever. They could only suggest and request. Every aspect of Tronko's physical keep had to be cleared through the Director's office, Sparrow insists, and then put into effect as a line order down through Security. So you see, Sparrow says, to claim that *we* tortured Tronko in some sense or other, *we* meaning *Counterintelligence,* is utterly unjust and inaccurate. Everything came down through other channels. Everything but the interrogation itself. In that only were we free to shape our own strategies.

"So now it's an interrogation again," says Kessler. Sparrow ignores him.

The facility itself, for instance. Sparrow and his people wanted Tronko in a wholly new place, a fresh context, away from the scene of Lentzer's efforts. They wanted better security, greater privacy, greater freedom for the debriefing officer to come and go without exposing himself to the curiosity of an Army sergeant in a guardhouse. They wanted Tronko more thoroughly isolated—and they wanted him to *feel* that isolation. Also there was the matter of duration. Sparrow himself already sensed, he says, that to dismantle Tronko's legend might take some real time. A year or more. Even he did not foresee at that point, though, just how *much* more it would take. No one guessed three years.

"Least of all, Viktor Tronko."

"No. No, that's wrong," says Sparrow, fastidious and cold. "He would have known exactly what he was stepping into. Perhaps better than anyone."

The facility was designed and constructed expressly for this single use. It met all the specifications. It cost Sparrow extravagantly—in more senses than one. The order had to go up from Counterintelligence to Eames's office and come back down through Security and Sparrow himself was required to raise a wild bureaucratic din, but he did that, and required also to pay the acquisition and construction costs from his own budget, and he did that too, and finally he got what he wanted. Tronko was moved during the last week of November.

"How?"

"By people from Security, under our supervision. He was blindfolded."

"Was he handcuffed again?"

Sparrow twists his head to see Kessler with both eyes. "Again?"

"Was he handcuffed?"

"Yes. Blindfolded and handcuffed. This was to be his passage beyond the pale."

"Moved by car or plane?"

"Both. Actually, we loaded him onto a military transport and flew him around for an hour, then landed again at a different end of the same air base. All for that sense of isolation, you see. Then it was by car." Sparrow, recollecting, grins like a guilty child.

"That's bizarre. Whose idea was it?"

"Mine, Mr. Kessler. And it wasn't bizarre. On the contrary, it was quite sensible and economical. We wanted Tronko to feel alone, remote, hopeless. But our own debriefing officer would still need to commute back and forth."

"Like Dante. Commuting to the far side of the grave."

"Like Dante in purgatory, yes," Sparrow agrees.

"I was thinking more of hell."

"But Viktor Tronko got out," says Sparrow. "Unfortunately."

"And you called this place the Vault. Concrete walls, concrete floor. A cot and a light. Nothing else. *Nothing*. Am I correct?"

"Mel named it that," says Sparrow.

Vault or crypt or whatever, Mel was the one who would know. It was Mel, after all, who spent so many hundreds of hours there over the next three years, sharing that concrete box with its chief inhabitant. In the first week of December 1964 Mel Pokorny began his divided life as a commuting inquisitor.

Thereafter, for just slightly more than three wearying years, he bounced back and forth two or three times a week between Langley and the Vault, between Claude Sparrow's company and Viktor Tronko's, carrying always questions in one direction and answers in the other, not much enlightenment either way, reviewing transcripts, brainstorming with Sparrow and the analysts, going back out to drag Tronko over old matters from a dozen different new angles, working long hours on too little sleep, consuming too much bad coffee and highway food, losing his marriage, burning himself unstintingly and with narrow focus, like an acetylene torch aimed for cutting a hole in a bulkhead, all of it just as Lentzer had done before, and Claude Sparrow himself back in the early days with Fedorenko. The difference was that Pokorny's ordeal went on so much longer, says Sparrow. And yet he seemed to be tireless. Indestructible. He seemed to thrive under this unwholesome regimen. He seemed to grow only more determined that Tronko could and would be broken. Mel was perhaps an example of the ideal personality for an interrogator, says Sparrow. He was very smart, he was quick, yet he could be fierce and tenacious as a pit bull—sometimes just shockingly fierce. At the same time there was that other side to him, the clown, the incorrigible comic, inventing silly nicknames and refusing ever to take himself or anyone else too seriously, cutting up in meetings like the classroom goon, a seemingly harmless and quite likable fellow who could charm a smile out of the most grim-minded individual. You would know about that last, thinks Kessler. Mel was the obvious choice for this chore, says Sparrow. He was in many ways the best I had.

Claude Sparrow is loyal. Kessler, seeing the slant taken, is distracted especially by one thing Sparrow has said. *Pokorny's* ordeal? *Pokorny's?* For Christ sake what about Viktor Tronko's?

After just two weeks they decided on another polygraph, says Sparrow. Brought the examiner out to Tronko, fluttered him right there in the Vault. None of that Holiday Inn business this time.

"Did you pull the EEG trick on him again?"

"No. We did not. Who told you about that?"

"A source," Kessler says. "I have several, besides yourself."

The logic behind this second test was entirely different, says Sparrow. The first had been a gimmick, yes. A little drama staged with the hope of breaking their impasse. Not a bad idea, says Sparrow—suggesting in Kessler's mind that again the inspiration must have been Sparrow's—but it didn't happen to work. The second was different. A straight polygraph, says Sparrow, as scientifically valid and accurate as we could make the thing. We called for it now, after only two weeks, because we imagined it might help us know how to proceed. Baseline data, was the general notion. We'd ask Tronko everything once again, let him give all his old lying answers once again, and then we'd look at the charts. The true emotional topography of his legend. That was the notion. We imagined this would give us coordinates on the weak points, you understand, and also identify the places where his tale must have had some framework of more solid factuality. Then we would proceed against the weaknesses. Flanking right around the points where he was solid.

Any good legend must contain *some* portion of real truth, *some* element of factual support, says Sparrow. The most persuasive lie, always, is a half-lie. Our thought was to let this flutter steer us toward Tronko's more vulnerable half. But again, says Sparrow, it didn't happen to work.

Under even the most scientific conditions, Viktor Tronko seemed to be lying about everything.

Everything—Sparrow stresses the word forlornly. Tronko's story seemed to contain almost no truth at all. No framework of real fact. Not even in the most banal details. Not according to the machines, anyway. As he had done before, when we intentionally made the test situation rather menacing for him, Tronko again registered spikes of cognitive dissonance against almost every statement he made. Spikes and more spikes, Sparrow says in a voice going shrill. Well, this itself was suspicious. Befuddling. It ran counter to what we knew or believed we knew about Soviet disinformation techniques. And of course it gave no help at all as to how we should focus our attack. Rather the opposite. It raised a whole bloody mess of new questions about what could or couldn't be taken for granted.

"Give me an example."

"Everything," Sparrow gasps again. "His job. His rank. His access. His special assignments and incongruous vacations, if any. His education. His language skills, or lack of. His relations with goddamn Rybakov. All of that was full of lies, the needles jumped right off the paper. Very well. Fair enough. The bugger had been sent over for a purpose, after all. His mission was to deceive us, presumably on a few crucial matters. Fine. But we had also asked him about these other things. Simple things, innocent. Who are you? What's your name? The needles were jumping already. What's your age? Are you married? Wife's name and age. Any children? One boy, all right, his name and age. Do you love your wife? Yes Viktor Tronko loved his wife. Good for him. Do you love your son? Pause. A straightforward query, is it not? *Do you love your son?* And dammit, these were supposed to be just the *control* questions"—Sparrow's fists shake like tiny maracas—"but the needles were going *everywhere!"*

"Easy."

"Yes. You're right." Sparrow catches his breath. He sits back against the bench and swings his legs in a willful rhythm; composes his hands into a still life on his lap. "I'm not supposed to excite myself."

"So he lied there too," Kessler says helpfully. "Even the personal matters. He had no wife and son."

"A wife maybe, but no son. Or something," says Sparrow.

"He invented a son. Or his bosses invented one for him. But why in the world should they do that?"

The little legs continue swinging. Sparrow works them as though he is pumping a bellows. "God damned if I ever knew."

So without the advantage of any particular guidance they began the long process of trying to comprehend Viktor Tronko —the process that Sparrow wants to think of as a "debriefing" but to which he can't seem to resist applying words like "attack" and "dismantle." Kessler recalls how Max Rosen put it: the idea was not just to incarcerate Tronko for a period of intensive questioning, but to demoralize him and break the man's will. Will to resist being equated with will to lie. Break the man's will and you also break open the legend. Break open the legend and find—aha!—Moscow's sinister little toothy caiman lurking inside. But the eggshell was evidently tougher than anyone foresaw. Sparrow even now seems prone to hyperventilate at the thought of that pliant toughness. Kessler also remembers a bit of Pokorny's description, so frustratingly foreshortened, and offered before Kessler knew how much he might care: Tronko in solitary for three years, surrounded by concrete and questions. No human contact except with his latest interrogator, said Mel, the cast-iron asshole yours truly. Claude Sparrow on the other hand seems to view the whole episode from a much different perspective than those two, Pokorny and Rosen. Sparrow's version is not so immediate, not so claustrophobic. Not so concrete. His powers of imaginative self-transport seem to have failed him here, or else been determinedly restricted. He may have spent half his working life on mental reconnaissance visits to the third floor of the Lubyanka in Moscow, out-of-body experiences that allowed him to test the feel of L. V. Nechaev's swivel chair, but he does not seem ever to have projected himself into the Vault. Kept his distance from that place, mentally as well as physically. The second hostile interrogation, in Sparrow's mind, seems to exist chiefly as a series of mendacious transcripts and a long-distance battle of wills. And the Vault itself was a vaguely imagined, mildly austere place where Sparrow himself never went—no more than Viktor Tronko came to Langley.

"Where was it?" says Kessler.

"Out. Outside the Washington area." Sparrow's hand makes a push at the air, implying the outland status of all America. "But as I said, within range."

"Where exactly?"

"Exactly? I won't tell you that."

"Why not?"

"Because I don't choose to. Just as I won't speak by name of Agency men who are still active. Never mind, Mr. Kessler. You couldn't go there and find anything now. Leave it."

"You speak about Jed McAttee," Kessler argues. He really does want a look at the place, the Vault, for no evidential reason but merely on principle. Go see for yourself, breathe and touch, before you describe. Maybe it's no more than a literary need. "McAttee is still active."

"Yes. Well. Jed is a *public figure,*" in derisive italics. "And he can damn well take care of himself."

For three years Mel made his commutes and brought back his tapes. The tapes were transcribed right there in Counterintelligence, under a designation of highest priority and highest restriction, then sent straight down the hall to Sparrow's personal office, where he and Mel and Roger Nye would work over each installment before Mel went back out. One copy of every transcript went also to the analysts, who dealt with it in their own curious way, and filed advisory reports that came back to Sparrow for whatever use he chose to make of them. The analysts themselves were not within Sparrow's section; they were separate, even remote, a small working group over in the Office of Strategic Research, but for the entire three-year period they were assigned to the Tronko problem and that only, and occasionally they saw something in the transcripts or offered an idea that Sparrow and his own people had missed. Otherwise the yield from Mel's ongoing interrogation was held to drastically limited access. Jed McAttee saw none of the transcripts. No copy to any other section or division. Even Herbert Eames got no copy—though that was at his own choosing, and he was kept abreast of progress by verbal briefings from Claude Sparrow delivered privately, just the pair of them, in the Director's office.

That last didn't demand much of Sparrow's time because for a long while, he says, there just didn't seem to *be* any progress.

Tronko was repeating obstinately all the same old failed lies he had told Lentzer. Tourist Department, under Rybakov. Rank of colonel. Oswald's KGB file, pure as snow. No such goblin as Dmitri. All the same tired nonsense, says Sparrow. Insulting to the intelligence. So we just had to keep squeezing him harder.

"Care to elaborate on that?"

"Certainly. We tried to drive Viktor Tronko insane with boredom. It was all we could do."

"Boredom."

"Yes, there you have it: the ultimate psychological weapon of the liberal West. Boredom. Sit in on a Board of Estimates meeting sometime and you'll see what I mean. In fact, perhaps we should have put Tronko through a few of those meetings."

"Did you ever use drugs?"

"No. Drugs were forbidden." On further contemplation, Sparrow adds: "Only the other side is allowed to use drugs. We're gentlemen, over here. Yes indeed. Meaning, we choose to fight standing on one foot."

"Were you ever tempted?"

"Of course I was tempted, always. Those things can be bloody effective. Might have made the difference. But I've told you. Drugs were forbidden."

As was the tapping of telephones, on U.S. soil and without a court order—Kessler recalls—but that evidently didn't dissuade you. The drug business continues to puzzle Kessler, though it seems a dead end. He scratches himself a note, quickly, while changing the subject.

"These analysts. Were they the 'Schnitzel Group'?"

"Yes, precisely. You already know about them, Mr. Kessler? From your many well-placed sources?"

"No. I don't. I'd like you to tell me about them."

"Three macrocephalic academic types alone in a room." Kessler waits for more. Sparrow just sits. He has had his say.

"But you admit they helped you. They contributed certain insights."

"I do admit it. I've got nothing against academic types, in their place."

"Names?" says Kessler. "Or are they still active?"

Sparrow ponders for a moment, presumably reviewing what he knows of the retirement schedule of the Schnitzel Group. Taking Kessler by surprise, he offers a name: "Sidney Gondel-

man. Large fellow, with a training originally in physics. I've
heard he went to a private think tank, somewhere up the Hudson. Better money. Mel called him Sidney Gondwana."

Kessler scribbles it all. "Thank you."

"For God's sake don't say I sent you."

But Viktor Tronko was a stubborn man, a rather strong man
in fact, Sparrow continues, and boredom in even its more extreme form was not enough of a weapon to readily break him.
He was not bothered by the fact that his hosts utterly disbelieved him. Nor by the impossible errors and contradictions in
his story, as those were thrown up to him. Nor by the physical
situation either. The Vault. Loneliness, sensory deprivation,
with seemingly no prospect of lying his way out. No. He held.
Damn his soul, he held, says Sparrow. A good soldier. General
Avvakian had chosen well.

Not according to Max Rosen, Kessler remembers. *If Tronko
was sent by Moscow, why wasn't he given more to offer? Why was
his dowry so meager? Ask yourself why Moscow should have chosen so badly.* Another variation on the central discrepancy of
opinion. Was Viktor Tronko a strong man or a muddled hopeless drunk? A good soldier or a deserter from the ranks? Was he
well chosen or badly chosen or wasn't he chosen at all?

"You made these assumptions," Kessler says. "One was that
Tronko had been sent. And not just sent. That he had been sent
by this General Avvakian. Which would mean it was all a *dezo*
operation—am I right? Or do I have Avvakian confused with
one of the others?"

"Not assumptions. Well-founded deductions. Yes, that's
right: Avvakian. *Dezo.*"

"Let's talk about the deductive process."

But instead Sparrow makes a leap forward, to begin talking
about the critical point of impasse, the point at which all his
own deductions and Pokorny's interrogations and Viktor
Tronko's stubborn lying finally converged with the impatience
of Herbert Eames. It happened in December of 1967, just over
three years after Tronko had entered the Vault.

"He *held,* damn him," Sparrow repeats quietly. "He held,
and we ran out of time."

Partly, says Sparrow, it had to do with political pressures
again. Lyndon Johnson had fallen into the last and enduring
foul mood of his presidency, and one day, during an NSC meet-

ing in late December that year, the subject of the Tronko case had somehow cropped up. Certainly Eames himself wouldn't have mentioned it. Someone else, maybe the National Security Adviser or one of our other bureaucratic enemies, says Sparrow. Johnson of course had forgotten all about Viktor Tronko. He was enraged when he heard that the matter had never been settled, that Tronko was still being detained, still being debriefed. Enraged and shocked, were the words Eames used when he told us of the President's reaction, though I personally found it hard to imagine Lyndon Johnson being genuinely shocked by anything, says Sparrow. Of the rage part, there was no doubt. Eames returned from that meeting ashen-faced. We could only guess what exactly the President had said to him. And all in front of a roomful of witnesses, Eames's own peers. So at nine the following morning Eames suddenly called both myself and McAttee into his office, says Sparrow, and told us that there must be a final, conclusive judgment on Tronko within sixty days. Sixty days, mind you, when three years had been insufficient. Eames still seemed a little pale and wobbly from his humiliation the previous afternoon. This occurred during the week between Christmas and New Year's, our busiest and most frantic time of year, everything in half disarray with the effort to compose budget documents. The budget is now a secondary priority, we were told. My God. Eames was passing along to us the same peremptoriness that he had gotten from Johnson—though not anything like the same rudeness, I'm sure. He wanted the Tronko thing settled. And not settled "as soon as decently possible," not "with all dispatch," not "by March 1 or thereabouts," no: he wanted it settled in sixty days, period. A definitive report should appear on his desk by the morning of February 27. It was quite unlike Herbert Eames as I had otherwise known him, says Sparrow. Furthermore we two —McAttee and I, that is—would be personally and jointly responsible for making this impossibility happen.

"How did you feel?"

"How? Crestfallen, of course," says Sparrow. "This was disaster. Madness. Total disaster." The legs go into motion again, short weighty pendulums counting off a segment of fleeting time: just sixty days.

"Did you consider resigning?"

"Yes. Definitely. I would have loved to do something so stupid and petulant."

"But you decided against that."

"Decided is hardly the word. I knew better. I couldn't afford any such childish self-indulgence. Flushing half a lifetime of effort down the commode."

"And conceding the victory to Jed McAttee."

"Precisely."

Under this ultimatum from Herbert Eames, a small panel was selected to conduct the review. Three men. These three would examine the entire documentary record of the case—all the transcripts from the various stages of debriefing, plus every other scrap of evidence—and then render a final assessment by Eames's deadline. They would be granted access to any file they might need, and to all other assets and resources of the Agency, with a single exception: Viktor Tronko himself. No further interviews, Eames decreed. No more visits, no more polygraphs, no more follow-up questions to puzzling answers to questions about previous answers. *No more.* Evidently Eames was concerned that the person in the Vault, whoever and whatever he was, might cast the same spell of confusion over this panel that he seemed to have cast over all prior inquisitors. You'll work from the documentation, God knows there's enough of it, Eames told them. The panel members came from three separate divisions within the Agency. They were all—they were *supposedly* all, Sparrow corrects himself—they were supposedly all men of the best fiber, much esteemed for objectivity as well as acuity of mind. Eames himself reviewed and endorsed the choices.

"Who?"

"Roger Nye from my shop. Even the unspeakable Jed couldn't argue with that. Everyone knew Roger for one of the finest and cleanest brains at the Agency."

Kessler decides to let pass the question of just what Sparrow means by a "clean" brain, and to stay for now on the track. "Someone from McAttee's shop too?"

"Scott Wickes," Sparrow says brusquely.

"Ah. The unspeakable Scott. I wondered when we'd come back to him." But Sparrow shows no sign of being amused. "Who was the tie breaker?"

"Sidney Gondwana. From the analysts."

"Gondelman."

"Gondelman, I meant. Yes. Sidney Gondelman."

And the impossible *was* accomplished, more or less. The panel of three hid themselves away for those sixty days, with that small mountain of self-contradictory paper, proceeding upon their assignment as though it were purely a problem of textual exegesis. They locked grips with the phantom of Viktor Tronko and with each other's view of that phantom. They had their own separate conference room, down on the second floor in a wing devoted otherwise to the Directorate of Science and Technology. They didn't discuss their progress or lack of it with anyone but each other—not even with Sparrow himself nor, so far as he knew, with McAttee. Herbert Eames had forbidden that. They were the jury on Viktor Tronko, these three, and now the trial was over, the closing arguments had been made, and they were *out.* Deliberating, and not to be tampered with. On February 27, 1968, a sheaf of typescript appeared, as demanded, on Eames's desk. It ran to 126 pages. There was no executive summary and, according to a cover note of transmittal, there were at that moment no copies in existence but this single one. It had been composed chiefly on Roger Nye's personal typewriter; it came to be known as the Nye Report. It was signed by Sidney Gondelman and Roger Nye.

"But not by Scott Wickes," says Kessler.

"Not by Wickes. No."

"Did he file a dissent? A minority opinion?"

"He filed a tantrum. We'll get to that."

There were two sections to this document. Following a dry recapitulation of the major points of evidence, the discrepancies among those points, and the various plausible or less plausible explanations for those discrepancies (all of which was necessarily concise at just 114 pages), the Nye Report spoke its conclusions in the form of numerical probabilities:

—The probability that Viktor Tronko had lied to his American debriefers, from the first contact at Rome and consistently thererafter, and not just due to drunken confusion, not just from an impulse of innocent self-inflation, but with the determined intention to deceive, was reckoned at one hundred percent.

—The probability that Viktor Tronko was (as he most recently claimed to be) a former KGB officer of the rank of colonel, lately assigned to the Tourist Department, as deputy to one Trofim Filippovich Rybakov, in which position he, Tronko, had handled the routine surveillance file of the expatriate Lee Harvey Oswald, could be put altogether at zero percent, in the opinion of the signatories.

—The question of whether Tronko had ever handled an Oswald file, routine or not, innocent or not, was judged indeterminable. The prospect that no direct KGB contact had ever been made with Oswald, despite his U-2 background, as Tronko claimed, was set at a ten percent likelihood of being true. The probability that the penetration agent code-named Dmitri did not exist, as Tronko claimed he did not, was put—for the very reason that Tronko claimed it—at ten percent.

—The chance that Viktor Tronko was a false defector, a dispatched agent, sent to Rome and then Vienna on an elaborate mission of disinformation, was figured at eighty percent.

Eighty percent, Sparrow repeats. Eighty percent. In our judgment, concluded the Nye Report, it is overwhelmingly probable that Tronko was sent across expressly for the purpose of deceiving this Agency and this country on the matters of Dmitri and Oswald. *Overwhelmingly probable,* Sparrow repeats.

"Was Eames satisfied?"

"No. Of course not. He'd wanted unanimity and certitude. The inachievable dream. Not a table of numbers. He certainly couldn't go back to Johnson with that sort of statistical gobble. 'Eighty percent chance we've been suckered, Mr. President. Ten percent chance that the Warren Commission got it right.' He'd have taken worse than a tongue-lashing. But Eames was stuck and he knew it. He himself had called halt to the interrogations. His panel had delivered. Now it was all on the desk of him, the Director. Now he had no way out but to pay his money, as they say, and take his choice."

"Except Scott Wickes hadn't delivered."

"No. That's correct," says Sparrow. "Not yet. Wickes refused to sign. He just went back up to Soviet Bloc and brooded. McAttee kept him out of view, protected Wickes under his own skirts, until the storm winds had died down and the Director's attention had shifted elsewhere."

"Where did it shift to?"

"Tronko himself. The problem of what to do with the body."

"The *body?*"

"Just an expression, Mr. Kessler. Don't work yourself up. The problem of what to do with the man."

"The man in the Vault."

"Yes. At that point he was still there."

"This eighty-percent-likely Soviet disinformation agent who had already served three years of solitary for no other crime than lying."

Sparrow shrugs. "If you care to see it that way."

"How did Herbert Eames choose to see it?"

Sparrow slouches lower within his camel-hair coat. The legs have stilled, the hands have disappeared again into pockets. If he were a tortoise, he would be gone altogether. The ears and the little nose are raw. He doesn't answer.

"What did Eames do?" Kessler presses.

"You'll need to understand," says Sparrow, "that at this point, the spring of 1968, Herbert Eames had already begun to leave us. Something like Lyndon Johnson had, I suppose. Though in his own very different manner." Sparrow doesn't take his eyes off the naked elms. They might all just be leafless with the season or, some of them, dead of blight. Only a man who comes to this park often would know.

"He was already sick then? Eames was?"

"No, not in the way you mean. Not like later. But he had already lost his vigor. He had lost the focus and strength that were necessary to the job. Getting himself a tumor, eventually, was just a symptom of that loss. Rather than vice versa."

Kessler waits.

"You should understand that Herbert Eames had once, in his time, been an exemplary Director," Sparrow volunteers. "Among the best we've had."

"What did he do about Tronko?"

"A very silly thing."

Kessler's opinion of the late Herbert Eames continues to be improved by new information. Eames accepted the assessment of the Nye Report, evidently, and then pointedly ignored the options presented therein for the "disposition" of Viktor Tronko.

"Wait a minute. *Disposition?*" says Kessler.

"Never mind," says Claude Sparrow.

"No. *Wait.* Like what sort of options? Burial at sea in an oil drum? Involuntary committal to an asylum? A lifetime in the Vault? I'm just asking. What options?"

"Options are not the same as recommendations."

"I understand. But *what options?*" Having raised his voice, Kessler glances self-consciously around the park. In all its desolate banality, this time of afternoon, it is theirs alone.

"Never mind. Forget that, Mr. Kessler. That's a blind alley, I promise you."

"Where can I get a copy of this Nye Report?" For the first time in days Kessler thinks of the empty Grand Central locker and the key from Pokorny's attaché case. For the first time he feels a sense of having been robbed.

"You can't. Forget about it."

" 'Highly classified,' " Kessler says scornfully. "For all the usual good reasons."

"Yes," Sparrow says. His chin is stuck out like a small plow. "Yes, exactly."

What Eames did was give Viktor Tronko his choice. A Solomonic choice, it was supposed to be, says Sparrow. To my own great surprise, to my own horror, says Sparrow, Eames had elected to take the findings of the Nye Report in a counterintuitive and utterly wrongheaded way. An eighty percent likelihood was not a likelihood after all. Eighty percent full turned out to be—in Eames's view, this fading Eames—twenty percent empty. *Overwhelmingly probable* was not probable enough to carry. Instead Eames decided, for reasons known only to him, that a narrowly legalistic standard of proof should be applied. By this standard, Viktor Tronko had not been found guilty *beyond a reasonable doubt.* If you can believe it, says Sparrow. His duplicity had not been established *beyond a reasonable doubt,* because there was still that twenty percent. So Eames proposed simply to send the man packing. Tronko was summoned in from the Vault and scrubbed up and given a fresh change of clothes, and then Eames actually met with him personally. Not at the Director's own office, of course, because Tronko still wasn't to be allowed inside the gates, but instead in a room of that very same Holiday Inn, the one at Tyson's Corner, where we had staged the first polygraph, says Sparrow. I myself was obliged to arrange this encounter, says Sparrow. Vodka and herring for two, and a little placative small talk. It was horrible, says Sparrow. And then the Director gave Tronko his choice.

He could accept a plane ticket to Vienna or one to Los Angeles.

If he chose Vienna, his original Soviet passport would be returned to him, and his other papers, in addition to which he would be given one hundred dollars in cash and a new suit. He would hit the street cold, in Vienna, and be on his own. Free to do as he wished—or at least, as he could. The four years in America would vanish as though they had been just a long somnolent blink; and here he would be, back where he started. No one would receive advance information of his arrival. He could walk into the Soviet Embassy, declare his identity, and announce that the mission had failed. Or he could bypass the embassy and take his chances otherwise—disappear, get as far away as he was able on that hundred dollars and that new suit. No one from this Agency, or this country, would bother him further. No one on this side of the ocean would come looking for him or care where he went.

Tronko's eyes hung out of their sockets as Eames described this option, says Sparrow. Tronko knew, as we all did, says Sparrow, that he wouldn't be good for twenty-four hours in Vienna, whatever the truth might have been about his mission. The Soviets would kill him just to show us we had been wrong —even if we had been right. Or he would find himself on a fast flight back to the cells of the Lubyanka. It was only Eames who didn't seem to grasp these realities anymore. Tronko grasped them perfectly.

Or there was Los Angeles.

If he chose the L.A. ticket, he would receive also a new identity, supported by an authentic American passport showing his own photograph and the new name, as well as a cashier's check for $86,443, and a letter of reference from a mythical employer stating that the man in question had served for four years as a reliable and satisfactory employee in whatever capacity Tronko cared to specify. The particular dollar amount represented back salary for the four years plus a few weeks that Tronko by then had spent in American custody, at a rate of just over $21,000 per year, which would have been his CIA pay in a position roughly equivalent to deputy chief of the Tourist Department. He would in this case too get a new suit. He would receive no physical protection from the Agency, and by the same token there would be no surveillance.

"I choose that. I choose Los Angeles," Viktor Tronko said quickly, according to Sparrow. Eames had not even finished explaining the arrangement whereby the letter of reference would be verifiable through a telephone number that rang at Langley.

"Are you quite sure?" said Eames.

Tronko nodded emphatically, by Sparrow's account. He was sure.

Less than a week later Viktor Tronko was drinking his way across Beverly Hills, says Sparrow. By June he was in Fresno, with a job as custodian at a set of apartment buildings and a solid alibi for the night Robert Kennedy was shot (which was very lucky for him, and also for Herbert Eames, says Sparrow). The part about no surveillance had been untrue, Eames's sole concession to trickery or, as Sparrow prefers viewing it, to normal sensible sound practice. The cashier's check was good. After a year Tronko moved back down to Santa Barbara, having managed somehow to land a part-time instructorship in the Russian department at UCSB. He supplemented that trickle of income with work for a dry-cleaning chain, though there was still also the large nest egg. After another six months we stopped watching. Sparrow is reciting these facts, now, in a weary droning voice. He has slumped still lower on the bench beside Kessler, so low that his neck rests on the back edge and his toes, pointed, touch the ground. He stares toward the elms.

It's ending, thinks Kessler. The last day of my three, and we're going to finish early.

And damn, I still haven't learned anything.

I've got nothing but a whole lot of tangled and useless information. I don't know the big Who, and I don't know the big Why. I have been snowed upon—Christ, I've been avalanched at—by an expert. God damn. For a moment Kessler feels the nervous despair of having botched a precious opportunity.

Sparrow goes silent. But it doesn't seem he has come quite to the end. He has caught himself in mid-sentence.

Kessler turns. He traces the vector of Claude Sparrow's frozen attention. From out of the bare woods along the far perimeter of the park, near the paved path but not on it, a figure has emerged. Kessler squints toward the figure, trying to make sense of some blurry, confusing details. It is a man in camouflage fatigues. Or a boy. No, it's a man, but a small man, and he moves as though feeble or very old. The man is bent over a long tool of some sort, holding himself hump-shouldered, head low, his own attention directed at the ground. He could be raking leaves. But he is not. Kessler and Sparrow together watch the man come, as he inches his way across the browned grass, seemingly oblivious to the fact that he might be observed, that he could possibly bring any conversation to a dead stop. Now Kessler can see him well enough: an old man dressed in camo fatigues, yes, a fragile pensioner, probably at least in his early eighties, mincing along with an electronic metal detector. Combing the park for lost silver and keys and interesting trinkets. He wears a baseball cap, and over it a pair of earphones. The dish of his instrument hovers back and forth above a narrow swath along the far edge of the path, putting Kessler in mind of some sort of psychic vacuum cleaner by which stray ideas might be sucked up, carried in through the earphones. Or maybe memories. The old man is looking for something, and apparently it doesn't much matter what. He will settle for whatever he finds. The search itself gives him purpose, no doubt. Kessler can't quite read the insignia on his cap.

"There's that asshole again," Sparrow whispers.

The old man takes an excruciatingly long time to angle past them across the park. He is thorough at his task. Kessler finds himself dreading that the man may turn, reverse, and work his way back up, along the near side of the path. But the old man seems to have gotten interested in the redwood chips under a jungle gym.

It's ending, thinks Kessler. He has started again to feel abused by the cold. "Before you finish, tell me about Scott Wickes."

"The hell with Wickes," Sparrow grumbles.

Kessler's mood sinks further. This fugue of gloom into which Sparrow has fallen seems to be contagious. Then, as though hauled back from some distant distraction, Sparrow brings his face around toward Kessler.

"Finish?" says Sparrow. "No no, not yet. Certainly not before we have done McAttee and Ivan."

"Ivan?"

"Ivan. See how appallingly little you know? Ivan was *McAttee's* greatest and worst folly."

The emphasis is so clearly on *McAttee,* the name, that Kessler is forced to wonder: as opposed to *whose?* Herbert Eames's greatest and worst folly, as just described? Or is Sparrow perhaps thinking about himself?

"Open your notebook, Mr. Kessler, and I'll give you a story to write."

Ivan began in 1967, during the middle stages of Tronko's term in the Vault. Sparrow himself was so absorbed with the debriefing, with the transcripts he was getting and the verbal reports from Pokorny, that he barely—

"Ivan began what?" Kessler interrupts.

"Began to happen."

"Was Ivan a person?"

"Ivan was a voice. A putative voice. A source. Whether it was a real person or not, we never knew. And never *will* know."

"A goblin," says Kessler.

"Yes."

"Much like Dmitri."

Sparrow scowls. "No. Take my word, Dmitri was indisputably real. That we *do* know. Ivan was something quite different."

Ivan, from the start, was McAttee's very own. Ivan grew from a seed that McAttee had planted and watered back in the middle 1950s, while Jed was still just a lowly case officer in Berlin. At least so goes the story, says Sparrow. It was only one seed among many, tossed out on untilled ground, and McAttee himself admitted to having had no special intuition that this one in particular would germinate, take root, grow into something. He had merely been operating on instinct and sound principles, playing percentages, trying to maximize possibilities. Any runner of agents, any field man worth his pay, functions just the same way, devoting some time and attention to long-range, low-likelihood prospects, each of whom might someday turn into a valuable asset but probably will not. In this case one did: and behold they named him Ivan. Or so goes the story, says Sparrow. McAttee had known this person originally during his own time in Berlin back before the Wall, but whether Ivan had been attached to the KGB already then, or perhaps to the GRU, whether under diplomatic cover or some other sort, whether in fact Ivan had been stationed in East Berlin or had only come passing through, were questions that Jed wouldn't answer. Or

would answer only to Herbert Eames, in private session; and
Eames wasn't sharing the answers with Claude Sparrow.
Whether McAttee himself had ever so much as *met* Ivan, in a
face-to-face contact, was even a matter of uncertainty. It was
merely known that they had somehow connected, McAttee and
the voice called Ivan. McAttee did a few well-calculated favors
for Ivan during the earlier years, toward consolidating that connection and reinforcing Ivan's ambivalent lean toward the West,
and then for more than a decade the connection lapsed to silence. McAttee forgot all about him. Ivan was still undecided as
to his own loyalties, or more likely as to his level of daring, or
else he was simply not in position where it was feasible for him
to act. Finally that changed. Suddenly one day Jed heard from
him. He heard in the form of a long-ago-prearranged signal
requesting contact. Presto, Ivan was ready. He had fetched up
as a desk officer at the Lubyanka, conditions had altered, inhibi-
tions were less, and he was now ready to place his career and
his life within the disposition of Jed McAttee. At least so goes
the story, says Sparrow.

The resumption of contact was itself an elaborate little
drama, if one is willing to credit Jed's later account of that part,
says Sparrow. He received the signal by way of a case officer
from the Berlin base, a man who had worked under Jed while
he was station chief in Bonn and whom he still trusted completely; this younger man had concocted a tale of family emergency in order to get three days' leave back in the States, and
then delivered Ivan's signal personally in an evening meeting at
McAttee's home. The younger man knew nothing of what the
signal entailed except that it came from the opposite side, that it
seemed to be potentially important, and that it was intended for
Jedediah McAttee alone. McAttee flew out of Washington a day
and a half later. The long-ago-prearranged rendezvous point
was in West Berlin, fortunate for McAttee but possibly a problem for Ivan, now that the Wall was in place. The time of day
was also prearranged; the date was specified in the signal he had
received. McAttee checked in with the current chief of the Berlin base, explaining with dire emphasis that he was there on old
business and that he wanted to be given a long tether. No tether
at all, actually. He wanted to be left alone. The base chief could
clear it by cable with Langley, if he so wished. But that cable
should go straight to the Director's office, no intermediate

quacking to Bonn station, no consultation with anyone else—
otherwise McAttee and the poor base chief would be at war.
This was so like Jed, you see, that it makes me inclined to
believe in the whole little episode, says Sparrow. He was such a
melodramatic fool, such a cowboy in a silk neckerchief, whenever he got into the field. He loved it so. Well, the base chief said
just about what I would have said, Sparrow tells Kessler: Be my
guest, Jed, go out and get yourself kidnapped. McAttee went off
in his Burberry to an appropriately seedy hotel. He made the
rendezvous point just on time, but no one showed up. No sign
of any Ivan.

He made the fallback two hours later, and still there was no
one. Returned to his hotel and waited a day. Showed up again
at the rendezvous point exactly twenty-four hours after the first
try, again no sign of Ivan, but this time a young German frau
with a child in a pram intercepted him as he was leaving. She
asked him for directions to the Zoological Gardens—clearly
just a pretext for an impromptu brush contact, Jed explained
later, because by her accent she was a Berliner herself whereas
he was unmistakably, by his clothes, an American. So he impro-
vised with her through a few lines of amiable street-corner chat,
to see what might develop. Did he like children? the woman
asked. Yes, he lied. My little boy is a very bright baby, she
bragged, very handsome, quite intelligent and communicative
for his age. Jed took the hint. He bent himself over the pram as
though to admire her child; he tickled the kid, he smiled, he
even spoke a bit of baby talk. And he discreetly removed the
piece of folded, sucked-upon paper that it was holding in its fat
little paw. Then he excused himself to the woman and went on
his way. The scrap of paper informed him of a new time and a
new place: Luther Bridge, where the Paulstrasse crosses the
Spree; nine-thirty the following evening.

Nine-thirty the following evening, at the Luther Bridge, Ivan
once more failed to appear. By now Jed was getting concerned
that something had gone seriously wrong. Perhaps Ivan, after
all those years of cautious delay, had been discovered and
squashed just on the very verge of his first useful act as an
agent. This possibility also implied a greater jeopardy for
McAttee himself. Maybe he *would* be kidnapped, and that base
chief would get the last laugh. Nevertheless Jed skulked back
out to the Luther Bridge at 3 A.M. the next morning. You ap-

preciate the motif of modest but intrepid professionalism, I trust, says Sparrow. Here was our Jed now in dungarees and a dark sweater, armed with a flashlight—a pavement artist again, in his middle age. He searched the undergirders and pilings of the bridge. It took him two hours, counting interruptions to wait out the passage of hookers and police patrols. He was obliged to do some rather athletic climbing; he might have fallen into the Spree and drowned, or at least caught hepatitis. But he found the magnetized box in which had been left the first of the Ivan messages.

This message consisted of a tantalizing sample of product from inside the Lubyanka, says Sparrow, as well as ground rules by which all further traffic would be conducted. McAttee arrived back at Langley wearing the smile of a baleen whale. Ivan had begun.

"And this was in 1967," says Kessler, putting it straight in his own mind. "While you were preoccupied with trying to crack Tronko."

"Spring of '67. Alas, yes. Evidently I *was* preoccupied. Jed had been feeding Eames full of Ivan material for almost six months before I became aware of it."

"Was that unusual? That you wouldn't have heard about the new source?"

"Highly unusual."

"McAttee was intentionally keeping you ignorant?"

"He was keeping all of us ignorant. With the indulgence of Herbert Eames. Eames allowed Jed to play Ivan as his own personal fish. I suppose that much might be explicable in petty human terms. It was still early, and Jed was excited and greedy; it appeared that he had pulled off a nice piece of work, with the trip to Berlin. So Eames indulged his possessiveness. But later there came a different slant to this possessiveness. Later, as you will see, there was a particular animus against me."

"How many times would Ivan have communicated, during that space of six months?"

"Two or three times at most. Not many. But each of those messages caused its own stir. Each one was taking us onto new ground." Sparrow wrinkles his face into a rodential sneer. "Putatively."

"You saw them, then. Those messages."

"Retroactively, I saw them. The early messages."

"What sort of new ground was it?"

"Inside the Lubyanka. Faces, names, résumés. Organizational structure. We had so seldom ever gotten a peek inside there."

"And when you had, it was thanks to Bogdan Kirilovich Fedorenko?"

"Chiefly him, yes. Certainly we were learning nothing from Viktor Tronko. Then again, even Bogdan Kirilovich's information was already a little stale by the time we got it. Whereas Ivan was broadcasting live."

"Putatively," Kessler adds, to save Sparrow the trouble.

"Right."

"What was the form of these messages? Radio?"

"No. You can't hope to use radio in downtown Moscow. It was all by dead-drops. Written matter, one-time pads. McAttee was permitted to choose a case officer from his own folk and place him in Moscow, specially for servicing Ivan. The messages came back to Langley by diplomatic pouch. Directly to Jed. None of it went over the air."

"Again like Dmitri," says Kessler, scribbling fast. Having taken Sparrow at his word, he is now making thorough notes. "Maybe they studied at the same school."

"Maybe they did, Mr. Kessler."

Mel Pokorny coined a nickname for Ivan, says Sparrow. The name "Ivan" itself was only a code name, of course, a marker, an arbitrary designation that Jed had given to this source. Pokorny nevertheless, in his unmistakable style, came up with another. His name for Ivan—snide and yet quite apt, says Sparrow—was "The Shadow." Who knows what evil lurks, et cetera. You follow, Mr. Kessler? Are you old enough to—

"Yes, I get it," Kessler says.

Pokorny had a knack for light mockery. Within a few months, "The Shadow" was general usage among everyone but Eames and the Soviet Bloc staff.

"That's very interesting," Kessler says.

McAttee didn't let it bother him. He remained all flushed and hearty, like a young man in love, from the thrill of working this new source. He moved through the corridors briskly, always too busy to linger, always on his way to Eames's office or back from there to an urgent closed session with his own people on the subject of Ivan's latest billet-doux. Always carrying an ac-

cordion folder or some other prop, the pretentious ass. Always
cheerful, says Sparrow, and always a little bit coy. Ivan had just
delivered again, say, and so Jed would be in a twitter, but he
controlled himself. "Another packet of wonders, yes, you'll see
some of it Monday at the section chief's meeting, Claude, I
think you'll be interested." Interested, Sparrow repeats. You'll
see *some* of it. He was riding high at that point, Jed was. He
went about in shirt sleeves, with the cuffs of his oxford-cloth
shirts folded up to the elbow, carefully. Not rolled but folded.
He began seeing a fancier barber. He was a busy man and could
afford for the present to forget about Viktor Tronko, the search
for Dmitri, and all that dreary old tired business. Because he
now had a voice whispering to him from ground zero at
Dzerzhinsky Square, Jed did. Many times that autumn, says
Sparrow, I wished him death in a falling elevator. And Ivan was
still on best behavior. Ivan was sending his blasts of insider's
material and asking for nothing more, so far, than the appreciative attention of the Archangel Jedediah.

"Another of Mel's coinage, as I recall. 'The Archangel
Jedediah.' "

"Yes," Sparrow says.

Ivan, at this stage, seemed to be placed within the Scientific
and Technical Department of the First Chief Directorate. That
was merely an informed guess, since Ivan himself wouldn't say.
He was ready to be helpful, to perform treason against his country and espionage against his colleagues, but not ready yet to
reveal much about himself. Neither his present position within
the Organs, nor his motivation for this reckless leap toward
McAttee. Based on the content of his first three or four messages, it could be deduced almost with certainty that he was
somewhere within the First CD, and the Scientific and Technical Department seemed a likelihood, being one of several subjects about which his knowledge appeared to be rather full. He
had described the leverage that department exercised over a
certain state committee, the GNTK, responsible for allocating
scientific resources and deciding which Soviet scientists would
be allowed to attend international conferences. He had supplied
a profile of the second deputy to the chief of that department, a
pathetic little drunk with a harridan wife and an imperious
mistress in the Bolshoi, who—this second deputy—might be
ripe for some form or another of subornation. He had also told

THE SOUL OF VIKTOR TRONKO 261

of an operation by which a Soviet agent under diplomatic status in Ottawa was harvesting valuable information about heavy-water reactor technology. Concerning this latter case, Eames and McAttee together determined that there should be no alert given, not yet, to the Canadian government; that it would be preferable for now to sit on that information, in the interest of safeguarding Ivan's position. But what position? demanded Claude Sparrow. I thought we've already admitted we don't *know* his position. For all we know he could be in the Department of Lutes and Balalaikas, merely gulling us into thinking he's over in Scientific and Technical. It might be his own means of covering his tracks, Sparrow argued. And we can't gauge how valuable his information is unless we use it, Sparrow said. Sparrow was heard and overruled. He had half a temptation to call up the Canadians and warn them himself, he tells Kessler. But he did not.

Interestingly, Sparrow says, the diplomat in Ottawa went back to Moscow a couple of months later. The Canadians had expelled him on their own initiative.

McAttee insisted, thereafter, that the Ottawa case went toward proving Ivan's authenticity, by confirming that he was giving them valuable stuff. This logic left Sparrow short of wind. In his view, Ottawa suggested precisely the opposite. The Canadians had already been onto that man. Ivan had given away nothing.

Meanwhile the period of Ivan's supposedly selfless generosity came to an end. For the first year he had simply offered his messages without demand for pampering or payment, a virtually cost-free agent; no longer. During the spring and summer of 1968, Ivan began wheedling at McAttee for some form of help. He didn't want money. Lumps of suspicious, extraneous cash would have been no good to him in Moscow anyway, says Sparrow. And he didn't want to escape to the West. Not yet, at least. He wanted advancement. A little boost up the corporate ladder. His career rise at the Lubyanka had proceeded swiftly enough so far, he was recognized as a capable officer, but the next major promotion might take a long time unless he happened to be fortunate in scoring some sort of remarkable coup. He might waste years waiting. On the other hand, such a coup could be arranged rather easily. And my gain will be your gain, Ivan reminded McAttee. McAttee granted the point in princi-

ple: yes, they were willing to help Ivan's career if they could.
What did he want?

What did he want? This, Sparrow declares bleakly, is how the
case of Daniel Petrosian entered into it.

"Petrosian the physicist?"

"Yes. You've heard of him, then."

"Barely. I recall there was a little stink when he disappeared.
Missing, under damning circumstances, and presumed to have
gone back across to the Russians."

"Aagh. That's totally false," says Sparrow. "We never made
any such presumption. We knew too well what had happened."

"Ivan had eaten him."

Sparrow flattens his hands together in prayerful fashion and
presses the fingertips hard into his upper lip, just below the
nasal septum. This is to indicate the great measures of patience
and reserve with which he offers his answer to Kessler. It might
also reflect a real depth of feeling.

"What we did to Petrosian wasn't funny. It was inexcusable."

Daniel Petrosian was a physicist, yes, that much Kessler has
got right. A very brilliant physicist, one of the world's leading
experts on the quantum theory of metals. He was also a courageous, forthright man. I met him only one time, Sparrow says,
but I was impressed by his personal force. "Rectitude" is an
old-fashioned word, Sparrow says, possibly even obsolete; Daniel Petrosian possessed rectitude. There was an aura of moral
authority to him that was quite strong. No blazing righteousness, no readiness to prescribe or to judge. He simply knew
what he himself thought to be proper, and had all intention of
acting on that. I liked the man very much, based on our single
short acquaintance, says Sparrow. I was disgusted and shamed
by what happened.

He had defected to us in 1961, says Sparrow, during an international conference of scientists that was being held in Vermont. Before that he had been one of the show dogs of Soviet
physics. He had won a Stalin Prize and a Vavilov Gold Medal,
and was elected to full membership in the Soviet Academy of
Sciences at age thirty-three, younger than anyone else had ever
made it except Sakharov. Petrosian had been a junior colleague
to Igor Tamm at the time Tamm did the work for which he
later received his Nobel, and he was working again under

Tamm, at the Physics Institute of the U.S.S.R., during the early 1950s when they produced the design for the first Soviet H-bomb. That was the little chore, of course, that earned Petrosian both his Stalin and his Vavilov. Afterward he was allowed to withdraw gradually from weapons work and devote himself to more theoretical problems. He remained at the Physics Institute. His chief interest was in the properties of electron emission among metals, I think it was, says Sparrow, but don't ask me to explain what that means. The authorities humored him, within reason, because they owed him so much for having helped put that one gadget into their hands, and because he was famous in the West. Famous among scientists, anyway. He had published three or four landmark papers. He was permitted to go abroad for the first Pugwash Conference in 1959.

It was probably Ivan's own department (at least the department which Ivan would be working in, or pretending to work in, eight years later, says Sparrow) that made all the decisions, by way of their puppet committee, about which scientists would be allowed to attend these Pugwash things. They liked Petrosian for that sort of role: he was eminent, he was articulate in English, and he seemed still at the time to be such a true believer. He could be trusted to promote the correct line. *Soviet weapons scientists urge their Western colleagues toward peace and disarmament.* It made for good headlines in the European press, says Sparrow.

That was the sole merit of the entire Pugwash movement, so far as the Soviet mandarins were concerned, Sparrow claims. To them, it was merely a fine forum from which to create misleading headlines. An opportunity to grease up their international image through the application of unctuous rhetoric. Notwithstanding the best intentions of Bertrand Russell and all his credulous friends, to the Soviet government the whole thing was just a charade. A ridiculous charade, but a potentially useful one. So the Soviets were happy to participate fully, send some of their top scientists, and try to give the impression that the real implacable warmongers were all in Washington.

"How do you know?"

"Petrosian," says Claude Sparrow. "We have this from him."

In September of 1961 a Pugwash Conference was held for the first time within U.S. territory—at a resort lodge just outside of Stowe, Vermont. The declared theme of the conference this year was "International Cooperation in Pure and Applied Science," or something to that effect, Sparrow says. The speeches, the earnest expressions of fellowhood and resolve, were presumably interchangeable with those from all previous Pugwash gatherings. Daniel Petrosian was in attendance, one of a dozen delegates representing the Soviet scientific community. Also attending, on the U.S. delegation, was a woman named Martha Gillespie, a biochemist from Boston University. Halfway through the conference Petrosian and this Martha Gillespie suddenly went missing. They had each disappeared sometime between lunch and the afternoon session. By six o'clock that evening they were in an FBI office in downtown Boston, having arrived there together in the woman's car. They had made good time down from Vermont because Dr. Gillespie, at the insistence of Petrosian, had driven like a maniac. Five days later the U. S. State Department granted political asylum to Daniel Petrosian.

Contrary to the hysterical assertions that came immediately from *Pravda* and *Izvestia*, says Sparrow, Martha Gillespie was an authentic and somewhat dowdy scientist, not a paid seductress under CIA control. Actually we weren't hiring seductresses that year, none at all, says Sparrow. And if we had been, we wouldn't have picked a frump biochemist with Pugwash leanings. Petrosian seemed to care for her, though, and that was what counted. They had met two Pugwashes earlier, in Austria, and had renewed their mutual infatuation at the previous year's conference in Moscow. Needless to say, in Moscow they were discreet. With the KGB watching everything, they must have confined themselves to professional dialogue and moony glances. Perhaps that restraint only helped their passion build steam, says Sparrow.

But the romance with Martha Gillespie was not the main factor behind Petrosian's defection, says Sparrow. The bolt down off that mountain and into Boston was not something done on an afternoon's hot impulse. Petrosian had been waiting to make his break. He had long since wanted to get out. I couldn't tell you whether this realization came before or after his first involvement with Pugwash, maybe Petrosian himself didn't quite know, says Sparrow, but I can tell you that for some time, at least since the Moscow conference, he had only been waiting. Maintaining appearances, careful to keep himself in good smell with the security thugs, so that his chance to travel wouldn't be jeopardized. Waiting for his moment to break. The choice of Stowe for the 1961 conference had come like a gift from heaven. This was not what you heard from the gossip columnists in *Izvestia* nor from the left-wing European press, of course, says Sparrow. From them you heard only about the tartish Miss Gillespie, the decadent Petrosian, and Petrosian's poor wife back in Moscow.

Admittedly, his situation was complicated. There was indeed a wife. But Petrosian was probably the least decadent, most conscience-ridden man any of us is ever likely to meet, says Sparrow. The first thing he did after the grant of asylum, even as he began submitting to all the various debriefings, was to file a formal divorce petition back through the Soviet courts. Of course the Soviet authorities laughed at him. His petition was not in order, they said; anyway, he had lost his citizenship and therefore had no standing to file; the marriage was indissoluble. If this seems faintly illogical to us, well, says Sparrow, the Soviet courts were in business to dispense revolutionary justice, not logic. The immediate reaction of Mrs. Petrosian was not reported.

Petrosian anguished about this woman, the wife, with whom his relations had long ago deteriorated to the level of bitter mutual toleration. He was worried much less about how she might feel than about what might be done to her. It was four or five years since they had shared any real emotional bond. She had drifted through several casual affairs during that time and he had had one, previous to Dr. Gillespie, but the wife had consented to maintain their pretense of marriage because divorce proceedings would have hurt his career and, worst of all, destroyed any chance of his traveling out to international conferences. She had played on with the pantomime, as a grudging favor to him. Now it was she who would suffer the reprisals. He had used her badly and he knew it—though the reality was much different from the melodrama of caddish betrayal that ran in the Soviet press. He consoled his own conscience with one hope: that they wouldn't kill her, because to do that would set him free of the marriage.

The first official announcement described Mrs. Petrosian as hysterical with grief, and under hospital care. That might mean anything. It covered the fact of her disappearance from their

Moscow apartment, but the true details of her absence were still
unknowable. The second announcement was that she had attempted suicide and failed. This was more ominous. Attempted
suicide was an entirely plausible prospect, unfortunately, since
she would understand that her life of privilege was now over,
and that the best she could expect was a future of ostracism
from her class, a return to hard living, and tireless bureaucratic
harassment. Equally possible was that she had been packed off
to internal exile, or to a camp. She might also be dead. Even if it
had truly been a suicide attempt, and she had succeeded, the
authorities would not release that particular information because, again, it would set Petrosian free. Let the traitor dangle.

Petrosian did dangle. His relations with Martha Gillespie
were in abeyance while he wrote endless letters to Moscow, filed
endless petitions through the U. S. Embassy, trying to learn the
truth about his marital status and the fate of his wife. He
wanted to proceed honorably. As honorably as possible, at
least, given what he had already done to the woman. Dr. Gillespie waited in Boston, ready to marry Petrosian or at least set up
housekeeping. Evidently the difficulty of obtaining a Soviet divorce decree came as some surprise to her; Petrosian, or maybe
her own politics, may have led her to assume there would be no
problem. Also unexpected was Petrosian's stubborn reluctance
to ignore the whole marriage question and move ahead with her
as they had planned, getting himself up to Boston and finding a
university position while she continued at BU. Martha Gillespie's affectionate exasperation became less affectionate after six
months had passed.

Petrosian meanwhile was still down in Washington, living
under protective guard and cooperating with every defense- and
science-related agency that wanted a piece of his time. Another
point of growing tension between him and Dr. Gillespie. Some
of his new associations must not have seemed very Pugwashly.
He was debriefed in succession by the FBI, the CIA, the State
Department, two thermonuclear experts from the Atomic Energy Commission, the Institute for Defense Analyses, the Pentagon's Defense Advanced Research Projects Agency, and
the—

"Also known as Darkest DARPA," Kessler inserts.

"Also known as DARPA," Sparrow says blandly. "In those
days it was just ARPA. The superfluous D for Defense was

added later. To indicate, I suppose, that these were not advanced research projects in agronomy."

"Darkest ARPA, then. Not very Pugwashly, no. I'd say that's a safe statement."

—and the National Security Agency, Sparrow finishes. He talked himself hoarse, Petrosian did. He knew a little something of potential interest to so many different folk in so many different areas, and his brain was so good, his memory so precise, that we gave him almost no rest for months. Everyone came away impressed, says Sparrow. He was an exemplary defector —not surprisingly, since he was in all ways an exemplary man. Around the time when the last of these sessions ended, the estimable Gillespie sent him a Dear John letter. She was marrying an osteopath from Framingham, she informed him. Petrosian took it rather well.

"Did you get a crack at him yourself?"

"You mean, did I debrief him?"

"Yes."

"No. It was others. My one encounter with him was purely social."

After all the debriefings and the publicity, after the smoke had blown off and Gillespie was gone, he quietly went to work for ARPA. They invented a consultancy for him. Although he was touchingly grateful to this nation for taking him in, and eager to be cooperative, he had stipulated from the first interview that he would not work on nuclear explosives. No thermonuclear stuff, no fancy fission, no bombs or warheads period. Take him or leave him on that basis. Fine, this small precondition was entirely acceptable to ARPA. They had a basic research program in materials, especially strategic metals, which they thought might interest him; another, in those days just getting under way, to investigate the possibility of particle-beam technologies. He could spend a little time in each and then take his pick. In the meantime their personnel people would work up a contract wherein the description of services was left intentionally vague, a one-year agreement but indefinitely renewable, and Dr. Petrosian could begin being paid. Would $19,000 annually be agreeable at the start? That was enough to allow him a nice apartment in Alexandria or a small house farther out, as well as a car for commuting to the Pentagon, and of course it would be adjusted with later renewals of the contract. They knew his reputation and were delighted to have him. Petrosian for his part, I have been told, literally broke down and wept with gratitude, says Sparrow.

So he was at ARPA, and happy to be, says Sparrow. Another year passed. I don't know what his personal life was like during this interlude, or if he had one at all. An apartment in Alexandria, a car, a job. A new name, and a bushy new beard that altered his appearance substantially, but no permanent escort of guardian angels, and the KGB goons could have probably found him and hurt him if they had been determined to do so. Evidently they weren't. This was the early sixties now, says Sparrow, not the thirties or the forties: Moscow probably understood that it wouldn't be cost-effective in terms of international publicity, assassinating Petrosian for the sheer spite of it. His chosen pseudonym was Daniel Schultz; he had insisted on keeping the Daniel despite advice to the contrary, and he wanted a last name that sounded American. Schultz-Petrosian lived his quiet new routine without wasting a great deal of energy on worry. He was alone much. ARPA treated him well but his isolated role as it evolved there (as a high-level critic of other people's ideas rather than a team member on one project) didn't make him a lot of cronies. In the evenings he read. From an impulse of self-improvement, he was reading his way right through American history and literature—Francis Parkman, Henry Adams, Melville, Dreiser, Penn Warren—Christ he was even reading Scott Fitzgerald, says Sparrow—and taking solitary little excursions to places like Atlantic City or Gatlinburg when he got a three-day weekend. He played chess with an old man he had met in a Russian bakery, until the man's daughter moved him out to join her in Phoenix. He continued sending those long letters and petitions for word of his wife. Such a patient and long-suffering man, says Claude Sparrow. Finally there was some news. Relatives wrote to notify him coldly that the wife had died, recently, at a hospital in the city of Gorky. That was all—no mention of the cause of death, how she had come to Gorky, nothing. It seemed to be authentic. If Petrosian shared the news that evening, we don't know with whom, says Sparrow. I imagine he felt only more bitterly alone. Two months later he got married.

The woman was a thirty-year-old secretary from the FBI office in northern Virginia, whom he had met back in 1961 while that office was still supplying him with a bodyguard. Back before he became Daniel Schultz. At just the moment, remember, says Sparrow, when his romantic bolt with Martha Gillespie was all over the newspapers. History doesn't record what the FBI secretary thought about that at the time, if anything. She herself seemed to have made some sort of lasting impression on Petrosian, though, and so later he tracked her down and they began seeing each other. It all moved quickly. Her boss, a special agent named Fiori out of the Alexandria office, stood in as best man for the ceremony, evidently because he was responsible for their first acquaintance and because Schultz-Petrosian had no other friends.

The astonishing thing about this marriage, says Sparrow, is that it seems to have become such a very good one. That was against all the odds. Petrosian's new wife didn't understand a word of Russian or of physics. She had a nine-year-old daughter from a previous marriage, to a hometown sweetheart, that had lasted less than a year. The ex-husband was dead in a heavy-machinery accident but divorce had come first. Her own family and roots were in West Virginia. She had two years of college and about six years of answering phones and typing reports for the FBI. If she was a stunning beauty, I never heard anyone mention it, says Sparrow. Probably we should assume that she possessed a wonderful smile. Petrosian may have clutched out rather desperately, after the Gillespie experience and then the news from Gorky, to seize the first American female who had been nice to him and whom he felt he could trust. In that case, he was very lucky. But probably it was at least a little more complicated, a little less slapdash, says Sparrow. Before long they had a daughter of their own. Also, Petrosian had legally adopted the nine-year-old. The wife's name was Joette. She quit her FBI job. Petrosian and she could never talk about any aspect of his work, for security reasons as well as educational ones. God only knows what they did talk about. But when I met the man, five or six years later, says Sparrow, he was still positively mush-headed over her. He called her "my Jo." Found occasion to invoke her name a half dozen times in the course of a stag dinner, says Sparrow, and then excused himself for a quick phone call. I mean the man was in love.

"These things always mystify me," says Sparrow. "I've been told it's a character failing on my part."

"Me too," says Kessler.

"I suppose I've got no quarrel with that interpretation."

They had their house out in Fairfax now, and Petrosian's contract with ARPA had indeed each year been faithfully renewed. He was reviewing a succession of highly speculative projects, writing critical assessments of each. He had passed along his views on the nuclear-powered-airplane idea, on the Sentinel ABM concept in its earliest form, on the Air Force's notion of putting millions of copper needles into orbit for some kind of communications application, others in that vein. Some dizzy things and some promising things, says Sparrow. Altogether, though, it was a function that could have been performed by any really bright systems engineer. Petrosian didn't complain. Not even to Joette, evidently. He was doing no original research. He wasn't publishing. But he didn't grouse. He did the work. Now it's 1968. We thanked him for all that, says Sparrow, by handing him over to Ivan.

Sparrow folds his arms on his chest and gapes belligerently at Kessler, as though waiting for a comment. Kessler has nothing to say.

"McAttee's goddamn little *voice.*"

Kessler remains prudently silent.

"Yes, certainly, they would be glad to give Ivan's career a little nudge," Sparrow repeats. "Willing to invest in his future. *What does Ivan want? How can we be of help?* Jed and his inner court of fools speaking, you understand. Offering away the whole candy store. Very well. *Petrosian,* said the voice. *Give me Daniel Petrosian.*"

"What, in a box?" says Kessler.

"No. Not yet. As an agent. Ivan's own agent within ARPA. He wanted to recruit Petrosian back. Or, at least, to seem to have done."

An operation of such baroque perversity required the collusion, of course, of all the worst brains at three agencies. The director of ARPA had to know, though no one else over there should be allowed to become even faintly suspicious of what Schultz-Petrosian was doing. J. Edgar Hoover had to be apprised of it, dangerous as that might be, so that he could keep his own people from stumbling in with an ill-timed investigation of Petrosian's security breaches. And McAttee did the real scheming, subject only to the gentle guidance (which by now was like no guidance at all) of Herbert Eames.

"And subject also to the protesting screams of Claude Sparrow?" says Kessler.

"No. I couldn't. I wasn't consulted. At this point in 1968, I was being cut out of it."

"Already?"

"On the matter of Ivan. Yes."

"Then how did you know about the Petrosian operation?"

"I never stopped knowing things. I just couldn't always *say* what I knew. I still had my pores. My capillaries. My various conduits."

"You still had your phone taps."

Sparrow nods indifferently to that, and continues.

The most difficult person to enlist, he says, was Petrosian himself. Petrosian reacted very negatively. He wanted no part of espionage against the United States, real or bogus, not even if the CIA were imploring him to play such a role. No. He was outraged at the suggestion. No. Bad enough that he was wasting half his time at ARPA on consummately foolish ideas. No. *No.* But gradually he was talked around. The telling argument went something like this: unlike his ARPA work, the ruseful espionage activity would be quite dangerous, a great personal sacrifice on his part, and important. At last he agreed.

They choreographed Petrosian's espionage career with great care, says Sparrow. Started him slowly, modestly, quite plausibly. He was to be the disgruntled expatriate, you see, underappreciated and underemployed in his new country, full of regrets, gazing back wistfully toward the Motherland. That was at the beginning. Later his supposed bitterness, and his rashness, would be made to escalate. They worked up each bit of this script as they went along and turned it over to him with little advance notice, no consultation, as though he were just an actor in a successful soap opera, highly expendable himself, who might at any time be written out of the plot in a plane crash or on a long vacation, according to the producers' whim. They led him along gradually, and left him ignorant of their real purposes. Petrosian knew only his own small, perilous role. He knew only what they asked of him. Never why. He was told nothing about Ivan, nor of the investment they were making in Ivan's future.

They began him with the usual, innocuous sort of thing. He
would steal an internal phone directory of ARPA employees.

"They is who?" says Kessler. "Hoover and McAttee and the
ARPA guy?"

"McAttee, yes. Hoover had jurisdiction, and token control,
by way of his own so-called Counterintelligence section. The
ARPA director stayed clear, leaving it to the two of them.
There was a muted turf battle, which technically Hoover should
have won, but McAttee was much brighter than J. Edgar Hoover, of course. He knew how to appease the old crocodile. And
McAttee alone was in communication with Ivan. So it developed as Jed's operation in every sense."

The phone directory was passed to a KGB field officer, Ivan's
man in the United States, who had come down from New York
for the contact. He and Petrosian met in a park. A public place,
not very much different from this one, says Sparrow. It was
only the second time they had set eyes on each other. On the
first occasion, the field man had heard Petrosian (whom he
knew only as Schultz, a pseudonymous émigré) confirm his
willingness to function as a Soviet agent. That was when the
field man asked him to pirate the directory. Petrosian's first
chore as a spy. The directory itself possessed no real significance; it was just a token, a gesture of irreversible commitment,
like a thumbprint on a receipt or a drop of Petrosian's blood to
seal the pact. On the second occasion Petrosian carried it, the
directory, rolled up inside a magazine. Just as the field man had
instructed him. After a casual conversation, they contrived to
exchange magazines, a *Time* for a *Newsweek*. Petrosian was
now compromised. He was trapped.

But by whom? says Sparrow, raising his eyebrows.

The field man's name was Bubnov. At least that's the one he
went under, says Sparrow, as a trade attaché to the consulate in
New York. Evidently he was a property of the Scientific and
Technical Department, Ivan's group back in Moscow, and had
been given this New York tour to see what he might cadge and
steal in the way of interesting high-tech hardware. Probably
Bubnov spent a lot of his time buying drinks at computer trade
shows. Certainly no one on that side would have expected him
to land such a catch as Daniel Petrosian. Least of all, no doubt,
would Comrade Bubnov have expected it himself. For the initial
meeting with Petrosian, Bubnov had merely been acting on a tip

from home, passed along by his desk officer. The tip had described a disgruntled émigré using the name Daniel Schultz, who held a sensitive position in Washington and was thought to be ripe for recruitment. Check it out, Comrade. The desk officer of course was Ivan, says Sparrow. The recruitment attempt proved successful, even surprisingly easy. Bubnov may not have known with whom he was dealing—that his Schultz was the infamous traitor Petrosian—until after the phone directory had been handed over, or later still, after their third or fourth transaction, when a terse message had come across the wire from Moscow and Bubnov's immediate boss, the KGB *rezident* in New York, had begun treating Bubnov with an entirely new degree of cordial respect. The Petrosian recruitment might have made Comrade Bubnov's career, says Sparrow. It would also have done well for the desk man, Ivan. There would have been glory enough to go around. At least that's the way we were asked to view it, says Sparrow. That's the version McAttee chose to believe.

"But it all rests on the assumption that Moscow ever *did* credit Petrosian's recruitment as real," says Sparrow. "And that Ivan was indeed an actual flesh and blood desk officer, not a committee of very senior ghosts. Who were cackling up their sleeves, as they sucked Jed and Petrosian along."

"Which is the version you choose to believe."

Sparrow is too engrossed to be testy. "Poor little Bubnov, no one knows what ever became of him. Called back to Moscow, finally, in 1972. I've always suspected that he finished his career in a camp."

But through the four years of Daniel Petrosian's life as an agent, it was poor little Bubnov who serviced him. Bubnov who traveled every month down to Washington, Bubnov who collected Petrosian's material, Bubnov who saw it into the pouch or filed reports back to Ivan by wire. Ivan provided the guidance, the wit, and Comrade Bubnov the legs and hands, by which Daniel Petrosian was developed into a precious source of information on certain arcane areas of American weapons research, a source highly valued by Moscow. Or an *apparently* precious source, Sparrow amends. *Apparently* valued. It was never clear who had been fooling whom, Sparrow says. Anyway Bubnov was the case officer. He and Petrosian established a new pattern after the first half dozen times. They would make a

brush contact, at noon on a Saturday in some crowded suburban restaurant out in Fairfax or Rockville, a place filled with
young parents and howling children and angry distracted wait-
resses, a different restaurant chosen anew for each meeting by
Bubnov from his apparently inexhaustible roster of such spots.
The worse and more hectic the restaurant, the more secure.
Evidently Petrosian loathed this arrangement, because it ruined
his weekends and forced him to eat entire meals of breaded
frozen shrimp while enduring obnoxious clamor. That's what
we are told, says Sparrow. That's the cartoon version. He had
other and better reason to loathe those occasions, however. He
was passing away American defense secrets. Scraps of them, at
least. Against all his own instincts of gratitude, loyalty, and
self-preservation. And he had never been allowed to know why.

The cost of this arrangement to Petrosian's working life made
it even more doleful. He was assigned to one nitwit project after
another—because what he worked on was what he would give
away, and what he gave away had to be expendable. He told
Bubnov all about the copper needles in space, and that was fine,
perfect, since by that time the copper needles were a dead idea
anyway. Under the careful supervision of McAttee and with the
ARPA director's reluctant consent, he told Bubnov what he
knew of the nuclear-airplane research. By then the nuclear air-
plane was also stone dead. In 1969 he was put to work on
another certifiable loser. This was the space mirror project—an
excellent example of what our lunatic fringe in the Pentagon
laboratories can come up with if we give them enough money,
says Sparrow. The notion was to send a gigantic inflatable mirror into high orbit and use it for reflecting sunlight onto the
night side of the earth. An enormous spotlight, you see, to cast
a beam down on those dark Asian jungles where there was a
war going on and we were only winning it during the daytime,
says Sparrow. Light up the bush with a cosmic aluminoid glow
twice as bright as the full moon. On *that* Daniel Petrosian was
made to squander his fine intelligence. Because it was expendable. Even the Pentagon planners, by 1969, had lost interest in
their giant mirror and begun draining away the budget. Even
little Bubnov must have shaken his head at the folly of that one.
And Ivan, for his part, had commenced to complain over the
quality of Petrosian's product.

Petrosian himself was the silent soldier, accepting everything, risking everything, slogging along, while Ivan if you can believe it had complaints. Couldn't they get the man out of these bizwhack, dead-end projects and into something good? Like particle-beam research, for instance?

ARPA in those days was indeed doing a bit of the earliest particle-beam work, Sparrow says. They also had several small programs to look at other directed-energy technologies, one of these being the X-ray laser in its most primitive form, another involving more conventional lasers that might be jumped up to huge energies. I don't really know what I'm talking about, you understand, says Sparrow, but of course Daniel Petrosian would have. Certainly he could have done valuable work for ARPA on lasers. Certainly. And that is exactly what Ivan lusted for. Petrosian himself may have wanted it too. A decent research assignment would have helped him salvage some peace of mind, some shred of pride. But no, it couldn't happen, no. Out of the question. This was an absolute, this was the line. The ARPA director was adamant: Daniel Schultz would be allowed nowhere near particle beams or lasers. He would stay over there with the copper needles and the inflatable space mirrors and the other exploding cigars, or he could leave, period. ARPA would surrender his services. It wasn't that the director distrusted Petrosian himself, necessarily. He distrusted Jed McAttee. A sensible man, says Sparrow. Well, of course Petrosian could not be permitted to leave ARPA and take his skills elsewhere—that would spoil everything for Ivan. So he stayed. He labored on in the kingdom of criminal silliness. And then still worse.

"Lord, what now?" says Kessler. "They assigned him to the United Appeal campaign?"

No. Worse. To cover the deadlock over Petrosian's access, to exploit it on Ivan's behalf, McAttee had a rumor leaked to select Pentagon and FBI people that Daniel Schultz-Petrosian was under suspicion of espionage.

"Oh," says Kessler. "Jesus."

Nothing could be proven against the man, not yet, according to this rumor. Petrosian himself didn't realize that he was suspected, according to the rumor. A very discreet investigation was under way; Petrosian's work and his security clearance were being reviewed; possibly he himself was being watched. If the current investigation proved eventually to establish his innocence, his loyalty, then Petrosian would come back into good standing and be allowed to continue in his present important position at ARPA, said the rumor. Meanwhile he was in shadow. Even little Bubnov seems somehow to have got a sniff of this rumor and canceled all contact with Petrosian for three months, later reestablishing it cautiously under a new arrangement that, mercifully for all, did not involve breaded shrimp.

To Ivan, in Moscow, the rumor provided a perfect explanation for Petrosian's stagnating career. Ivan could use that explanation on his own Lubyanka superiors: the asset was under suspicion, therefore extreme care must be exercised, at least temporarily; afterward, if the crisis was successfully weathered, there would still be a chance of getting at those particle-beam projects. This little drama would also help Ivan by making the whole Petrosian recruitment seem more vividly authentic. Petrosian's very jeopardy would seem to give him, in his role as a Soviet agent, greater cachet. All of that being the theory, at least, behind McAttee's latest machination. And upon Petrosian also the rumor had an effect. It nearly ruined what remained of his life.

His coworkers heard he was being investigated. His division head turned cold and vague. Special Agent Fiori from the Virginia FBI office, who with his own wife had become Mr. and Mrs. Schultz's closest family friends, began to seem uncomfortable about maintaining the contact. The four of them still met for dinners and went together to Orioles games, but there was a new uncertainty in Fiori's eyes. This look suggested not so much accusation as concern, and even pity. Petrosian didn't like it. So he found excuses himself to gently but completely close down the friendship with the Fioris. Joette thought he was crazy. It affected their relationship also, though he had no reason to believe that Joette herself had heard the rumor, that she suspected him of reversing his loyalties back to Moscow. He couldn't talk to her about any of this. And he may have wondered, paranoiacally, what his two daughters thought of him now, says Sparrow. The younger of the two was barely aware that her father had ever been a Russian. Furthermore his only other—

"I do feel bad for the man," Kessler interrupts, "but could we roll this soap opera forward?" Evening traffic is in full scream again along Old Dominion, dusk lowering, yet Kessler still has so damn many unanswered questions. For instance:

what does the Daniel Petrosian case have to do, if anything, with Viktor Tronko? "Could we jump ahead to the plane crash or the long vacation or whatever it was?"

"A kidnapping," Sparrow says icily.

"A kidnapping?"

"Or possibly he was just murdered, right there in Vienna. But no corpse was ever found."

"Petrosian."

"Yes," Sparrow says.

"He went on a trip to Vienna. All right, yes, I recall this part. He went to Vienna and disappeared."

"His first trip outside U.S. territory since he had defected," Sparrow says. "He had been very careful, until then."

"I remember now. Sure. Then the Vienna trip, and bingo, he vanished. Presumed to have defected back to the Russians, because of professional disappointments."

"That was just for the newspapers," Sparrow says.

"But you say they jumped him. Murdered him."

"No. I said that more probably he was kidnapped. Dragged back to Moscow for torture and interrogation," Sparrow says. "They would have gotten him out of Austria as a comatose patient on a stretcher, if it was by plane, or else in the trunk of a car. Quite a coup, it was, for someone. Glory enough to go around. In Moscow, they might have marched him through a secret trial. Or possibly not. They might not have bothered with that. Then in a very lonely corner of the Lubyanka cellars, when they were finished with him, he'd have had a rubber ball shoved into his mouth, and then the bullet. Smallish caliber, one shot, in the back of the neck. The rubber ball catches the slug and spares mess. Or possibly, too, he might still be alive, somewhere. Although that isn't likely."

"Why the hell did he go to Vienna?"

"It was scripted. You say you want the concise version, Mr. Kessler? It was scripted."

"There was supposed to be some sort of secret rendezvous?"

"Precisely. A meeting with Ivan. Face to face. Their first. Ivan had requested it."

"Wasn't that risky for Petrosian? Foolhardy, even?"

" 'Foolhardy' implies Daniel Petrosian was given a free choice. But of course it was risky, yes. Yes indeed."

"Did he see Ivan?"

"We don't know. Petrosian left his hotel, went to the rendez-vous. Never reappeared. But if there *was* an Ivan—then yes, very likely Petrosian saw him, eventually."

Kessler pauses. He has gotten it all in the notebook. He sets the notebook down on the bench. He puts the ballpoint behind his frozen right ear. "Now I'm supposed to ask you: *Who scripted this trip to Vienna? And then you tell me: Jed McAttee.*"

Claude Sparrow holds his elbows pinned against his ribs, his shoulders hiked up around his neck, conserving warmth. "And then what do you say, Mr. Kessler?"

Sparrow is suddenly on his feet, not pacing, exactly, but executing a series of small restless cha-cha sidesteps back and forth in front of the bench. His hands have come out of the deep pockets, he is using his arms like a Signal Corpsman on semaphore duty, and if the temperature—which is falling fast, a much more serious and palpable cold filling the air now as twilight seeps away, filling their lungs too, visible as vapor with each breath and each exclamation—if the temperature bothers Claude Sparrow half so much as it bothers Kessler, that fact doesn't show. Sparrow is very much preoccupied. He is reacting to Kessler's latest statement.

Kessler has said: "What I say is, I get a strong feeling you want me to believe that Jed McAttee is the mole Dmitri."

Sparrow hasn't answered yes or no. Instead he seems to be changing the subject. He seems all at once to want Kessler to forget about the matter of Dmitri's identity. More important issues may be involved, it would appear, and more complicated ones. How can that be? thinks Kessler. Haven't you just devoted three long days to convincing me of exactly the opposite?

"There are two ways to be an agent," Sparrow is saying, bland words spoken excitedly. "At least two. There are two ways of damaging the security of an intelligence service. You can do it wittingly. Or unwittingly. Sometimes the unwitting agent can be the more destructive."

"Which kind was McAttee? Pardon me: *is.*"

Sparrow seems not to hear. He can't even stand still.

"When Eames retired in 1972," he is saying, "it was foreordained that I would be out. Soon. You oughtn't be so naive as to imagine that Joe Delbanco had much to do with it—except as the unwitting agent of Jed, our new Director. McAttee used him rather adeptly. I know that you journalists prefer to believe in the myth of your own autonomy, your own faultless and inviolable sense of purpose functioning as final guarantor of the public welfare. But that's a delusion, I assure you. We all have our own, and that's yours. Anyway the Delbanco stories were only a convenient pretext for what McAttee himself already intended: Claude Sparrow simply had to be got rid of. I was causing certain problems. It was imperative that I be sacked. This was foreordained, I say. And not just from the moment of Eames's departure. No, long before that. Years. There had been a concerted campaign, over years, to destroy my position. My influence. To negate me. It went straight back to the early phase of the Ivan operation.

"That disembodied voice, Ivan, had been murmuring against me. I've told you I was already being cut out of it by the spring of 1968. The same period of time when Roger Nye and the two others on Eames's little panel were trying to reach a conclusion about Tronko. Everything was quite tense just then. We were working under great pressure. There was discord. Eames's own energy had begun to wane badly, and that would pass soon into the waning of his health and his leadership. The entire Agency was in a state of roiling turmoil. Even more so than usual. After Lentzer's try at debriefing Tronko, and sometime during the early stage of our effort, McAttee's skepticism had finally succumbed and he became a convert: a convinced and dogmatic Tronkovian. He believed now, Jed did, that the man was a real defector with real stories to offer. He believed in Rybakov, he believed in the Tourist Department, he believed in *Two Russians Contemplating the File of Oswald.* He allowed himself to disbelieve select parts of Tronko's testimony, the most implausible parts only, the proven falsehoods and the real hooters, excusing these away as innocent misstatements and fibs by a desperate drunk. On the subject of Dmitri (who of course did not exist, by Tronko's account, except as a figment of our paranoia) McAttee took up a straddling position, which turned out to be just very damn opportune for his future needs. It turned out to be a brilliant stroke of prescience. On the subject of Dmitri, Jed reserved judgment. He held out that Dmitri might or might not exist, regardless of what Viktor Tronko was telling us. Regardless of what Tronko himself might believe. Jed's stated view was that Dmitri could be real and among us, yes—and that, never-

theless, a KGB officer of Tronko's middling status might not
have been cognizant. Might even have been actively misled, on
that point, by the larger mullahs above him—that is, by
Samoylov and Nechaev and his own dear paternal Rybakov.
After all, said Jed, if you've got a deep penetration into the
opposition's service, a priceless but very perishable asset, you're
not going to blab the fact around to your own foot soldiers, are
you? Tronko of course claimed to have been much more than a
foot soldier, but never mind. Let that pass. The beauty of this
position, for Jed, was that it allowed him to embrace both
Viktor Tronko and Ivan. Both. Whereas I was at a distinct
disadvantage. I had no pet Russians of my own to counter him
with. Fedorenko by now was dead.

"So Jed made his swashbuckling trip to Berlin," Sparrow is
saying, "and then Ivan was suddenly there, our man on
Dzerzhinsky Square. Giving away baubles, such as the agent in
Ottawa who stole reactor technology, others in that vein. More
importantly, he was offering an over-the-shoulder peek at current procedures and personnel within the First CD. And with
the prospect of advancing himself still higher. Ivan, I can tell
you, was the hottest new piece of action in many moons.

"At first McAttee kept Ivan's little love notes all to himself,"
Sparrow is saying, "and that seemed natural, or at least predictable, because the operation was only barely begun and Jed
could be considered to have certain finder's rights. Then a few
months passed and Jed was having his whisper sessions with
Eames but still none of the rest of us had been brought in on the
Ivan product, and this seemed less natural. Even given Jed's
standing, by then, as favorite boy. In fact it seemed a glaring
breach of good practice. If Ivan was supplying anything worth
courier costs, then by God let's share it around. Counterintelligence obviously had every reason to want to know what the
KGB's First Chief Directorate might be up to, and so did the
top people in a few other divisions. But no. It didn't happen.
Jed remained stingy. Eames indulged him. And then a few more
months passed, until one day I discovered with a great sickening jolt that the deputy director for Foreign Intelligence and the
division chiefs of Western Hemisphere, Near East, and Special
Operations had all been let into the know on Ivan. Everyone
but me.

"I charged off to confront Jed, of course, got no satisfaction,

and then went straight for Eames. Actually barged past the
secretary and thumped my fist on his inner door. I was admitted. I refused to sit, I stated my piece. Eames merely looked
pale and rolled his eyes back in his head before giving me,
quietly, just the two of us in there alone, the following piece of
breathtaking news: 'Claude, you were excluded by stipulation of
the source. It was a ground rule.' Seems that, from the very
beginning of contact, Ivan had specified that there must be no
access to his material by anyone in the Counterintelligence section.

"My section. He had explicitly sealed us out. No access to
the CI section, full stop. Any violation of that rule would put
Ivan himself in *unacceptable jeopardy* (this is what Eames told
me that Ivan had said) and would therefore be cause for termi-
nation of contact, completely and irreversibly. Of course it
could only be taken one way. Ivan was pointing his finger.

"He never made a direct accusation," Sparrow is saying.
"Not to my knowledge, anyway. He never claimed outright that
Dmitri was lurking somewhere in my shop. It wasn't necessary.
Probably he got much more attention, much more credence
even, doing it just as he did. *No access to Counterintelligence; I
don't trust them to know about me. Signed, Ivan.* What better
weapon could Jed and the rest of my enemies have received? It
was clever, I must say so myself. *Whose* cleverness, I don't
know, but it was gracefully simple and it was clever. It was
effective. We were quarantined off, I and my whole staff, from
all reports by and deliberations concerning what was either the
most important Soviet source that the Agency then had, or else
the most harmful *dezo* agent then working against us. Among
other consequences, this made it impossible for me to do my
own job. I was powerless. I was grounded and blinded and
featherless. It should have been manifest that I could never
locate Dmitri if everyone else knew things from Ivan—from
inside the opposition—of which I was to be kept ignorant. I
wouldn't have a prayer of succeeding. Unless I took exceptional
measures. So of course this led to the wiretaps, of which you
seem to derive such joy in reminding me, Mr. Kessler. Granted,
they were technically illegal. Obviously it was a reckless step.
But I was desperate.

"And then the Scott Wickes episode," Sparrow says, pausing
only for breath.

"What did he do?" says Kessler. "A tantrum, you said."

"Wickes refused to sign that report. The one Eames had demanded, for a final resolution on Tronko. Instead he went back up and hid out with McAttee, oh, four months, five months. Nothing was heard from him. Evidently he was relieved of all line responsibility in the Soviet Bloc Division—or rather, those duties that had been shifted away while he worked on the panel were never afterward reassigned to him. He was left with a bare desk, Wickes was. At the time it was implied that this might be some form of bureaucratic punishment. Eames seems to have been under that impression. Late in the summer of 1968, Wickes resigned from the Agency. Abruptly, and with ill feeling, it was said. To his letter of resignation, which landed first on McAttee's desk and then was passed along to Herbert Eames, he appended a fifty-page document. The subjects of this document were Viktor Tronko, Claude Sparrow, and Dmitri. Wickes claimed to believe that the last two were a single person. He had concocted quite an elaborate theory, really, during his five-month sabbatical."

"He denounced you. As being Dmitri. Yourself," says Kessler. "And then he quit."

Sparrow nods once.

"And that was the campaign to destroy Claude Sparrow," says Kessler.

"Not only me. My section. It was the end of Counterintelligence."

"Right. Counterintelligence had to be purged. Razed and rebuilt."

"Or just razed."

"Sounds pretty nefarious," says Kessler. "Also, as you say, pretty clever."

Again Sparrow nods, minutely.

"But aren't you telling me it was Jed McAttee's work?"

Now Sparrow pins his lips tightly together and shakes his head. He appears very agitated. Then he says: "Partly."

"And Wickes's own, of course."

"A lackey's role."

"Who else? Who else *was* there?"

"Ivan."

"Ivan, again. But he was McAttee's agent."

Sparrow can barely restrain himself, though he seems to be

trying hard. He looks almost lightheaded from the effort. Kessler doesn't think it's a performance.

"Or vice versa," Sparrow says.

He turns and begins walking quickly away up the paved path toward the trees. Five yards off he stops, and turns back. Kessler opens his own mouth but nothing comes out.

"Good luck to you, Mr. Kessler," Sparrow says.

20

This is insane, Kessler thinks.

He has found a pay phone in the foyer of the restaurant across from the park, but there is still no answer at Barry's house and the switchboard at Georgetown Law School has closed. He calls the Tabard for messages and recognizes the voice of the woman in black mohair, assuring him that he has gotten none. No, no unmarked parcels either. By now she may be sizing Kessler up as a remittance man whose check is late. The hell with her, she has already run a print of his credit card, she's got nothing to worry about. No calls, no couriers, no visitors resembling lizards or any other form of wildlife—no, huh-uh, zero. Guess they don't love you anymore, she jokes. How long have you been there? he presses her. Maybe Barry's call came in right after I left to meet Sparrow, he thinks.

"Twelve wonderful years, honey," she says and then asks Kessler if he can hold but doesn't wait for an answer.

Sure I can, he says to the dead air. He hangs up. This is insane.

For another full minute Kessler stands there beside the phone, his mind almost empty of everything but fatigue. The foyer is at least warm. His toes and his ears begin to hurt, a good sign that those appendages may survive. His sinuses hurt. Now he has a headache also. That might mean he is sliding down into the far trough of his hangover following an afternoon of healthy diversion, the letdown effect, or else to the contrary Claude Sparrow is directly responsible. It's out of character, Kessler is thinking, for Barry Koontz to be careless about an appointment or a promise.

Somewhere a piece of linkage must be down.

Kessler decides to drive straight to Rockville and find Barry at home, or at least leave a note. The direct approach. Just go, just show up. Barry should have arrived back by the time Kessler gets there. Possibly. If Kessler's luck happens to be running good, Barry has perhaps even left the law school early to swing by his bank and retrieve that other item from his deposit box. That other bit of relevant material. Item, document, some such —what exactly did Barry call it? What did he tell Kessler about this other thing, before Kessler realized how interested he might be? Duh. Blank. The whiskey is making you stupid, Michael.

"Is *that* what's doing it," Kessler answers himself aloud. Two teenage girls halfway in the door glance at this man by the telephone, conducting his conversation with the receiver cradled.

He stops at a Wendy's for a bag of fish sandwiches and a Coke the size of a beach bucket which he drinks for its restorative value as he drives. First thing he sees along the Beltway, of course, are the signs for Langley. A reminder, an omen. Amid this foul traffic somewhere is Jedediah McAttee himself, perhaps, riding homeward in his bulletproof limousine. Undoing the bow tie, slipping off the pumps, after a hard and vigilant day's work. But work for whom? Kessler thinks about the Nye Report on Viktor Tronko. He thinks about the fifty-page appendix to Scott Wickes's resignation letter. If it isn't one of those two that Barry has squirreled away, Kessler will be very surprised. But which one? And which document was it that Mel stashed at Grand Central? The Nye Report, or Wickes's *J'accuse*? Dmitri and Ivan, Sparrow and McAttee, was it the lady or was it the tiger, which one which one. The thought of tigers brings a new wave of depression down over Kessler, and in a moment he understands why.

Tigers remind him of termites, naturally. The unfinished book. Rather, the inchoate pile of pages that may or may not be a book, now sitting abandoned at home on his desk. Northbound traffic has tightened down to a slow grind and only at this point, finally, after half an hour, is Kessler crossing the river. He eats one of the fish sandwiches. On the basis of that one he decides he will save the other three for Barry. He eats all the french fries.

The house is lit when Kessler pulls up, and Barry's Subaru stands in the drive, two encouraging signs. He rings, peeks expectantly through the door's leaded window, rings again, peeks.

Barry does not appear. Kessler can see into the living room, bare of life signs and furniture just as it was last night. He puts his thumb back to the bell and tips his weight against it. By this hour of evening even a workaholic lawyer should be home. Unless he's got a dinner date, unlikely, or has elected for reasons of self-castigation to spend another night on the floor of his office. Kessler tries the door. It is unlocked.

The dirty plates and wineglasses are still in the sink. The gin bottle stands on the counter. Kessler touches the bottle: room temperature. Yesterday when he arrived it had been in the freezer, placed there expressly in expectation of Kessler's martinis, no doubt, since Barry himself seldom drinks gin. Kessler sets the bag of cold sandwiches beside the warm bottle.

"Barry? Yo, Barry. It's Kessler."

He walks back to look in the bedrooms. At the master bedroom he knocks first. Nothing in there but a mattress, dirty socks crawling out of the closet, a suit jacket hung on a doorknob. The boys' room is bare and clean. The little study contains only a card table, a mate to the one they ate on last night, though this one is covered with bills and bank statements and torn envelopes all in wild disorder, spilling onto the floor. I hate this, Kessler thinks. But he can't stop now. He does the whole drill, the whole macabre search, even snatching aside the shower curtain while his pulse thumps loudly in his ears. Then he goes to the basement.

Barry is there on a pallet of file boxes. His clothes are unchanged since Kessler last saw him, the same wrinkled gray trousers that go with the jacket upstairs, the same wrinkled blue shirt. He is in stocking feet, and if socks could be wrinkled too, Barry's would be. There is hardly any blood. Barry's right wrist is cocked around at an extreme angle. His hand is closed on the pistol in just that slightly awkward position required for getting the muzzle not merely into his mouth but all the way back to his soft palate. Behind where he lies there is an ugly mark on the wall. Nothing garish—just a chip out of the concrete, and a rusty spatter. The gun must be small, a .22 or some such.

Kessler stands gazing at this for probably ten minutes. The muscles in his throat are clenched like a fist.

Then he picks up the Cutty Sark bottle. It has been set on the floor beside Barry's foot. Dead soldier, emblem of emptiness and despair. But Kessler happens to know that it was already empty, and lying on the carpet upstairs, before he left Barry alone.

Fleur-de-lis, Barry had . . . Dexter rather uselessly completes and repeats. But Kessler doesn't let him. That's precisely what's nagging at the back of his— cerebrum, cortex, no, left . . .

21

Dexter Lovesong has taken up a position inside the Dumpster in the darkened alley behind the National Rifle Association building, an excellent spot in that it allows him a view of the exit ramp from the underground lot on Scott Circle where Kessler has been parking his car, as well as a line of sight half-way up N Street toward the lights of the Tabard Inn. The Dumpster is almost empty at one end, fortunately. Lovesong stands on a pair of cardboard peach crates which he has set into place for that purpose amid the fermenting funk. The peach crates came from a pile beside the Dumpster, and Lovesong picked two that were fairly clean. With arched knuckles he supports the lid of the Dumpster off the rim, leaving a gap of two inches through which he can see out. Knees bent, back hunched, he crouches there in the posture of a constipated skier on a subzero day. It is uncomfortable, but Lovesong doesn't mind. What the NRA is doing with all those peaches, he has no idea. Buddyboy is looping the area in search of a parking space. With luck, Lovesong thinks, maybe he'll have to drive all the way to Bethesda.

It isn't strictly a part of Lovesong's assignment—preventing Michael Kessler from being killed. Merely a point of independent professional pride. It happens so fast, anyway, that Lovesong is functioning mainly on instinct.

He has watched patiently as Kessler appeared, walking up the ramp into the amber street lighting. He has noticed the shorter man in the rust-colored jacket emerging from darkness beyond the Scott statue, converging with Kessler's path like a panhandler stalking a mark. As the two of them exchanged words, Lovesong has become mildly curious. What, a new contact? Another little bird, eager to sing into Kessler's notebook? But now Kessler begins backing away. The movements don't look right. When he sees Kessler fall, Lovesong stands straight up, lifting the Dumpster lid with his head.

He vaults out of the garbage and breaks into a sprint up the alley, making no particular effort to stay quiet. He gets angry as he runs, and angrier with each stride, gathering speed on adrenaline carburetion. This sort of business here, this bullshit, he takes it as a personal affront. He pushes the pace, he leans. For all his belly, for all his age, Lovesong in a cheap suit and wing tips and with a full head of anger can still move as fast as a linebacker.

Kessler has tumbled sideways into a bush. Gotten himself tangled in there, but he seems to be still alive because Lovesong can see his feet thrashing, kicking out desperately toward the shorter man, as this man comes back in close. From twenty yards off Lovesong notes the quick little arm movement that seems to indicate a knife, though the knife itself he cannot yet see. Kessler will be liverwurst in a second or two so Lovesong, at full gallop, shouts: "Hey, asshole. *You*"—thereby surrendering the advantage of surprise. The shorter man turns and now Lovesong sees the wink of a blade and Lovesong dips low, like a runaway bobsled, hitting the man in the groin with his head.

They both go ass-and-teakettle into the shrubbery. Unfortunately Lovesong's aim was imperfect, or the knife man had time for half a step, and Lovesong has merely given him a hard bruising blow on the hip instead of a hernia and heart failure. Lovesong rolls onto the man and tries to pin his arms with a bear hug, the only option since Lovesong can't see the knife and doesn't know whether or not the man has kept hold of it. At the same time Lovesong jacks his knee up and down and up again, hoping to do more damage in the man's groin. Lovesong would prefer to concentrate on the throat and the eyes but can't dare release his hug. This asshole in the rust-colored jacket is meanwhile grunting and snarling in a language Lovesong doesn't recognize, not English and not Spic and not, if Lovesong knows anything, Russian. Okay, just another of Washington's many East European muggers—except that Lovesong doesn't believe for a minute that this guy is a common mugger; the coincidence would be strained and there are just too many other wallets in the city besides Michael Kessler's. The asshole gets an arm free and delivers a stunning smack across Lovesong's cheekbone, a serious right hook that recaptures his full attention.

But during the instant it takes Lovesong to absorb that
stroke, he feels Asshole squirming to pull himself away, lurching and wiggling like he needed only inches for a touchdown,
stretching that free arm toward the sidewalk. So aha, the knife
is gone. Thank you. Lovesong loosens his hug in favor of jam-
ming a hand up under Asshole's chin, grabs the throat and
squeezes it like a tennis ball, driving the man's head down backward into the snapping bush stubble, if possible to plant it there
permanently. Then from somewhere comes a very quick chop at
the point of his own chin that slams Lovesong's jaws together
with a nasty jarring porcelain clack and could have done far
worse if the range had been maybe an inch less. He might have
bit off his own tongue like pastrami, he might have had a man-
dible shard driven halfway into his brain. This blow has made
Lovesong very much angrier. It has also served notice that he is
dealing with a dangerous bastard, likely a professional. Lovesong bears down harder on the throat, but now a problem arises
—his own arms are so tired that they have gone almost numb.
He can hardly hold his grip. Lovesong is an old fart, after all,
who can't carry on this way indefinitely. Asshole on the other
hand seems to be young, or at least in excellent physical shape,
besides which he hasn't just run a hundred-yard dash. Lovesong
wishes dearly that there was something hard and heavy, preferably with edges, to hit this guy with.

He raises all his weight up over the fork grip on Asshole's
throat. He loosens the grip for a second with the notion of
changing hands, and in that second Asshole delivers another
flashy cross that blinds Lovesong and makes him momentarily
stupid and, he realizes at once, has almost certainly broken his
nose. Now Lovesong himself is snarling in a language he
doesn't understand. He lets go with both hands and tries to
stand. The idea, in so far as there is one, is to jump up and
down on Asshole's face. But Lovesong stumbles, tripped by the
branches. Asshole is up faster. He shoves Lovesong headfirst
back into the shrubbery. He takes a delicate little prance backward to set himself, strides forward, and kicks a forty-yard field
goal against the padding of Lovesong's stomach. Then he jogs
off down Massachusetts Avenue, this athletic stranger, ignoring
and ignored by Buddyboy, who kneels in the grass wrapping a
cotton handkerchief around Kessler's arm.

* * *

"You're bleeding too," says Buddyboy.

Lovesong wipes the back of a hand across his nostrils and glares at the blood. He says nothing.

"And your nose is crooked," Buddyboy tells him.

Lovesong touches it. "Broke. That's the fourth time. Wonderful. Where were you, Buddyboy? If I might ask." But Lovesong doesn't hear the answer because he has been wrenched over double with another spate of vomiting, his second in three minutes. When that's finished, he wipes his mouth on his sleeve. "Where were you? You worthless goddamn twerp."

"Helping Kessler. He's got a pretty bad wound here, Dexter. Stop horsing around and give me a hand."

"Helping Kessler. And I was doing aerobics."

"Come on. We should get him to an emergency room."

"That again." Lovesong spits. "Kessler, how did you get so accident-prone all of a sudden? You're keeping us busy."

"It seems that way, doesn't it?" says Kessler. His voice is unsteady.

Lovesong notices that Kessler has gone pale as wood putty and his good hand is trembling wildly on Buddyboy's arm. Evidently unnerved by the sight of his own blood in these quantities. But Lovesong doesn't think Kessler is in danger. Not from this particular wound, anyway. Lovesong ignores him, turning back to Buddyboy.

"Dammit, you should have jumped in. Use your head. I wanted that guy, Buddyboy. Wanted to mount him on a board. Now we got nothing. A mashed nose and a cut arm. Empty hands. Nice piece of work."

"Give me your handkerchief," says Buddyboy. "If it's clean." Lovesong digs, then thrusts out a blue bandanna roughly the size of a dish towel. "The car is back up on New Hampshire," says Buddyboy.

"Who was he?" says Kessler and now, with a glance traded quickly, they both ignore him.

Lovesong doesn't know the answer himself, though he could hazard a few plausible guesses. If he did know, there would be no particular reason for telling Kessler. He helps Buddyboy steady Kessler to his feet, in the process getting a large smear of blood on his own jacket.

"Maybe you can tell *us*."

"Later," says Buddyboy. They move off along Massachusetts Avenue with Kessler balanced gingerly between them. Buddyboy can sprint ahead for the car if he wants to but Lovesong himself is damned if he'll volunteer.

"There's something I don't understand," says Kessler, whose voice is still weak and shimmery.

"What."

"Aren't you wearing a gun?"

"Of course." Lovesong swings back his lapel to flash the ivory grip, gleaming moon-yellow under the streetlights. While he's at it, he straightens back the holster strap. Miracle of good luck that the damn piece didn't fall out into that asshole's hand.

"Why didn't you use it?"

"You can't solve everything with violence," Lovesong says.

22

It's the same doctor tonight, with the same crooked wire-rim glasses and the same curly hair.

"But you got a haircut," says Kessler.

"Hello, Mr. Kessler. What is it now? Oh Jesus, that's a nice one. How long have you been bleeding? Come in here."

The questions continue while the doctor and one nurse give Kessler's exposed gore a good irrigation, douse it with some sort of benign blue solution, and then wrap the whole thing temporarily in a very thick swaddling of gauze. Kessler is seated on a chair next to a scrub sink. He is slightly dizzy but the interrogation keeps him occupied and he avoids looking at the place where his pulpy pink muscle tissue smiles out at him from deep near the bone and from which blood still flows like summer rain.

"How did you do it?"

"Uh. Um, a knife," Kessler says stupidly, trying hard to focus but wondering in his haze how much he should tell.

"You cut yourself like this on a *knife*?"

"No. No, I had help."

"Was it a clean knife or a dirty one?"

"I didn't get time to ask."

The doctor's face floats down to the level of Kessler's and hovers there like a balloon on a string. Young as this doctor is, he nevertheless seems to despise nothing so much as a wasted minute. "Who helped you? What happened? Mr. Kessler, don't jerk me around. We're busy people in this hospital."

"I was attacked," Kessler says. "Mugged. On the street, right near my hotel. I've been stabbed, for Christ sake. I'm a stab victim, is what." Now Kessler himself is getting a little hot. "What's going to happen to my arm? Will the hand still work?"

The doctor says: "That's what we're about to find out."

Yes, Kessler can move his left hand at the wrist. He demonstrates. Yes he can make a fist. He does. Again, says the young doctor, who this time lays three of his own fingers across Kessler's palm. Do you have any strength? Show me how much. Kessler squeezes feebly on the fingers. He would like to crush them like breadsticks but he is afraid his own blood and sinew might come splashing and popping out through the gauze. Some bit of force, not much, says the doctor to the nurse, and she writes on a clipboard. All right, now open it wide, he tells Kessler. Wider. Kessler spreads his hand out flat. He turns it this way and that. It seems to be functioning almost normally, praise God. After a few more simple tests (can Kessler feel the touch of this Kleenex on the back of his hand? does he feel one caliper point or two?) the doctor says: "Okay, I think it's good news. The muscle isn't severed. Not quite. The nerve doesn't seem to be either."

"Just a flesh wound, as they say. Just flesh."

"You were lucky, Mr. Kessler."

"I know I was, Doctor. I couldn't agree more."

"Now we'll get you sewed up."

Forty-five minutes later Kessler is all stitched and gauzed and taped back together. His shirt sleeve has been cut away just above the elbow. He has been advised to do no strenuous pushing or reaching and to let the arm simply dangle as much as possible. He should be gentle with it, go easy, use common sense. There's no need for a sling. He has gotten a tetanus booster and been given a prescription for some fancy antibiotic. He is under instructions to return tomorrow afternoon for a second exam. He has taken ninety dollars in cash out of his wallet, clumsily, using only his right hand, and presented the money to a nurse at a desk. You can bill me for the rest, yes, fine. He has shoved her receipt, crumpled, into his right trouser pocket. Lovesong and Buddyboy are still there, at the far end of the corridor, sitting patiently on plastic chairs. Lovesong hasn't bothered, evidently, to have anyone look at his nose.

Kessler is eager to leave. He wants to go. He wants to get out of this hospital and this city. He has no intention whatsoever of coming back here tomorrow, though he has promised solemnly that he will. He just wants to go. To get in a car and drive. The young doctor emerges from another examining room in time to catch Kessler gently by the elbow, the right one, pulling him aside into a doorway where they are out of the gurney traffic and beyond earshot of Lovesong and Buddyboy and the admitting nurse. He looks Kessler soberly in the eye—a favorite tactic of this particular young doctor. He should get an optician to straighten those frames, Kessler thinks.

"May I say something, Mr. Kessler?"

"Okay."

"It isn't my business. Except it is, really. Trying to keep people healthy. Keep people alive."

Kessler waits. The doctor glances off down the corridor, hikes his chest for a deep breath, shuffles his loafers.

Then says: "The drug trade can be very unhealthy. Serious people out there. Bad dudes. I'm sure you know. It can be honest-to-God fatal."

"I know it can," says Kessler. "But I'm not in it."

The doctor comes back at him with a sad man-to-man skeptical smile, so Kessler adds: "Honest to God. That's not who's trying to kill me. I'm a journalist. Not an importer."

"Then who is?"

"You wouldn't believe me. You'd think I was just being snotty."

"Try me."

Kessler sighs. He says: "I really don't know. But it's either the CIA or the Russians, I think."

The doctor's smile changes. He looks almost respectful. He is delighted to be brought in on this confidence. "What're you, some sort of investigative reporter?"

"Not me," says Kessler. "I write about termites."

23

He drives. He is checked out of the Tabard by 1 A.M., and he drives. Somewhere along the Baltimore Beltway he stops for gas, pulling up to the full-service island and then watching furtively from behind a magazine at the station news rack, with the vague notion of seeing if someone has followed him. He feels pathetically amateurish. And he spots no one, not even Lovesong and Buddyboy. He has had a hard time talking himself free of those two, and it wouldn't surprise Kessler if they were still with him somewhere (well camouflaged, in the cab of a bread truck and wearing false beards and Budweiser caps, maybe), though it is also just possible that they have believed what he told them and gone home. Kessler assured them, as he did the doctor, that he would be available tomorrow. Lovesong wants to show him some file photographs of faces, one of which might belong to the murderous man in the rust-colored jacket. Gladly, Kessler has said. He has promised to meet Lovesong and Buddyboy in his room at the Tabard at nine the next morning. He leaves the gas station with a quart of coffee in Styrofoam on the dashboard and a handful of chocolate bars on the seat, and by 3 A.M. Kessler has passed Philadelphia.

He pulls into New Haven about the same time Lovesong and Buddyboy are turning up, he hopes, at the Tabard. Dropping the car off in a Budget lot at the airport, he takes a cab to his apartment. Unlocks the door in a state of some trepidation. Pads his way quietly through to the living room, the bedroom, the bathroom, the office, on an inspection tour for lurking intruders. He checks the closets, he glances out onto the fire escape. No one. He walks back to the door, which is already closed and locked; Kessler throws the extra bolt. In the living room, he sinks into the good chair and sets his feet on the coffee table.

Just exactly the way Mel was sitting, he thinks. Kessler is more exhausted than superstitious so he doesn't move. But with a small jolt, then, he becomes aware that it is less than seven full days since the evening Pokorny visited him. My God. That was just Tuesday night, this is Tuesday morning. The thought of his past week makes Kessler still more weary until, with a second jolt, he recalls the date with Nora. Wednesday: tomorrow. He has promised to be back in town, so that he can take her to see the film about Eugène Marais. Such a nice little trail of promises Kessler has left. Such a nice little trail of promises and death.

Pokorny's murder was bad enough—it was startling and menacing in a cold way—but the matter of Barry Koontz is quite different. Barry was not just a player in some spooky professional gambit, a contact, a source, a person with whom Kessler was dabbling. Barry was an old and treasured friend. Barry was like a brother. He was also, in this Viktor Tronko business, an innocent bystander. His only mistake, the fatal one, was that he knew and trusted Michael Kessler. If Kessler hadn't called him, hadn't gone out there to soak up booze and information and then dance away safely back to the Tabard because he found the empty house depressing—if Kessler hadn't gone visiting, Barry would still be alive. The full impact has been slow in arriving but now Kessler feels it like a hatchet blow to his own chest: Barry is dead. Murdered. A light pistol shoved into his mouth in that cruel, outrageous pantomime of suicide. Barry has been shamelessly used, by Kessler among others, and though nothing is going to put life back into the pathetic lump of meat Kessler found in the basement, still some sort of recompense is demanded. What sort? Personal revenge? Kessler does not even know who pulled the trigger, and anyway physical violence is not his own strong point. Penal justice? Publication of the truth? Maybe. At least. Possibly. But Kessler has small confidence at this point in his own ability to deliver either of those. Justice could never be more than a fortuitous by-product of anything Kessler might write, and the truth is just something to be set atop Barry's grave, weighty and useless as a headstone. No, what he himself owes Barry in a very personal way, Kessler realizes, is much more straightforward and immediate and difficult. He has got to call Patsy in Colorado and give her the news. *Patsy, this is Kessler. Listen. Uh. Barry is*

*dead. Yes. I'm sorry. The police will tell you he killed himself,
Patsy, but it's not so. Take my word. He missed you badly, he
was depressed, but not to the point of suicide. He was murdered.
Someone killed him for talking to me. I'm sorry.* Nice sort of
comfort that Michael Kessler can offer his friends.

Kessler's arm wound is throbbing fiercely. It seems to have
bled again during the mild abuse of driving a car. Furthermore
he forgot to stop at a pharmacy for his antibiotic. His brain
aches. He pushes off his shoes. He walks out to get a beer and
remembers, with the refrigerator standing open, that there has
been no beer in the house since Pokorny and he drank the place
empty. Kessler considers the bottle of sour mash. But he hasn't
had breakfast and he isn't that desperate. Maybe he should eat
something. Why? He's not hungry. A cup of coffee? It might
cure the headache but, no, better to sleep. He has been up the
whole night, after all, and now feels miserable—sore and sick
and guilty and lonely and very tired—yet he doubts that his
mind will let itself rest. Too much still that has got to be figured
out. Too much to decide. Is he going to call Nora at all? Or
would that be dangerous for her at this point? Kessler is deeply
worried and, dammit, very confused.

He drops back into the chair. Within five minutes he is
asleep.

But it only looks worse by the light of a Connecticut winter
afternoon.

Now he does make a pot of brutal coffee. He breaks a bagel
loose from the package in the freezer and toasts it. After one
bite of the bagel, he decides it would be a good idea to take a
shower. Clean skin might help him think. He wraps his left
forearm in a plastic garbage bag to avoid soaking the dressing
and washes himself awkwardly. Afterward he puts on fresh
clothes, not from the suitcase but from the closet—his baggiest
pleated chinos and a cotton long-underwear shirt, just as
though he were staying in for a serious day of work. It's a bluff.
It's for his morale. He drinks the coffee out of his favorite mug.
Kessler is trying to soothe and calm himself. To focus.

He goes into the office and closes the door and puts himself
down in the swivel chair, feet up again, this time on the desk.

"All right," he says aloud. "Now." But it doesn't help much.

All of the prospects are terrifying, and all of the options are unsatisfactory. Period. Kessler sees the situation lucidly. The only sensible course of action is panic. Probably he should begin drinking seriously.

Barry dead, Pokorny dead, both of them murdered by a person or persons unknown. Kessler himself will be next. Clearly he too has earned a place on the list of targets. He wishes he knew just *how* he has earned it, but obviously he has. He doesn't know who is after him and he doesn't know why. Indeterminate strangers require his death because he has learned something important, or else simply because they *believe* he has learned something important. Kessler on the other hand can't recall having learned a single damned thing that seems worth dying for. Maybe it's only a question of what someone fears he *might* learn. After all, two of his oldest friends have been killed, each of them almost in mid-sentence, evidently to prevent them from talking to him.

Correction—one of his oldest friends, Barry, and one of his oldest and most unlikely acquaintances. Mel Pokorny. Kessler snaps on the desk lamp. He sits forward. This little move is unfortunate, since it brings his attention onto the pile of typescript that rests accusingly on a rear corner of the desk. He sits back. Mel Pokorny.

Kessler has long harbored queasy feelings about his early relationship with Mel, despite the fact (and in a sense it's *because* of the fact) that that relationship launched Kessler's career. Mel was his first and best source, back in the time and the place where confidential sources meant everything to the kind of work Kessler was choosing to do. Sources made stories, on the intelligence-community beat. Sources made careers. Cultivation of a good set of sources wasn't sufficient alone, of course, not even in that cloistered and melodramatic branch of journalism—not sufficient, no, but certainly necessary. Besides the key sources you still needed tireless ambition, luck, a measure of meticulousness, a boyish joy at the whole game, and some brains. Kessler had all of those, at the time. After quitting law school he had come to Washington for a Detroit newspaper and then gotten on, after less than a year, as a city reporter for the *Post*. That was the luck. Almost immediately he had begun pressing his case to be allowed to cover Langley or the Pentagon, and at the same time he drove himself to exhaustion trying to do a little magazine free-lancing by moonlight. It was hard

and it was touchy, because his city editor felt that the *Post*
owned Kessler's moonlight as well as his daylight; nevertheless
he did it, and that was the tireless ambition. But his assignments for the *Post* remained boring. He was not allowed to
cross the river. And his early magazine pieces were modest,
marginal, amateurish. He knew he was only playing around the
edges of the spy world, the subject that so intrigued him; he was
no more than a hobbyist, having never yet gotten inside the
great outer wall of conspiratorial clubbishness. He was still only
twenty-three years old. Then in early 1968 he got to know Mel
Pokorny.

Kessler couldn't say at this point whether that was a matter
of luck, or of ambition, or of good professional instincts, or just
what. Though he does have his suspicions.

They met sometime that winter or very early spring, before
the assassinations. Kessler doesn't recall the exact time. He
doesn't recall the circumstances. And as a matter of fact this
gap in memory became troubling to Kessler later, when he began to reconsider his professional choices, and has continued to
trouble him whenever he reflects back—this one small gap especially: his inability to remember just when or how he and Mel
Pokorny first met. What the gap means, Kessler suspects, is
that the initiative came from Pokorny.

He liked Pokorny, young Kessler did. Pokorny was funny
and he was quick. He played a buffoon's role sometimes (and he
did seem to have a streak in him that was genuinely, incor-
rigibly unserious) but Kessler prided himself on having recognized fast that the man was really very bright. It would be a
mistake to underestimate him, Kessler saw. An easy mistake to
make. But only a fellow of uncommon gifts could have risen
into the higher levels of CIA governance, as Pokorny had, despite being burdened with the face of a pug and the soul of a
clown. He was not a pretentious sobersides like the few other
Agency officers Kessler had met, and he was not righteous. He
was also not overtly indiscreet—Kessler got almost nothing
from him for what seemed, back then, like a long time. Reflecting now, Kessler cannot imagine why it did seem long; it can't
have been more than three or four months. Kessler's first major
story, on the illegal mail-intercept program, ran in *Harper's* in
August of 1968. As Claude Sparrow so accurately remembered.

Pokorny of course had been his chief source. Pokorny had almost led him by the hand.

By that time he and Mel were seeing each other every two or three weeks, for barbecued ribs and beer by the pitcher and shuffleboard bowling, at a roadhouse that Mel had known of on the old Manassas highway. Kessler loved the sense of convivial subterfuge. Ground rules were that Kessler would never show a notebook while they were together in any public place, that Mel would mention no names or code names, that Mel would not introduce subjects but only respond—sometimes—to percipient questions, and that Kessler would publish no single fact heard from Pokorny if he couldn't confirm it elsewhere. There were some additional rules, equally romantic and meaningless, to all of which young Kessler adhered slavishly. And there was the unvoiced understanding that they would not spend *all* their time talking about intelligence work, that tired old subject—that Kessler had better make himself a good conversationalist and a congenial drinking pal during those hours when Mel Pokorny was wearied blind by the whole silly realm of spookdom. Kessler did. He loved it all. But he saved his receipts from the roadhouse and used them on his taxes. This was research. This was genuine work. Michael Kessler was cultivating a source.

Poor dangerous young fool. Who was cultivating whom? is what Kessler has wondered for years.

These people, the cleverest of them, have a hundred different purposes all on line at once. Total secrecy serves some of their purposes at some times. Talking coyly to journalists, when they choose to do that, serves others. It doesn't need to be lies. Half-lies are quite useful occasionally and even whole gobbets of truth can be given away to good and well-calculated effect. Witness Jed McAttee's use of the Joe Delbanco staff against Claude Sparrow. But Michael Kessler was a slow learner. He didn't begin to appreciate this multiplicity of means and purposes until about 1972. Then he started to measure how much he owed to one man—the mail-intercept thing, the Laotian heroin-trade thing, several others—and to wonder what might eventually be asked in return. He was quietly horrified to realize that, as a respected young journalist specializing in intelligence-agency exposés, he was virtually the creation of Mel Pokorny.

Then again, maybe nothing would ever be asked in return. Maybe Pokorny's compensation was already being received.

How? Somehow. Kessler didn't know, but in the meantime his feelings toward Mel changed drastically and he went stiff with dread, a sense of impending ruin and damnation. He passed through a crisis week during which he barely left his Georgetown apartment. He lost the nerve to write up anything from his notebooks, or to follow further along any of his promising leads. He was terrified and, equally, puzzled.

He no longer viewed Mel in the same naive way he had—as a zealous but disgruntled CIA officer, a conscientious cold-war professional who believed in the Agency's primary mission but despised certain tactical abuses, and who was willing to act indirectly, risking his own position, to emend those abuses. A nice portrait but, no, not hardly. Mel was too smart and too crafty and he wouldn't have *needed* Kessler for that. What other way to see the man? Kessler didn't know. But he came to suspect that Melvin Pokorny was not nearly so disgruntled, not nearly so divided in loyalty, not nearly so much the impetuous maverick, as he liked to seem. He was above all a deft operator. And Kessler was now tyrannized by the hunch that his own precocious success might be somehow a move in a larger Pokorny operation.

By then he had heard about this man Claude Sparrow, Mel's boss. Sparrow was demented. He was paranoid and devious beyond imagining. That was his reputation, anyway, as it reached Kessler. Suddenly Kessler was faced with the entirely plausible notion that this famed Claude Sparrow might have sacrificed certain Agency secrets—thrown them into Kessler's hungry young jaws, by way of Mel Pokorny—for some greater, more opaque purpose. Entirely plausible. Kessler just didn't know.

And still doesn't. Even now, safe at home in New Haven, it makes him highly uncomfortable to contemplate all this. He would much rather give his attention to man-eating cats, grotesque marine creatures, bird-eating spiders. Termites. Kessler goes out to the kitchen for more coffee.

There must be something to eat around here, isn't there? No. Very well, he decides to live dangerously. He walks up to Biaggio's grocery for salami and pesto. He returns with salami and pesto and beer.

24

He finishes the six-pack in lonely squalor, pitching the last empty bottle down the length of his living room, in imitation of Mel. By then it is midnight and he wants badly to call Nora, or maybe just show up at her door, but he is still sober enough to know that he shouldn't. Can't. Not unless he wants to horrify her, make an ass of himself, scuttle whatever small chance he seems finally to have of coaxing her open to his attentions. And not unless he wants to put her in danger.

With Barry gone, with Nora beyond reach, Kessler feels a heart-chilling loneliness.

He is weary of the Viktor Tronko case, weary of Claude Sparrow and Dmitri and Pokorny, disgusted with the whole stupid quest and disinclined to continue. It has become a gruesome annoyance. He doesn't need it. Isn't interested. Be gone, Satan. Having cost Barry's life, any possible results of Kessler's efforts would already be exorbitantly overpriced. Besides which, this thing represents another wedge pushed down between him and Nora. But at least Nora, for the moment, is still alive.

It would be irresponsible, Kessler realizes, to go anywhere near her. He wants to stumble over there right now. But knows he cannot.

She is a noncombatant, defenseless, and for Christ sake there is also the little daughter, Emily, myopic and cute and nine years old, shy as an owl. Women with slumbering nine-year-olds are not likely, in Kessler's experience, to welcome drunken men on their porches at midnight. Especially not this woman. Anyway the last thing that Nora needs, or desires, is to be pulled into the web of Kessler's cloak-and-dagger capering. She has made that clear: she judges him to be wasting his time and talent. Symptoms of arrested adolescence. One of Nora's foremost attractions for Kessler, and at the same time a big problem, is that she possesses a sensitive and ruthless antenna for crap. She is unforgiving of moral drift. She knows what she values and what she doesn't; she knows at all times what she thinks. Such clarity, to Kessler, is mystic and terrible. Methodically raising one foot, he upsets the telephone table onto the floor.

God forbid that he do anything irresponsible. The phone yammers at him for a moment, then stops. Kessler fetches the sour mash and carries it to the office.

He picks up the Eugène Marais typescript, flips a few pages, reads a few scattered paragraphs, can barely recall having written them, and sets the pile back.

Then he forages in his suitcase for the three ring notebooks that should be there. Slaps them onto the desk. Opens the third, flips pages, reads a few lines of his own scrawl. Viktor Tronko appears in these notes as *VT*. Claude Sparrow also goes by his initials and Dmitri is simply *D;* everyone else gets at least three or four letters of a last name. Paging on quickly, Kessler lets disconnected phrases catch his eye as they might. Fedorenko dead. Lentzer's cigarettes. Ivan the friendly ghost. Petrosian bye-bye. Schnitzel Group. Eames bye-bye. Wickes bye-bye. CS bye-bye.

An hour later he notices the time.

He carries the whiskey bottle, still unopened, back to the kitchen. He takes two sleeping pills and sets an alarm. This time he sleeps in the bedroom.

By nine-thirty the next morning, after a half hour of imaginative phoning, Kessler has located Sidney Gondelman. He has spoken to Gondelman's secretary, asking her to arrange an afternoon appointment today and informing her that he will be showing up regardless. By eleven Kessler is on the road toward Cold Spring, New York.

25

What he said to the secretary was: Tell him I want a few words with Sidney *Gondwana*. And then he spelled it. Kessler has no idea what that will get him, if anything.

Having stopped for directions at a framing gallery in downtown Cold Spring, he finds Gondelman's institute easily. A mile north of town on the two-lane toward Poughkeepsie, it sits up above the river on the crest of a long sloping meadow of snow, at the apogee of a horseshoe drive, stone gateposts flanking the drive and only a laconic brass plate on one of them to provide identification: JANUS CORPORATION. Remind me, Kessler thinks, not to ask how the name derives. The building itself is a large pile of cut granite in the Romanesque vein, complete with multiple turrets and bartizans, leaded glass and slate shingles and rain-spout gargoyles, balcony parapets notched for crossbow archers. In other words it looks like an early neurosis of the same architect who later went crazy designing Yale. But this Yankee castle seems a little older than all that cut stone back in New Haven; probably it was once the home of some grand nineteenth-century family, the place where a railroad or shipping baron stashed his wife and kids and the rest of his private collection. Hidden up here on the Hudson, it is the sort of estate to which Franklin Roosevelt as a young man might have come to play tennis and flirt. Yet the stonework and the roofs are still in perfect condition and the grounds, despite winter, look carefully groomed. Janus Corporation must therefore be solvent. Gondelman and his colleagues seem to be doing—whatever it is they *are* doing—quite well.

"Michael Kessler. To see Sidney Gondelman. I called this morning."

"You have an appointment, Mr. Kessler?"

"That's what I'm here to find out. You can check with his secretary."

"Yes. Have a seat, please."

But Kessler prefers to hover. Once you deposit yourself into one of those big red leather sofas, you have surrendered advantage, accepted a supplicative posture; you're liable to sink out of sight and be lost for days. Instead he pretends to inspect the fox-hunting prints. To his surprise, he is left waiting less than five minutes. A matron in gray tweed appears and says: "Mr. Kessler?"

"Yes."

"Follow me."

They climb a carpeted stairway as wide as the one at Tara. On the second floor she leads him back up the corridor to a front corner office, overlooking the lawn and the bare trees and, beyond, the river. This turns out to be her own office, merely an antechamber for the boss. Oak paneling and a muted watercolor of a covered bridge and banks of IBM hardware. Kessler is intrigued. He almost wishes he had worn his suit. At the smaller of two desks sits a younger woman, who glances up from her green electronic screen and over her tortoiseshell frames for a peek at Kessler. The peek seems to satisfy her, and she doesn't lose a beat on the keyboard; he suspects that she is the underling to whom he was brusque by telephone, since the matron's husky alto isn't familiar. Kessler expects to be invited again to sit but the matron marches across toward another door, another slab of oak, in this case lined with brass rivets and padded with leather. On the jamb is a buzzer button. The matron ignores that. She knocks twice, then opens the door without waiting, and Kessler is ushered into the presence.

Gondelman is even larger than he expected: six foot two and just short of obese. He wears a Hutterite beard along his wide round jaw, like the corona of a full solar eclipse. He comes out of his chair with remarkable spring for such a big man, extending his great fat hand to be shaken. But the oddest part, for Kessler, is that he is grinning cordially.

"Mr. Kessler. My pleasure."

"Thanks for seeing me."

"Of course. What the devil happened to your arm?"

"A storm-door accident," says Kessler. "I did something stupid. Too embarrassing to describe."

"That's a pity. Does it hamper your writing?"

"Probably not. Just my typing. Why is it your pleasure?"

"Pardon?"

"Seeing me."

Gondelman stops. For a moment he stares like a stern Santa Claus.

"You're direct," he says. "Good for you. Good." Smiling again, he waddles away toward the bookshelves lining one wall. Two other walls are also covered ceiling to floor with books. Otherwise Gondelman's office is done all in high-tech modern, smooth lines of stainless steel and rectilinear Plexiglas, blacks and silvers and whites, a startling contrast to everything just outside. The desk looks to have been cut from a block of obsidian, and except for a single legal pad it is bare. A large organpipe cactus stands in a silver pot. There is a white sofa, a matching white chair, a coffee table with a mirror surface and, beyond this area, what seems inexplicably like a steel spiral staircase twisting up through the ceiling—maybe it's just some sort of advanced decoration. While Kessler admires the furniture, Gondelman reaches high on the wall for a book. Gets right up on his toes, he does, dainty as a performing elephant. "Because I'm rather a fan of yours, Mr. Kessler. That's why."

Kessler feels warning alarms ringing, but the grin and the cordiality appear to be real. He recognizes the volume that Gondelman has taken down: *A Fearful Symmetry,* by Michael Kessler. It's a book about Bengal tigers and a man who loved them, until he was killed by one. A true story, as the careless saying goes. On the back is a photo of Kessler, squinting into sunlight.

Gondelman clicks a ballpoint pen. He extends the book as ingenuously as he extended his hand. "Would you? And then we'll go upstairs for a talk."

"Sure. Of course," says Kessler.

If this is all an elaborate tactic to disarm me and fatten my head, he thinks, I will give you great credit, Gondelman. It seems within the realm of possibility that the man has sent his junior secretary scampering out, two hours ago, to a bookstore. A bizarre notion but not inconceivable. Kessler wants another look at that particular shelf where his book was stashed. Meanwhile he hesitates awkwardly, as he always does, over the title page.

"If you like, you could make it: 'To my friend Sidney *Gond-wana*,'" Gondelman coaches him. "Our little joke."

So Kessler does. After signing it, he opens the book casually to a middle page and finds the spine already well broken. On the shelf above Gondelman's head he sees George Schaller and a half dozen other books on the big cats.

They have climbed the spiral staircase and are now seated in Gondelman's private aerie, a tiny glass-walled cupola that juts up above the north roof of the building like a conning tower. There is room enough only for two captain's chairs and a small table, but the view sweeps out grandly in all directions over the Hudson Valley. No telephone jack up here, Kessler notices. No typewriter, no pads or pens, not so much as a sheet of paper. The table is a slab of hardwood, gleaming with spar varnish and just large enough for a chessboard, or perhaps for Gondelman's two huge feet. "This is where I do my thinking," he has told Kessler. "The real stuff." As distinct from what other sort of thinking, Kessler isn't sure. But it seems clear that pure cogitation, the real stuff, is an important and no doubt highly remunerative part of whatever services Sidney Gondelman offers. Kessler wonders, in passing, whether Janus Corporation does "risk analysis" for the multinationals.

"So you knew Mel Pokorny."

"He was a friend of mine," Kessler fibs.

"Awful thing."

Kessler waits. Then he says: "You're talking about his murder, I assume."

"I saw a notice in the Hartford paper. A little one. They gave him two column inches and called him an insurance counselor."

"You read the Hartford paper?"

"I read everything," says Gondelman. "They described it as a grocery holdup. An unlucky bystander. Tell me what really happened, Mr. Kessler."

"What makes you think I know something?"

"Because you're here," says Gondelman. "You either know something or you want to."

"Actually, both," Kessler says.

For reasons not wholly rational, he has a good feeling about Sidney Gondelman. Maybe that's just the crude flattery having its calculated effect, but Kessler senses something else. The man seems to be pleasantly forthright—impatient with mystification and more interested in asking blunt questions himself than in maintaining secrets or protocol. He has dragged Kessler up into this tower as though for the first welcome diversion in an otherwise dull week. By appearance Gondelman is merely a three-hundred-pound professional sage, highly paid, highly poised, with a head like a pumpkin and a smirk like Buddha, but down inside all the flesh Kessler detects a thin restless skeptic. Possibly Gondelman, like Pokorny, has discovered the private sector to be a golden bore. No, Mel was no unlucky bystander, Kessler says.

"He was a target. The grocery was the unlucky bystander."

"You have some evidence?"

"Not a shred," says Kessler, and Gondelman nods to indicate that his attention has nevertheless been engaged.

Kessler describes the night Pokorny was killed. He relates in bare outline what Pokorny told him about Viktor Tronko. We had just gotten to the second hostile interrogation, says Kessler, when Mel left the apartment. He mentions the locker key from the attaché case and the empty Grand Central locker. I think that was the Nye Report, says Kessler. I think Mel had a copy that he intended to give me, if I accepted the bait. Kessler tells of his three days with Claude Sparrow. You've got to spend money to make money, he has reminded himself, and sometimes it is the same with information. He is betting on Sidney Gondelman—*investing in* would be putting it too mildly. He omits any reference, though, to what happened to Barry.

"Sparrow gave you three days?"

"Yes."

"He *talked* for three days?"

"Yes. Does that surprise you?"

Gondelman tips his head noncommittally. "No. I suppose not. Sparrow is complicated, God knows what his purposes were. A brilliant man. And just mad as a goddamn hatter."

"It was Sparrow who gave me your name," Kessler volunteers.

"Bless his soul."

"I wasn't at all sure you would talk to me. Maybe you won't." This sounds like an afterthought but is offered carefully by Kessler in a tone of gentle challenge.

"Are you here as a bereaved friend of Pokorny or as a journalist?"

"You should assume it's the latter. Whether I'll ever write anything is an open question at this point. But you should assume that I might."

"Everything I say is off the record." Gondelman lifts one hand and his eyes sparkle and he twiddles his fingers like W. C. Fields. "A zephyr whispering through the willows."

"Fine."

"But I was never a spy, you know. Nor even a counterspy. I sat in a room and shuffled paper."

"Exactly," says Kessler. "The analysts. That's what I want to hear about. The Schnitzel Group."

Gondelman tilts his chair delicately back. He raises his feet one after the other onto the table. The table holds.

"Three of us," says Gondelman. "We were brought over from the Office of Strategic Research. That's way the hell off on a far side of the Agency, OSR is. No connection to Counterintelligence. Part of a whole different directorate, devoted mainly to conventional intelligence processing. By which I mean open sources. Legal. Reading newspapers, scanning the fine print in budget documents, that sort of thing. You don't care about the organizational chart but we were separate, is my point. Outsiders. Claude Sparrow was never our boss."

"We," Kessler says.

"Yes, they plucked us up individually and threw us together, for that particular case. We worked as a team. Sort of a special study group. Leo the Dubious, Big Al, and myself." Gondelman smiles faintly at the recollection. *"Sidney Gondwana."* He clasps his hands over his navel. "Actually, I was smaller then. I've put on a few pounds."

"Nicknames courtesy of Pokorny?"

"Yes. Mel was the name-giver, that's right. He had a silly side."

The Tronko case was their sole assignment for three years. None of them had imagined it would go on so long. An intense collaborative effort, not quite like anything else Gondelman has ever experienced. Very intense. Just the trio of them, alone together for most of three years, talking and play-acting in a couple of conference rooms. Just them and the script. Occasionally

they were called over to meetings with Sparrow and his people
—Pokorny and Nye, that is. But not often. Mainly they communicated with Sparrow formally, through their advisory reports. Mainly they stayed away, alone, sequestered. That was
the way Eames liked to arrange these things; no contaminating
the analysts' views with extraneous reinforcement or disputa-
tion, was the idea. Let them work it out among themselves. See
what they might turn up. Gondelman scarcely knew the two
others, Leo and Al, when this assignment began, he says. Nor
did those two know each other. A nodding acquaintance from
the halls of OSR. Then for three years they all shared an in-
tensely centripetal life. And then pop, dispersion again, everyone flying apart. I haven't spoken with either one of them in a
decade, says Gondelman. He sounds wistful.

"The *script?*" says Kessler.

"The transcript of the interrogation. Yes. Pokorny and
Tronko. As the tapes came in and were transcribed, we got a
copy."

"But you did say *play-acting?*"

"That's what I call it. An analytic technique. We took roles
and reenacted the whole interrogation, day by day. While it was
happening. That's how we proceeded. Acted it out, like a little
courtroom drama, and then discussed what we had seen. Or
felt."

"So you each got a chance to be inside Viktor Tronko. Or at
least, to try to be."

"Each? No," Gondelman says. "No, the roles were permanent."

"Who did you play?"

"Nobody. I was the eye in the sky. I watched the other two.
That was important. Sometimes I noticed things that they, in
their involvement, had missed. You needed three people."

"Who played Tronko?"

"That was Leo."

"And Big Al was Pokorny."

"Yes."

"Did he know Mel personally?"

"He who?" says Gondelman. "Now you've lost me."

"Big Al."

"Oh, I'm sorry. I didn't mean to mislead you," says Gondelman. "But Big Al was a *she.*"

Her name was Rosalind Alpert. She was one of the more senior analysts within OSR at that time, though she couldn't have been much past her mid-thirties. A very brainy broad, says Sidney Gondelman in his jokey tone. She had been with the Agency ten or twelve years, having signed on, oh, probably straight out of graduate school. Her doctorate was from Hopkins, if he remembers right. She was a mathematician, that much Gondelman knows for sure. Had been a mathematician, rather. When OSR hired you on, those sorts of specialty were never more than door openers. They liked people who had been trained in the sciences, but often enough they would turn you back into a generalist. Leo had started out as an electrical engineer. I myself was a physicist, says Gondelman, in an earlier incarnation.

"There was no bias against her within the Agency?"

"What, for being a mathematician?"

"No. A woman."

"Oh yes. Definitely some of that," says Gondelman. "Which particular sort did you have in mind?"

"She was allowed to role-play the Pokorny part. Casting her against gender. It seems a little surprising."

"Only because you don't know Rosalind Alpert."

"I would have thought that it might affect the dynamic. A woman analyst, trying to do Mel Pokorny. Or, at very least, that someone else would have raised that objection."

"Well, in a general sense you're quite right. Ordinarily there would have been howls. But not with Big Al. Nary a grumble nor a woof. It testified, I suppose, to the genderless ferocity of her mind."

"Why did you call her Big Al?"

"That was friendly," says Gondelman. "She was statuesque. Tall. Nothing more."

They had a small suite of rooms on the sixth floor, at the far end of one corridor, where people left them alone. And a locking outer door, actually, to guarantee that privacy. The Tronko-Pokorny transcripts were supposed to be very closely held. And so they were, says Gondelman, suddenly emphatic as though someone has questioned his probity. So they by God were. One copy went straight to Claude Sparrow, and one came to us. As a matter of fact it took a special order from the Director's office to get us permission to make another duplicate. We needed two, you see: reading scripts for Leo and Al. That was a struggle. Finally it was settled by them giving us our own photocopy machine and our own shredder, right there in the suite. And of course we had our own safe, into which both copies went overnight. God help you if even a single page of this leaks, they told us. And by *leaking* all they meant was that Jed McAttee or some other unauthorized person might catch a glance. Well, no page ever did leak. Not from us, anyway. Not from *der Schnitzels,* says Gondelman.

"Who is *they?* This *they* who threatened you about leaks."

"Claude Sparrow, naturally."

We designated one of our rooms as the Vault, Gondelman says. Then he stops himself. Do you know about the Vault? he asks Kessler.

"Yes."

"Tell me, then."

"A concrete cell where Tronko was kept. Somewhere outside the Washington area. Three years of solitary confinement. Sensory deprivation and hard conditions, but no active physical torture, and no drugs. I have all that from Pokorny and Sparrow."

"All right," says Gondelman, easily assuaged. He seems to want to believe that it is within the bounds of discretion, sharing his recollections now with Kessler. He seems, after all these years, to relish the chance. "So we had this one room, and we called that the Vault. Got rid of all the furniture to make it sufficiently grim. Even tore up the carpet. Nothing was left but three folding chairs."

Gondelman himself took one of those chairs and sat inconspicuously in a far corner—at least, he amends, it was as inconspicuous as he could be. I had a note pad but no script, he says. I kept quiet, each day, until they were done. Leo and Al had center stage. They worked through the transcript. Al tried to be as tough and as cunning and as pitiless as Pokorny seemed to be. Leo argued back from Tronko's side. Tronko's own exact words now, you understand. He did it with conviction, Leo did. Tried to. That was crucial to this whole exercise. As much conviction as possible. Assume the role, walk a mile in the man's moccasins; see where his footsteps might lead you, and what you might notice along the way. And when conviction was utterly impossible, says Gondelman, then Leo would say so, afterward, and we would talk about that. That itself would be a datum. This was our procedure beginning in, what, late fall of that year. It must have been I suppose about 1965, says Gondelman. Ancient history. I don't remember exactly, but whenever Pokorny began on Tronko.

"November of '64," says Kessler.

"Sixty-four? Are you sure?"

"Yes. The assassination, and then Tronko appeared three months later. Lentzer did the first debriefing, but it was short. Mel got him at the end of that same year."

"Of course. You're right."

November of 1964, then, Gondelman and his colleagues began. But they had gone on for barely a week in their original arrangement before it became clear that something was wrong.

"Me," Gondelman says. "I was an intrusive presence. Little Sidney in his corner. Ambience was very important, we thought, so we moved my chair out."

"Out of that one room."

"Yes. Then Leo and Al had the space to themselves. I took up a position behind the door to the room adjoining. It had a plastic window, and we got some holes drilled in that so I could hear. Like watching everything through a one-way mirror. This improved the ambience greatly. No distractions. It helped Leo in imagining Tronko's sense of total, hopeless isolation. The lousy part was that, for most of three years, I had to stand."

By the time we began working, says Gondelman, Tronko had already taken and failed two polygraph tests, and we had those also. The transcripts as well as the cross-referenced charts. We could match each statement against the variance in physiological parameters. Compare what he said with his mouth against what he said with his heartbeat and with his skin. Then we could generalize, sorting the statements according to subject matter and trying to find trends or patterns in the man's cognitive dissonance. This was part of my role, says Gondelman. I worked up the analysis of all the polygraph data, put it into charts, and identified a number of subject areas where there seemed to be particular strain. Then those categories could serve us as search-images while we went over the material that Pokorny was—

"Sparrow told me he lied about everything," Kessler interrupts. "Uniformly."

"No. Oh, that's far too simplistic," says Gondelman. "You have lies and then you have anxiety and you have doubt. Shame. Regret. All very difficult to distinguish, using just these tricky machines. You have about ten grades of ambivalence. No, Sparrow had no call to say that."

"Sometimes he told the truth? Tronko, I mean."

"Of course. Apparently so, anyway. But you can't X-ray a man's soul. Not even with polygraph technology."

"Did Tronko feel all ten grades of ambivalence?"

"His test results showed a whole rainbow of variations, yes. From maximal dissonance all the way to a flat normal reading. On many points he seemed to be speaking the purest gospel. Or at least he thought that he was. Clear conscience and true belief."

"Name one."

"Beg your pardon?"

"One of those points. With a flat normal reading."

Gondelman shrugs. He tilts his head back to gaze at the ceiling. "Well, Rybakov's daughter."

It was too pathetic to be invented, says Gondelman. Also it tended to reflect badly on the Soviet regime. Tronko might conceivably have cooked up the whole story from his own imagination, just to make himself look like some sort of sensitive, openhearted guy, but I don't think so, says Gondelman. I don't think he had that much imagination, for one thing. And for another, what did he care if we believed he was sensitive? What was that going to buy him? Nothing at all. Not from Claude Sparrow and company. So I think it was mortally real, this part. And the point is, both polygraph examiners agreed. They gave him high marks on the matter of Rybakov's daughter. It happened while he was doing his student internship with the diplomatic service.

"In Prague," says Kessler.

"You've heard this, then."

"No," says Kessler. "No, please go on."

Prague it was, says Gondelman. Tronko was in his last year at the Institute of International Relations and therefore eligible for a six-month posting at one of the embassies. His first chance to get beyond Soviet borders. He spoke a little Czech. So the powers that controlled his destiny sent him down there, to

Prague, to get his feet wet and his ears dry, in the role of a very
very junior attaché. Roughly twenty-three years old, says Gondelman. He wasn't yet married. Though he did have a nubile
young friend waiting back in Moscow, we're told—the same
one who later became Mrs. Tronko. This would have been in
autumn of 1952, that he took up the assignment in Czechoslovakia.

The purge trials down there were just hitting full stride in
'52, by the way, says Gondelman. They were about fifteen years
behind Moscow. The numbers weren't large, but some Czecho
heads had begun falling into the basket.

Tronko's winter in Prague seems to have been mainly un-
eventful, says Gondelman. Young Viktor did just what he had
been sent there to do—generally, very little. He attended a few
receptions and shook a few hands but spoke only when spoken
to; he ran a few innocent messages back and forth between the
embassy and the Czech Foreign Ministry; he got to try his hand
at translating a few boilerplate proclamations from the
Gottwald government into Russian for cabling home; he might
even have done the original translations of those same proclamations from Russian to Czech; and he kept out of trouble.
When the ambassador said jump, he pole-vaulted. He was just a
small widget in the Soviet occupation machine that was discreetly but firmly running the country. He knew almost no one
outside the lower ranks of the diplomatic community, and very
few diplomats outside the Soviet and Czech services. He stayed
away from the cafes and saloons of Old Town Prague because
Russian voices were so unwelcome there. He drank imported
vodka in privacy with a code clerk who had befriended him,
watched Czech girls pass on the street but didn't speak with
them, and waited for his tour to end. He adjusted himself com-
placently to the pinstripe ghetto life. In other words, says Gondelman, his internship fared well toward being a total success.
He had made only the most cursory acquaintance with
Rybakov's daughter.

That encounter had happened back in late autumn. They met
at an embassy function and exchanged a couple polite sentences. There had been no reason to say more, since Tronko at
that point didn't yet know her father, and he and the daughter
had nothing evidently in common. She was ten years older than
Viktor, after all, and a married woman. Truth be known, she

seems to have made no particular impression on him. At the same gathering Tronko had also been introduced to her husband, a pleasant man named Yuli Landau. Him Tronko remembered vividly.

Landau was a doctor, a surgeon trained at the best schools and hospitals in Moscow, and he was considered to be quite brilliant. A rising star in his profession, Gondelman says. He had been sent down to do pediatric surgery at the St. Ignatius Hospital in Prague, where his very presence was meant as a sort of personified aid and public-relations program to help shine up the Soviet image. He was that good. Landau himself had no quarrel with the assignment, since the children of Prague were afflicted with more than enough punctured eardrums and cleft palates to keep him feverishly busy. His wife, Zina Trofimovna Landau, was herself an obstetrician, also attached to St. Ignatius; but she wasn't such an icon as her husband. Viktor Tronko remembered meeting Yuli Landau because (despite the fact that Landau was much celebrated and fawned upon in Prague while Tronko was just another swatch of the diplomatic wallpaper) the doctor had looked straight into Tronko's face as they talked. He spoke with Tronko for five minutes, at that embassy party, and seemed to care about the answer to every question he asked. Tronko didn't recall afterward what they had discussed. But he remembered that Dr. Landau had black curly hair with flecks of premature gray, and brown eyes that burned like phosphorus fires, full of intelligence and compassion.

He also remembered mentioning Dr. Landau, shortly thereafter, to one of the more senior consular officers. Yes, absolutely, said this older man, Yuli Landau is a very deft surgeon. No one could deny him that, said the man. And the children seem to like him well. Prague is a good place for Landau, said the man; it was a stroke of great wit to ship him down here. All this sounded a little odd to Tronko. And intelligent? he asked. Isn't Dr. Landau supposed to be brilliant? The other man's face altered slightly. "Yes, I suspect he's quite clever, for a Jew."

Landau was arrested the following February. First there were no explanations at all. He simply disappeared from the hospital one day, in the custody of officers from the Interior Ministry and two of their Soviet advisers.

He was being questioned, it was said. For two weeks not a rumor of more, and even his wife didn't know whether he was

still in Prague or had been taken back to Moscow. When the
rumors did come they spoke of profiteering, conspiracy to commit sabotage, treason, and other formulaic slanders. Zionism
wasn't even mentioned. But the "Doctors' Plot" had just been
uncovered at home and—putatively uncovered, Gondelman
corrects himself—and, though Yuli Landau had no connection
with any of those men, it was an especially bad time for Jewish
doctors. In Prague itself, Rudolf Slánský and a half dozen other
Party officials, all Jews, had just been executed. For a month
Landau's wife could only wait and worry. No one at the embassy would see her. The Czech Interior Ministry ignored her
demands for information. Eventually there was another rumor:
that Yuli Landau had been found guilty of a lesser crime, unspecified, and in accordance with Czechoslovak justice was being sent for a term of forced labor to the Jachymov uranium
mines. By this point, his wife might have taken that news as
cause for relief. But how long a term? Then almost immediately
she received a dry official notification that the convict Yuli Landau had been executed, mistakenly, at Hlinko Crossing, with a
group of other prisoners.

The subsequent events seem to suggest that Landau was indeed the very exceptional man that Tronko had taken him for,
says Gondelman. If you can judge anything at all from the grief
of the wife. Caesar is always least honored by his own spouse,
or however that saying goes, says Gondelman—but not in this
case, evidently. Evidently Landau and Zina Trofimovna had
had a fierce and total marriage.

She was wild with anger, she was inconsolable, hysterical,
beyond control. She went to the Interior Ministry day after day
and pounded at closed doors with the flat of her hands until her
fingers and palms were swollen like sausages. She screamed at
some powerful men. Twice she was removed from the embassy
grounds by militia. No one from the Soviet colony would talk to
her. No one would even give the illusion of help or sympathy.
They couldn't afford to. Didn't dare. She was a pariah. She was
the widow of a traitorous Jew doctor. Get away, disappear, was
what people were thinking. But she wouldn't and she didn't.
Not yet. She wanted her husband's body, at least give her that,
his cold body, was what she screamed at the stolid men and
then at the closed doors and eventually at the rooftops and the
pigeons in the gutters. She wanted his body. She demanded her

right as a Soviet citizen to bury the body of her murdered husband. She was unraveling horribly, the madwoman of Prague. She had loved that man—how she had, says Gondelman. But she got nothing. No body. No explanations. Two or three weeks went by like that and then suddenly she fell silent.

She didn't appear anymore at the ministry offices. Didn't make scenes. She began to wash and eat again, reportedly. No more weeping. That's it, the squall has passed, she's come back to her senses, people thought. She even showed up at St. Ignatius and resumed her rounds. A couple more days, everyone breathed out, and then they found her late one afternoon on a cobbled courtyard at the hospital. She had thrown herself out of a window. But it was only three stories, unfortunately. She lived for another week.

Her father, Rybakov, was on assignment in East Berlin and even under normal conditions he would have had slim chance of getting down there to her bedside—but the current conditions were far from normal. It happened to be a moment of dire confusion within every branch and twig of the Soviet bureaucracy throughout the entire bloc. Everything stood still in a frozen instant of chaos. Everyone was paralyzed with caution and dread. Because her timing had been so very inopportune, you see, says Gondelman: she had managed to die the same week as Joseph Stalin.

Probably that fact would have given small consolation to Zina Trofimovna Landau, says Gondelman.

Up in Berlin, the father heard only that his daughter had been stricken with "serious illness." By the time even that skewed bit of information reached him, she was already dead. And he heard no more. There was nothing he could do. He may have tried to leave Berlin for Prague, on a transport flight or some such, and been denied permission. She was his youngest of three daughters, so we're told, says Gondelman, and the mother was dead. She was, we are led to believe, his heart's little treasure. But there was nothing he could do. Possibly. Or possibly his own nerve faltered during that dangerous moment and he didn't ask to leave. "Serious illness" might not have been anything so immediate, after all. We don't know. This part of the tale remains in ellipsis, says Gondelman. All we know is that everyone was petrified. Motion had stopped. Business had stopped. They were all frozen to their footprints with fearful uncertainty. Possibly even Trofim Filippovich Rybakov. Meanwhile his much-adored daughter Zina, by now, was a lump of cold clay down in Prague. The unclaimed carcass of the widow of a traitorous Jew doctor.

Her body spent two days on a shelf in a large meat locker at the Soviet Embassy compound. No one dared dispose of it, and no one dared take the initiative of shipping it back to Moscow. Everyone was vaguely aware that her father had been an important man in the security apparatus but no one knew how he stood with the new regime—if there was a new regime yet. He might be out or he might be up. No way to know. Any action with regard to his daughter's remains was therefore a rash one. Most of all, right now, no one wished to guess wrong. So they just left the body on ice. Two days. It might have stayed there for two months, until explicit instructions could be received from above or the embassy chef demanded the shelf space. But it didn't, says Gondelman.

Two days were long enough. Her skin had already turned a pale suety gray, we are told, says Gondelman. Young Viktor Tronko barely recognized the body when he saw it. But then again, he had barely known her.

According to his own testimony, Tronko acted on impulse, says Gondelman. And the polygraphs tended to confirm him here too. Twenty-three years old, remember, says Gondelman. Stars in his eyes over Yuli Landau yet this woman, the wife, had made no special impression upon him. He hadn't been in love with her. He wouldn't even claim he had liked her. She was a stranger. What he did, it might easily have wrecked his career, or worse—but when does a twenty-three-year-old ever stop to consider that? It was an impulse, Tronko said, and he never would say more. Maybe he was just modest, says Gondelman. Don't ask me. Sometimes the most potent human acts are the ones that transcend rational motive. The most potent and, I should add, the most credible, says Gondelman. Anyway. So he sold his watch. The kind of melodramatic thing a young man does. He possessed no money otherwise, we are told. He sold his watch. With the proceeds he bought a black dress and a coffin.

"And he had her buried," says Gondelman. "That's all. Simply saw her into the ground."

"What, he took the body away himself? He dug a hole?"

"Yes. Almost like that. He pushed open a few doors. Hired some men. Yes. He put her in a Jewish cemetery near the river."

"And he wasn't punished?"

"Neither punished nor rewarded. Not immediately, anyway. No repercussions whatsoever. Just more of the same embarrassed silence. There was still that raging epidemic of caution."

"You believe that this really happened," says Kessler.

"I do. The flutter technicians did too. Tronko himself believed it, evidently."

"No wonder the old man loved him."

"Yes," says Sidney Gondelman. "No wonder at all."

Gondelman has interrupted himself to lumber off down the spiral staircase, taking the steps like a gorilla, and returns after several minutes armed with two bottles, which he carries pinched by their necks among three of his fat fingers. He is wheezing happily. He sets an old and no doubt highly distinguished brandy on the table before Kessler; beside it, a fresh bottle of soda water. From the deep fold of his other palm appear a pair of crystal glasses.

"Sure," says Kessler. "Thank you."

Gondelman pours two fingers of brandy into a glass and then plugs the bottle. He fills the other glass with soda. He pushes the brandy glass toward Kessler. Nevertheless he looks more cheerful than ever.

"You're not joining me?"

Gondelman raises the other glass. "Vicariously," he says. "My doctor says it will kill me. And my doctor is a smart old man."

"But you didn't need to get this for me."

"I got it for me," says Gondelman. "You savor it. Please. I'll watch."

So Kessler says, "Cheers," and Gondelman sips sybaritically at his soda. To Kessler's ignorant but appreciative palate, the brandy seems very fine.

"Tell me the truth," Gondelman says abruptly, "about your storm-door accident."

Just as abruptly, Kessler hears himself admit: "Someone tried to kill me." It's another matter of impulse and fast character judgment, confiding that fact to Gondelman. "For pursuing this story, I think."

Sidney Gondelman nods, satisfied.

"So you were outside the room looking in," Kessler says. "Through a plastic window. Leo the Dubious and Big Al were inside, working their way through the transcripts, like it was a reading rehearsal."

"That's right."

"Leo was trying to summon an empathy with—by the way, how did he get saddled with that nickname? *Leo the Dubious.*"

"I told you. Pokorny's little joke."

"But why *Dubious,* rather than something else? You were large—Gondwanaland, okay. Rosalind Alpert was tall. What was it in particular about Leo?"

Gondelman ponders this, almost as though for the first time. He puckers his lips and takes a full minute. "Leo . . . Leo was a little strange," he says finally. "Though I suppose we were all, each of the three of us, a little strange. From the standpoint of someone like Pokorny or Sparrow. Our position was so different. We were analysts—meaning, we were never responsible for results, in the same way as a case officer was. Certainly not in the same way as an interrogator. Or a section chief. We were responsible only for producing ideas. Mere ideas," Gondelman says ironically. "Of course it's actually quite a stupendous demand. But not everyone appreciates them, these mere ideas. Our anointed role was to look over people's shoulders, and to second-guess, and I suppose Mel Pokorny had some sort of feeling about that."

Kessler waits.

"And of course, there's the fact that Leo's last name happened to be Dupuyre," Gondelman adds.

"Spell that," says Kessler, and Gondelman does, though Kessler is taking no notes.

Leo was trying, yes, to summon an empathy with Viktor Tronko, Gondelman agrees. For much of three years he sat on that folding chair in that drab little room and gave it the most ferocious concentration. He recited all the same fabulous stories and contradictions and recantations that Tronko (off in the *real* Vault somewhere) was delivering to Pokorny, and after so very much time it began to seem often that Leo himself truly believed them. He appeared to have hypnotized himself just a little. Some sort of transference had occurred. Or at very least he had succeeded—

Kessler intrudes to say: "You didn't happen to know where that real Vault was?"

"No. Never did. And if I had, I'm not sure that I could tell you," says Gondelman, so Kessler is happy to let the subject drop. He inhales the fumes off his brandy.

—or at very least he had succeeded, Leo had, in making that leap of empathic imagination. In some sense or another—and I don't mean this to sound mystical, says Gondelman, because I assure you I have a highly unmystical disposition—in some sense, he had entered into Viktor Tronko's brain. Leo had. Or maybe you could equally well say Tronko had entered into his.

He would recite still again, for the tenth or the twentieth time under Pokorny's relentless questioning—Pokorny in our version being Al, you recall—he would recite the story of his career, hitting all the familiar steeplechase jumps that by then everyone knew so well. First meeting with Trofim Filippovich Rybakov, the man who would become his spiritual father and patron. That was roughly two years after the Prague business, when Rybakov finally came home from Berlin. Recruitment to the KGB, and his training in Novosibirsk. Promotion to captain at age twenty-seven. Transfer from the Eleventh Department into Rybakov's shop. And then that all-important scene over the Lee Harvey Oswald file. You know about that, I assume, says Gondelman. You certainly must, or else none of the rest of this would even hint at making the dimmest sort of sense.

"I know about it," Kessler says. "That's the one Sparrow calls *Two*—"

"Let me guess," Gondelman interrupts. *"Two Russians Contemplating the File of Oswald."*

"Yes. Was it general usage?"

"No. He got it straight from me," says Gondelman. "Claude Sparrow doesn't know beans about Flemish painting."

And the question of Tronko's rank at the time of defection. And the discrepancies between those early Rome tapes, the ones that McAttee had got, and everything later. And the apparently sudden decision to come across, at Vienna, complete with the telegram of recall which Tronko himself was by now

admitting had been a total fabrication. And of course Dmitri—
Tronko's consistent stonewalling on the subject of Dmitri. He
had never heard of any such penetration, was what Tronko
swore. Almost certainly he would have heard, at least a rumor,
a small smug wisp of gossip leaking its way like the perfume of
a fancy woman through the upper corridors of the Lubyanka,
he claimed. If any such wondrous creature as Dmitri had truly
existed. Tronko firmly adhered to the view, therefore, that Dmitri did not. That we were wasting our time and our resources,
crippling ourselves, with a great goose chase. Needless to say,
this sort of vague disclaimer persuaded no one, says Gondelman. Give us some proof, he was told. He couldn't. Or he
wouldn't. One cannot prove a negative, Tronko answered—and
that's true enough, says Gondelman, so far as it goes. Believe
me, your Dmitri is a fantasy, an imaginary demon, he told us.
Well, no one did believe him. Virtually no one. Claude Sparrow
certainly didn't, Pokorny didn't. Al didn't. Oddly, though, the
polygraph boys gave Tronko rather high grades for sincerity on
this matter too, Gondelman says. Anyway we covered it all, all
of that and more, in our little game of charades, Gondelman
says.

Leo would march through the latest reiteration, under Al's
ungentle goading, maybe five hours' worth of transcript in an
average installment, and then we would adjourn to another
room of the suite, with our bag lunches. Sometimes Leo would
dodge down the hall for a shower first, and change his shirt;
then he would join us, freshened and revived from his trance.
We would eat sandwiches and drink cola from cans and discuss,
Gondelman says. Just we three. Nobody here but us Schnitzels.
The tone was relaxed and dispassionate now. Cerebral. Seated
around a conference table in a comfortable room, we would
analyze the morning's drama. Gondelman stretches back in the
captain's chair, clasping his hands behind his head. We would
discuss, he repeats. Kessler wonders suddenly whether any
other offices along the plush corridor downstairs contain people
like Sidney Gondelman. Colleagues. Partners. Maybe not.
Maybe there are no other large thinkers at Janus Corporation.
Maybe Gondelman is the sole grand and glorious wizard of this
outfit. There are no other lookout towers, Kessler has noticed.
And Gondelman sounds downright lonely.

"We would discuss. Usually I would propose the first observations, from my notes. Al would comment. She generally had a very strong sense of the points where Tronko seemed vulnerable—where Pokorny had extracted or maybe just come close to extracting some new admission, or even, sometimes, where Mel had failed to pursue an opportunity that looked to her promising. Meanwhile Leo would inject Delphic comments like 'How in the world could a nice guy like me go from senior lieutenant to colonel in eighteen months? I don't think I've got it in me.' Or he would announce: 'I can't believe I really forgot about Trofim Filippovich, during those sessions back at Rome. I couldn't have been *that* drunk. I think I was protecting him. But why aren't I protecting him *now*?' Or he might gaze straight across at Al and say: 'You don't scare me, Pokorny. I know you're just the personal stooge of Claude Sparrow,' and then Al and I would have to pounce on him for committing logical fallacy, since it was manifest that Tronko knew nothing of the kind. There was no reason to suspect that he had so much as heard of Claude Sparrow. And then another time, which I remember quite well, Leo simply proclaimed: 'I feel very strong today. I feel a great deal of inner force.'

" 'What do you mean, Leo?' we asked him.

" 'I feel strong,' he said. 'I think I'm stronger than all of you. More stubborn. I think I'm going to win.'

" 'Stronger than Pokorny?' we said.

" 'Stronger than Pokorny and Sparrow and McAttee, yes.'

" 'You don't *know* from Claude Sparrow, goddamn it. Remember?'

" 'Stronger than Eames. Stronger than Langley and Moscow. I'm a clam. You can crush me but that doesn't mean you can pry me open.'

" 'Come back to earth, Leo, and explain what you mean.'

"He looked blank, then," says Gondelman. "And he said: 'I don't know. It's just a feeling.' "

That was all during the first twenty months or so, says Gondelman. Leo would snap in and out of the role, and make these cryptic pronouncements off the top of his head, offered for just whatever they might or might not be worth, and then he would return to us, fully and soundly, joining Al and me for prolonged analytical discussions of the character of the testimony thus far. We were working in the realms of psychology and epistemology as well as verifiable factual evidence, and we knew that, says

Gondelman. Some of it was verifiable, anyway. And we knew that, I say. Nevertheless we used symbolic logic and a blackboard, sometimes. We chalk-talked at each other, we jawboned, we twirled the body of evidence to expose it from every angle and we peered and we delved. It was the ultimate intellectual puzzle, if you like, says Gondelman: trying to solve the mysteries of just one human soul. Gondelman stares out toward a red band of sky low over the Hudson.

It was quite grand, actually, he says.

After a glance at Kessler's brandy and a taste of his own soda, Gondelman continues. But as I say, he says, that was earlier on. Toward the end of the second year, there came to be some gradual changes.

God knows, none of us had expected the thing to drag on so long—two years. Let alone three. That's a piece of time, out of any life. Leo was getting tired. We were all three tired and frustrated, naturally, but for obvious reasons especially Leo. He grew moody. He had always been the quietest of the three of us, says Gondelman, not a bombastic fool like me or quick and trenchant and delicately, murderously bright, like Big Al. Leo had a different style of intelligence. I suspect he would have made a great auto mechanic—and I mean that with no condescension, Gondelman insists—because he was the type, Leo was, who could listen to the sound of an idling engine, his head cocked to one side, and then correctly diagnose that there was an electrical short somewhere between the alternator and the right taillight, if that's possible.

"I doubt it," says Kessler.

"But you see what I mean. For the same reason, he might have been a fine veterinarian. Working with patients who can't talk. I respect those capacities."

"I think I see, yes," says Kessler.

He grew moody and then plain sullen, Leo did. He seemed to be suffering an extended funk. He contributed less to the group discussions. And here was another symptom, says Gondelman: he gave up the showers. He came to lunch sticky. He didn't smell, you understand, says Gondelman. Not especially. But it was a thing I noticed. Like when an old cat finally loses interest in cleaning herself: the first dingdong of mortality. I don't know whether Leo was even showering, anymore, when he went home.

"Was there something wrong in his personal life?"

"He had no personal life," says Gondelman. "He was an aging bachelor, like me. He was wedded to the job. Like all of us. He had a collection of jazz records and a ham radio, I think. I never saw his apartment. No, it wasn't that. It was Viktor Tronko's personal life that was dragging him down, not his own. Tronko who also, of course, had none whatsoever."

At one point in the later period, Leo came forth with: "I've *told* you. I don't *know* why we didn't debrief Oswald. I don't *know* why we didn't contact him. But I saw the file. And we *hadn't.*" His eyes were fixed on a spot on the floor. The voice was stiff, cold, angry. And this wasn't a reenactment of the transcript, says Gondelman. This was spoken over lunch.

During the third year it only got worse. Leo never anymore made statements like "I feel strong." He volunteered little, says Gondelman. He sat hunched at the conference table and deferred languidly, with a wave of his hand, to ideas offered by Al and myself. He left the building promptly at night, sometimes even early, and wouldn't accept rides from the two of us during a week when his Karmann Ghia was in the shop. He had a friend in Security, Leo said, who would drop him at the bus stop. There was this distance now. As though it had become him against us. As though Leo were truly the clam and we were the ones determined to open him or crush him. Somewhere along the way, he had gone over to Viktor Tronko. I suppose the same sort of thing might happen to an actor who spends too long in a very successful play, says Gondelman.

Much of the interrogation that year was focused on two subjects: Oswald in Russia and Dmitri. What Pokorny liked to refer to, hectoringly, as Tronko's pair of big lies. More and more, Pokorny left the other unresolved matters swept off to the wayside and concentrated upon just these two. Oswald in the days before Dallas, the days of his expatriate life in Minsk; and Dmitri, the phantom agent. He went after Tronko relentlessly on each of these subjects.

Over and over again they covered the same ground. Pokorny asked the same old questions framed eight dozen different ways and Tronko made over and over again the same responses—or occasionally mixed in a slight variation, by innocent or less innocent mistake, which Pokorny would then instantly seize upon and try to exploit for new leverage. *Why do you say so-*

*and-so, if two years ago you said such-and-such? Why do you
keep changing your story? Who do you think you're kidding?* It
might have been something so potentially crucial as the weather
in Minsk on that twenty-third of November, says Gondelman.
Or it might have been something minuscule, like the names of
Rybakov's surviving daughters. And when there were no prospects of new leverage for weeks at a time, no variations, then
Pokorny would resort to browbeating, psychological bully tactics, strident demands for still further repetition, until a fresh
angle might finally turn up. It got to be quite tedious sometimes, let me tell you, says Gondelman. But Pokorny seemed to
possess the right talents.

I suppose he made an excellent interrogator, says Gondelman. Certainly he had stamina. He was quick-witted, his memory for detail was impressive, and he could be cruel. Affable and
engaging in his clownish way and then, just moments later,
cruel. Merciless. Absolutely predaceous. I suppose those are the
requisite traits, says Gondelman. Of course all I know is what I
saw and heard from the transcript. But even our Al was hard
taxed, sometimes, filling the role.

"Mel told me himself that he was a cast-iron asshole, as an
interrogator," says Kessler.

"That was self-knowing."

We returned endlessly to the *Two Russians* tableau, for instance, says Gondelman. Pokorny seemed to feel that this was
the linchpin to Tronko's edifice of lies—assuming as he was,
Gondelman adds, that it was indeed an edifice of lies. And not
just a random garbage heap of lies.

"Or an edifice of truth," Kessler says.

"Well, that seemed unlikely."

"All of this seems unlikely to me," Kessler says.

The *Two Russians* tableau was scrutinized minutely, obses-
sively, like a brilliant art forgery set for auction at Sotheby's.
Tell me again, Pokorny would say. Tell me again about your
adventure with Oswald's file. Wait, what was the layout of the
office? he would demand, interrupting before Tronko could get
started. Tronko had already described the office layout. He
would describe it again, and if he were lucky the words he used
would be the same exact words as last time, and he would
therefore be allowed to continue. Whose office was it,
Rybakov's or Tronko's own? Tronko would answer. What sort

of lighting in the office? Tronko would answer. Did the table
lamp have a shade of green glass? Was the lamp itself made of
brass? Was the brass polished? Tronko would answer these
things docilely. Why had he called it a table lamp, if it was
placed on a desk? Why not a desk lamp? Was it a desk or was it
really a table, upon which the file had rested, there in
Rybakov's office—or did Tronko perhaps not know what it
was? Tronko would answer: a table lamp that happened to sit
on a desk. A desk lamp, in his mind, was different. Though he
could be mistaken. How large was it, this file? Was it thick or
thin, one volume or several? Tronko would answer and again
Pokorny would pounce: why was it one volume now if it had
been several volumes last year and again only one volume back
when he told the same tale to Sol Lentzer? Where were the
missing volumes? What was this—the multiplication and distribution of loaves and fishes? From the transcript as we had it, of
course, Gondelman says, you couldn't tell which of these questions had merely been asked of Tronko and which had been
screamed at him. Al had to guess. She had to play from context.
If the file was just one thin volume, why did it take you and
Rybakov so long to go through it? Tell me again what Rybakov
said to you. Tronko would answer, quoting: "We must see,
Viktor Semyonovich, whether we have gotten ourselves implicated. Do you pray?" Wasn't it rather unusual, Pokorny would
demand, for a major-general of the KGB to talk like that?
Tronko would answer: yes, it was.

He drove Tronko like a sled dog, Gondelman says, through
the entire chain of events surrounding that tableau, the entire
twenty-hour period leading up to the inspection of Oswald's file.
What time of day was it when Tronko first heard the news out
of Dallas? Twelve o'clock midnight. Exactly twelve midnight?
No, not exactly; just roughly twelve. How did he hear? Trofim
Filippovich called him by telephone, woke him, and told him
this horrible news. He had a private home telephone, then? Yes,
of course. Did Tronko's wife wake to the sound of the phone?
Yes, she did. Although on another occasion, says Gondelman,
Tronko said she did not. Pokorny of course roughed him up
over that. Tronko tried to clarify it by explaining that she had
slept through the ring but she came awake when she heard the
sound of Tronko's voice, the tone of alarm, as he spoke with
Trofim Filippovich about the assassination. Then what? Po-

korny was not easily appeased. Then what happened—did
Rybakov tell Tronko to get his ass right down to the Lubyanka?
No. No, he told Tronko to get dressed but to remain at home,
by the telephone, until he, Trofim Filippovich, called back. And
did Rybakov call back? Yes, Tronko would say; though a full
hour had passed before Trofim Filippovich did call, and that
had been the longest hour of Tronko's life. Was it longer than
this one, you lying piece of pickled herring? and here Al's voice
would go deep and quiet with menace, says Gondelman. I can't
speak for how Pokorny himself might have played it. Tronko
would answer: yes. It was longer, yes. And what did Rybakov
say when he called you back in an hour? He said I must go to
Minsk, Tronko would answer. Exact words, Pokorny would
demand. "You are going to Minsk," Tronko would say, quoting.

"It went on and on like that," Gondelman says. "Pokorny
would take him over the whole story, minute by minute. Word
by word. Like a good bastardly trial lawyer conducting a cross-
examination. I think perhaps Mel missed his calling."

"I don't," says Kessler. "I think he found it perfectly."

They did the same sort of workout over that Ilyushin-28
transport that had supposedly taken Tronko down to Minsk.
How many propellers? asked Pokorny. None, said Tronko, not
to be so easily fooled. All right, how many jet engines? demanded Pokorny. Tronko didn't remember, or remembered
wrong, and so they had another tussle. There were similar exchanges about the architecture and the interior layout of the
KGB office in Minsk where Tronko had supposedly impounded
the file, about the landing conditions at Vnukovo Airport when
Tronko's plane arrived back, about the physical weight of that
one volume or those several and the question of how many
would have fit into Tronko's briefcase, about whether Tronko
during all these long hours had understood the significance of
his mission, about whether he had peeked at the file before
delivering it up to Rybakov, about whether anyone else but the
two of them had been present in that office when Rybakov
began turning the pages and, if not, why not. Tronko contradicted himself on a dozen different points, all of them seemingly
small, seemingly meaningless, and Pokorny punished him over
each of them. Tronko made minor corrections when he was
forced to, but no major recantations concerning this particular

episode. Merely brush strokes here and there, says Gondelman. Brush strokes that left the essence of the picture unaltered. *Two Russians* was still two Russians and the file of Oswald was still that. It was still just a routine surveillance record, a log of the subject's movements and a sheaf of wiretap transcripts such as would have been collected by local officers of Rybakov's Tourist Department for any visiting or expatriate American, even a maladjusted and unwelcome young man who had offered himself as though he were some type of important political defector and then been shunted off to help manufacture radio circuits on a production line in Minsk. Nothing more. It was still blessedly empty, the file was, of any evidence that the KGB had ever recruited or even approached Lee Harvey Oswald, for any purpose whatsoever. Tronko's story in that regard had not been subject to modification. He had not wavered on any of the crucial particulars, Gondelman says.

But then Pokorny himself didn't seem truly concerned over the particulars, crucial or otherwise. Those seemed merely to serve him as points of leverage. He seemed to have his own larger theory—or call it a predisposition, Gondelman says, or a bias—about the *Two Russians* matter. Perhaps it was really Claude Sparrow's theory. Sparrow's bias. That's hard to know. Anyway, Pokorny was not haggling for modifications. He wasn't exerting himself this hard over a few brush strokes. His goal, evidently, was to knock the whole damn painting down off its easel. He was trying to make Tronko confess that the entire episode of the Oswald file was an utter concoction.

To admit that, of course, was for Viktor Tronko the same as admitting that he had been sent. That he was a phony defector. A dispatched agent of Soviet disinformation. And Tronko couldn't or wouldn't make any such confession—no matter how badly he contradicted himself, no matter how much Pokorny badgered him about General Avvakian.

"Avvakian?"

"General Avvakian was the chief of the KGB disinformation department," says Gondelman.

"I know. Sparrow told me about him," says Kessler. "How did Avvakian figure in the *Two Russians* episode?"

"There was no evidence that he figured at all. Avvakian was really just a name to blame things on. We knew virtually nothing about the man. But that was the favored hypothesis: if

Tronko had been sent, then it must be General Avvakian who had sent him."

"Pokorny's hypothesis?"

"Pokorny's or Sparrow's, yes. And, sure, it was logical enough. There just wasn't any evidence. No confirmation. Viktor Tronko would never admit to it."

Likewise with what Pokorny called the second big lie, says Gondelman: the question of Dmitri. Tronko professed his own total ignorance of any such penetration and claimed adamantly that therefore the penetration did not exist. But how could he be so positive? Well, he bragged about the breadth of his own official access, Tronko did; he bragged about the sensitivity of his antennae for gossip; not to mention that he was the trusted assistant of T. F. Rybakov, a major general who was himself closely associated with KGB Chairman Shelepin. It simply wasn't plausible that Dmitri could exist and Viktor Tronko not have got wind of him. So said Tronko. To Pokorny, on the other hand, it was quite plausible. Pokorny came back at him with—

At which point, Kessler feels himself slide.

Maybe it's the brandy without lunch, maybe it's the pain in his arm, maybe the vertiginous view from this glass tower causing Kessler to fear for a bad moment that he might be ill, right here, right now. How embarrassing. Terrible faux pas, to toss Gondelman's prize vintage up on the carpet. He is woozy. Unsure of head and stomach. He stares down into his glass, as though listening thoughtfully, until these gravitational wobbles begin to fade. Maybe it's the brandy and the arm and the whole subject of Viktor Tronko. Or maybe, more specifically, it is the single grotesque suspicion that has just flickered through Michael Kessler's overcrowded brain. Dmitri. How would I hide myself, if I were Dmitri?

Kessler doesn't recall exactly what statement by Gondelman triggered this mental derailment; and of course Gondelman was merely quoting Big Al, who had in turn been mouthing the words of Pokorny, who had himself been . . . et cetera. Anyway, whatever, there was some mention again of General Avvakian. Then came Kessler's sickening thought, his nasty and paranoid notion, passing its way suddenly along arteries and synapses like a jolt of drug-induced nausea.

How would I hide myself, if I were Dmitri?

With a riddle of high quality, always go for the least obvious answer. Turn this drawing upside down to locate three chickens, two goats, and a mole.

After a moment, Kessler feels better. Stable, at least. Those glands at the sides of his jaw have stopped firing their juices. But he finds himself wanting to change the subject. Let his brain and his belly have a chance to settle, please. A chance to adjust. Gondelman's monologue has meanwhile left him behind.

"But you weren't actually there," Kessler says haphazardly.

"Me? No. Never."

"You got it all third hand. Through a plastic window."

"That's right. As I've said."

"So how was poor Leo the Dubious doing, by this point?"

Gondelman comes to a full halt. He shakes his head at the memory. "Not at all well."

It had been such a long and laborious process, three years' worth, says Gondelman, yet at the end it seemed to have happened so abruptly. In December of 1967, Herbert Eames decreed that the Tronko interrogation was over. He demanded a final assessment. He appointed a—

"The Nye Report," says Kessler.

"Yes."

"Roger Nye and Scott Wickes and you. Eames appointed a panel consisting of you three. Sparrow told me about this too."

"He told you a lot."

"I think he liked me," says Kessler. "And you had a rigid deadline. Also decreed by Eames. Sixty days."

They did indeed. Gondelman immediately left the suite on the sixth floor and began meeting with Nye and Wickes. The sessions of the Schnitzel Group simply ended, bang, that suddenly. Too suddenly. They were never given the chance to compile a final report of their own. Gondelman had to speak for them all, through the Nye panel. In some ways, though, that was probably for the best. Leo at this stage was barely conversable. Big Al seemed to be turning her attention to other things. After the Nye Report was finished and delivered, Gondelman himself took a month's vacation, much needed, his first in three years.

He went to Majorca and then Monte Carlo, on a package

tour; played the tables, in a very modest way. When he got back to Langley, Leo Dupuyre was gone.

Once again Kessler waits. He watches Gondelman take a drink of soda and experiences a vicarious swell of discomfort. His mind is still elsewhere. But he can hear the words and he now expects to be told, perhaps in melodramatic terms, where Leo Dupuyre went, and why. Instead Gondelman says: "Within a month, Big Al was gone too."

"*Both* of them?"

"Leo left voluntarily. He shook the dust of the place off his feet. Al, on the other hand, was forced out. She was put into a position where she could only resign."

Kessler leans forward. "You haven't told me much about Rosalind Alpert."

"No?"

"No. A tall mathematician. Very bright. A delicately murderous intelligence, I think you said. That's all. Who was she? Another aging bachelor? Did she have jazz records and a ham radio, like Leo?"

"I doubt it. She did own a piano, I believe."

"A piano. She lived alone with her piano. Lord, you people. And a house full of cats, I suppose." But then passingly it occurs to Kessler: What would they say about me? *He lived alone with a typewriter and a liquor cabinet. Traveled often. Is mourned by his agent.*

"No. No cats, so far as I knew."

"And she never married?"

"No," says Gondelman.

"What happened to her?"

"I couldn't say. We haven't spoken—"

"In a decade, I know. I mean back then. Why was she forced to resign?"

"Because of tawdry rumors," Gondelman says. And he has poured a stout refill into the brandy glass before Kessler can flag him away.

Gondelman himself never knew the real logic behind Rosalind's plummet from grace, he says. *Logic* is probably saying too much, actually. He never knew the real reasons. She never confided in him and he didn't care to pry. He saw her a couple of times, in the hallways of OSR again now, and in each case they exchanged friendly words but no significant personal news. They had scarcely ever exchanged personal news anyway. The second of these hallway encounters occurred, just after he got back from the Monte Carlo trip, on the day she had come to clean out some last private effects from her office. She seemed to be cheerful. She acted shocked and delighted at the incongruity of Gondelman with a tan face. She seemed herself. She fooled him totally. Gondelman had no inkling that she would be leaving, permanently, that day—he wasn't aware until later, when she had already gone. Only about three hours later, it was. He put his head into her office with a wry comment ready and found the room a shell.

That was merely the day when she had transferred her things over to the cubicle they had given her in the Office of Finance, but it represented Rosalind's true departure more than any other moment did. The reassignment to Finance was just a transparent and temporary thing, a humiliation that would lead inevitably to her resignation. As the powers in charge well knew. You don't consign an extraordinary mind like Rosalind's to the Office of Finance, says Gondelman, unless you want to drive her away. It was almost a bad joke. With the background she had in mathematics, I mean, says Gondelman. If she were a prize-winning playwright, they could have accomplished the same by exiling her to the typing pool in Personnel. But this joke wasn't funny at all. They hurt her. That wasn't easy, with Rosalind. They mortified her. That wasn't necessary. They could have simply fired her, if they felt so compelled to get her out. But firing would have demanded a measure more of decency and a measure more of moxie, says Gondelman. Kessler is acutely aware that Gondelman has begun finally to use her first name.

The reassignment to Finance coincided with the end of her security review. She had been allowed to keep her clearance, says Gondelman. That can only mean that she had been found blameless of any willful breaches or careless mistakes. She had come under some degree of suspicion, evidently, but the review officer or the board—if she was given a full board—must have found nothing to fix on. Nothing solid. Nothing supported by even a flimsy bit of evidence. It wouldn't have taken very much. But no, her clearance was allowed to stand. I never knew whether she did have a full review board, says Gondelman. A person doesn't gab about those things with one's workmates. Especially a person doesn't if a person is soon afterward out the door.

"How long did she stay in Finance?"

"Less than a month, I believe."

"Then she quit. Left the Agency."

Gondelman nods.

"Was there still any chance for her? I mean, might she have been reinstated? After a period of bureaucratic quarantine or some such? You say she had been allowed to keep—"

Gondelman wags his head slowly.

"Why not?"

Gondelman says nothing. He sits. He flicks an eye toward Kessler's untouched brandy.

"Why not?" Kessler repeats. "Because of the tawdry rumors you mentioned?"

"That was my view, yes," says Gondelman. "It would have been very hard for Rosalind to do anything but what she did. Very improbable."

"These rumors involved something more than a little security breach, didn't they. Something more than taking classified documents home at night. Didn't they. Or maybe I should say, something *other.*"

"Of course they did."

"Her private life."

"Mm."

"Could you tell me, please," Kessler says gingerly, "what it is we're talking about?"

"Oh, she had been linked romantically with Jed McAttee," is Gondelman's pristine formulation. The breezy tone he has applied to it sounds totally artificial.

"That's all?"

"That was all, and it was enough, Mr. Kessler."

"Why should it be enough? This wasn't the Victorian era, this was 1968."

"This was also the Central Intelligence Agency. Not a campus somewhere in California. And there were damaging conclusions to be leapt to. Matters of some professional pertinence."

"Namely, that she was leaking the Tronko transcripts to McAttee," Kessler posits. "If she were sleeping with him, she must also be sharing information."

Gondelman cringes. He answers: "Yes."

"Did the rumors go that far?"

"No. Never. Maybe it was addressed by the security board. If it was, they evidently dismissed it. I myself never heard any such accusation made. Not even in a whisper."

"But it didn't need to be. Only that she was"—this time Kessler is more careful—"romantically linked with him."

"Yes."

"And you think that was a lie."

"What *difference* if it was a lie?" Gondelman barks, laying his fat palm onto the table with enough force to rattle the glasses.

Then at once he is milder: "But probably it was, yes. I think so. Based on nothing except my knowledge of human character. Anyway, I always suspected that as the reason she was treated so badly. Getting rid of her was a means of announcing, true or not, that the rumors were false. Possibly McAttee himself was to blame. He may have demanded her head."

Gondelman's arm moves out across the table like a thick graceful python, snatching away Kessler's brandy. He drinks off half of it in a gulp. Then he swirls the rest, privately admiring its color.

"There was a double standard in those days, I suppose," says Kessler. Even to himself, it sounds feeble.

"Yes, at least two," says Gondelman.

The castle below them may be empty by now. Car headlights have gone away down the drive. The river is dark and the sky above it is a dim silver-gray. Cold Spring is a speckling of yellow dots to the south. God, you can see everything from up here, Kessler thinks. Maximum visibility and the illusion of lonely wisdom. Maybe Gondelman's smart old doctor should have warned him against heights.

26

"I had a long talk with Sidney Gondelman," Kessler is saying. "He was very helpful. And he's very protective of you, by the way."

From the far end of the line there is only silence.

"An extremely loyal man, was my impression. Forthright and loyal. I'm sure he's also hugely intelligent, in his own way. I liked Gondelman. But I got the sense that he might have missed something."

Only silence.

"Something that passed almost under his nose," Kessler adds.

The woman's cold voice says: "And?"

"And so I'd like to see you."

"How did you find me?"

"Gondelman knew the name of the town," Kessler says. "You've been there a dozen years now, I gather."

"Eleven."

"I would take an hour of your time. I'd ask some questions, any of which you could choose not to answer. I wouldn't harry you. I wouldn't quote you. I'm just trying to fill in a few gaps. Background. I wouldn't be intrusive."

"Of course you would," says Rosalind Alpert.

He is in a booth on the darkened street of downtown Cold Spring, holding the phone with a cramped shoulder and balancing his pad on the shelf. His breath shows in frosty little puffs. Kessler at this moment is desperate not to lose her, but he feels the connection stretched thin, failing. His own silence is like a fatal admission.

"Let me intrude, then. Briefly."

"Why should I?"

"Maybe you owe it to yourself?"

Even cast as a question, it is presumptuous and risky. She doesn't answer.

"You left Washington abruptly," Kessler says.

"Long ago. Without any regrets."

"But maybe there was something left unsaid. No one asked you. Or no one could be trusted. Maybe no one would have believed you, at that particular point."

Again she doesn't answer, which this time seems encouraging.

"Say it to me and be rid of it," Kessler says.

"Where are you?"

"New York. Up on the Hudson. I have a car," Kessler says eagerly.

He drives north on the parkway in a state of nervous excitement. For the first time since Pokorny barged in on him last week, Kessler feels his own intuition charging out confidently in advance of the evidence. He can't clear his mind of Dmitri— Dmitri who now finally seems a real person, not just a name, a phantom, a Siberian wild goose. He can't forget what Gondelman said about those moments when Tronko argued otherwise. He can't stop thinking about Leo, who became unconversable, and about Big Al herself, whose attention was turning to other things. Short of Albany, Kessler exits.

He heads back into western Massachusetts on a two-lane through manicured countryside, a high half-moon making the snowfields glow like lambent ivory. Up here the Housatonic is still a free-stone trout stream. He reaches the town of Great Barrington in time to find room at an egregiously overpriced motor lodge, and then dinner. Coming straight up tonight seemed to make more sense than going back to New Haven. Rosalind Alpert has agreed to meet him tomorrow at noon.

He takes four aspirin for his arm and sleeps reasonably well, despite a dream pageant of looming menacing faces, like balloons come untethered from a Macy's parade. Possibly he is running a slight fever. He should get that prescription filled. And he should do something soon about the dirty bandage. But the first thing is to clear his brain of distressing suspicions. He wakes early, feeling manic. Over a long breakfast he reads the Times minutely, absorbing nothing. In late morning he asks directions for walking to the school.

She came up here a year after leaving Langley—he knows that from Gondelman. It was virtually all Gondelman himself knew. And Gondelman only knew it from the same gossip network that had carried the damaging rumors. This time the gossip said that Rosalind Alpert, horrible to relate, had accepted a job at a finishing school. Teaching mathematics to debutantes, snicker snicker. Gondelman never heard how it actually came about, or whether it was as bad as it sounded, since he never again talked with Rosalind. Presumably it was a job that would not even have been offered to her—because she was grossly overqualified—if she hadn't made clear to the hiring committee, with some sacrifice of pride, that yes indeed she would grab it if offered. That she would be glad to get it.

And after eleven years, evidently, she remains glad enough to keep it. Maybe the cloistered, Minervan atmosphere is part of the appeal, Kessler thinks, though not necessarily for the reasons that gossip would have presumed. Maybe she just wanted a drastic change. No question, she got that. The place is hardly to be confused with Langley.

The buildings are of red brick and cedar shake, genuinely old but impeccably kept, like bond certificates stored in a safe; all the filigreed cast-iron railings have recently been repainted with black enamel. There is a proliferation of ivy. There are paddleball courts and a hockey field, broad snow-covered lawns and rectilinear hedges and a tame creek running through the campus. Kessler notices a huge naked hardwood tree, probably an oak or a catalpa, so ancient and weary that one horizontal limb, thick as a phone pole, has rested its elbow against the ground. The walkways and the lane are deserted, at least until just a few minutes before twelve, when comes a sudden flush of five dozen girls all in plaid skirts and blue blazers. They gabble for a minute and then disappear into other doors. Kessler finds the particular building that has been described to him, unmistakable with its black shutters and its white Doric columns and its widow's walk. On the wall to one side of the entrance is a brass plaque:

MISS USSHER'S SCHOOL
1843

PUELLAE VENERUNT
ABIERUNT MULIERES

I'm sure that much is true, Kessler thinks. It continues with a hopeful brag about the pursuit of truth, knowledge, humanity. Yes, don't we all like to think so. He goes inside.

To the frowzy young woman seated at the desk, a matron before her time, he says: "My name is Kessler. I'm expected. Dr. Alpert."

This one lifts her head enough to look at him through the lower crescents of bifocals, though she isn't wearing any. She points down the corridor with a pencil.

"Miss Alpert," she says.

It is a faculty common room, not a private office. Two walls are lined with old books, one wall consists of windows over-looking a back lawn, and one is full of coats hung on hooks. The room smells of cigarettes and, if his nose is right, soggy jelly sandwiches. A coffee urn gurgles listlessly. Kessler expects a half dozen bleary teachers to come stampeding in any moment, escaping their students to this sanctum. He has closed the door behind himself, though, and it stays closed. Rosalind Alpert stands in a corner near the windows. She is not so tall as he imagined her, only about five foot eleven, the same as him. Nevertheless she holds herself straight and, in a pair of spike heels, she might seem to tower. Kessler doubts that this woman has ever owned a pair of spike heels. She is handsome, but not so handsome as to embarrass herself, and if Kessler didn't know that she is about fifty years old he would guess that she is about fifty. She consents to a handshake. There are chairs but she doesn't offer him one.

The lack of guaranteed privacy is clearly no accident. She has chosen this room, for meeting him, as in some way a measure of protection. On the other hand, she could have refused him altogether. She didn't. So Kessler is optimistic. And he remembers his own promise: he has not come to harry her. He has come to listen.

But when she opens her mouth, his impression changes radically. She speaks in a warm quiet voice, very alive, almost sympathetic, not the least stiff or edgy. She lets her hands rest in the pockets of her long sweater-vest and leans backward, now, against the window ledge. She has evidently decided in advance of his arrival how much she is willing to say, which turns out to be rather much. She anticipates some of his questions. Her memory for the relevant facts is precise, quick, not noticeably bitter. Occasionally she even pulls a smile. She congratulates Kessler on his own line of deductions, in a tone that seems gently condescending, and then a few moments later she runs a hand up the back of her neck and tosses her brown sleek hair, an extraordinary relaxed gesture. Kessler sees now that the word "handsome," with its severe and mannish intimations, is all wrong for Rosalind Alpert. She is not what he expected. And she seems virtually undamaged by the events of her own life.

After just five minutes of mild preliminaries, news of Gondelman, the less mild news of Pokorny, he has sensed that this will have been no wasted trip. *Veritatem, scientiam, humanitatem hic repperunt.*

They talk for an hour, until a bell rings jarringly.

27

But it's going to take at least one more conversation before Kessler has anything that he would ever dare publish.

Maybe he won't dare publish it anyway. Or maybe his friendly contact at *Rolling Stone* will back away and Kessler will have no better luck coaxing anyone else to take the leap. It certainly will be a leap. On a story like this, so provocative, yet by its nature so subterranean, you can never really provide proof beyond doubt—or for that matter beyond plausible action for libel, if someone decides to press it. All you can do is say: *Two knowledgeable people told me the same exact damn thing, independently, and I have reason to believe they weren't lying.* After that, reliable sources and carefully dated notes can't help you; fact-checkers and lawyers definitely can't help you. After that, it's more like a religious conversion than an epistemological judgment: you bet that a heaven exists, also a hell, and act accordingly. Kessler himself is almost ready to bet.

But he still needs that other voice. He needs confirmation. He drives south toward New Haven not quite like a maniac.

He intends to stop home only long enough to throw clean underwear into his bag and be gone again, but as he elbows the car up Chapel Street in five o'clock traffic there comes another unpleasant jolt.

"Damn it. *Damn* it," he says aloud, thumping his palm against the steering wheel. This new shock is not so grotesquely concussive as the one that hit him in Gondelman's tower, but still it is bad, yes, and he feels it even more intimately, an assault to the stomach. One casual glance at the Yale Art and Architecture building, here on the corner by the stoplight, has triggered his memory: the Athol Fugard presentation on Eugène Marais. Film, lecture, baby-sitter, date. At the A and A building, 8 P.M., Wednesday. Last night.

He has stood her up cold. Without so much as an unctuous last-minute phone call. His ass is grass.

He tries Nora's home number as soon as he gets inside his door and of course there is no answer. He tries her office, nothing. She is in transit. Or else this is the day of the week when she chauffeurs little Emily to gymnastics class, ballet, Tae Kwon Do, whatever it is the kid is taking, and they go downtown afterward for mother-and-daughter pizza. Kessler can't remember the particulars. Today is Thursday, he knows that much. Thursday and he is, ouch, twenty-four hours late. Nora is in transit. Or maybe, too, she has yanked her phone out of the wall.

No, don't flatter yourself with that notion. A phone is a phone; if anything has come asunder, Kessler, it is just your own personal connection. *I see your lips moving, Mr. Kessler, but I can't hear a word.* He has been in Washington playing cowboy, and he has concealed important facts from her, and now he has stood her up. Kessler realizes what he can expect, whenever he does reach her: merely the cold polite voice and the fast good-bye.

He makes his other calls. This doesn't take long, and again Sidney Gondelman's memory for gossip proves to be very helpful. Gondelman has supplied a suggestion as to where he might find Roger Nye.

After the great purge of Claude Sparrow and his close accomplices, back in 1973, when McAttee tossed them all out and got himself a new Counterintelligence staff, Nye evidently went off to live in the boondocks of Shenandoah County, Virginia. He had a piece of family land, it was said. A useless but genteel stump farm. So far as Gondelman knew, he stayed out there. "I doubt that he would talk to you, though," Gondelman said. "From what I've heard about his state of mind." Naturally Kessler pays no attention to that part. And there turns out to be only one Roger Nye with a listed telephone in the county.

"I don't know," says an arid faraway voice that has answered to the name. "No. I don't know. Talk about what?"

"Counterintelligence," Kessler says vaguely. "The reorganization. When you left." It has come time to be careful about what he says over the telephone; anyway, Nye should be able to read through this language.

"I can't speak about that."

"Claude Sparrow has." Kessler's only point of leverage. Ordinarily he would be much more discreet on behalf of a confidential source. Circumstances are no longer ordinary, but even that is no excuse. I'll make it up to you somehow, Mr. Sparrow. If not in this life, then the next.

"Are you calling from Washington?"

"No. But I'll be there tomorrow."

"Don't come down on my account," says Roger Nye.

"I'll be there regardless."

"I don't know," Nye repeats still again, sounding faintly less negative. "Call me tomorrow, then."

28

Going back to the Tabard Inn might be a mistake but he does it anyway. If Lovesong and Buddyboy are still eager to find him, let them find him. Kessler doesn't care. He will gladly take a half hour to look through their mug book, sure, so long as they don't interfere with his own researches. Let them find him, let them watch him, let them follow him; let them try and stop him.

The ferocious little man in the rust-colored jacket is another matter. By him, Kessler would much prefer not to be found. Possibly a change of hotels might help. Or not. If Kessler really wanted to be safely invisible, though, he should have stayed up in New Haven and dismissed the whole affair from his attention —and at this point even that might be insufficient. Kessler is not philosophical about the prospect of getting stabbed to death or thrown off another tall building or next time who knows what. Shot, maybe. Like Barry. On the contrary he is quietly, grimly terrified. The danger has made itself too real to be thrilling, and he doesn't consider mortal peril as any part of the romance of his profession, or even a necessary evil. It ain't necessary to him. Granted, he feels a strong compulsion over this story and now also a giddy sense of momentum—but to die for it, Kessler judges, would be just dumb. Banal. So conceivably he is making a bad mistake, coming down to Washington again at all. That's as far as his thoughts on the subject have carried. He intends to be careful. The grebelike woman checks him in and gives him his old room back.

"I'm not here," Kessler says.

She stares across vacantly, so he repeats: "I'm not here. Anyone calls, anyone stops by, you do not have a Michael Kessler registered. Earlier in the week you did, fine. But not now. Is that all right?"

She shrugs an indifferent yes.

"I need total privacy this time."

"Total privacy," she echoes him, a little sardonically. Yeah, played this game a hundred times, is the implication. Then she adds: "What if it's a woman calling?"

"Same thing," Kessler says. "Though it won't be an issue." He lays out his credit card and three twenties. "I can pay cash if that'll make things easier. Here's one night. I'll go to a bank tomorrow and get more."

"Never mind," says the desk clerk. She takes his card only, and rolls her eyes. "Trust me."

Early in the morning he calls the Roger Nye number again.

Nye still sounds timorous and distant, more distant than just three hours west into the foothills of the Alleghenies; what he really sounds like is a case of bad nerves at the end of a weak party line somewhere in rural Nebraska. But to Kessler's surprise, to Kessler's joy, he consents to talk. Evidently eight hours of good country sleep (and very likely a phone consultation with Claude Sparrow, Kessler suspects) have made Roger Nye more willing to share his memories. It pleases Kessler to imagine that Claude Sparrow may have personally endorsed him, Kessler, as an innocent journalistic idler to whom one could safely tell old war stories. Neither Sparrow nor Roger Nye can know that Kessler is now downright dangerous. Or so he fancies.

Nye proposes a time and a place. Fine, Kessler says, though he will have to hurry. By all means, he thinks, I'll be out there before you can change your mind. He scribbles down the long shaggy-dog set of directions that Nye drawls to him. Then he reads them back and Nye says: "Mm. That should get you here. Unless you get lost." Half an hour later Kessler stops, just short of a ramp onto the Beltway, for gas and a map of the state of Virginia.

Then he points himself toward a town called Strasburg, beyond the Blue Ridge, in some halcyon woody hollow of Shenandoah County.

Kessler is cautiously, breathlessly optimistic. Intuition tells him that Roger Nye could settle this whole chase with a few sentences. With just a nod of the head, possibly. *Here's what I think I've discovered, Mr. Nye. Yes or no, Mr. Nye.* But will he?

It was Gondelman's guess that Nye would not want to talk, not to a stranger, certainly not to a journalist—and the very fact that Nye is granting Kessler an audience seems therefore promising. When the stones speak, they do not lie. From what Gondelman said, Roger Nye is an embittered man who wouldn't waste his words, if he chose to offer any at all.

The gossip, as it reached Gondelman, had suggested that Nye never recovered from being fired. He seemed to have taken it quite hard, harder than others who fell at the same time. The end of Claude Sparrow's Counterintelligence section was not simply, for Nye, the end of a job. Maybe in some ways he took it harder than Sparrow himself. And certainly he was more affected than the likes of Mel Pokorny, who turned up a lucrative new situation in the private security business within months. Roger Nye merely went off to the country and sulked.

He had been slightly older than Pokorny and the other deputies, already in his late fifties then, a contemporary of Sparrow, and that could have partly accounted for the difference. Personal history and character explain the rest. Nye was a serious, fastidious, unflaggingly loyal man, by Gondelman's account, well suited to providing the day-to-day execution under a difficult boss like Sparrow. He was old enough to have been in the Agency all its existence and in the OSS before that. He had done a tour as a desk officer in Covert Action, run agents for a while somewhere in Latin America, then served under Claude Sparrow at the station in Vienna, and come back to join the Counterintelligence staff at the time, in 1955, when Sparrow became its chief. He had family money and a doctorate in economics from Chicago. Without question he could have found consulting work after the purge, if he had wanted to, Gondelman told Kessler; maybe he could have picked up a faculty appointment, if he preferred academia, or a dignified sinecure at some right-wing institute. But none of that happened. He didn't need the income or, evidently, the further aggravation. He was just purely soured, Gondelman said. He had taken his dudgeon off to the Alleghenies and he stayed out there, devoting his time and his energy and his anger, Gondelman guessed, to reading Seneca and splitting firewood, or whatever it is that country squires do. So far as Gondelman knew, he was alone. Nye's wife had been an uppercrust Venezuelan woman of half-German extraction, brought back from the duty down there, but she was now dead. Gondelman could say that much for sure because he had gone to the funeral himself, during that period when he and Nye served on the panel together. Nye in his grief had been private and self-contained; he had thanked Gondelman for showing up; Gondelman never did hear what the wife had died from. There were grown children, Gondelman thought, though he didn't know where or how many. Roger Nye had been much respected and even fairly well liked at the Agency, not just within Counterintelligence but along the other corridors too. Gondelman himself had nothing bad to say. They had worked smoothly together, Nye and himself. Nye was brisk and professional without being a robot, and at least in the early phase of the panel he seemed to be trying hard to produce a report that Scott Wickes would be willing to sign. It was notable that, despite the big schism, even Jed McAttee would usually hear Nye out. Some people were surprised, in fact, Gondelman said, to see Nye's career get washed out to sea along with Claude Sparrow's. Some people thought that Nye would be spared. Some even thought that he was the logical replacement, the best choice as a new Counterintelligence chief. Kessler recalls all these potentially useful details as he drives west on the interstate, remembering also one other bit of data that leaves him puzzled.

Are you calling from Washington? was the question.

No, but I'll be there tomorrow, was what Kessler answered.

Don't come down on my account, said Roger Nye, although Kessler to the best of his recollection had not mentioned where he was.

There is only one exit for the town of Strasburg. Kessler takes it and then pulls aside on the gravel shoulder, consulting the directions in his notebook. He continues. A half mile on he passes the No Frills Food Warehouse, as promised, and comes to a T-junction, with gas stations on two corners and a road sign pointing left for the village of Lebanon Church. Kessler goes right. He drives slowly along the commercial drag of downtown Strasburg, all three blocks of it. He takes note of Pangle's Barbershop and then the Hi Neighbor! Restaurant, a storefront cafe with yellow curtains and a pillared balcony and a wrought-iron bench out front. Nye or the Nye ancestors seem to have picked a cozy town. Farther up the hill he moves

through a zone of grand old clapboard homes left behind by the
founding families, then again out into countryside. The road
swings around south, climbing higher along a ridge slope, with
the waters of the Shenandoah River now below on the left, a
pretty trickle winding among bare trees. Kessler glances at the
odometer. He passes the Old Mill Steakhouse, as promised.
Parking lot empty and windows frosted, it has either closed for
the season or failed, though the little mill wheel is still functional, turning slowly on an afternoon's meltwater drippings.
Kessler is glad for the break in weather, this gleaming and
hopeful February day. He will not take it amiss, however, if
Roger Nye (unlike his old boss) prefers to be interviewed in-
doors. Almost exactly at two miles from town Kessler spots the
turnoff ahead and slows.

The green sign gives a county road number. The other sign
says FISHER'S RUN, as promised. Kessler heads up the ridge
slope on this little road.

The directions seem to be good—meaning that Roger Nye is
a precisely observant fellow who can communicate when he
wants to, meaning in turn that perhaps Kessler has come to the
right place.

He winds uphill watching for a granite cutbank and, after
another bend, sees the cutbank just as described. Beyond it he
sees the stonework trestle. Kessler drives under the trestle and
then pulls aside, onto an eddy of brown grass. He parks there in
front of the other car. He gets out and walks back. Roger Nye is
seated behind the wheel.

Kessler has a sudden bad moment, expecting to find Nye
dead: bolt upright, seat belt fastened, eyes aglaze, shot through
the heart. But the bad moment passes. This seems to be merely
the man's customary expression. He shakes hands with Kessler
through the car window.

"Not here," says Nye. "We'll go on up to the house."

"Fine. Shall I follow you, or leave mine where it is?"

"Bring it," says Nye.

Now, following at a distance behind Nye's aging Ford, Kessler pays less attention to landmarks. He becomes almost unaware of mileage and turns. He is thinking instead about what
he has come out here to ask Roger Nye, and about the elaborately disingenuous preliminaries that may be needed to lead up
to it. He wants to take Nye off guard but not shock him badly.

He wants the interview to move toward an unexpected but ineluctable point, bearing Nye along, on a swell of memory and
frustration and bitterness. Then he wants to say: *Is it true that
Mel Pokorny was Dmitri? I have good reason to think so. Is that
why he finally had to die?* But how do you lead up to such
questions? What can be done to extract a truthful answer?
What sort of man is Roger Nye these days, and how is he going
to react? Kessler is still frantically thinking out strategy. They
cross a culvert and creep through a backwoods hamlet of five or
six houses and drive on. Keeping the Ford in view, Kessler
might as well be in a trance. He registers nothing but a pressed-
tin sign on the side of a small grocery, the sign's paint fading
gray from age and weather. WE GIVE FAMILY STAMPS, it says.
His brain is full.

And it is exactly this deep concentration that allows Kessler
to be so heartbreakingly stupid.

For several more miles they continue alongside a creek, presumably the one known hereabouts as Fisher's Run. Farm-
houses spaced widely, browned bottomlands and leafless woods,
no other vehicles meeting them on the gravel, and Kessler has
time to grow curious again about the hermit's retreat in which
Nye has chosen to take his retirement. Then he sees the Ford's
brake lights come aglow.

Nye turns, coaxing his car up a steep lane to the right that
proves, when Kessler tries it, scarcely better than a jeep trail.
Kessler climbs for a hundred yards at a bad angle, all in first
gear, and then lurches off into a horseshoe driveway that is
muddy and weed-grown but at least flat. Nye is there, standing
beside the Ford.

He is taller than he seemed at first glance, and older than the
mental image Kessler had of him: a thin erect patrician in his
late sixties, with stone-gray eyes and a severely trimmed stubble
of white hair, a man of corporate bearing who looks slightly
incongruous wearing jeans and a plaid flannel jacket. The boots
are well broken in. The hands, as Kessler noticed back at the
trestle, are slender and steady and unbent, but carry liver spots.

The house itself seems another odd match. Kessler expected
something much finer. He takes care not to show his reaction
but the place seems to him dreary at best, ramshackle, tawdry.
Almost pathetic, in fact. If Nye's old colleagues imagine that he
withdrew to a baronial estate, they would be shocked by the

reality. It is just an old two-story clapboard of the family farm type with defeated paint and ragged shingles and blank, disconsolate windows. The yard has been vanquished by an insurrection of thistles. There is a rusty burn barrel. The porch sags. The concrete stoop is crumbling and to each side sits a smallish cast-iron lion, gazing off toward some sorry dream of grandeur. The lions look ridiculous. Kessler wonders, with some pity, whether Nye found them himself in a junk shop or they came with the house and Nye just doesn't notice or care. Tact prevents Kessler from asking.

"We'll have privacy," says Roger Nye.

"I appreciate it."

Kessler follows him up the steps. Nye unlocks the door and stands aside. At least the locks are new, Kessler notices. Maybe Nye has a security fetish, last remnant of his old career. Or maybe, give him a chance, he is gradually fixing the place up. Kessler walks in to find nothing but bare hardwood floor coated thickly in dust, naked lath showing on one wall, and a derelict reading chair pushed into a far corner, and only at that moment does he grasp that it is all very wrong.

But of course he is too late. Not even close. He turns. The wave of nausea is like what he felt in Gondelman's tower, except now much worse.

Roger Nye is holding a gun. Kessler hates himself.

It is a sizable automatic, maybe a .45, and the thought dances into Kessler's brain that possibly this is the very weapon that killed Pokorny. He manages to restrain himself from raising that question, which might only be suggestive and fatalistic. The gun looks strange, but no less terrible, held in a gracile hand that happens to be spotted with age. Kessler realizes his bladder has leaked. It only makes him more scared.

"We'll go back here," says Nye, pointing.

"Do I put my hands up?" Oh Christ oh lord, not like this. Not in a sad-ass little house on a back road where they won't even find my body until the beetles have been all in and out.

"I really don't care," says Nye.

With bovine docility Kessler walks down a corridor toward back bedrooms. Meanwhile his mind crackles with desperate disorder. No, this is wrong, I should do something. Shouldn't make it easy for him. Resist. He's going to execute me, the bastard. Or maybe not. Maybe not. At what point, dammit, does sheer suicidal panic become appropriate? At what point do I have no more to lose? I'd rather go out stupid and wild than compliant and simpering, Kessler thinks. Rather make a run or try to fight or dive through a window or even just wave my arms and scream angry things. Any of those is better than letting the man just put that muzzle against my neck and fire, Kessler thinks. But *when?* What's the last possible chance? Do I get a goddamn moment's warning? Kessler comes to a doorway. The room beyond is dark. He stops. This is the moment, he thinks.

"Go on," says Roger Nye from a dispiriting ten feet behind. Kessler could never reach him with the fanciest karate move, even if he were trained for this nonsense.

"Go into the room," Nye says precisely.

Kessler complies.

He hears a door grind shut sonorously, and then he is in total blackness. He waits. He expects to be dead within five seconds. But there is no sound except the wheeze of his own breathing. He waits. After an endless half minute he becomes aware that he is alone. Nye has left himself on the far side of the door.

Kessler reaches out. When he feels the rough concrete of the wall, he understands where he is.

29

The man who calls himself Max Rosen knows the way. He has been here before, after all. That was only last weekend, when he went up and left the note for Kessler and then retired out to the scaffold to wait.

This time he prefers not to expose himself by passing through the lobby and the bar and then climbing the stairs. The bar is teeming with people at this hour on a Friday night. He prefers to stay clear of it. But in fact the traffic of strangers back and forth through the lobby, the festive confusion, helps him. Having ascertained that Kessler is using the same room as before, he sets the ledger carefully back into place by the switchboard and leaves again before the woman in the shabby sweater can return from her errand.

He walks down N Street toward Connecticut Avenue, makes a right turn and then another, comes back up the darkened alley. He avoids the construction site and the scaffold this time; he avoids that end of the alley altogether. Instead he finds an aluminum shed that puts him within reach of the fire escape on the back of a building adjacent to the Tabard. He climbs the four stories to that building's roof, which leaves only a little scramble up the copper mansard. But the slope is steep, so the little scramble is more than a little problematic. He requires the aid of a piece of lumber, a length of dirty two-by-four scrounged from a corner of the rooftop. Balancing on one foot with the board for a stilt, his belly flat to the copper slope, like a snake climbing glass, he gets another four feet of reach. Which is enough. He pulls himself up onto the Tabard. By now his lungs are raw and he is spitting nicotine-flavored phlegm. Fortunately the hatchway to the stairs is still unlatched.

He lets himself into Kessler's room, as before, with a simple lock blade. But this time he sits down to wait.

Only a very dim glow leaks in through the window from N Street. In the darkness he cannot find an ashtray, so he gropes quietly around the porcelain sink, which shows itself as a faint lambent shape, and comes up with a water glass. The man who calls himself Max Rosen does not want to turn on a light. He smokes the first cigarette while his lungs are still sore from the exercise.

30

Hours pass. Kessler doesn't know how many hours because as usual he isn't wearing a watch. Anyway he would need a luminous dial; his cell is still dark as blindness. Lots of hours, is how many, and they have gone by very damn slowly. It must be well on into the middle of the night. His ass hurts from sitting on the slab. Under the rank bandage his forearm hurts too, throbbing and pulsing, with occasional sudden rips of acute pain that travel straight up through the shoulder and into the back of his brain. Maybe that's part of the healing process for a bad cut. On the other hand, God knows what could be growing in there by now. Kessler was busy, Kessler was stubborn, Kessler did not take his antibiotic. Now Kessler is cultivating a microbial experiment in the warm pink agar of his own muscle. But no sense in worrying over the arm, since it may be moot. Kessler right now would jump at a chance to walk away from all this as an amputee. Roger Nye hasn't yet reappeared.

Possibly Roger Nye doesn't intend to.

Possibly the front door of the house is locked and the man is gone and Kessler has already been permanently entombed. Nothing left but to wait awhile, then die and then rot. No one in the world (he has realized with a disheartening shock) knows even vaguely where Kessler is. No one except Nye and whatever accomplices there are, if any. Worse still, no one is likely soon to wonder. A child who has gotten himself locked inside a junkyard refrigerator has better prospects—at least someone will come looking. Then again, a child locked in a refrigerator hasn't been quite this dumb. Kessler is trying to stay calm.

He has explored the room thoroughly, groping his way four times around the walls, crossing the open floor with cautious steps, then crossing again on hands and knees. The good news is that there seem to be no vermin; he hasn't set his palm down on a scorpion or a centipede or felt the skittering bump of a rat. Evidently this place has been sealed too tightly for vermin. Nothing to tempt them here anyway. Viktor Tronko has been gone for thirteen years and Kessler detects no sign of any more recent inmates. The walls are lined with concrete, sure enough, extending at least beyond his reach and probably straight to the ceiling. The floor also is concrete. The door is a sheet of steel, heavy, windowless, and Kessler has derived neither response nor solace from whomping his fist on it. He has found no drains, no bricked-over windows, no ventilation grates. He has found nothing, period, except an old cot that lay overturned near the center of the floor. At first, in the dark, he couldn't make out what this thing was. Then he got it onto its feet. Ah yes, the prisoner's cot, of course. Several hours later, when he was ready to try sleeping, he groped back to it, brushed it off, and lay down. The canvas split, opening like a zipper. Very low comedy, and in the jumble his injured arm took a painful mashing. Kessler untangled himself, stood up in rage, and heaved the cot at a wall. Then with a second thought he retrieved it, methodically stepped off his line of aim, and threw the cot at the steel door. A dull *thunk* sort of sound, like the tap of a wood spoon on a cast-iron skillet. It also seems clear that he will not dig his way out with a Swiss Army knife.

He has emptied his bladder twice into a chosen corner. He hopes that the floor is level enough so that his piss won't flow back to where he sits and, cruel indignity, soak his rump. He doesn't care if it flows down the other way and leaks out under the door. Let it. Kessler has passed beyond embarrassment into a starker range of the emotional spectrum. He wants water badly. He hasn't thought about food. But he wants water. He has been cold all day, all evening, all whatever, with the concrete sucking his warmth away, sucking it down into the unplumbable frozen indifference of the earth itself, and as night or whatever advances he is getting still colder. Unheated for thirteen years (and longer, come to think, since Tronko got no heat either), this cube of concrete holds the chill like an icebox. It could sap away every erg of Kessler's bodily heat and not raise its own temperature a degree. The only way to keep warm is to minimize contact. With the cot torn, that means standing up.

So he stands. He paces back and forth, beating the chill but making himself only more thirsty. He pounds again on the door. No whisper of a hint that anyone hears. He stands. He leans. He would very much like to sleep.

A little sleep would make the time pass more quickly. Of course Kessler still doesn't know for sure whether he wants the time to pass quickly. He may have too little left, not too much. He doesn't know whether he has anything to anticipate—a fresh phase of tribulation, a challenging new danger—besides his own slow but too proximate end. Doesn't know whether he should kill these hours or better treasure them.

And the other thing about sleep is that it would allow him to empty his brain, which also might be either good or bad. He would love to make even a brief mental getaway, forgetting Viktor Tronko and Pokorny and Nye and the whole cavalcade of poor judgments by which Kessler has brought himself here; but he has a sense that, right now, this minute, his mind should be bubbling with ingenious ideas for escape. Cut the canvas of the cot into long strips and tie them together and then do something or other with them. But do what? Anyway the canvas is rotten, asshole. Then break a wooden leg off the cot and use it to, um, well, use it to bash Roger Nye's head open when he steps back into the room. If he ever does step back into the room. If not, there is always suicide by bludgeoning, a fate that Kessler richly deserves. Or he could stand the cot on its end, maybe, and climb up it like a stepladder. Good, but a stepladder to where? These are just a few of the ingenious ideas he would be missing if he were asleep. He sits down again on the cold floor, spine to the wall, coat wrapped up around him, and lowers his head onto his knees.

Not long afterward the light comes on, blinding him with its cheery glare.

The man who calls himself Max Rosen consults his watch. He has waited an hour, and there is no sign of Kessler. He has not heard so much as a footfall on the stairs. All right. He is prepared to wait longer—a great deal longer, in fact. He knows how. But it has come time to allow himself to open a fresh pack of cigarettes. By a habit of parsimony, he realizes, he has been unconsciously rationing his supply.

True, he may be here half the night. No matter. After thirteen years and more of keeping his peace, he can certainly wait another few hours. If the cigarettes run out, they run out. He is indulging a reckless instinct tonight, in disregard for the practices of habit and caution.

He suspected at first that this Michael Kessler would go away, like the other journalists who over the years have come sniffing. There have been enough. He has spoken with a few of those others himself, and in a single instance the man even knew his identity. His former identity. But that man was the crude slapdash type, a bounty hunter of strident headlines and startling leads merely, a daily reporter with a great reputation and all the worst traits of his breed and not someone to whom any sane individual would entrust delicate personal revelations. Maybe it isn't sane ever—through even the most carefully chosen conduit—to make that sort of revelation. Maybe it just isn't. The man who calls himself Max Rosen still feels enormous wariness about this. He feels distrust, cynicism, a remnant of mortal fear. He could probably lose his job simply for being here, in Kessler's hotel room. Lose the job and he would lose also his protection, such as it is, at exactly the moment he might most need it. But he also feels the same pressure from inside, the same bitterness and frustration at events, at appearances, the same abyssal loneliness, that he has felt for thirteen years and more. He suspected at first that Michael Kessler would just go away like the rest—inconclusively, settling for a lesser though more dramatic truth or even none at all. And that may still be the case. Or maybe not. Maybe Kessler is the one.

Ask yourself, he told Kessler, why Viktor Tronko was not given more to offer, if he had come on a mission for Moscow. Ask yourself why his dowry of useful secrets was so meager. I have been, Kessler said. The man who calls himself Max Rosen remembers their words precisely.

I have been, Kessler said. *I get nowhere.*

Then ask Claude Sparrow.

I will.

He liked that. He liked Michael Kessler for that directness. Of course Kessler will not have learned the answer from Sparrow, if only because Sparrow himself never learned.

I will, Kessler said. *What about you? Do you have an opinion?*

Ask yourself, he said, *how could it serve Moscow's purposes to send a man who lied so poorly? How could it satisfy Moscow, for Viktor Tronko to spend three years in a concrete cell?*

I assume that they wouldn't have planned on that three years,
Kessler said.

Don't assume. Ask yourself, he thinks. The man with the
habit of patience glances again at his watch.

Kessler shields his eyes with a hand but still they won't open.
After all these hours of total darkness, the glare of the overhead
bulb is like vinegar on his corneas. He only knows by the sound
of the door that someone has entered.

He assumes that the pistol is once again pointed at him and
hopes that the damn thing doesn't have a jumpy trigger. Before
this experience Kessler never realized that the mere pointing of
a loaded gun in one's direction does not seem in any sense a
formality, a gesture of coercion, but instead itself represents—
just the goddamn *pointing*—an outrageous, life-threatening act.
That sucker could go off. It makes him angry. It inspires him
with a strong urge to drive his fist, eventually, against Roger
Nye's splintering teeth. Meanwhile of course he is again very
scared.

"What," Kessler says sullenly.

"Stand up," says the voice of Roger Nye.

Kessler stands.

"Take off your coat and toss it aside. Not at me. Aside."

A careful man. Kessler obeys. Squinting fiercely, he is getting
his vision back. Nye tells him to turn toward the wall. He
obeys. Lean into it, Nye says. No, not with your hands—brace
against your head, arms out wide. Kessler obeys. Obviously
Nye knows what he is doing because Kessler feels helpless in
this gimpy position, and his forehead hurts against the concrete.
Now empty your pockets, Nye says. Kessler moves slowly,
dropping his car keys and his pocketknife and his wallet and his
handkerchief and about two dollars in change onto the floor.
The latest notebook is in his coat.

"Fine. Arms out again, now."

Nye's hand dodges in to pat over his body thoroughly,
searching no doubt for those derringers in trick holsters and
switchblades strapped on with duct tape that any sensible journalist carries. Kessler is unarmed. If I were smart enough to
have brought a weapon, Mr. Nye, I would have been smart
enough not to come. When Nye squeezes the arm bandage,

Kessler yelps but does not pull away. Nye squeezes it several times more—not sadistically, merely to assure himself.

"Nothing in there but gauze and pus," Kessler says.

Nye steps back and Kessler stays as he is. This body search has brought Kessler a new small flush of hope, seeming as it does to imply that he will be alive a while longer. You don't frisk a person right before shooting him dead, correct? Much easier to reverse the order. And there is relief also in knowing that he hasn't been trapped and abandoned, as he feared. Altogether, Kessler is glad for the attention. He hears the door scrape again.

But he holds his position dutifully, head forward, rear arched, arms out, like a timorous child caught by the camera's shutter at the lip of a diving board. He holds it to the point of pain. Then he says: "Can I turn?"

No answer, so he straightens himself gently and turns. Nye is gone. The door is sealed. For that one too I'll get you, Kessler thinks. His wallet and his keys and his pocketknife are gone also. Worst of all, so is his coat.

This time the light stays on.

It is no more than what he was asking himself, throughout those three years of arduous lying and those thousand lonely confused nights. He had nothing else to occupy his brain, so much of that time, except memory and regret and the unfinished business of solving this grotesque riddle that had been made of his life. So he wondered, yes. He asked. *How can it satisfy Moscow for me to rot away here, abused and disbelieved, in a concrete cell?*

He was genuinely bewildered. *How can such epic futility be of use to Dmitri, if there is such a person, or to anyone else?* The man who calls himself Max Rosen remembers all those pertinent questions which he posed to himself and offered to Michael Kessler, and remembers them verbatim, as precisely as if they were part of his own legend. *Ask yourself why Moscow should have chosen so badly. If they chose Tronko at all.*

This last was in fact easy to answer, having never been in doubt. They did not choose him, no. Viktor Semyonovich was the one who had chosen, and badly. They merely chose to exploit him, after he had delivered himself up.

He was lost the moment he stepped on the flight to come back from Rome.

Because in Moscow they knew, somehow, of his first contact with the Americans almost as soon as he had made the decision himself. It took them six days to find out, possibly less. They knew that fast, yet they were cagey. No peremptory telegram (like the one he later concocted, on instructions, in Vienna) had summoned him back, nor was there any ominous hint, and he left on his scheduled flight from the Rome airport. He was understandably nervous as he boarded that plane, but nevertheless confident, still utterly unwitting. Only to be arrested when his foot touched the tarmac at Vnukovo.

He supposes, in retrospect, that it must have been Dmitri himself who betrayed him so promptly. Six days would have been roughly sufficient, given the famous refusal to use radio. Time enough for a drop to be signaled and made, and then for a courier to travel between Washington and Moscow. That was quick work but not hasty. Anyway Moscow would have had more time if they needed it, since Viktor Semyonovich was returning voluntarily. What difference if they had arrested him in his office a day or two later? He was coming home regardless. Tanya was there; the boy was there. He could fathom treason against the Motherland, perhaps, but not desertion of them.

It was a routine arrest and a routine interrogation. He spent three days in a cell at the Lubyanka and then close to eleven months at Lefortovo.

The eleven months of abuse and interrogation were actually rather longer than average, but still this phase could be considered routine in the sense that Viktor Semyonovich was one of the stubborn type, of which there were always a few, and was dealt with the same as other stubborn ones, and his interrogation progressed inexorably albeit slowly to its foredestined conclusion wherein Viktor Semyonovich's personal interrogator got what was wanted: a complete confession. The confession as written was also routine, even formulaic, for the articles under which Viktor Semyonovich was charged. His interrogator was a certain Morozov, whose first name and patronymic Viktor Semyonovich never knew.

Morozov was a major and a law graduate with the soul of a thug. Viktor Semyonovich found cause during those eleven months to suspect that Major Morozov was not just grotesquely

cruel, sick with evil, but also imbalanced in a more clinical way.
Besides the rest, Morozov in moments of raging frustration
sometimes spat on him, frenetically, like a hysterical child.

Of the two prisons, Viktor Semyonovich much preferred the
Lubyanka. It seemed horrific at first but after a month in
Lefortovo he looked back on it almost fondly. His cell at the
Lubyanka was larger, the food ration more nearly adequate; he
was allowed use of the toilet whenever he wanted and, most
importantly, they were still letting him sleep. Obviously the
cells of the Lubyanka, limited in number but conveniently located, were devoted only to temporary uses. Either you were
shot there in the basement or in the courtyard, as in the old
times, or you were processed on. Viktor Semyonovich was processed on. Another merit of the Lubyanka stay was that there
was no Morozov.

After his three days of benign neglect he was marched back
up to the courtyard and put in a van. On the side of this van,
Viktor Semyonovich noticed, were painted the words DRINK
SOVIET CHAMPAGNE but in the back it carried only himself and
a guard. The ride across the city to Lefortovo didn't take long.
He was admitted past a desk at which sat a businesslike officer
who required Viktor Semyonovich to sign himself in. He signed
a large ledger, writing through a narrow slot in a metal plate
that had been clamped into position there over the page, ob-
scuring every name but his own. This and certain other quaint
measures, both at Lefortovo and at the Lubyanka, were evidently intended to reinforce the illusion that he was utterly
alone in his fate. The strip search was more thorough here at
Lefortovo. While Viktor Semyonovich stood watching, naked,
the seams of his jacket were slit open, the shoulder padding was
pulled out, the cuffs of his trousers undone; his trouser pockets
were slashed, not to discover anything there but presumably
because he wouldn't need pockets anymore; his clothes when he
got them back were rags and tatters. His belt was impounded.
Before he could dress again, they shaved his head and his arm-
pits and his pubic area. Then a doctor was brought in, a curt
woman wearing a white coat and rubber gloves. She peered
around under his tongue, under his scrotum, between his buttocks, looking for contraband. Finding none, she left without a
word. Viktor Semyonovich was taken to his cell, where he immediately learned the rules about sleeping.

The rules about sleeping were diabolically simple. It was forbidden—*nye polozhna!*—for the prisoner to lie down or even to
close his eyes at any time during the day, from first rousing at
six in the morning until ten at night. This was enforced by a
guard who glanced at regular intervals through the wolf's eye
in the door—every minute or so, all day long—and shouted
minaciously at any sign of napping. Refusal to heed the first
shouted warning could lead to a week in a hard-punishment
cell, down in the basement. Sleep was permitted only between
the hours of 10 P.M. and 6 A.M. That schedule did not seem so
bad to Viktor Semyonovich until he realized, after another few
days, that the interrogation itself would be conducted chiefly
between 10 P.M. and 6 A.M. At about midnight the first night he
was shaken awake and led off on a hike, along the catwalk and
down a stairway and then through a carpeted corridor, to meet
a burly man in uniform.

"My name is Morozov," the man said. "I am a major in the
Organs of State Security. You will sit there, and then we can
begin."

So they began.

Always these sessions took place in the same nondescript
room, furnished only with a desk and a comfortable chair and a
telephone for Morozov, stark fluorescent lighting, and a
straight chair for Viktor Semyonovich. Sometimes Morozov
would unholster his Tokarev pistol and let it lie within view on
the desk, or even, in more vehement moments, brandish it at
Viktor Semyonovich and slap him across the cheekbones with
its barrel while threatening to shoot him right there in the room
for his intractable refusal to cooperate. Morozov would demand
that Viktor Semyonovich sign the statements, the confessional
depositions (the "protocols," as Morozov called them) that the
major had written out in his own laborious but sloppy long-
hand, and before long Viktor Semyonovich was obliging him.
He signed a page describing his agreed-upon signal code with
the Americans, for instance, which code there had never been
time for him to use; and a page confessing the anti-Soviet attitudes that had led to his act of treason. Unsatisfied by these
admissions, Morozov only demanded more, a full confession, a
complete account of the conspiracy into which Viktor Semyonovich had supposedly entered—by which the major meant,
other names. He wanted other names. Who had recruited

Viktor Semyonovich for the Americans? Who had counseled him to make contact through the economic attaché at the embassy in Rome? With whom had he shared his plans and ideas, here in Moscow? Who were his accomplices? "We already have these names, of course," Morozov would say. "We know these people. We know who they are. Most have already been arrested. But it will go easier on you if you confirm what we know. Such a service to the people's justice will certainly mitigate your own sentence. For your sake, Viktor Semyonovich, I advise you to confess fully before those others do." It wasn't convincing. And, convincing or not, to this Viktor Semyonovich said no. He could not confess any more than he already had. There were no other names. There was no conspiracy— except the pathetic, incipient one between himself and the Americans. No one had recruited him. He had recruited himself: a walk-in. He had chosen the economic attaché at random, there having been no other American in Rome with whom Viktor Semyonovich got an opportunity of contact, and the fact that this man himself proved to be a CIA officer should be understood as a matter of pure luck. Good luck, Viktor Semyonovich had imagined at the time; now he saw that it had been very bad luck indeed. But only luck. There were no other names. If there had been, Viktor Semyonovich would be only too eager by this point to supply them. Morozov would then embark on a fit of shouting, or lurch to his feet and stride the four steps from his desk to whack Viktor Semyonovich across the face with his pistol.

Viktor Semyonovich's nose was broken during the second week and never repaired. No medical attention was given in Lefortovo to such minor complaints. The nose healed or at least fused back on its own, leaving just a lump along the bridge and a slight crook to the left, imperceptible to anyone who didn't look into his face carefully from straight in front.

The man who calls himself Max Rosen rubs his fingers down the line of that lumpy bend now in the darkness of Kessler's room. Morozov was left-handed.

At first Viktor Semyonovich had resolved to deny everything, to hold firm against all the charges, with a notion that this might somehow protect Tanya and the boy; but he discovered quickly that it wasn't possible. At least it wasn't possible for him. Another man, maybe. Or maybe it would have been im-

possible for anyone. Viktor Semyonovich himself, in any case,
was a stubborn type but no prodigy of physical and moral
strength. Without sleep and without adequate food, he just
couldn't stand up against the insistence of Morozov. So he
broke. He gave Morozov a series of confessions and he signed
them. Article 64 of the criminal code: Yes, I did that. Article
58, Section One: Yes, I am guilty. It happened shamefully soon,
Viktor Semyonovich felt at the time—within twenty days of his
transfer to Lefortovo. He was a weaker wretch even than he
had imagined, or else Morozov and the techniques of interrogation were much stronger. Viktor Semyonovich had composed in
his dulled fuddled mind a rationalization whereby he could pretend to himself that Tanya and the boy might not be harmed by
his admissions of treason and espionage—they might even
somehow be helped—and then he offered himself up. Morozov
was pleased and complacent. Viktor Semyonovich was rewarded with one full night's sleep. He fell into a gloom of self-
loathing that lasted for only the next day, a long quiet day in his
cell, to be jarringly interrupted the next night when it became
clear that Morozov was far from satisfied. The confessions of
personal guilt were, to Morozov, just a tantalizing start. Now
the major wanted those other names. He wanted details of the
conspiracy. But Viktor Semyonovich was too stubborn and too
stupid to invent any.

In retrospect, it could be seen as a failure of imagination.
Viktor Semyonovich was a straightforward man of moderate
intelligence and, notwithstanding his profession, never a tal-
ented liar. He could have given Morozov some real names and
some faked-up conspiratorial details, certainly, and thus destroyed a few innocent lives, but his dimmed brain couldn't
come even close to providing him with a rationalization for
that. So he stuck with the truth because it was simple and sure
and, over another ten months, he suffered miserably for it.

His daily food ration throughout all this time consisted of
four hundred grams of sour black bread in the morning, along
with two cubes of sugar and a cup of very weak tea; a bowl of
fatless gruel at noon; and a cup of hot water at night. He lost
weight quickly and his hair, as it grew back from the shaving,
fell out in tufts, probably from lack of vitamins. His gums bled.
His teeth loosened in their sockets. His fingernails broke like
flatbread. On an average night he got no more than an hour of

sleep, spending the other seven hours seated upright in the chair in Morozov's interrogation room, subjected forever to the same repetitious questions and the same fits of screaming abuse, and trying desperately not to nod off. Sometimes he did nod off and fell backward out of the chair, waking on the floor to the roar of Morozov's voice and the spray of Morozov's spittle on his face, and to the burst of excruciating pain when Morozov's boot toe came slamming into his kidneys. On these occasions the five or six seconds of sleep that had been snatched between when his lids closed and when Morozov's boot struck seemed almost (but not quite) worth the punishment. During an average day in his cell he stole a total of another twelve or fifteen minutes of sleep, sitting up, between the guard's glances in through the wolf's eye. He shrank down to about one hundred pounds, then his weight stabilized there. He had no flesh left to his buttocks. His knees and elbows stood out like knots in a rope. He and Morozov had sunk into a stalemate of repetitions and it began to seem possible that Viktor Semyonovich might die or lose all mental competence before Major Morozov succeeded in extracting anything new. Viktor Semyonovich was by now utterly docile, a walking invalid in the last stages of generalized physical decay and a model prisoner, with no stubbornness left in him except the somatic stubbornness that kept his heart thumping, barely. He would have confessed to anything and implicated anyone, at this point, if he had just had the requisite focus and energy to create a lie. But he didn't. He was ready to die, and vaguely aware that it shouldn't be long now. Morozov on the other hand was not ready for that. Viktor Semyonovich's death from interrogation might not have hurt the major's career but neither would it have helped. Presumably Morozov could not abide having eleven months of effort end inconclusively. So as Viktor Semyonovich slipped closer to death, Morozov's rage and frustration increased. He swung the Tokarev more frequently, sometimes knocking Viktor Semyonovich unconscious and then summoning a guard to revive him with a bucket of cold water. Viktor Semyonovich grew puzzled and annoyed, in his faraway sense of the whole matter, that Major Morozov would not simply use the pistol to shoot him. Then at some point in those final weeks Viktor Semyonovich was conscious, hazily, of being examined by another doctor. He couldn't recall later whether this one had been a woman or a man. He remem-

bered no face, only strong cold fingers tapping and pinching
him, and a stethoscope. Next thing he knew he was in a bed
with real sheets, at the Serbsky Institute.

They were feeding him intravenously with a nutrient solution. After a few days of that they switched him to solid food—
wholesome food, food that had taste, and given to him in modest but progressively larger quantities. There was a bowl of cabbage soup with bits of meat, for instance, which he would never
afterward forget. They were nursing him back, at this place. He
didn't understand why and for the moment he didn't care. A
miracle had occurred, and he was saved—he set himself to be-
lieving that, difficult though it was.

He regained some of his weight and his brain began to clear.
He spent the first week in his bed but after that he could stand
and walk again, and it was permissible for him to leave his
room, even to take a stroll down the length of the ward. There
were guards here too, but these guards dressed in white jackets
and functioned also as orderlies, and none of them shouted at
Viktor Semyonovich, not even when he stayed in his bed by
daylight and slept. The windows were shielded from inside with
heavy wire grates. Viktor Semyonovich did not know where he
was. Obviously, though, it was some sort of prison hospital.
Only later, on the train that took him to Kolyma, did he learn
the name of this facility where he had been treated, and its
reputation. The stairways were off limits. He was instructed to
confine his explorations to the corridor that ran past his own
room, and he obeyed. The doors of the other rooms were usually closed. He saw few other prisoners—few other patients, or
inmates, or whatever they were called here—except the four
men who shared his room, and those four didn't communicate.
Three of them acted feral and shy, keeping their distance from
Viktor Semyonovich when they could, avoiding his glance, ignoring his direct questions, and the fourth seemed to be in a
coma. The doctor now attending Viktor Semyonovich was a
man, a young fellow about his own age, handsome, with swept-
back hair and an unctuous manner. This doctor visited daily.
He himself never examined Viktor Semyonovich, merely read
the chart that was kept current by a nurse. One morning he set
the chart back on its hook and said:

"So. How do you feel, Viktor Semyonovich?"

"Very much better."

"Exactly. So. I will be sending you some medication now. You will take it obediently."

"I feel good. It's the food," said Viktor Semyonovich. "What medication?"

The doctor's smile stiffened like cold fat and he walked away.

They started on him with pills. Viktor Semyonovich was given two different kinds, and the dosage each morning amounted to a cupped palmful of capsules. These were counted out into his hand by a nurse, who also provided the water and stood by to watch, then demanded he open his mouth and raise his tongue so that she could be sure they were all gone. Viktor Semyonovich did not know at the time what it was he was taking. He only knew, after the second morning, that the stuff made his mouth and his throat go dry and burned in his stomach like some sort of corrosive bile. Nevertheless he swallowed the capsules as he was told. That seemed far preferable to the prospect of being sent back to Lefortovo. And maybe these side effects would disappear, he hoped, when his body adjusted to the medication. But he began to feel sicker again. Continuous headaches, dizziness, faintness when he stood up out of bed. Although he was still drowsy much of the time, his body wouldn't let him sleep; the nerves in his legs tingled maddeningly, his calf and thigh muscles twitched and spasmed. He couldn't lie still. During daytime he walked endlessly up and down the corridor. But at night such pacing was forbidden and his legs tortured him. He waited desperately for each dawn, when he could get up again and walk. The nerves of his face were soon tingling also, and his jaw muscles grew sore from a constant involuntary clenching and yawning. After ten days Viktor Semyonovich grasped that he was being poisoned.

When he told the nurse that he would swallow no more of those capsules, she replied in a firm cold professional tone that, yes, he would indeed. Anyway he would get the medication one way or another, she said. To Viktor Semyonovich's own surprise, this flat statement by her brought him to tears. He sobbed uncontrollably for a quarter of an hour.

But he refused to swallow more capsules. So the injections began. Each day he was held belly down on a metal table by three guards in white, while the nurse raped him repeatedly with hypodermics. The stuff was shot into what remained of his buttocks. It required several syringes to deliver the full dosage.

During these brief moments Viktor Semyonovich would thrash piteously against the guards' strong grip and moan like a tortured cat. For the rest of the day, then, he would be well behaved. Sometimes he didn't find his way back to his bed at night and a guard would come out to retrieve him. When that happened, Viktor Semyonovich wept childishly from fear of punishment, but evidently there was no punishment for getting lost in the corridor. More and more often, he was incontinent with his urine. He would dry his legs with the hospital gown. No one gave him a fresh gown, and the guards scolded him for his puddles. The scoldings put him in tears. His eyesight seemed to be going foggy. Finally one morning there was a man's face at the foot of his bed. Viktor Semyonovich had trouble focusing, but this face seemed too round for the unctuous doctor. When he saw that it was Major Morozov, he wept with the joy of recognition.

Twenty-six days had passed since Viktor Semyonovich left Lefortovo.

He still had enough of his wits, barely, to give Morozov some names. He denounced two of his colleagues back in the Eleventh Department, two men he knew only slightly, each of whom had been in competition with Viktor Semyonovich for favor and promotion, and each of whom had in some petty way treated him badly. These two, he told Morozov, had been his accomplices. One of the two, the elder, had been influential in forming Viktor Semyonovich's own anti-Soviet attitudes. The other man had alerted him about the American economic attaché at Rome. Complete lies. Viktor Semyonovich despised himself as he said these things to Morozov and even more so afterward, but he didn't hesitate. For a margin of safety he also told Morozov about his own closest friend from his years at the Institute of International Relations, the son of the Politburo member.

This young man, now a desk officer at the Foreign Ministry, had played a role in encouraging his treason, Viktor Semyonovich said. He and this young man had often exchanged counterrevolutionary ideas. The young man was a secret admirer of the West, Viktor Semyonovich said, who kept his real views concealed from everyone but his closest confidants. He listened to recordings of Duke Ellington and Charlie Parker. He received smuggled goods that came in from America, especially books and magazines, and was under the spell of what he read in them. During private conversations, he expressed his contempt for the leadership of the Soviet state and of the Party. All of this was at least half true. His friend at the Foreign Ministry might not be destroyed, Viktor Semyonovich consoled himself, thanks to the position of his father. Or he might be destroyed anyway. Probably it depended upon how the father currently stood with respect to the Politburo's majority faction. If he were in good smell, the son was invulnerable; if not, the father himself might be ruined by these statements too. Viktor Semyonovich wished them the best. The other two men, however, from the Eleventh Department, were definitely finished. Major Morozov wrote all three names greedily into a little blue notebook. He also wrote the names of Duke Ellington and Charlie Parker.

Then again Morozov disappeared. This final degradation had taken less than an hour. Viktor Semyonovich went back to sleep and allowed himself to dream it hadn't happened.

Next day he was transferred back to a cell at Lefortovo, not the same one as before but identical. The ration of bread that arrived for him now was slightly larger. He was allowed to sleep. It took him a full twenty-four hours to realize that the sleep rules had been canceled, for him, and so through that first day he slept sitting up. No one shouted through the food slot. Evidently no one cared. The following day he tried it lying down. Not a squeak of reprimand. They weren't even peeking in on him anymore. They had ceased to care. Viktor Semyonovich went through another phase of stark despairing self-hatred and thought seriously about how he might kill himself. But there were no means available to him in this little cell that were likely to be better than gruesomely inefficient. He wasn't interested in bashing his head open against the iron corner of the cot, only to live on as a helpless drooler—and when this thought was given words in his mind, he remembered the boy. His son. At least Viktor Semyonovich had not named his wife as an accomplice in anti-Soviet attitudinizing; at least he had not done anything, so far, he hoped, that would leave the boy unprotected. Instead of suicide, Viktor Semyonovich slept.

He retreated from consciousness that way, sleeping as much as his body would accept, he didn't know how much, probably sixteen hours a day. He no longer scratched off a calendar on the wall. The day count didn't matter. And he didn't see

Morozov again. After another ten days or perhaps two weeks or a bit more, an officer in a uniform just like Morozov's (but this man was a stranger) came to Viktor Semyonovich's cell and informed him of his sentence.

He had been given "twenty-five, five, and five": twenty-five years of corrective labor, five more of exile, another five after that before his full rights of citizenship were restored. My full what of what? he thought.

It didn't surprise Viktor Semyonovich. It was a standard sentence, for its time. This was during the thaw. If Stalin were alive, Viktor Semyonovich knew, he would certainly be shot. He was glad now to be unburdened of the pressure and the suspense. He was glad to have those arduous preliminaries with Morozov all out of the way. And the sentence did not seem especially shocking, given his offenses. After all, Viktor Semyonovich would have expected to get twenty-five, five, and five merely for confessing to treason and espionage; and he had not only confessed to those things, he had actually *done* them. Fine, let the rest begin, he thought.

Two days later his wish was granted. He was taken by champagne van to the Yaroslavsky Station and mustered into a prisoner convoy bound for the East.

It was September when he left Moscow on this train. He traveled for thirty-seven days in a Stolypin railway car under conditions of unimaginable crowding. Some prisoners were offloaded at transit prisons along the way, others were picked up at siding stops and packed into the car even when it seemed there could not possibly be space for another human body. Generally the head count in that car hovered between five and six dozen, not including the guards, who had their own compartment on the far side of a partition. Viktor Semyonovich got no chance to be lonely. As they crossed the high Siberian plain during early October, the cold weather came on them like doom. It began so abruptly—with crosswinds that rocked the car and fine driven snow sweeping across land that was still autumn brown and the breath of sixty men coating the iron meshwork of their cage with frost—it began so abruptly that they seemed to have traveled into it, as though riding an ore car down into a mine. And they *had* traveled into it, of course, but through both time and geography: the season had broken. The actual mines would come later. Viktor Semyonovich still didn't know that he was destined for Kolyma. He had heard of the goldfield camps there, vaguely, but like everyone else he had been led to believe that they went out with Stalin. A temporary aberration, which had resulted from certain abuses of power during the period of the cult of personality.

There was no stove in this Stolypin car except a small one on the guards' side of the partition. While the train rolled eastward, toward that temporary aberration, the days grew colder and shorter.

Sometimes the train went on for a week without making more than the briefest stops; then sometimes it pulled onto a siding and stood for an hour, or two, or forty-eight. No prisoner was permitted to leave the car, during such stops, except those who were taken off permanently. And then on one occasion the rest of the train pulled away again while this particular Stolypin, with Viktor Semyonovich and his cohabitants, was left behind on the siding, eventually to be coupled onto a different train. Naturally no explanations were made, ever, to prisoners.

After he had been robbed of his good boots and his decent trousers, then left otherwise unmolested by the common criminals (who had enough other political prisoners even weaker than Viktor Semyonovich to focus their menace upon), his life in the moving boxcar became almost tolerable. He clung to his patch of space on a high bunk—a desirable bunk near the ceiling, and shared with only three other men. The rations were meager and no one got enough water, true. Toilet privileges were restricted at the whim of the lazy guards, true, and some men fouled the bunks. But at least there was no labor, yet, and no interrogation, anymore. Viktor Semyonovich himself had recovered control of his bladder. All day and all night, he and the rest of the prisoners simply slept or talked. He made two friends among the other politicals. One was a former general from the Army, and one was a dentist. Each of them tried to tell him things that would be helpful for surviving in camp.

The general was a tall man with a large frame and it appeared as though he had once been burly as a bull walrus; now his skin hung slack at the jowls and his wrists were delicate. He coughed. His eyes were constantly moist as a beagle's. The general was educated. He spoke Ukrainian, though he was not himself Ukrainian, and he had been trained as an engineer. In

his proudest moment of youth he had commanded an artillery
battery at Stalingrad. He advised Viktor Semyonovich that in
camp it would be necessary, whatever the risk, whenever possible, to steal extra bits of food. Otherwise a man would weaken
and be unable to work, the general said, which would get him
cut back to invalid's ration and then he would die for sure. The
general was debarked at Irkutsk. Viktor Semyonovich never
saw him again. The dentist, on the other hand, was left in the
car all the way to Vanino. So they had thirty-seven days to
share company.

The dentist knew poetry. He carried in his magical memory
long sections of Pushkin, among others, which he would recite
to an avid audience of prisoners in exchange for small privileges
like bunk position and freedom from general molestation. The
dentist was a frail little man who would have been helpless, but
even the common criminals were gentle with him because they
as much as anyone enjoyed the recitations. This was their only
entertainment, besides stealing and fighting. So the dentist was
favored, in the car, as a sort of pet. His hair grew back out into
a woolly tangle of black ringlets, during the course of the trip,
and his eyes were a deep ruby brown. He smiled more than
most. To Viktor Semyonovich, he seemed in some ways like a
clever child, this dentist. He had been arrested for ownership of
gold—an occupational hazard for a dentist, the dentist would
say, his eyes dark and shiny with wit. The real reason for his
arrest was still a mystery to him. He came from Leningrad, of a
half-Jewish father who taught chemistry at a technical institute
and gave slavish obeisance to the Party, and a Latvian mother.
His name was Yuli Landau. He counseled Viktor Semyonovich
to find some skill or trade, in camp, by which he could make
himself useful and earn a trickle of personal income. That was
the only way one could hope to survive, the dentist said. And
this trade had better be found quickly, the dentist said, before
Viktor Semyonovich got weak and they put him on invalid's
ration.

"Something like dentistry?"

"No. There is no dentistry in camp. Something like sewing.
Or dealing tobacco, somehow. Or poetry."

The dentist was cheerful, confident, popular. He seemed to
have the game beat. Each night across Siberia he would give a
performance. Sometimes it was Lermontov, sometimes Nikolai

Nekrasov, sometimes the frazzled verses of Mayakovsky, which the dentist would animate with wild hammy arm gestures and crazy faces; most often it was Pushkin. Always it was poetry that could only be judged politically safe, because there were informers in a Stolypin car just as anywhere. That was another bit of counsel that the dentist offered Viktor Semyonovich: there were informers everywhere, even in camp, and a man could always have an additional sentence tacked on. Landau the dentist was serving his second, and he intended that it would be his last. He knew two hours' worth of *Eugene Onegin* by heart.

The early stanzas about Eugene's decadent life, with its costume balls and its duels and seductions and other nineteenth-century pleasures, were by acclamation the favorites. The dentist repeated these stanzas so often, on demand, that half the prisoners in the car eventually had them by memory too. The thugs would make everyone hush. The dentist would begin, and recite for twenty minutes, raising his voice alone over the clack of the rails, before he came to:

> The ball's wild gaiety was wearing,
> So turning morning into night,
> To darkness' kind abode repairing,
> Now sleeps the scion of delight.
> By afternoon he will be waking,
> He'll then resume till day is breaking
> The merry and monotonous round,
> And then once more till noon sleep sound.
> But was true joy to Eugene granted
> Then, in the flower of his youth?
> Was pleasure *happiness* in sooth
> 'Mid all the conquests that he vaunted?
> When in the banquet-hall he beamed
> Was he the carefree soul he seemed?

This was the point where dozens more voices would chorus in, chanting in full throat as the train rattled along through Siberian darkness:

> No, soon the world began to bore him,
> The senses soon grew blunt and dull,

> In vain the belles might clamor for him,
> He found the fairest faces null;
> Seduction ceased to be amusing!
> And friendship's claims he was refusing,
> Because he could make no *bon mot,*
> Could not wash down with Veuve Clicquot
> The beefsteak and the Strasbourg patty!!
> When his poor head began to ache;
> And though he was an ardent rake!
> An exquisite both bold and natty,
> The time came when he quite abhorred
> Even the pistol and the sword!

And then the guards would pound on the wall.

The man who calls himself Max Rosen cannot help smiling at this recollection. He remembers those two stanzas of Pushkin indelibly, and quite a few others. He even used them to amuse himself, later, over here, in the concrete room. Probably he will never forget them. He hopes he will not. He sets his feet up on Kessler's bed, making himself more comfortable.

They reached Vanino in mid-October. This was the terminus of the rail line, and of the continent, on the Tatar Strait just a spit from Japan. By now it was unmistakable where they were being taken. But first they were marched overland six kilometers to the Vanino transit camp. They spent a few days there in a huge compound with thousands of other prisoners, under no work regimen yet, merely standing around and growing colder and more hungry, waiting for the ship. The ship arrived. They were marched back to the harbor and put on board. It was a huge rusty old steamer, called the *Felix Dzerzhinsky* now though Viktor Semyonovich heard from another prisoner that this was a second name for what had long earlier, under a different set of winds, carried registry as the *Nikolai Yezhov*. The ship lived up to both its names. The open hold was divided into a number of very large cells, simple cages of heavy iron grate, each cage holding several hundred prisoners; the cells were set in tiers, with no solid floors, so that refuse from an upper cell rained down on the men below. Viktor Semyonovich and the dentist were both so fortunate as to be shoved into an upper cell. Nevertheless the dentist was ill during the voyage—not badly ill but afflicted with some sort of seasickness or flu or a recurrence of dysentery. He gave no poetry recitations. Their passage up the coast to Nagayevo, gateway to the Kolyma basin, took eleven days. Across the last few kilometers and into Nagayevo Harbor, the *Felix Dzerzhinsky* was breaking ice.

The dentist, with his usual morbid good humor, said something casually during the ocean passage that Viktor Semyonovich did not forget. "Think of the irony, Viktor Semyonovich," he said. "Here I am, sentenced for owning gold. And now soon I'll be standing on top of the biggest lode in the Soviet Union." As it turned out, the dentist was wrong. At Nagayevo they were put ashore onto a pier and then mustered immediately for another overland hike to the transit camp, this time about ten kilometers. It was early morning, no promise of daylight yet, and quite cold. Before they left the harbor a guards lieutenant had warned them that rest breaks would not be allowed, no stopping and no stragglers would be tolerated, on this march to camp. After a couple kilometers Landau the dentist was having another crisis of the bowels so he scampered off quickly to the edge of the gravel and dropped his pants. A guard shot him.

Viktor Semyonovich stopped walking. He stared at the dentist's body, small and crumpled on the edge of the road. Its pants down. Then the same guard who had fired the shot said a word to Viktor Semyonovich, and Viktor Semyonovich marched on.

Of the final three or four weeks what he mainly remembers is being cold. He had never been so cold for such a long stretch of days. Of course he realizes that three or four weeks was really nothing, just a wink of time, a relative moment—relative not just to his twenty-five-year sentence but even to the actual period most prisoners in Kolyma served before dying or, in the rarer case, being released. Still it was enough time for Viktor Semyonovich to grasp that he himself would not have survived long. Not twenty-five years, which was laughable, nor five years nor probably even two. It was enough time to make him understand, later, how lucky he had been. Most likely even a single full winter would have killed him.

He spent less than a day at the transit camp. He was added to a truck convoy that was leaving at once, before the road became impassable, for labor camps within a few days' hard driving along the nearer headwaters of the Kolyma River; the more northerly camps were already snowed in. He was deposited sev-

eral days later inside the gate of a compound, a zone of dirty
snow surrounded by high fences with guard towers. The compound contained only a handful of log buildings and maybe a
hundred tents. It was one of the gold camps, devoted to dredge
operations there on a small tributary of the main river. It had a
proper name, this camp, but it was more familiarly known to its
inmates as "Kilometer 299." Two of the log buildings were
occupied by guards, one belonged to the commandant, the rest
were for machinery. Viktor Semyonovich was assigned randomly to a tent. Each tent was furnished with wooden bunks
but no bedding, and a stove but no stove wood. Prisoners were
allowed to scrounge what stove wood they needed from the
taiga during their free time, which was also nonexistent. Another option was to burn the bunks in the stove and lie down on
the snow. The real intention, Viktor Semyonovich saw clearly,
was that he and these other men should die here, mining a little
gold in the meantime. Viktor Semyonovich was fortunate in
that his assigned tent already housed some sturdy stubborn vet-
erans, men who had piled snow and moss against the tent walls
outside and over the roof, for insulation. These men also knew
the illicit ways to get stove wood.

And by still greater luck, on his first morning of work he was
given a steam hose. The steam hose helped save his life. The
dentist, with his bright-eyed optimism, should have had half so
much luck.

Another man had been running the steam hose for months.
The day before Viktor Semyonovich arrived, that man had died
—simply sat down in the snow and coughed a pint of blood into
his lap and that was all. Viktor Semyonovich by good timing
inherited the man's job. On the first morning his work-brigade
leader took him out to the placer site, showed him how to light
and stoke a large wood-fired boiler, how to regulate pressure,
how to control the nozzle. Each day thereafter it was Viktor
Semyonovich's task to use this steam hose for melting the frozen stream gravel long enough so that it could be dug up and
sifted. He himself never had to dig. He just wielded the hose
like a wand. His lungs stayed damp but unfrozen and the rest of
his body had a source of heat while everyone else got frostbite.
He was warm but wet as he worked, and only suffered badly
during the hike back to camp and the half hour of waiting
outside the gate for evening head count. Each night he could

warm himself briefly again by the tent stove, then he slept in his soggy clothes. He was one of few prisoners eager, each morning, to get to the work site. Eventually the steam hose would have killed him as surely as anything, and he knew that. Pneumonia, probably. But for three or four weeks at Kilometer 299 it saved him from the quicker physical wreckage of pure brutal cold. As events unfolded, that much was sufficient.

One afternoon they came out and found him at the placer site: a guards lieutenant from camp, and two strangers.

The strangers wore unsoiled fur parkas with fur hoods, good felt boots that seemed to be new, uniform trousers unsuitable for serious cold. They looked miserable, these men. Viktor Semyonovich was reluctant to surrender his steam hose. But he was ordered by the lieutenant to accompany these strangers back to camp. *Accompany,* the lieutenant said. Viktor Semyonovich left Kilometer 299 that same afternoon, seated between the two strangers, in a truck equipped with tire chains and a heater and a plow. One of the two strangers had presented him with a sheepskin coat; Viktor Semyonovich wasn't sure, but he believed that the coat had belonged to the camp commandant. He was mystified. They had food, which they shared with him. Sausage, smoked fish, a thermos of strong hot tea. He was astounded but didn't dare to ask questions. If he was being taken back to Nagayevo to be shot, for some meaningless reason, let him at least enjoy the last meal in ignorance. They didn't look as though they would answer his questions anyway.

At Nagayevo a ski plane was waiting. Also a fresh supply of food; the food evidently came from the Nagayevo commandant's kitchen and was already boxed for air travel when the truck arrived. They flew down the coast to Vanino, just the three of them and a pilot. Viktor Semyonovich was growing guardedly more optimistic. He could imagine not even the most farfetched reason why he should be taken to Vanino or Vladivostok, in luxury, to be executed. Something else was happening.

Someone had died, he guessed.

He remembered all the turmoil and crazy caution after Stalin's death. Khrushchev has died, he thought. The old peasant has choked on a turnip. Viktor Semyonovich couldn't dream how it might have come to involve him, by even the silliest misunderstanding, but that had to be what was what.

Nothing happened so swiftly unless someone had died. At Vanino this time there was no forced march between the camp and the harbor; they didn't go to the harbor at all. Another plane was ready, a big one, there on the airstrip.

It was an Ilyushin-28 transport. It took off immediately and flew west. Aside from his two escorts, Viktor Semyonovich was the sole passenger. He was given a double armload of fur rugs on which to sleep. He was given more food. The plane stopped only once for refueling. It landed finally at Vnukovo Airport late on a clear cold afternoon, the last day of November 1963.

Kessler's neck is sore. His buttocks are sore. He is hugging himself at the rib cage and shivering steadily now. His shoulders are sore from the unconscious effort of hunching them up, trying to use them as earmuffs. His head is throbbing like a chime doorbell. Probably he is running a fever, he suspects, thanks to the infected arm. He is tired of pacing the room in a half-assed attempt to stay warm and very damn tired of being cold. Very damn tired of waiting. The arm is throbbing also, of course—sort of a syncopation of throbs. His attitude is negative. He has resolved to buy a watch.

Then again, Nye would probably have taken the watch also. But maybe not. How long has it been now? Kessler estimates five hours since the last visit, when Nye deprived him of his coat. Possibly longer. The time by now must be close to dawn. It could even be bright winter sunshine outside, a new day, and in here he wouldn't know it. Five hours of frigid misery in just a khaki shirt, five hours to ponder the loss of his dear heavy frayed wool overcoat, with the notebook in its inside pocket.

Kessler had a few seconds of terror when he first remembered the notebook. But then he relaxed, aware of what may be the week's only merciful happenstance—that this particular notebook is a fresh one, nearly empty. He snatched it from the drawer just before leaving New Haven again. Nye will have found it in the pocket, yes, and it will have told him nothing at all except the phone number of one Roger Nye, and directions from Washington to a certain stonework trestle outside of Strasburg, Virginia. For this narrow escape Kessler can claim no credit of foresight. The notes that he made after talking with Gondelman—and the few terse crucial phrases that he put down after seeing Rosalind Alpert—had simply filled out the previous notebook, so he left that one behind in New Haven, with the two others. In fact he tucked all three notebooks away securely, in the spot to which Kessler by habit consigns irreplaceable papers when he is leaving town in a hurry: the freezer compartment of his refrigerator. So there is a God after all, even if He does seem more often inclined toward sick humor. Nye is welcome to the empty notebook.

Thoughts of the freezer only amplify Kessler's shivering. And thoughts of the other notebooks only amplify his anxiety.

Maybe that's the reason for all this delay—maybe Nye has sent someone up to New Haven, to ransack Kessler's apartment. Will they find his notes, so cleverly hidden among the potpies and the bottle of Beefeater and the frozen lasagna? Only if they have at least the intelligence of a raccoon. On the other hand, maybe Nye doesn't need the notes if he has Kessler himself, held hostage without hope of rescue. *Ve haff vays of mecking you tok, Mr. Kessler.* Better still, we have ways of keeping you evermore silent. How in the dancing devil, Kessler wonders, am I going to lie my way out of here?

How do I hide the notes that are on ice in my brain?

Pokorny, he wrote on the page below Rosalind Alpert's underscored name. Just that single word. He was not likely to forget what question it answered. Kessler was sitting in his car, back at the overpriced motor lodge, after his hour with her. He had not taken any notes while Rosalind Alpert talked—not because he was worried about spooking her, but because it just wasn't necessary. Highly unlikely that he would forget anything she had said. Now in the car he scratched down a few phrases hurriedly. Even these phrases were not for memory but to reassure himself, later, that he hadn't hallucinated. *Rosalind's epiphany,* he wrote. Having met this imposing woman, he no longer could think of her by the lampooning nickname. A slash after the previous entry, and he added: *Mel's mistake.*

Kessler's bag was stowed in the back seat and he had already checked out of the motel. But he didn't yet start the engine. He thought of that day in the Vault, halfway through the third year, when Pokorny was badgering Tronko with special insistence about the imputed connection to General Avvakian. He thought of Rosalind Alpert reenacting that session with Leo the Dubious, under the eyes of Sidney Gondwana, and he thought of what she had described to him as her own very private instant of dire recognition. Pokorny had finally slipped. He had gone a step too far. And he knew he had. Viktor Tronko seemed to know too. Probably Leo the Dubious had grasped the import of the moment, in replay, and Rosalind Alpert certainly had. Everyone noticed but Gondelman, outside his plastic window, and the rest of the Central Intelligence Agency. Then the moment passed. It was interred within thousands of pages of transcript. Rosalind Alpert had taken her suspicion—her knowledge—with her up to Great Barrington, Massachusetts, and never again spoken of that moment until someone came asking.

Kessler wrote *the stammer man* in his notebook, and drew a fat line across the page.

He sits up awake, suddenly, in the chair. But despite drowsy confusion and a mild sense of alarm, pulse drumming in his ears, he doesn't move. He waits for his brain to clear. He listens for sounds outside the room, on the landing and stairs, meanwhile breathing silently through his mouth. He listens for a long time and hears nothing. He thought it might be Kessler, returning at last. Evidently not. Seems to be no one out there. Probably it was just his own drooping head that startled him back awake.

The man who calls himself Max Rosen can still doze comfortably while sitting upright but, even asleep, his body remembers when a drooping head was enough to earn a beating.

From Vnukovo Airport they took him straight to a hospital in the center of Moscow. It was a special facility of some sort though not, mercifully, of the same special sort as the Serbsky Institute. He was wary again by now. He was guessing that perhaps they had brought him back for a confrontational interview, to use him as a stooge in some other poor man's interrogation; maybe to use him against his former friend, the son of the Politburo member. But in this hospital there were no iron grates over the windows. The nurses and even the doctors were cheerful and servile. He had a room all to himself with a door that was kept closed, guarded constantly by one or the other of the two lockjawed men who had fetched him back from Kolyma. He slept long hours. He was given books to read. After a few days of intravenous supplements he was shifted entirely to a solid diet, and the food was shockingly good. Roast birds, sturgeon, beefsteak, priceless tender tomatoes from God knows where. When he finished one dinner tray, the nurse would ask him if he wanted more, and since of course he did, she would immediately deliver additional delicacies, steaming and tasty, the best food he had ever eaten. It was the quality of these meals by which Viktor Semyonovich deduced that he was in a hospital normally reserved for the Party bosses. He still didn't know why. At the end of a week of such pampering he woke in the afternoon to find a man standing at the foot of his bed. This time it wasn't Morozov.

Nor was the man a doctor. He wore a charcoal suit of fine twill that must have come at least from East Germany. He held his hands clasped patiently at his belt. He was unexceptional physically, neither tall nor short, a middling fellow of middling age and possessing the gift of stillness, with inexpressive gray eyes and thinning hair combed back. His eyeglasses were unmistakably Soviet, and didn't flatter him so well as the suit: ungainly frames, with a thick silver bar across the brow and only thin rims looping under the lenses, like some apparatus a jeweler might wear. He spoke with a mild, intermittent stammer that sometimes left him unmolested for whole sentences. Viktor Semyonovich had no idea who he was.

"Welcome back, Viktor Semyonovich," the man said. "I'm glad to see you looking so much b-b-b—" The man stopped himself at once and glanced at the floor. Then he glanced up again and said crisply: "Better."

Viktor Semyonovich said nothing.

The man smiled. Not a menacing smile at all. His mouth was a small line curled gently. He came up alongside the bed, pushing this friendly new smile before him. He picked a bright Jaffa orange off Viktor Semyonovich's tray and began peeling it with fast sure fingers. He rolled the entire peel off in only two pieces and set the pieces back on the tray. Then he split the orange down into sections, setting those on the tray. He dipped his head toward them. Obediently, Viktor Semyonovich put an orange section into his own mouth. The man wiped his hands on a white handkerchief.

"We'll wait until you are completely healthy. That comes first," the man said.

"Before what?"

The man nodded indulgently. "Everything will be all right now, Viktor Semyonovich," he said in lieu of answering. He opened his mouth again and then closed it, having decided, evidently, that further elaboration was not called for at the moment. His purpose this afternoon seemed to be limited: peel oranges and smile and take his own firsthand look at Viktor Semyonovich Tronko.

"I want to see my family," said Viktor Semyonovich, feeling reckless.

The man stared back. Again not a menacing expression, though neither did it seem meant to reassure. "Yes. Naturally you do. Still, for a while you will need to be p-p-p—" His eyes went to the floor, lingered an instant, and came up. "Patient."

"Who are you?"

"You will know me as Trofim Filippovich Rybakov," the man said precisely.

Viktor Semyonovich was allowed nine days of this luxurious and idle recuperation, throughout which he felt like a goose being fattened for Christmas. The nine days were a great concession of precious time, he understood later, grudgingly allotted not only to restore his strength for coping with the hard work ahead, but also to rid his body as completely as possible of the visible effects of Lefortovo and Kolyma; likewise the intravenous supplements had been discontinued early, he guessed, because of concern about lingering needle marks. They wanted him healthy and whole, and yet they were in a hurry. After nine days he was judged fit to begin. That morning the two lockjawed angels brought him a suit of civilian clothes. They told him to dress and they waited there in the room while he did. Viktor Semyonovich had the suit halfway on before he recognized it: one of his own, left behind in the apartment sixteen months earlier because it had been much too heavy for Rome in August.

"Where did you get this?"

The lockjawed angels didn't answer. He hadn't expected they would.

They took him across the city in a ZIL limousine with smoked windows and armor plating and a driver screened off from them by glass partition. The car was also equipped with a telephone, first such that Viktor Semyonovich had ever seen, but nobody made any calls. He gaped out through the smoked windows at the familiar street corners of Moscow. He saw pedestrians, hobbling over the frozen slush, who couldn't see him.

There seemed a wild chance he might catch sight of Tanya. He didn't. At the Lubyanka they drove through a gate that opened magically before them and closed behind. It was a different courtyard from the one he had seen sixteen months earlier, on his march from the cell to the champagne van. This courtyard was smaller and cleaner; all the snow had been cleared off the cobbles. They walked to an elevator and rode, this time, up.

The third floor was also new territory. During his working years in the Eleventh Department, Viktor Semyonovich had never had occasion to visit these holy corridors, spanning the junction of the old building and the annex, so near to the Chairman's office. Along the floor stretched a pink and green runner. He and his escorts followed the rug around three corners and for what seemed like hundreds of meters. Finally a door. It was held for him. He was ushered across a large antechamber, past a male secretary in blue uniform, through a swinging gate in a low wooden railing and into an inner office. The light here was softer. The furniture was elegant: an oak desk, leather armchairs, brass lamps with shades of green glass, and an Armenian carpet. On a table were a half dozen telephones. The man of the silver eyeglasses looked up as Viktor Semyonovich entered. He smiled his benign smile. He motioned Viktor Semyonovich to a straight chair pulled up beside the desk, and then he waved the two lockjaws out.

On the edge of the desk was a thread-bound file.

"Open it, Viktor Semyonovich," said the man.

Viktor Semyonovich obeyed. He ran his eyes over the first page, recognized his own handwriting, turned on to the second page and then the third while the man waited patiently. Viktor Semyonovich had sewn in each of the pages himself. It was the file from a visa investigation concerning a poor fellow in Leningrad, a professor of philology, who had called himself Lavrushko for years but was actually the son of a Jewish laborer named Giterman. Giterman the son had been a genuine war hero and was a genuine philologist, though a genuine Lavrushko he was not. Viktor Semyonovich had uncovered that little deceit five years earlier. Giterman had been denied his visa for the foreign trip and then lost his job at the university. But it had not been a case possessing any special importance, so far as Viktor Semyonovich knew.

"We begin here," said the man of the silver eyeglasses. He

tapped two fingers on the open file. "With Lavrushko. With your brilliant and zealous investigation in the Lavrushko affair."

Viktor Semyonovich looked at him vacantly.

"Congratulations on your p-p-p—" The man glanced at the floor and then up again. "Promotion to captain."

Viktor Semyonovich wagged his head, still not comprehending.

"I have a chore for you, Viktor Semyonovich," the man said in a tone that was more stern and direct. "Pay the closest attention to what I say, and everything will work out well."

For the seven weeks of his briefing, Viktor Semyonovich did not once leave the Lubyanka. But he wasn't kept in a cell. He spent his nights in a princely two-room apartment on the fifth floor, with one or the other of the lockjawed angels always on watch at his door. His breakfasts and his suppers were brought to him there. The food was excellent and abundant, though not so extraordinary as what he had gotten at the bigwigs' hospital. Lunches he ate off a tray in the office downstairs, while the man of the silver eyeglasses left him alone for an hour. With the noon meal he was also served a small paper cup of pills, of which he was terrified at first, but which turned out to be only vitamins. They wanted him healthy, fast. And he was given a thick pile of *Izvestia* and Soviet magazines, dating back into November, by which to acquaint himself with what had gone on in the world recently. In the early mornings and in the evenings he was allowed to take exercise on the roof, so long as no prisoners were up there at the time. Viktor Semyonovich had heard the man of the silver eyeglasses use that very phrase, in giving the instructions to a lockjaw: "—so long as no prisoners are up there at the time." Evidently Viktor Semyonovich himself wasn't considered a prisoner. Then again, he certainly wasn't free. During the long days he listened intently and answered the questions thrown at him, while the man of the silver eyeglasses rewrote the script of the last five years of Viktor Semyonovich's life. It was only the two of them in the office, working over files or notes at the oak desk or, in the later weeks, seated more comfortably in the leather armchairs. There was a large body of information to master and the repetitions demanded were seemingly infinite. The precision of memory demanded was seemingly impossible. In the evenings Viktor Se-

myonovich drilled himself further. Marching up and back on
the roof in his sheepskin coat, with a lockjaw guarding the
elevator, he repeated aloud the various intricate details of his
revised biography, conditioning himself to hear these new facts
spoken confidently in his own voice. The man of the silver eyeglasses had suggested this sort of practice. The man had also
suggested that he add some knee bends and toe touches to his
exercise regimen, in the interest of restoring his atrophied buttocks. Viktor Semyonovich obeyed. He was eager to satisfy the
man. He still feared what would happen if he didn't. He performed the knee bends and the toe touches, he chuffed back and
forth on the roof with his arms swinging high, his breath puffing
out white in the frozen night air of December and then of January, his voice rehearsing the lies. He learned to know himself,
by rote, as a somewhat different person from the Viktor Semyonovich Tronko who had boarded a plane for Rome. He made a
dogged pupil.

He learned to know that the Lavrushko case had been a turning point in his career. He learned to know that, in early summer of 1959, following a commendation for his work against
Lavrushko, he had been promoted still again, from captain to
major, and transferred to the Tourist Department of the Second
CD, where he took up service as deputy to the departmental
chief. He learned to know that the departmental chief was a
man named Trofim Filippovich Rybakov, and that this Comrade Rybakov had been Viktor Semyonovich's own patron and
protector for some years, since even before his recruitment to
the Organs. He learned to know the basis for that paternal
relationship. He learned to know the routines and functions of
the Tourist Department, the layout of the offices, the size and
decor of his own personal office, the view from his window, the
route to the elevator. He learned to know the size and decor of
Comrade Rybakov's office. None of these offices was Viktor
Semyonovich ever permitted to see; they were merely described
to him, until he could describe them back. His new living quarters were also described to him: a larger apartment for Tanya
and him and the boy, in a desirable building on Maksim Gorky
Embankment—and not even sharing a kitchen, but theirs alone.
Having memorized the apartment, he found he could delude
himself with hopeful fantasies that perhaps, by some miracle of
folded reality that passed his understanding, his wife and son

were actually living in such a place, unmolested. He learned to
know about hidden microphones at the U. S. Embassy. He
learned of his later and final promotion, to lieutenant colonel.
And he learned to address the man of the silver eyeglasses as
"Trofim Filippovich," just as if this man himself were Comrade
Rybakov of the Tourist Department, though Viktor Semyonovich felt certain he wasn't. The familiar form of address had its
place in an atmosphere of gentle but firm tutelage that had been
set between them; in each case when Viktor Semyonovich re-
verted to calling the man "Citizen Colonel," as he had at first
and as any camp inmate would address a commandant, he was
corrected to say: "Trofim Filippovich." Gradually the name
came to feel natural on his tongue. Maybe it belonged to a real
living man, maybe not. But Viktor Semyonovich never believed
it belonged to the man of the silver eyeglasses, no more than he
believed in himself as a deputy departmental chief who lived on
Maksim Gorky.

   In the seventh week he sensed a culmination of some sort.
His story was being polished like a lens, and a new passport
photo had been taken. So he said again: "I want to see my
family."

   The man of the silver eyeglasses shook his head.

   "I insist," Viktor Semyonovich said daringly.

   The man had a steady and ever measuring disposition. After
a moment of stillness he left the room. The day's session had
ended, early. Viktor Semyonovich was taken upstairs. Next day
there was a full session and the subject of his family was not
mentioned. Viktor Semyonovich judged that the prudent thing,
now, might be a little patience. That night after his exercise and
his shower and his solitary supper he was brought back downstairs, an exception to the normal routine. The man of the silver
eyeglasses was waiting in his office, that room being now totally
darkened. They sat in the armchairs. There were no questions,
no drills, no repetitions. They just sat. Within a few minutes
Viktor Semyonovich's eyes had adjusted to the dark, and then
the other man summoned him to the bank of windows. The
man pressed an electric control that opened the steel shutters of
one window. Together they stared out at the night. Finally two
figures appeared, walking along the pavement of Dzerzhinsky
Square: Viktor Semyonovich's wife, guided at the elbow by one
of the lockjawed angels. These two walked the length of the

block, turned, walked back. The Lubyanka building loomed over them, and Tanya was painting it with her gaze, sweeping her eyes imploringly along the rows and tiers of windows. She gave no special attention to the window at which Viktor Semyonovich stood. One circuit down and back, and she disappeared beyond view.

"Where's the boy?"

"A defective child cannot be out at night. He needs special attention," said the man of the silver eyeglasses.

Viktor Semyonovich looked at him in the dark. Only the silver frames caught any light from the street.

"Neighbors," the man said.

They were finished polishing him. Evidently he had learned his rote lessons sufficiently well. A suitcase full of his own clothes had appeared, and a tailor was brought in (though healthy now, Viktor Semyonovich was still twenty-five pounds lighter than at Rome) to do alterations. He knew his lines. Without a superfluous word spoken by the man of the silver eyeglasses, he knew what was implied by parading his wife, alone, up and down Dzerzhinsky Square. He knew that Article 64 of the criminal code was applicable not just to defectors and traitors but also to their families. He knew the kind of facility his son would end in, if his wife were taken away to a camp. He understood exactly what was expected of him, he thought. He had no inkling of the reason or the logic behind it, if indeed there was any reason or logic.

Then another night session, the second and final one of those. Viktor Semyonovich was told to dress in his (newly retailored) work uniform and then brought downstairs. The man of the silver eyeglasses was standing over his oak desk. Turning the pages of a thick file. For a moment Viktor Semyonovich thought again of Lavrushko. But this was different. On a corner of the desk sat three other file volumes bound identically. The man looked up as Viktor Semyonovich entered.

"You have just come from Vnukovo Airport," he said.

He described the night in November when Viktor Semyonovich had flown back from his mission to Minsk. He described the weather in Moscow that day and evening, the unseasonable warmth, the slush in the streets, the fog. He described the phone call from himself that had been necessary to cow the traffic controller into allowing Viktor Semyonovich's plane to land. He described the trip's larger context, the midnight call twenty hours earlier by which he had waked Viktor Semyonovich at home, the tense conversation that had passed between them, the thoughts they had together been almost too frightened to think. This is the surveillance file on the American lunatic Oswald, he said.

"Good Lord, Viktor Semyonovich," he said. "We must see how much, if at all, we have gotten ourselves implicated. Do you p-p-p—" He glanced down at the file and up again into Viktor Semyonovich's face. "Pray?"

The following afternoon Viktor Semyonovich was put on a flight to Vienna.

This time, in place of the gun, Roger Nye carries only a folding chair. Possibly that means he feels secure in here with Kessler because of accomplices outside the door of the Vault. Possibly it means no such thing. Maybe he knows kung fu. He opens the chair and sits, directly in front of Kessler, who is on the floor again with a cold aching ass and his back braced in the corner of two walls. Nye pushes his hands into his pockets. With the snowy hair and the lean genteel features and the flannel jacket and the boots, he could be a professor emeritus of forestry at some New England college, or perhaps E. B. White. He says: "Are you ready?"

"Yes."

"Good. Let's talk about what you know, Mr. Kessler. And what you think you know."

"All right. Let's."

Kessler has given this moment a great deal of advance meditation. He has concluded, with the lucidity of the angry and scared, that he has two options. He can tell the complete truth and then hope for the best, or he can spin out some elaborate total lie, trying to conceal the extent of his own knowledge with a muddle of distortions and ignorant mistakes and bad guesses all designed to persuade Nye that Michael Kessler needn't be taken as a threat—and *then* hope for the best. The second option seems safer, which is not to say safe. Unfortunately, no such elaborate total lie has occurred to him. His brain feels as if it's full of cold bacon grease. He has no idea what he will say until he hears himself saying it.

"Start with what you know."

"Everything," Kessler says.

He begins quacking about Mel Pokorny, the clown-faced arch deceiver. Mel was Dmitri and he fooled you all, Kessler says. Not just Jed McAttee and Eames but Claude Sparrow and you yourself, Kessler says, who had worked beside him for years. But don't feel bad because he fooled me too, Kessler says. I think he had plans for me, the gullible young journalist who would be an eager conduit for his leaks. That could have been very embarrassing. I shudder. It might still prove to be. Of course I would never have killed him for it, Kessler says.

Roger Nye draws his hands out of his pockets and clasps them on his lap.

Whoever did kill him was someone he knew, Kessler says. I know that from Mr. Biaggio, the old grocer. Mel recognized the voice and he understood what was coming and so he panicked. I know it was a white man in a gaudy ski mask. I don't know whether or not the man had liver spots on his hands, Kessler says, but I suppose Mr. Biaggio might remember. Kessler grins masochistically.

Roger Nye folds his arms.

"I also know about Ivan, in Moscow. McAttee's own precious bird. I know that Ivan has fallen silent. Missing, presumed dead. The KGB finally caught him and squashed him, evidently."

"How do you know that?"

"Because otherwise Claude Sparrow would never have told me about him." It's a small bit of deduction for which Kessler takes no special pride. "And because, otherwise, Mel himself would still be alive. In a funny way, they were linked. Ivan had scuttled Mel's career, but Ivan's own delicate position in Moscow also left Mel with a strange sort of immunity. Immunity from prosecution for espionage. Also from death. Probably Mel never even knew he had been found out. Now we're into the realm of speculation, admittedly. What I only think I know. You want to hear this too?"

Roger Nye nods politely.

"Okay. I think Jed McAttee got something from Ivan. It was something of very exceptional value. Not just an offering of information, most likely, but an actual physical item. An artifact. McAttee paid for it with the life of Daniel Petrosian, the physicist. What it was, I think, was the proof of Dmitri's identity."

Roger Nye makes a stolid audience.

"A thumbprint on a receipt, for instance. But then Mel didn't do what he did for money, is my guess, so there probably weren't any receipts. A photograph, maybe. A grainy old photo of Mel Pokorny and another man, say, conferring together on a park bench in suburban Virginia or Maryland. The date of this photo that I'm imagining would be March of 1958. The other man would be a Russian. He would be a beetle-browed guy in a pair of clunky eyeglasses. His name would be L. V. Nechaev. How am I doing?"

Roger Nye says nothing. That doesn't matter because Kessler now has his own manic momentum.

"Or maybe it wasn't a photograph. But something. A piece of physical evidence, solid and incontestable. Something damning enough to convince even Claude Sparrow, when McAttee pushed it in front of his face. God, how Jed McAttee must have relished that moment. And how Sparrow must have hated it. *Two Americans Contemplating the Identity of Dmitri.* The problem then was to get rid of Mel without blowing the game for Ivan. So people had to be sacrificed. Not just Pokorny alone. You all had to be thrown out together. The great purge of Counterintelligence. Forced retirement for everyone in the vicinity, with wiretap abuses as the plausible pretext. I commend you for your self-abnegation, Mr. Nye."

"Claude Sparrow didn't tell you this."

"No. Of course not. I've got a half dozen sources. Different bits from different people. I've left my footprints all over Washington."

"I know a little something about your footprints."

"Yes. Then you know I've been a busy boy. And it's all in my notebooks," Kessler says proudly.

Roger Nye reaches into the side pocket of the flannel jacket. Oh lordy, here comes the pistol again, Kessler thinks. He feels another instant of gut-clutching terror before Nye pulls out the empty notebook and drops it on the concrete beside Kessler's feet.

"Three others," says Kessler. "Those other three are full."

"Where are they?"

The advantage of surrendering so perilously much truth as he has, Kessler hopes, is to buy credibility for one good little lie.

"I mailed them to myself," he says. "Registered packet, care of my editor at *Rolling Stone*. He expects me to show up there sometime Monday. His name is Terry McDonell." Kessler spells the last name for a touch of verisimilitude, though suddenly Nye doesn't seem interested. "You can call him and confirm that, if you want."

In a half hour it will be dawn. He can't afford to wait until dawn; he can't afford to be seen climbing back out over the roof. Evidently Kessler has found female companionship somewhere, or else drunk himself stupid and spent the night asleep in the back seat of his car. The man who calls himself Max Rosen is mildly annoyed. He will have to try again tonight. Maybe this time he should take the chance of making contact by telephone first. Or maybe Kessler is just the wrong person after all.

He doesn't really know anything about Michael Kessler. Maybe the prudent thing is to forget Kessler, forget about one journalist versus another, forget about talking to anybody. Go silent to the grave. But he doesn't *want* to be prudent—only cautious. And he *does* want to talk. In any case, he now has another full day to reconsider. He empties ashes and butts from the water glass into the side pocket of his suit jacket. He rinses the glass in the sink, wipes it out with his handkerchief, sets it back exactly where he found it. Of course Kessler will still smell the stale smoke and know that someone has been here, if Kessler has any wit at all.

He does want to talk. There is so much he has never told anyone, so many large and little things each adding to the pressure within his brain: from the champagne van, to the death of Landau the dentist, to that afternoon of the last year in the Vault when Pokorny forgot himself momentarily and—

This thought is interrupted.

As he steps out the door of Kessler's room he sees a man walking toward him across the landing.

For an instant in the dim light he thinks of Kessler himself, arriving back. But this man is shorter than Kessler. This man wears a rust-colored leather jacket. This man raises one hand, in which is held a long-barrel .22 pistol, and fires a shot.

He hears the nasal slap of that shot, despite everything. Then he is on the carpet, twitching and coughing just briefly as disorder pours out into blackness through the raw channel torn in his heart. The amber spectacles have been jarred off his face. The man in the leather jacket leans over his body. The muzzle of the .22 pistol is pressed hard into the socket of his left eye, forcing the eyeball aside. But even before the second shot has been fired, Viktor Tronko is dead.

31

Kessler has slept. He doesn't know how long. Long enough to flatten his right hip against the concrete and put another good cramp into his neck. He sits up again, sullen and desolate, into the corner of the two walls.

Still no food, still no water, and his body is still quaking in a continuous spasm of cold. He dreads the prospect of spending another day or two in this place—dreads it almost as much as he dreads seeing Roger Nye reappear with the gun. Kessler doesn't know whether he said the right things or whether Nye believed what he did say. He knows that Nye certainly won't be foolish enough to call the magazine, and that Terry McDonell wouldn't tell him anything if he did; but he doesn't know whether that really matters. He doesn't know whether he even wants to guess what Nye is likely to do. There is quite a lot that Kessler doesn't know. He sits for another half hour in his self-piteous stupor before he notices the door of the Vault. The door is slightly ajar.

Kessler stands, a difficult maneuver in itself. For a long while he simply stares. Then he shuffles across the cell, moving lamely on one good leg and one that has suffered some temporary neurological outage. The heavy steel door is unlocked, yes, and a crack of daylight showing. Kessler hooks his fingers into the gap. Gently, slowly, he pulls the door open until it makes a small grinding chirp against the floor. He stops. Possibly he should call out. He doesn't want to startle Nye and be shot unnecessarily. Unnecessarily? Bullshit, it will be highly unnecessary from Kessler's viewpoint no matter how it happens. He slides through the opening.

He pads quietly down the corridor. He readies himself to do something exotically daring, like wrestle an old man for a loaded .45 automatic, or break into a hysterical sprint. He wishes suddenly that he had ripped that leg off the cot after all, and brought it along, but too late now. Approaching the archway into the front room, he goes dizzy from forgetting to breathe. Again he stops. Draws some air into his lungs. All right, what now? Feeling idiotic and at the same time scared mightily, he peeks around the corner. The room is bare. Empty of every trace except that, near the front door, draped over the folding chair, is Kessler's long wool coat.

My coat. Kessler walks over, picks it up. He looks out the window. Nye's old Ford is gone. His own car is still parked among the weeds, sunlight banging off its windshield. A crisp and gorgeous February morning has unfolded upon the Virginia countryside.

Favoring his bandaged arm, Kessler gets himself into the coat. Warmth at last, but now he is shivering worse than ever. He begins to relax. In one pocket he finds his car keys. His wallet and his knife are there also. In the other pocket his hand comes upon a piece of stiff paper, smooth on one side. By touch he knows immediately that this is a photograph. Oh joy, Nye has left him a photographic souvenir. Kessler stands paralyzed with both hands in his coat pockets. For a giddy instant he expects to see the faces of Pokorny and L. V. Nechaev.

No, not Pokorny, not L. V. Nechaev, not Kessler on a park bench with Claude Sparrow. The photo is of Nora.

It is a candid shot, black and white, taken with a good camera. Nora is shown talking to an older man whom Kessler does not at first recognize. The man is gaunt; he wears a turtleneck and a goatee. Not her type. Is Kessler supposed to be jealous or something? On the other hand if they had kidnapped her, Nora and the gaunt man wouldn't be looking so amiable. Then Kessler remembers Athol Fugard, the Afrikaner playwright, who was in town Wednesday with his film about Eugène Marais.

I know a little something about your footprints, Nye said. The message is clear enough.

Kessler does not linger to admire the fine country morning. He drives back down the winding gravel and under the trestle and then on through the town of Strasburg without paying much heed to its only stop sign, getting himself onto the interstate and clear of Shenandoah County as quickly and quietly as possible. He is still dazed. His brain is clanging away with a renewed version of the same headache he has had for most of five days; no doubt dehydration and caffeine deprivation have by now added themselves to the causes. He pushes up past the speed limit and opens his window. He drives that way for an hour. At a Dunkin' Donuts in Fairfax, just a few miles from the Beltway, he stops for coffee. His hand shakes as he raises the cup.

He asks also for a large glass of water. Gulps that one and asks for a refill. Hunched like a gnome at the counter, he gets several minutes of peace before Dexter Lovesong slides onto the stool beside him and orders coffee and three maple bars.

"Where were you?" says Kessler.

Lovesong appears mildly amused by the question. Like Kessler, he hasn't shaved recently. His nose is still crooked, and shows a small discoloration along the bridge. "I was around. At a distance."

"I thought you might stage some sort of dazzling rescue."

"No. Really? That's kind of flattering, but no. This time, Kessler, a dazzling rescue was definitely not in the cards."

"I was in serious danger."

"Correct."

"I could have disappeared permanently. Never a trace."

"That isn't so. If they killed you, I was going straight to the FBI." Lovesong pushes a maple bar halfway into his mouth and mashes it off. He talks while he chews. "As it is, I'll just resign."

Kessler absorbs that information silently. The coffee is strong and scorched and several hours old and it tastes glorious. He orders a maple bar for himself. "Who do you mean by *they?* All I saw was Roger Nye."

"There was a small confab. Nye and McAttee and that little prick partner of mine. Former partner."

"Buddyboy?"

"Buddyboy, yeah. But he was just there to open doors and run messages. It was Buddyboy who drove McAttee out from Langley."

"What about Claude Sparrow?"

"No. No sign of him. I think Sparrow isn't part of that club anymore. I think Sparrow these days is only just what he seems: an old guy who sits on park benches a lot."

"Talking to any fool who will listen," says Kessler.

"Talking to journalists, yeah," says Lovesong.

They finish their breakfasts. Kessler lays out a twenty and motions to the waitress that he is paying for both. He leaves her two dollars. He begins struggling into his coat. Lovesong says: "A smart person in your shoes, Kessler, will not go back to that hotel."

"Why won't he?"

"They had a death there, early this morning. A murder. Cops everywhere right now."

Kessler's shoulders drop. He feels very tired and bruised. He wants the lurching behavior of his stomach to stop. "Anybody I know?"

Lovesong nods. "Under the name Max Rosen, I suppose. He was coming out of your room. It looks like a piece of professional work. Might of been, he was mistaken for you."

Kessler sits back down. He is more upset than he would have expected. It must be cumulative. He thinks of the frigid evening on the rooftops and of the cigarette pack and of the man he takes to have been Sol Lentzer. After a moment he says: "They'll want to talk with me."

"Who?"

"The police."

"That's being fixed."

"They'll know who I am. I was registered."

"Forget about it. Trust me."

"My bag is still there."

"Anything irreplaceable in it?"

Kessler considers. "Not really."

"Buy a new bag," says Lovesong.

So Kessler turns north at the Beltway and keeps driving. He feels barely fit to be on the road. He stops often for more coffee and eats a big greasy lunch and spends an hour asleep on the front seat at a rest area, finally limping into New Haven sometime after dark. It seems a prudent idea to go straight to the hospital and let someone look at his arm. From a phone in the waiting lounge of the emergency room, he dials Nora's number. He wants to confirm in his mind that she is still safe, still unwitting and unmolested, in the little house on the far side of town. He isn't sure what he will do if there is no answer. But there is an answer.

"Are we on speaking terms, you and I?" says Kessler.

"Of course," Nora says. "What happened? Are you all right?"

"I'm sorry I stood you up."

"Yes. Right. I was pretty annoyed for a couple of hours."

"I have a long woolly excuse, which I'll spare you for the moment. The short version is, I was working, and I forgot. I'm sorry." He pulls in a breath and waits.

"Let's say you owe me for the baby-sitter. Roughly equivalent to a spaghetti dinner."

"Tomorrow night."

"That would be nice," she says. "How was Washington?"

Kessler says: "Don't ask."

32

⟶

He should call Patsy Koontz in Colorado. He should call the
Rockville police and alert them about Barry's body. He doesn't.
Kessler faces the new day feeling morally and mentally dishev-
eled. He should make the required phone calls and see Nora
and then disappear on a week's vacation somewhere for the
sake of putting his thoughts in order. He should be good to his
body, especially the arm, and rest his brain just enough to restore its usefulness. He should reach some decisions and take
some precautions. Instead he drinks two cups of coffee, stares at
his mail without opening any, and finally goes out for a long
walk, avoiding the vicinity of Biaggio's grocery.

Around noon he returns. He remembers to take his antibiotic. He makes a third cup of coffee, this one roughly the consistency of transmission oil, and carries it into the office. Seating
himself very straight at his desk, he pulls forward the two-inch
pile of typescript.

The story, as Kessler has been trying to tell it, begins at the
end. Eugène Marais killed himself with a shotgun in March of
1936.

In the course of his sixty-four years he had been a journalist,
a newspaper publisher, an important Afrikaans poet, a medical
student, a lawyer, a gunrunner during the Boer War, and a
morphine addict. He had also spent three years living out of a
hut in the Waterberg mountains of South Africa, among a troop
of wild chacma baboons, making observations and developing
some eccentric ideas about primate behavior. And he studied
termites. Marais is mainly remembered today, by those few who
remember him at all, as the author of two books, neither of
which appeared in print during his lifetime. The first of these
two was *The Soul of the White Ant*, his mad masterpiece about

termites, a paperback edition of which caught Kessler's attention on a rack in a drugstore in Kenya.

The second book wasn't published until thirty years after Marais's death. Either the manuscript had been genuinely lost or it had been placed safely away and there was no interest in finding it. This manuscript had been written in the 1920s but was unfinished; evidently Marais had gotten distracted by morphine and fits of depression, or suffered a failure of confidence, and had never gone back to it. When finally published, in its incomplete form, the second book was titled *The Soul of the Ape.* It was an essay on the evolution of human consciousness, and it was based on the chacma baboon studies although, notwithstanding the title, a baboon is not strictly an ape. Kessler found his copy at a used-book store in Georgetown after six months of looking. That edition also carried a biographical foreword that told him a tiny bit more about Eugène Marais.

Marais came from Dutch and French Huguenot ancestors who had helped pioneer South Africa; his own earliest formal schooling, though, was in English. He had spent years of his young adulthood in London, studying medicine and law, and he wrote English prose fluidly, even gracefully. Nevertheless in his middle age, from resentment over Britain's war against the Boers, he renounced English and composed his poetry in Afrikaans. *The Soul of the White Ant* was written in Afrikaans; *The Soul of the Ape,* earlier, had been written in English. It is entirely typical of the warps and wobbles of factuality in the Eugène Marais story that the first of those two is not actually a book about ants, that the second is not actually about apes, and that the pair were composed in two different languages. Kessler has now spent almost three years trying to chart those warps and wobbles.

He has not been attempting to do an objective biography. He has thought of the work rather as a biographical essay, a personal meditation on Marais's life and ideas. The partial draft on his desk runs to three hundred pages, large sections of which may have to be thrown away as Kessler locates further documentary material, if he ever does. His working title is *The Soul of Eugène Marais.*

Kessler likes the title but has sometimes wished he had never begun this project. Today, just back at the work following a disruption, freshly stitched and bandaged and drugged, he is having particular trouble concentrating.

He has tracked down and corresponded with Eugène Marais's granddaughter, a middle-aged woman in Pretoria, who was generous enough to send him photocopies of a sheaf of old letters. After some coaxing she also loaned him a diary, a fascinating field journal from the years of the termite observations, which the United States Postal Service managed with divine intervention not to lose. He also traced the original English translator of the termite book to her gravestone in London and then to her next of kin, who knew nothing whatsoever about Eugène Marais. On the same trip he spent a day at the British Museum reading the letters that had passed between Marais and that translator, and to Kessler's surprise the curator even allowed him to carry away photocopies. Kessler still isn't sure why Marais, a fluent English stylist who only avoided the language for political reasons, should have needed a translator at all; but that's the least of Kessler's problems. The letters date mainly from 1935, the year before Marais died.

During that year Marais seems to have suffered physically, from recurrent attacks of malaria and also presumably from his morphine addiction. In one letter he described himself as writing in bed, "under the spur and inspiration of enduring pain." In a following letter he was much more cheerful, buoyed by the dream of seeing both his termite and his primate books published at last. "You see that your kindly enthusiasm has infected me!" he told the translator. "The thought of reaching a bigger public intrigues me." That was the last letter.

Five months later he shot himself. But whether the suicide was provoked by his illness, or by a transient spell of narcotized gloom, or by unendurable bitterness over the world's neglect, or some other possibility, Kessler is not in position to say.

Gin, he thinks. Two hours have passed and Kessler has reread his way fifty pages back into the typescript. A single minuscule alteration has been made by pencil, barely more than the correction of a typo. He intends to keep reading all afternoon if his body will stand it. Lunch he can do without. Lunch would just make him sleepy. A little gin, though, will help focus the brain.

He walks to the kitchen. But there is no gin to be had.

The freezer compartment is barren except for one tray of ice, a bag of bagels, a turkey potpie, three ring notebooks wrapped inside a plastic bag and bound tightly with duct tape, and a pair of Groucho glasses, which stare vacantly back at Kessler while the frozen white vapors foam and tumble.